Beyond the Rio Grande

BEYOND THE RIO GRANDE

Steve Shaw

To: Marilyn & Dobi Carey,

A real cowboy & hero of mine, and his lady.

I hope you enjoy this adventure.

Steve Shaw

April 2006

iUniverse, Inc.
New York Lincoln Shanghai

Beyond the Rio Grande

iUniverse books may be ordered through booksellers or by contacting:

iUniverse
2021 Pine Lake Road, Suite 100
Lincoln, NE 68512
www.iuniverse.com
1-800-Authors (1-800-288-4677)

ISBN-13: 978-0-595-37374-1 (pbk)
ISBN-13: 978-0-595-67492-3 (cloth)
ISBN-13: 978-0-595-81771-9 (ebk)
ISBN-10: 0-595-37374-7 (pbk)
ISBN-10: 0-595-67492-5 (cloth)
ISBN-10: 0-595-81771-8 (ebk)

Printed in the United States of America

Dedicated to my wife, Marcie, for her love, friendship, patience, and unwavering belief in me during the writing of this book.

CHAPTER 1

"You cheatin' us, greaser?" The cattle drover angrily spat.

Pulling his winnings toward him, the young Mexican glanced at the man and smiled. But he said nothing.

Ramming his fist in the center of the table, the drover stood with his right hand resting on the butt of his Smith & Wesson. "I asked y'all a question!"

"No…I not cheat," the Mexican replied, shaking his head for emphasis. Rojas hadn't planned on winning. In fact, he had intended to lose this evening, as he had every evening. He hoped his streak of good luck would soon end.

"Trust me, sir. He's not cheating," the dealer added.

The drover stared at the dealer. "I ain't talkin' to you, Billy Yank. Goddamn carpetbaggers." The drover sat down, mumbling under his breath.

Jack Wood, United States treasury agent, leaned his elbows on the round, wooden card table and glanced at the other four players who had elected to squander their money and Saturday evening playing monte. The drover's remark did not surprise him. Even though the Civil War had been over for eleven years, animosity toward either side, especially toward those who had fought for the North, was intense, particularly in Texas.

Wood glanced at his cards. Overhead, four immense, crystal chandeliers illuminated the cavernous saloon and gaming parlor. Ubiquitous cigar and cigarette smoke clung tenuously to the overhead rafters. A swarm of dirty, dust-covered men crowded the innumerable gaming tables, bellowing at the dealers when losing and guffawing when they won. Female entertainment from the stage at the rear of the saloon created riotous jubilation from the audience. It was just another ordinary evening at Rosita's Cantina in El Paso, Texas.

Wood peered from under the brim of his hat and scrutinized the men at his table. The man who had challenged the Mexican sat to Jack's left. He had introduced himself as a cattle drover from the JX Ranch. From his sullied clothes, weeklong stubble covering his tawny complexion, and dirty, thick fingers constantly probing his discolored teeth, Wood suspected the man was nothing more than a cowpuncher.

The tall, thin, pallid-faced man sitting to the cattle drover's left had been elected the designated dealer by a cut of the cards. He was meticulously dressed in a dark gray, double-breasted frock coat; black string tie; and white, starched shirt with French cuffs and expensive cuff links. The man's long, delicate, ashen fingers competently shuffled the deck of cards. He was unquestionably a professional cardplayer, a man who frequented one town to the next while cunningly plying his craft against those less skilled at the game of chance. Wood doubted the man was honorable. Obviously proficient at his trade, the man cut the deck of cards into two equal sizes on the table. He brought the corners together with his thumbs and rifled the cards downward, flawlessly interlocking the cards. The cards slid together into one perfect pack. The man briskly executed the task of shuffling the cards three times.

The next man to the left sat directly across from Wood. This man, the Mexican vaquero who the drover had challenged, was whom Wood had deliberately attempted to make friends with over the last several days. His name was Francisco Rojas. Three nights ago, Rojas had been losing carelessly. From all appearances, Rojas was just another poorly paid laborer or cowboy. But, the night he was losing, he had an infinite supply of twenty-dollar gold pieces. Wood figured the Mexican had lost $300 that evening. It was a staggering loss to any man, but it was a small fortune to those who lived and worked in El Paso. Nevertheless, the losses seemingly unfazed Rojas. Not only did Rojas play poker, faro, and every other game poorly, Wood noticed he enjoyed drinking heavily. The following night, Wood sat in on a game of five-card stud poker. He purposely lost whenever the winning hand went to Rojas, giving him the opportunity to jokingly chide Rojas on his good luck and befriend the Mexican. Toward the end of the game, Rojas was drunk and lost several hundred dollars—all in twenty-dollar gold double eagles. Wood and everyone else at the table procured several of the coins through their winnings. In his room that morning, Wood verified his suspicions. The gold was counterfeit. El Paso was the fifth Texas border town Wood had visited during the summer months where he had encountered counterfeit twenty-dollar gold coins. In El Paso, he hoped to find the source of the counterfeit money, and that source appeared to be Rojas.

The man sitting between Rojas and Wood, to Wood's immediate right, had introduced himself as an El Paso merchant. A small-framed man with a withered left arm that was half as long as the right spoke as if the other players intimidated him. He had an annoying habit of laughing nervously while his beady eyes darted from one player to the next. The merchant's clean-shaven cheeks possessed the ruddiness of an adolescent, yet his deeply wrinkled neck and hands and thinning, gray hair belied his childish appearance.

The man shuffling cards had introduced himself as Carl. Carl placed ten dollars in the center of the table. Having finished shuffling, he offered the deck to the drover, the person to his right, to cut. The drover waved the cards away, insinuating to the professional cardplayer that he trusted him. Wood doubted anyone else at the table would have done the same.

Holding the deck face down, Carl drew two cards from the bottom and placed them face up on the table in clear view of the players. A queen of hearts and a two of spades were showing. Carl then took two cards from the top of the deck and placed them face up. Revealed were the jack of diamonds and the ten of clubs. Each man hesitated while watching the other players. No one trusted the other. Each slowly placed a bet on the card, or combination of cards, up to the ten-dollar limit the dealer established. The drover, the last man to place a bet, glanced menacingly at the others, reached over, and dropped ten dollars on the jack of diamonds.

Carl placed the deck on the table face up. Each player glanced at the top card. It was the king of clubs, the suit of which determined the winning bet. The merchant, having bet on the ten of clubs, annoyingly giggled as he was paid his winnings. Expressionless, Carl reached over and raked in the pot of coins and currency bet on the other cards, sliding them to his side of the table.

"All bets are settled," Carl announced, discarding the four cards. He then turned the deck face down and discarded the old top card. Just as quickly, he placed two fresh layouts on the table and waited for the others to place their bets. It would continue like this until the deck was exhausted.

Wood yawned, removed his hat, and brushed his left hand through his long, dirty blonde bangs. He then knuckled his thick, handlebar moustache. He found the game of monte tiresome and terribly boring. However, he hoped to win a few bets and be paid in part through Rojas' losses. The only reason he played was to acquire more of the counterfeit coins belonging to Francisco Rojas.

As the game progressed, no conversation passed among the participants. Toward midnight, Rojas started losing. By two in the morning, he had lost nearly $400. The losses had not escaped the attention of the men at the table. The small, fidgety man with the withered arm continued laughing nervously, irritating Wood. The drover incessantly picked at his teeth, occasionally wiping a found fragment of food particle on his dirty vest. Carl sat with the largest amount of cash in front of him, mostly from Rojas. If Carl had known his winnings were counterfeit and utterly worthless, Wood doubted he would have the same arrogant attitude. On the other hand, if the drover knew of the Mexican's scam, Wood knew Rojas would not live to see sunrise.

An hour later, the party of five called it quits. Not every man walked away with winnings. Carl remained seated at the table, counting his profits. The drover stood and cursed himself for his losses. Turning, he exited through the batwing doors as the abatement of his spurs signaled his departure. Twisting his body awkwardly and dipping his left shoulder, the merchant rubbed his hands together. He smiled at his seventy-five dollar win. He apprehensively chuckled, attempted to shake hands with Carl, who rebuffed him, picked up his winnings, turned, and left. Rojas stood and staggered. He was drunk. Wood helped him to the bar and propped him against it. Wood feigned inebriation to befriend Rojas. Both laughed at their losses, cursed the professional gambler, and shared their feelings about him as he walked away with more than $300 in winnings. Wood estimated at least $200 of which was counterfeit.

Wood's Spanish was better than Rojas' English, and they communicated without trouble. Wood jokingly referred to Rojas' bottomless source of funds. Rojas indicated there was more and offered to buy drinks for the two of them. After several drinks, Wood was anxious to free himself from Rojas for a moment in order to wire Washington a telegram. Wood surmised that Rojas could confirm his suspicions of a Mexican counterfeit ring and knew the origin of the counterfeit money. Wood needed to keep Rojas drunk and encourage him to talk.

Rojas wanted a prostitute and offered to buy Wood the services of one as well. Wood delicately declined, informing Rojas he would return momentarily. Wood did not give any excuses because Rojas was already climbing the staircase with an overweight *señorita*.

Wood sent an encoded telegram to Jonah Walsh, deputy director of the Treasury Department, his immediate superior in Washington, DC. He then hurried back toward Rosita's Cantina. Rounding Utah Street, he headed north on San Antonio Street. He then saw Rojas talking to the drover who sat at their table earlier that evening. The two men walked into a dark alley. Wood's instant mistrust was validated as he neared the corner of the alleyway and San Antonio Street. The drover was robbing Rojas. Rojas began crying, telling the drover he did not have anymore money on him, but he could acquire more from his room. The drover threatened to kill the vaquero if he tricked him. Agreeing to go to Rojas' room, the two men turned to exit the alley. As they walked onto San Antonio Street, Wood coldcocked the drover with the barrel of his revolver, unintentionally more forcibly than he should as he subconsciously remembered the drover's remark about Yankees. Rojas began thanking Wood profusely.

"Put your hands up, boys!" the deputy sheriff called out.

Wood and Rojas turned toward the voice and saw the badge pinned on the man's vest. Both men reacted differently. Wood put his hands in the air, knowing he could convince the deputy of what had occurred. Rojas froze, staring at the sheriff.

"You boys weren't tryin' to rob this man, were ya?"

Wood smiled, knowing what the situation looked like. Rojas pulled his gun.

"No!" Wood yelled.

Firing first, the sheriff hit Rojas in the left shoulder. Jerked off his feet, Rojas fired his revolver at point-blank range. He hit the sheriff in the center of the chest, killing him instantly. Wood knelt down to confirm the deputy was dead.

"Move and I'll blow you both to kingdom come!"

Slowly turning his head, Wood saw an old man wearing a deputy badge. His sawed-off shotgun was pointed directly at them. The large blast from the twelve-gauge could kill both Rojas and Wood simultaneously.

"We ain't moving, deputy," Wood said as he stood, placing his hands over his head once again.

The old man motioned for Wood and Rojas to back away from the prone deputy. The old man took several steps forward, leaned down, and confirmed the sheriff was dead. Yelling for help, twenty men from neighboring saloons promptly surrounded the two suspected murderers and marched them to jail while the deputy sheriff's body was taken to the undertakers.

In the same cell, sitting on a flimsy, wood cot and soiled mattress, Wood and Rojas waited.

"Do not worry, my friend. We will be…er, how do you say? Taken from here?"

"Yeah, by a vigilante committee and hung," Wood retorted.

"No…You do not understand. I have friends. They will come. You will see."

"Your friends know we're in jail, *amigo*, huh?"

Rojas wanted to explain to his new friend about the army south of the Rio Grande. He wanted to explain they were his friends and knew he was in El Paso, had been away too long, had been expected back by noon that day. The leader of their army would notice his long absence. It would be very bad for him, but his friends would not allow him to die at the hands of the people of El Paso.

"My friend, they will come for us, very soon." Rojas leaned against the adobe wall and closed his eyes. Perhaps his new gringo friend would join their cause, their army. Rojas' thinking wasn't clear. The drinking had confused him, and the superficial bullet wound that had been hastily bandaged dazed him. But he wanted to tell someone his secret. Perhaps this new friend, Jack Wood, could keep a secret.

CHAPTER 2

"Shhh!" Kincaid placed his right forefinger to his parched, cracked lips and quietly issued the unnecessary warning to Stetson; unnecessary because she knew the danger they were in.

Motionless, the two lay side by side, hidden from the scorching desert sun in a narrow, shallow subterranean cavern. The sand beneath them was a fine powder that covered every inch of clothing and exposed flesh. Remaining silent, yearning to be invisible to the naked eye, they hugged the ground. Their hunters were near.

Kincaid glanced in her direction. He still thought she was the most beautiful woman he had ever known. Whether she was wearing satin and lace or buckskin and leather, she was the envy of most women, coveted by all men. Yet, here she was, in this desolate desert, facing death. He had only himself to blame.

They had left their horses in a ravine a hundred feet away, found a crevice in the arroyo wall, and squeezed themselves into it. Fortuitously, they wound up in a shallow cave. Kincaid knew their horses would be eventually discovered. Their tracks, leading to the crevice, would be followed. They crawled one hundred feet through the underground corridor to distance themselves from their horses.

Above them, a cleft in the desert floor permitted the sun to suffuse their rocky-walled sanctuary, creating clever shadows that would partially obscure them if anyone should look into the constricted chamber. Five feet above them, the rolling Texas desert stretched for hundreds of miles. The red, dusty landscape was dotted with clumps of grama grass, soapweed, and three-foot mounds of the pink-purple verbena bush. Above ground, the images breaking the sizzling shimmer of heat as it glowed and oscillated upward from the hot, sandy soil were not mirages, but Kiowa Indians. Kincaid knew twelve young braves were near, and the braves knew their white man prey was within their grasp.

For four tedious days, Kincaid and Stetson had drifted southwest across the Texas panhandle, from Lubbock through the high plains of the *Llano Estacado*. Commonly known as the Staked Plains, thousands of buffalo once occupied this vast, dry, treeless area. Buffalo hunters and the United States government killed them off to force the Indians to live on reservations, coercing them to rely on the white man. West of the couple's position was the Pecos River and the Rocky Mountain range that housed the Sacramento and Guadalupe Mountains. Kincaid planned to make camp at the Pecos River before nightfall. There they'd recuperate. He and Stetson, especially their horses, would savor a good, long bath. Making the Pecos River now seemed doubtful.

Their journey toward El Paso, Texas, was the result of a rumor, an offhanded comment. Lubbock's sheriff told Kincaid that Jack Wood had been arrested on charges of murdering a deputy sheriff in El Paso. He said the coconspirator was a Mexican. The murdered man was an influential, popular deputy sheriff in the Tularosa Valley area. Kincaid knew Jack was not a murderer, yet, if falsely accused, Kincaid also knew Jack could be in big trouble.

Jack was Kincaid's childhood friend and a cohort ever since their adventurous days riding for the pony express and fighting side by side for the North during the Civil War. They had promised to always protect and defend the other, regardless of the cost. Hence, Wood had saved Kincaid's life on numerous occasions; Kincaid had done the same for Jack over the years. Having lost touch with Jack, Kincaid was unaware he was needed, so he appreciated the sheriff's tip. Now knowing of Jack's fate and where to find him, he silently swore to honor his pledge.

Stetson's and his journey had been torturous with the lack of rain and insidious summer heat. Several times, they were forced to double back on their trail to evade Comanche and Kiowa renegades, Mescalero Apaches, and the murderous Comancheros. The Comancheros were a feared group of ruthless white men and half-breed Mexicans who traded amiably, albeit illegally, with the Kiowa and Comanche tribes. Comancheros bartered firearms and rotgut whiskey for stolen cattle and horses, used captured white women for slave labor, and eventually sold those women into prostitution, if they survived long enough.

The young Kiowa bucks hunting them were runaways from their reservation. They were well south of the territory they normally traveled. Obviously, they were not on the warpath. They were playing a deadly game of hide-and-seek. Kincaid knew their intention was to capture them, torment them, and trade them to the Comancheros. Stetson was assured rape by them and the Comancheros. Death for Kincaid was also a certainty.

Rummaging for roots and snakes to cease their hunger, the Kiowa braves had seen the two, mounted "white eyes" appear on the horizon. Then, just as suddenly, the image disappeared.

They fanned out and searched through every thicket and around every bush, no matter how small. The white man and woman had evaporated into thin air. To capture the "white eyes" and trade the woman to the Comancheros would give them great prestige and power over the younger members of their tribe. To tell of counting coup and raping the white woman would permit them to come of age and be recognized as true warriors among their tribe, that is, if they decided to return to the dreaded reservation. When they had left, their elders ridiculed and mocked them, warning the others that following the young braves off the reservation would bring retaliation from the soldiers. But it did not matter. It was better to die roaming the open plains free than live an agonizing life as a prisoner on the reservation who was forced to farm dry, stale soil for food that did not provide nourishment.

The disappearance of the human prey baffled the braves. There was not enough vegetation in this drought-ridden area, few arroyos, and little ground swell to hide two riders and their horses.

"Maybe they were ghosts," they argued. Maybe they were a sinister omen the tribe's shaman sent as punishment for leaving the reservation. No, Black Raven, the oldest youth, had seen the two riders. And so had Red Eagle.

"It is a trap," insisted Little Fawn. It was like the ones their elders had used against the half-witted white soldiers. They would be tricked into following the trail and suddenly discover their enemies surrounding them.

The braves talked incessantly, sounding like confused chipmunks. Black Raven pointed out that the more experienced warriors at the reservation knew this land much better than they did. Those warriors could easily find the white couple's hiding place. The Kiowa's were agitated. Their talk grew louder by the minute. Their continued frustration at not finding their prey would guarantee the couple unending torment and agony.

As the bucks moved away in their search, their voices grew distant. Kincaid told himself it was time to make a move. To stand and fight was one option. He had detected the tomahawks, lances, and bows and arrows, but he hadn't seen any firearms. But there were too many of them to fight hand-to-hand. Risking a loss of his own life would be foolish enough, but risking Stetson's life was unthinkable. A man's creed on the frontier was never to allow a white woman to be captured by an Indian. It was better to kill her than let heathens abduct her.

Kincaid searched Stetson's emerald green eyes for a hint of fear. He only saw the self-assuredness he had fallen in love with when they first met. He smiled and reached to shift a few strands of blonde hair that had fallen over her eyes. Her skin flushed at his touch. She smiled back, a knowing smile that said all would be well.

Kincaid decided he would make a run for the horses that were hidden thirty to forty yards away in the ravine, directly opposite the hunters. When they had initially seen the Kiowa braves, he and Stetson could have attempted to outride the Indians. His stallion could easily outdistance the Indian's stout ponies, but he worried that Stetson's horse would have been overrun.

He now feared, if he backtracked through the small cavern, the braves might hear him and be waiting when he emerged. His only choice was to make for his horse and lead the Indians away from the area and away from Stetson in her secure hiding place.

Kincaid extended five fingers, signaling her to wait five minutes. Stetson nodded in acknowledgment. Alert for any Kiowa movement, he slowly pushed himself up from the carpet of dust. Standing erect, he wedged his head and shoulders through the fissure in the ceiling of their hiding place until his forehead and eyes gradually rose from the desert floor, just as a prairie dog would peer from his earthen burrow.

Turning gently in an effort not to disturb the shrubbery and loose rocks around his head, he looked north and then west. He counted nine warriors twenty yards away. He continued his turn around the compass without sighting more of the enemy. Where were the other three braves? He assumed they had ridden to the reservation to bring back others.

Kincaid slowly hoisted himself up through the chasm, dragging his perspiration-soaked body over the thorny bushes masking the exit to their hiding place. "Move!" he told himself. "Before they discover Stetson!" He stood and began running as fast as he could, no longer concerned about making noise. The Kiowa's heard him, turned, and then saw him. The ghost had reappeared! Their shrieks perforated the still air. They bolted on foot after the white apparition.

Stetson's fingers clutched the coolness of her holstered Colt .45. The Indians grew louder. Looking up through the hollow of her potential grave, she only saw blue sky. Bare-chested Indian runners jarred her from her still-life watercolor as they passed over her hideaway. They had no idea she was a mere five feet below them. The sound of pounding feet soon faded.

Kincaid ran. The heels of his boots dug deeper and deeper in the soft reddish-brown sands. They were gaining on him. Struggling for each breath, the arid air scorched his lungs. His thighs began screaming.

The fastest of the bucks was just behind him. Kincaid heard the Indian's moccasins slapping the sand. He heard him panting and smelled his unwashed, odorous skin. The runner reached out and grabbed the soft cloth of Kincaid's cotton shirt.

Reaching around, Kincaid clasped the brave's wrist and jerked his assailant. The buck lost his footing and fell, but he maintained his hold on Kincaid. His grasp slipped down to Kincaid's waist. Being dragged, the pumping movement of Kincaid's legs and the heels of his boots pummeled the Indian. With an agonizing groan, the fastest Kiowa runner released his grip.

Kincaid whistled once and then twice while continuing his long-legged stride ahead of the charging Kiowas. At the sound of the whistle, the black stallion's ears bent back along his head. Bounding from his hiding place, the stallion rose from the arroyo, his muscular hindquarters elevating him momentarily off the ground, and bolted toward his master.

A lance sliced through the air, landing several feet in front of him. Kincaid knew the next lance or arrow would not miss. Kincaid stopped and turned to face his enemies. The Indians fell on him instantly. Kincaid jabbed with his fists, knocking the first and then the second off him. They circled him, pulling at his legs, hair, and clothing. More capable warriors would have slashed his throat and scalped him. These inexperienced bucks enjoyed the contest. They were counting coup. Unlike the more skilled warriors of their tribe, they coveted the challenge of delivering their captive alive. Kincaid had just bet his life on this assumption.

The hooves of the black stallion carved through the collection of human flesh as Kincaid and the Kiowas wrestled on the hot, desert tarmac. As the Indians moved to escape the black beast, Kincaid grabbed the pummel of the saddle. With the familiar weight, the stallion moved away swiftly. Kincaid seated his left foot in the stirrup and wrenched himself into the saddle.

He rode back toward the direction he and Stetson had come, back toward the distant, rolling terrain to the east. The Kiowas, several bleeding from wounds inflicted from the horse, ran toward their waiting ponies. They knew the white man's horse would be no match for their swift, lightweight pintos. In their haste, they had forgotten about the white woman.

Not wanting to discourage them, Kincaid rode at a slowed gait, giving them time to mount their ponies and catch him. Although the Kiowas rode swiftly and expertly, Kincaid and his black stallion, Cimarron, could maintain a safe distance. He occasionally allowed his pursuers to close the distance, encouraging them to stay on his trail. The youthfulness and inexperience of these bucks had been Stetson's salvation.

Stetson waited five minutes and then an additional minute. The sounds of scuffling had disappeared. Ensuring no other Indians were around, she followed Kincaid's earlier movements and pushed through the gapping hole. Pulling herself from her shelter, she kept flat to the ground. She scrutinized the area to confirm her safety.

Stetson cautiously trudged toward her prized appaloosa. She knew Kincaid would ride for hours, exhaust the Kiowa Indians and their ponies, and easily lose them. She smiled to herself, thinking of Kincaid and his untiring black stallion. It was what dime novels had written about as fable.

She spotted her beautiful horse, Sweetwater. Walking up to the appaloosa, she ran her hand over the moist nose. As she tightened the cinch on Sweetwater, a bloodcurdling cry punctured the air, sending an apprehensive shudder through her soul. Without hesitation, Stetson turned, drew her revolver, and fired. The gun bucked in her hand as the Colt .45 spat three times. The muzzle flashed as the 250-grain lead bullets struck their intended targets. As smoke rose from the hot barrel, three Kiowas lay dead within ten feet of her. She had learned well from Ellsworth T. Kincaid.

CHAPTER 3

"Dismount!" Major Weldon L. Cavendish shouted to his men over the bloodcurdling shrieks of the Apaches warriors now encircling them. As he hastily dismounted, an arrow penetrated his horse's neck. Wrenching her head around, the mare came crashing to the ground. Cavendish fell behind the dead carcass, using the body as a shield against the many arrows fired from the mounted Indians.

Cavendish's plan, approved by General Phil Sheridan, was falling apart. Two days before, Cavendish, leading three companies of the Sixth Cavalry, headed north from Fort Bayard, located ten miles northeast of Silver City, New Mexico, toward Horse Springs. Simultaneously, several cavalry patrols under the command of Major Ernst Stills from Fort Wingate, near Gallup, New Mexico, headed south, while two companies of infantry and three cavalry units led by Captain John Ormand headed west by southwest from Fort Sumner, situated on the Pecos River. All units were to converge five miles north of Black Springs. Cavendish strategically theorized their triangular advancement would form a net, hemming in the Indians around Horse Springs. The Fourth Cavalry Regiment at Fort Huachuca in eastern Arizona would ensnarl any Apache fleeing west from the entrapment.

Cavendish had not expected to encounter any hostiles before he met up with the other units. As he and his men labored northward through the Mongollon Mountains along the twisting Gila River, they had spotted fifteen to twenty warriors on horseback that appeared surprised.

The Indians raced northward. Spurring his horse into action, Major Cavendish and his men followed. As the cavalry exited the river canyon, several hundred Indians, hidden in the mountain crevices, emerged. It had been a simple trap, one Major Cavendish should have anticipated. The cavalry's only hope was to gallop toward Horse Springs, with the prospect that the other units had already arrived.

The Indian ponies were swift and more than a match for the heavily burdened army horses. Over the next few miles, the Indians darted in and out of the cavalry formation, riding ahead and then turning on them, shooting both horse and rider. Strict military tactics forced Major Cavendish to order a dismount. They couldn't possibly outrun the heathens or their arrows. They had to form a line of defense and trust, if another detachment was near, they would hear the sound of guns and come to their defense.

Major Cavendish wondered which Indian leader he was up against. Cochise, the great Chiricahua Apache chief, had recently died on an Indian reservation. Victorio, current leader of the Mimbreno Apaches, had retired to the Ojo Caliente reservation in New Mexico. Taza, son of Cochise, had escaped from the San Carlos reservation and headed for Sonora in June. Geronimo and Juh were with Taza. Quanah Parker, chief of the Comanche, had surrendered at Fort Sill a year ago. It could be Lone Wolf, chief of the Kiowas. No, Lone Wolf was imprisoned in Florida. From their apparel and lack of finery, these were clearly Apache warriors, not Kiowa. Major Cavendish was convinced it was the renegade the army had been tracking for months. The butchers had killed settlers and destroyed farms, forts, and supply wagons in the Arizona and New Mexico territories. In recent weeks, these attacks had increased as more than 150 settlers and their families had been massacred. This rebel Apache, known as Blue Dog, had declared war on the United States Army. Now, the government intended to bring him to trial.

"Major! Some of the boys want to try to make it to the ravine other there!" His blue uniform powdered with dirt, First Sergeant Jacob Brokowski threw himself down next to Major Cavendish near the dead horse carcass. The stench of dead horse flesh rose to greet him. Major Cavendish looked where the sergeant was pointing, where the flat ground began breaking into small crevices.

"We can hide down there, sir!" The sergeant mopped the blackened blood and dirt from his forehead with his neckerchief. It was approximately two o'clock in the afternoon; the blistering sun was burning the sweat-soaked men.

"They'll never make it, Brokowski. It's too far to run!" Major Cavendish shouted in reply. The crevice area was fifty yards away. It would be suicide. Major Cavendish expected the sergeant to know better. Scared, men in combat make foolish decisions. Major Cavendish scanned his troops. Formed in a tight circle, saddles, bedrolls, and dead horses, anything that would stop an arrow, comprised the outer circumference. Even though the Indians had seized the mule team carrying the provisions for the journey, his men had plenty of ammunition with them. They could make it until additional troops came, if they kept their wits about them.

"Sergeant, tell the men to hold at all costs! Do not break the line of defense! You hear me, sergeant?" Major Cavendish shook the sergeant, who stared into space.

"Sergeant! Sergeant!" Major Cavendish cried repeatedly, but First Sergeant Brokowski had drifted off.

"You hit? Sergeant!" First Sergeant Brokowski shook his head in the negative, yet a strange countenance covered his face. Sunstroke or fear gripped him. "Perhaps both," Major Cavendish surmised.

"Yes, sir. Right away, sir!" First Sergeant Brokowski stared blankly into the steel blue eyes of Major Cavendish, his response not making any sense. First Sergeant Brokowski crawled back to the other side of the defense perimeter.

Expert marksmen, the Indians circled the formation of soldiers, firing arrows into their midst. Seeing that many of the Apache carried the new Winchester repeating rifle, Major Cavendish swore to himself, damning the Comancheros. The Indians were better equipped than his own men.

Major Cavendish and his men were caught within an eye of a tornado. The dust and dirt the Indian ponies kicked up swirled in a brown arc over their heads. Major Cavendish moved from his location, scurrying in a crouched position to the other side of the perimeter.

"Men, hang on! Reinforcements are coming!" His words of encouragement fell short. They did not pay any attention. They were in shock. Major Cavendish had learned about it at West Point and had experienced it during the Civil War. Scared, not knowing if they would live or die, men froze and stopped fighting. They huddled around the group leader, hoping for mercy, only to be killed. He listened to their anguish outcries as the Indian arrows and bullets filled the sky and fell upon them. Their Springfield carbines were jamming, the .45-70 copper cartridge failing to eject properly. His troopers tried prying out the bulging cases with their knives as the Indians circled closer and closer.

Major Cavendish grabbed one of the soldiers who had stopped fighting and screeched at him, slapping him to come around.

"Go to blazes, Major!" The man stood erect. With a wave of his arm, he shouted, "Follow me, men!"

Three arrows struck him in the back before he took two steps. Several more men began standing. A group of men began running toward the ravine.

"Stop! Stop or I'll shoot!" Major Cavendish looked at First Sergeant Brokowski, who stared as the men ran, shaking his head and mumbling incoherently.

Major Cavendish silently swore at the men breaking rank and running. The men made it over the barricade and continued running. "Run, men. Run as fast as you can," he thought to himself.

"Run!" Major Cavendish yelled. "Run!"

The Indians waited and permitted the men to run. When the soldiers were halfway to the ravine, a savage yell was heard. Twenty Indians on horseback swooped down on them. It was over within minutes. Indian riders clubbed the few who had escaped the arrows. Those soldiers who were still alive were dragged out of range of the soldier's rifles and mutilated for all to witness. A few were scalped while still alive. Several of Major Cavendish's men remaining within the defense perimeter vomited at the sight.

Major Cavendish visualized his wife and young daughter standing on the far side of the defense perimeter. They were smiling at him. His beautiful wife and delightful daughter were holding hands and smiling. Maria had been so supportive of his desire to head west. She had been supportive in his every endeavor. When they first arrived at Fort Bayard, she had busied herself with decorating their assigned officer's quarters in the latest Victorian styles. She had assembled an officer's wives club. Before long, dances, socials, and afternoon teas had made life in this remote territory so much more tolerable. She had been his whole life, and he had loved her dearly until cholera had taken her from him. He smiled back at them.

"Major!"

Major Cavendish looked at First Sergeant Brokowski. Clear-eyed, he had come out of his stupor. He was lying behind a McClellan saddle propped up against a dead mare. Against his shoulder was the stock of his Springfield rifle.

"Here they come, Major!"

Major Cavendish saw the Apache warriors gathering near the fallen soldiers. "Men!" he ordered. "On the line!"

* * * *

Blue Dog closed his eyes and breathed in deeply. He sat cross-legged, perched high on a mountain peak overlooking the flat-topped plateau surrounded by the Gallinas Mountains. He had foreseen the encounter with the United States Army in a dream and had warned his people that many soldiers were coming.

Blue Dog felt the brisk wind coming from the northwest surround his naked body. He sensed his spirit ascend to the heavens. He wished to speak with the great spirits of those who had come before him. In his dream, he saw Juan Jose and Mangus Colorado, both great chiefs of the Mimbreno Apaches. There stood Eskiminzin, leader of the Arivaipa Apaches. With him was Black Knife, leader of the Warm Springs Apache. Chuntz, Chaun-desi, and Cochine, leaders of the Tonto Apache, smiled at him. All were exalted, noble leaders who died believing in their way of life.

He was told there would soon be more soldiers and more killings. The spirits forewarned him of more white man treachery. The dead elders advised him that his direction was true and righteous. The United States Army was his and his people's enemy. The white man continually broke the peace and violated the treaties forced upon the Apache, constraining them to live on reservations in poverty and hunger. The soldier could never be trusted. Yet, he could never be stopped. Their numbers were too overwhelming. The soldiers would continue to kill women, children, and old people; destroy their villages; and eradicate the remaining buffalo. Blue Dog and his people did not have a choice except escaping to Mexico and joining Geronimo. The Great Spirits told him that vengeance and the preservation of their way of life was his path. Before vanishing, they prophesized he would gain great honor before his death.

Thinking of his wife, Blue Dog's chest expanded. He emitted a grave sigh. Captured by the Mexicans, his wife and five-year-old daughter were taken from him and his village years earlier. They were delivered across the border to a Mexican soldier named Juan Rodriquez Felipe de la Caza. The Apache warriors from his village joined him to rescue his family, but the United States Army met them at the Mexican border and drove them back to the reservation. He had prayed to the Great Spirit to bring his family back to him alive.

One moon after they were captured, one solitary man, a white man, rode into the Apache camp. It was early evening. The wind howled, and the smoke from the many fires within the village made it difficult to see. The warriors heard the hoofbeats of a single horse. They armed themselves, thinking soldiers must be coming once again to kill innocent women and children. One man rode through the shroud of smoke, carrying a small child in his arms. The child was *Chat-ta-ke*, daughter of Blue Dog. Unafraid, the man rode between the many wickiups and delivered the small girl to Blue Dog's lodge. Blue Dog waved his arm for the man to dismount, and the man did so. Armed warriors surrounded him, but he did not show any fear. Blue Dog took his daughter from the arms of the white man. He hugged her and kissed her hair, thanking the Great Spirits for her deliverance, holding back his tears of happiness. He motioned to one of the old squaws to take the intruder to a wickiup near his own. Consenting, the man followed the old woman inside the dried grass-thatched dwelling. A fire for warmth burned in the center. The old woman told him to rest and said she would come for him later.

Late that evening, the constellation of stars known to the white man as Cygnus the Swan, Aquila the Eagle, Lyra the Harp, Capricorn the Goat, and Sagittarius the Archer occupied the black autumn sky that was drifting westward. The chiefs of the village gathered and sat around the great lodge fire of Blue Dog and conversed with the white man. Speaking the Apache language, he told them of rescuing the small girl and of the rape, torture, and death of the woman belonging to Blue Dog. He had not been able to kill any of her captors. He only had time to rescue the small girl. The chiefs asked him what he wanted in return for saving Blue Dog's daughter.

He thought for several minutes. When he spoke, the older chiefs listened intently. The white man then asked for the lives of the settlers and farmers living in the New Mexico, Arizona, and Texas territories.

"Why do you not ask to save your own life as well?" they asked him. "We can agree to your request, kill you, and ignore our pact with you. Have not the white chiefs lied to the Apache?"

"I trust your word," he told them.

"Why should we not kill you now?" an older chief asked.

The white man hesitated, thinking of his response. "I trust you will honor my courage in bringing back the small girl."

They looked at him through the smoke made from the fire. Several older chiefs shook their heads, agreeing to his response. Many moments passed without a word spoken. One of the elders, Kicking Wolf, pointed to the revolver on the white man's right hip.

"Have you killed many Apache?" Kicking Wolf asked.

The man looked directly at the old chief. Without hesitation, he replied, "Yes, I have killed many Indians. Some were Apache."

"Have you killed Kickapoo?" Kicking Wolf asked. Courageous in his response, the trespasser responded he had.

"Many Kickapoo?" Kicking Wolf asked again. The white man nodded in the affirmative. Kicking Wolf began laughing because he and all Apache loathed the Kickapoo. The other chiefs joined in the laughter.

Blue Dog, unsmiling, stood solemnly. To those sitting around the fire, he said, "We must give much thought to what the white man has requested."

The chiefs counseled. The stranger who had entered their camp had knowledge of the Apache as no other white man. They agreed he sensed the Apache's spirituality, dignity, and proud identity.

Blue Dog spoke first. "My war is with the United States Army, not of innocent white people."

Blue Dog looked to the heavens, to the Great Spirit, the divine creator who had returned his daughter safely to him. He swore he would honor the white man's request. He then turned to the chiefs who sat before him that evening and the white man who had liberated his daughter from death.

"I will no longer kill harmless homesteaders unless they raise their weapons against me. I speak for the Apache, the chiefs of this village, and the Great Spirits. From this evening forward, I war only against the United States Army and the Mexicans."

The other chiefs nodded in agreement, especially the Mexicans, whom they had hated for centuries. Blue Dog then silently swore an oath of vengeance against the man who had killed his wife.

The white man left their village that evening. Before leaving, Kicking Wolf took him aside, asking if he intended to kill more Kickapoos. "Only if I have to," he replied. Kicking Wolf grinned. The crinkles in his old face enlarged. The elderly chief retorted he had faith the white man would be forced to kill many times.

Blue Dog closed his eyes again and saw the face of the young white man who had crossed the Mexican border to rescue his daughter. He did not understand why a white man, an enemy to the Apache, would risk his life to save his daughter. He had not asked the man. Perhaps it was for the purpose of saving settlers' lives. But Blue Dog did not think this was the reason. He believed this white man had a good spirit and somehow learned of the kidnapping. Blue Dog believed this white man saved his daughter and attempted to save his wife because it was right. This man would remain his and the Apache's friend.

In his dream, Blue Dog saw the images of the fighting that took place that day near Black Springs against the United States Army. He knew of Major Weldon Cavendish. His spirit was strong, stronger than those who died foolishly. Major Cavendish and those who fought bravely and did not run were allowed to live so they would tell the white generals of what they saw. Blue Dog and his warriors fight like no other Indian. They do not attempt harmless coup on soldiers, the act of merely touching a living white man to test an Indian's bravery. They do not drink firewater or smoke the leaves of the peteta bush before battle. Blue Dog and his warriors fight with a clear head and with much fearlessness. Only when the battle is won will he permit the scalping and mutilation of their enemy.

Blue Dog stood and raised his arms so they were perpendicular to the earth. He turned and faced the cold wind and allowed the Great Spirits to envelop his body, making it pure. There was to be much killing. The United States Army was coming, and Blue Dog was prepared—both in body and spirit—to protect those he loved.

Chapter 4

"Tom, sure hate seein' you and the missus leaving us," Wagonmaster Buckskin John Peterson leaned down from his saddle and offered an outstretched hand.

Tom Anderson squinted from the sun bearing down on the wagon train as he looked up, using his hand as a shield to cover his eyes. His family and their wagon had moved off the trail so the others could pass by and continue their journey. He took Peterson's callused hand and shook it. The grasp was firm, the grasp of a stranger who had become a good friend over the last two months. The competent, hardworking frontiersman Peterson had, once again, successfully led a wagon train without incident over the Santa Fe Trail.

"Thanks, John. My family and I owe you an awful lot. The little ones will miss the company of the other children. But we best be moving on to El Paso."

"Head south, south by southwest. You'll pick up a trickling of the Pecos River. Then turn due west to the big waters of the Rio Grande. Follow it south. Without much rain this past summer, the river will be shallow. The small tributaries shouldn't prove to be a problem crossing 'em. Stay close to the Rio Grande. It heads directly for El Paso. Two, maybe three, days journey. Move quickly, keep that old flintlock of yours at the ready. Watch for Injuns. Hear they're causing trouble down that way. Good luck, and Godspeed."

Peterson glanced at Sandy sitting on the buckboard, her shoulder-length, wavy, dark hair blowing in the warm breeze. She smiled at him, a nervous smile that belied her steady hand on the reins controlling the six oxen. He took a quick glance at young Mark walking toward his father. He closed his eyes for a brief second, murmured a small prayer under his breath, and then pulled the reins of his steed around in the direction of the moving wagon train. With his hand held high for the Anderson family to see, he waved good-bye. The fringed sleeve of his soiled deerskin jacket sashayed with the movement. Spurring his horse, Peterson galloped back to lead the wagon train on its final leg around the southern tip of the Sangre De Cristo Mountains and on to Santa Fe.

With the wagon train rolling toward Santa Fe, Tom understood this was the first time since leaving Independence that they'd be on their own. He sensed Sandy's uneasiness and hoped it would diminish as they got closer to El Paso.

Tom tucked his thumbs in his suspenders, turned, and strolled slowly toward their wagon, waving off insects buzzing around his face. The chirping of birds could be heard in the background as the sound of creaking wagon wheels dwindled as the wagon train passed.

Sandy sat tall, almost stiff, on the buckboard. Her back was arched, and her shoulders were back. She was scared, truly scared for the first time since leaving what civilization she knew in Missouri. She thought to herself how she had been terribly apprehensive as the wagon train set out from Independence. She remembered watching the town, framed by the white Osnaburg, horseshoe-shaped canvas opening, disappear on the horizon as the wagon train moved west. She became immediately homesick for the glistening lakes, verdant farmlands, and huckleberry patches left behind. But others were just as fearful as she was. The thought of sharing her trepidation with them was comforting, just as the sound of children playing each night was consoling. Now the traveling community she had grown accustomed to was gone, and they were alone. The safe haven their many new friends represented was no longer there to calm her nerves. There were only she and Tom; twelve-year-old Mark, a man in his own mind; and baby Katy Marie, merely five years old as of three weeks ago.

Sandy smiled as she pensively recalled baking a huge flour biscuit sweetened with sorghum as a birthday cake for Katy Marie that special night. It was the evening Buckskin Peterson had bartered with the Crow Indians for safe passage. After dinner, she brought out the cake with a lighted twig serving as a candle. All the children began singing songs. Katy Marie's eyes were as large as silver dollars, a capacious smile beaming on her angelic face over the surprise. Whatever fears Sandy harbored finally disappeared that evening. It seemed as if a lengthy time had passed since then. Had it just been three weeks since Katy's birthday and two months since they had left Independence? And now, she had heard Peterson tell Tom that it was only three more days to El Paso. They would buy land and build a nice two-story home for the children to grow up in. Tom's dream of a cattle ranch would be realized. The $3,000 in cash she had inherited from her father on his passing last year was hidden in the floor of the wagon and would ensure their dreams. Perhaps there was a school in El Paso. If not, she could establish a good one. She missed teaching, missed the children she had taught in St. Joseph. Her dream to resume teaching and surround herself again with children inspired her to move on. She would not allow her children to sense her fear. It was simply the fear of the unknown. After all, she told herself it was only three more days.

She gave Tom a big, broad smile as he approached the wagon. She loved this tall, handsome man of hers and knew she had to be strong for him. She straightened her skirt and pulled her bonnet on her head to cover herself from the unrelenting sun and the gritty dust that shifted in the air, left in the wake of the now distant wagon train.

"Let's move on down toward the Pecos. We'll bed down for the night. Tomorrow, we'll get an early start. It won't be long, honey," Tom returned her smile, spun around quickly, and pinched at Mark's trousers, teasing him.

"Come on, son. Grab the lead oxen there."

Mark laughed and artfully dodged his father's pat. He loved his father and enjoyed the antics they played on one another. Tom Anderson doted on both children, but the boy was obviously his pride and joy. Mark ran to the lead oxen on the left and pulled on the reins. Mark had a name for each of the six large, Durham steer and called this one Moses.

"Come on, Moses. Move!" Mark shouted as he leaned forward, pulling on the harness while the team sluggishly moved ahead. Sandy maneuvered the three yoke of oxen in the direction Tom was walking. She glanced behind her into the wagon and saw Katy Marie napping soundly, sucking her thumb. No matter what she put on that thumb, vinegar, hot sauce, or bitter herbs, Katy just licked it off and continued sucking. Sandy worried that sucking her thumb might give Katy buckteeth.

Once the Anderson family bedded down, Tom busied himself helping Sandy start the fire.

"The wagon train is probably arriving in Santa Fe about now," he said to Sandy. By the frightened gaze in her eyes, he wished he hadn't said anything about the wagon train. He knew she worried and had worried since leaving Missouri. Although they were alone for the first time since leaving Independence, they had the protection of Fort Union to the north. With soldiers stationed just north of them, Tom didn't worry about their safety on the plains that night.

Mark maintained the fire with the available wood and clumps of yucca he could find in the dry desert. Hating it, Mark scooped up as much prairie fuel as possible. The smell of oxen and other animals' manure was detestable to everyone, especially to Mark, who had his family chuckling at his upturned nose while carrying arms full of it to replenish the fire. Tom didn't have the heart and was enjoying himself too much to tell his son that the drier manure didn't smell. He'd tell him in the morning.

With a light supper of ham, dried fruit, coffee, and tea finished, Sandy read to Katy Marie until the toddler fell to sleep. Mark hobbled the animals. Tom cleaned and stored the dishes and utensils. They slept peacefully that night, even Sandy.

The next morning they followed the Rio Grande south, traversing the east bank. They were making great time. The arid air and warm breeze kept the ordinarily moist river soil dry and solid for the wagon wheels. Tom rode in the wagon with his family. Their horse was securely hitched to the rear. The mountain peaks had received a trifling amount of moisture the night before, which had turned to a milky white snow in the higher elevations. The riverbed was flat for thirty yards on either side of the river. Small clumps of cottonwood trees lined the river's perimeter. Their leaves were turning yellow and orange in the September climate. In a week or two, the leaves would start falling as autumn deliberately advanced into winter. The soil was wetter closer to the water, and Tom steered clear of the dampness to avoid getting bogged down.

Mark held the reins and controlled the oxen remarkably well. Tom watched his son nimbly guide the animals. He was proud of him, this boy who had earned the right to be considered a man. To Tom, Mark had grown in stature and maturity. Someday, Tom surmised Mark would be as tall as him, maybe taller. During the journey, Mark had assumed the responsibilities of a mature man. His adolescent years were behind him. Mark took pride in caring for his little sister. Thanks to his ma's teachings, he read well and read to his sister every boring evening during the trip. He enjoyed reading excerpts from his favorite books, *The Life of Daniel Boone* and *Robinson Crusoe*. The animals had also become his full responsibility. He harnessed them, cared for them, and walked alongside them for most of the trip. His disposition was excellent. It was more like his mother's with a keen sensibility and good humor. In just two months, he had become trustworthy and reliable. He developed a sense of self-worth, a knowing conviction that hard times could be endured and overcome.

As they headed south, Tom began worrying, having difficulty rationalizing the need for putting his family in harm's way for a few dollars. He had heard land was less expensive in El Paso. Santa Fe had grown so large that they'd not be able to purchase a sizable piece of property, build a house, and have a herd of cattle with the cash they had. They were not rich people. Far from it! El Paso was developing slowly. He had heard the Southern Pacific Railroad had plans to run straight through it. There was enough water from the Rio Grande to irrigate thousands of acres. Picking the right parcel of property, they could have a prosperous life in Texas. He worried about Sandy and the two little ones. El Paso was not a family town. It was rough with saloons, gambling, whoring, and rowdy cowpokes. Yet, so were many towns that had grown into prosperous cities. He would form a town council and prohibit hard drinking and gunplay. He was a patient man and a strong-willed one at that. It would all work out. In God's name, he knew it would all work out.

Tom smiled while watching Mark. "Son, let's stretch our legs for awhile."

"Sandy, take the reins for a bit, darling," Tom said into the bed of the wagon. Sandy sat in the back, stroking her daughter's long, blonde hair and humming "Skip to My Lou." Katy Marie's hair was the color of Tom's. Sandy thought Katy Marie's hair was much thicker. She giggled audibly, knowing Tom was angry that God had allowed his hair to thin so early in life.

"All right, Tom," she replied. Sandy climbed up and over the rear of the buckboard, wiggling herself between Mark and Tom. Katy Marie played with her dolls and sang to herself.

"We'll walk a spell up ahead," Tom whispered to Sandy as he kissed her on the cheek and handed her the reins.

Sandy brushed a tassel of hair from Mark's forehead. "Keep an eye on your pa, young man." Mark jumped to the ground.

"Sandy, at this rate, I believe we'll be in El Paso tomorrow afternoon!" Tom yelled over his shoulder. The mountain elevation was beginning to decrease. The river began widening and stretching to the township of El Paso, eventually delineating the Texas and Mexican border.

"Mark," Tom said as his son caught up to him. "I've been meanin' to tell ya. Well, me and your ma are quite proud of you. The way you've grown since we left St. Joe."

Mark smiled broadly. Mark pulled the cavalry cap given to him by a soldier when they had passed Fort Larned, Kansas, from his trousers. He slapped it on his head.

"Thanks, Pa." Mark concentrated on maintaining his pace with his father's longer stride.

"When we get to El Paso, I…er…we, your ma and me, that is, intend to buy you the finest horse." Tom felt awkward praising his son. His awkwardness was readily broken.

"Can I pick 'em?"

"Yep, son, you sure can."

Mark's walk became a touch sprier. His posture was more erect. His shoulders were broader, and his smile grew enormous.

"Tom! Tom!" Sandy's cry for help stopped Tom in his tracks. Turning, Tom saw he and Mark had walked a good distance ahead of their wagon. He also noticed the wagon had gotten too close to the river and had bogged down.

"Come on, Mark. Let's go take a peek."

Mark ran toward the wagon. The left front wheel had sunk more than eight inches. Tom ran his fingers through his thinning blonde hair.

"Well," he thought, "El Paso just got further away."

"Mark, help me unload the wagon."

"Look, Ma. Look. Pretty Indians." Both Mark and his father heard Katy Marie's voice.

Perhaps the innocent tone of a child caused Tom not to react instantaneously. His eyes moved from the sunken wheel to the buckboard where Katy Marie had joined her mother, standing just behind the buckboard. The terror on Sandy's face shifted Tom into action. He turned westward in the direction of the rolling hills in which Katy Marie was pointing.

"Sandy, get Katy Marie in the back of the wagon. Hide, get low, and cover yourselves with blankets. Mark," Tom's voice was commanding and immediate. "Get with the womenfolk…now!" Mark ran to the back of the wagon and climbed aboard, looking in the same direction his father had begun to walk.

"There has to be fifty, maybe a hundred," Tom thought.

Riding swiftly toward them, the colors Katy Marie had called pretty were abundant—reds, blues, and yellows. Some wore neckerchiefs tied around their foreheads. Their faces were covered with war paint. The sound of horses' hooves became the resonance of thunder. Tom felt the earth grumble with the pounding as the horses came closer, now just several hundred yards away. They would have to cross the shallow Rio Grande River.

"Damn the lack of rain," he thought. "The river should be swollen at this point and difficult to cross."

Yet, he couldn't fight them all. Tom's mind was racing. He walked ahead of the wagon. He hoped he could beg for their lives, or at least the lives of his wife and children.

"Pa!" Tom was surprised at the sound of the voice. Glancing to his right, he saw Mark, standing along side of him. The old, useless flintlock rifle was in his hands, and his cavalry cap was pulled down tight on his head.

"I'm a man now, Pa. You said so yourself. I don't hide with the women. I'll help ya." Tom smiled at his brave, fearless son.

"You do that, son." Tom placed his right arm over his son's shoulder. Tom choked back a tear. Mark's most important lesson about life during this journey would be death.

Within moments, the yelling and shrieking band was upon them.

CHAPTER 5

Bent over with his head slumped forward until his chin almost touched his chest and his forearms crossed in his lap, the old, frail Indian sat completely motionless on the black-and-white pinto. A multicolored blanket was wrapped and drawn around his lower back. His tattered deerskin shirt and leggings were his only possessions. Leaning to his left, he was within inches of a tall mescal plant that grew abundantly in southern New Mexico. He stole whatever shade fell from the eighteen-foot-high cluster of stalks. Fatigued and starving, the old man's half-closed eyes gazed at the spine-covered, gray-green leaves of the plant. He vaguely recalled Apache warriors making lances with this deadly shrub many years ago.

He had been hallucinating for several days about different events in his youth. He concentrated as he tried bringing back one particular hallucination. He wanted to relive that one episode again. Shivering, he tried blocking his hunger, closing his senses to the fever that clutched at him. Then he smiled. Squeezing his eyes tighter, his mind swirling in the murky clouds of chimera, the pleasurable vision reappeared. He could see the cascade of water falling into the pool. There, in the center of the lagoon, he could see the beautiful, dark-skinned Apache women bathing naked in the deep, blue water. The clear, pure liquid beaded on their silky skin. The water ran like small tributaries over their breasts, buttocks, and thighs. One was pulling a hairbrush made from the thorny mescal stalks through her long, dark, shiny hair. The women lathered themselves with soap made from the pulp of the same bush. He continued smiling. A man never forgets these images, no matter his age. He recalled the potent drink he had made from the thick, juicy sap of the bush he now leaned against. Warriors called it *aqua vitae*, firewater. It made them foolish and imbecilic. For him and those who fell ill in his village, this drink, in moderation, was a healing medicine.

He was known by the Mimbreno Apaches as *Mon-do-layo*, or White Eagle, the spiritual leader of the fiercest tribe of Apaches. Now he was alone, aged and withered, with no village to support him. No sick or dying needed his cures. No warrior beseeched him for his magical shield of power. The scarcity of rain was an ominous omen. Old women and small children grew sick from the deprivation of the life-giving water. The rains had ceased for many moons, and the dreadful drought brought famine and death to his tribe. His people had implored the Great Spirit to return the waters of life to them. But the Great Spirit was not listening. All summer, they danced, chanted, and waited. Still the rain did not come.

The lodges of his village became a death camp. Only a mother's anguished weeping for her dying babies could be heard within the village. The earth became scorched, and the men no longer had the strength to hunt for food. The animals that relied on water for sustenance lay dead or had departed the plains in search of it. Finally, after all else had failed, the old medicine man climbed the rocky hills surrounding their village. For two blistering days, he climbed the razor-sharp rocks. Cut and bleeding, parched and hungry, he reached the top of the mighty mountain. There, *Mon-do-layo* made offerings of the jojoba bush and seedpods from the ironwood tree to the Great Spirit. The Great Sun set and rose again and again while the shaman communed with the Great Spirit. His people prayed and waited.

Finally, on the fourth evening *Mon-do-layo* descended the rocky cliffs and lethargically hiked back to his village. The chiefs surrounded him, asking when the rain would come. But the brooding countenance of the shaman caused alarm.

"Will not the Great Spirit allow us to drink ever again?" they asked.

"What have we done to make the Master of Life angry with us?" they implored.

Mon-do-layo prepared the sacred pipe. After inhaling deeply, he passed it to the circle of prominent chiefs sitting cross-legged around him. Each council member smoked the pipe, allowing the thick haze of smoke to rise as another offering to the Great Spirit. Then *Mon-do-layo* spoke as the tribunal leaders listened solemnly.

"The Great Spirit has given me a vision from the spirit world. I have been told that we have become lazy. We have taken an abundance from Mother Earth and have given nothing in return." He turned to each leader and shook his head slowly. "The famine is a warning," he told them.

The village grew silent as every man, woman, and child stared at one another, searching for an answer to this hideous sign. *Mon-do-layo* placed his hands on his thighs and emphatically stood. He stepped to the center of the circle while holding his arms over his head as his open palms pointed toward the sky.

"The Great Spirit demands a sacrifice to express our remorse. We must choose our most valued possession and offer it. We must rid ourselves of our one great possession as testimony of our atonement," the shaman said. He returned to his lodge while his people counseled with one another.

What imaginable sacrifice could they make that would demonstrate their repentance to the Great Spirit? What one prominent belonging does the village possess that they could surrender to the Great Spirit? The men and women of the village were perplexed. For three days, they pondered the demand of the Giver-of-Life.

On the fourth day, *Mon-do-layo* exited his lodge and called for the council of chiefs. He advised them and the village that he had experienced a vision in which the Great Spirit told him of the one possession most valued by the Mimbreno Apache.

"What is it?" they demanded. "Tell us, medicine man. We shall cast it out so the rains may come again and sustain us."

The old man glanced in the eyes of each of his people. "It is I the Great Spirit wants."

The women gasped and began weeping. The tribunal met to discuss their options.

Mon-do-layo bundled what little belongings he owned and lashed them to his pony. Then he paused near the center of the village, anticipating the tribunal's decision. The leaders came forth and proclaimed to all that the Great Spirit was indeed all knowing. The Mimbreno Apache had honored and held sacred the shaman for many years. He, and he alone, was the one possession the Apache cherished the most. It would be a considerable sacrifice to permit him to leave. And so, they resolved to favor the Great Spirit with the departure of *Mon-do-layo*. He was never to return.

The many creases around the old man's eyes deepened as he squinted at the sun high overhead. He rocked unsteadily on his horse. For two moons, he had been apart from his people. The supreme penance had been made. Still, no life-giving rain came from the Great Spirit. Every day, he prayed for the health of his people to return. The wildflowers no longer bloomed. The dry dust pervaded his and his pony's nostrils. His stomach was empty, and his mouth was parched.

His strength and energy were eroding. Why would the Great Spirit ask such a great sacrifice and then not deliver the much-needed gift of rain?

He nudged his pony with the heels of his moccasin-covered feet. Wearily, the horse moved northwest in the direction of the Rio Grande River. Although stifling hot, the old Indian felt cold and drew his wool blanket over his shoulders. His body shook from the coldness, and he understood he had the fever. He knew death would come his way with the winter winds. He longed to see the rain first, to know his vision was true and his people would not forget his great wisdom and sacrifice with the passage of time.

The pony drifted aimlessly. He rode hunchbacked and bent over. His eyes were scarcely able to scan the first few feet ahead of the pony's hooves. His hearing had remained sharp, and he heard a familiar, pleasant sound. The pony moved swiftly, rounded an arroyo, and then stopped. There, before him, lay the shoal waters of the murky Rio Grande.

Aware that death was drawing near and perhaps only his death would satisfy the Giver of Life and allow the rains to come, he was apathetic over such a discovery. Yet, he moved closer. His horse was also thirsty and needed to drink. Then he saw the wagon. His body tensed. Cautiously, he moved closer. The pony was as cautious as its rider. The old man saw the bleached white mound. He easily identified the well-known shape and color. A corpse lay ahead. He counted. Two certain. Carefully, he moved toward the wagon.

"Even for an old man," he thought, "it would take several men to fool me."

He hoped the wagon contained food or fresh water. The shallow Rio Grande River had brought death to his people in the past. The United States Army had purposely contaminated the water to destroy the Apache. He would not be fooled again.

The pony stood to the side of the still intact wagon with its white canvas covering. White Eagle's head turned to his right, facing east. The sheer granite hills were 1,000 yards away. Looking north, from the direction the wagon had come, the area narrowed. For anyone to approach, he would quickly see them and could escape. He trusted it was safe to look for food and fresh water.

* * * *

The strong, thick fingers of the man's massive hands slowly pulled the Sharps Model 1874 Creedmoor single-shot rifle from its hand-tooled, floral-carved leather sheath. The rifle had been meticulously cleaned, oiled, and cared for. The sun shone on the polished, blued thirty-four-inch octagon barrel bearing the maker's stamp, "Sharps Rifle Manufacturing Co., 1874." He had chosen the Sharps over the Remington & Sons long-range, rolling block rifle and the Peabody-Martini hammerless rifle the Providence Tool Company manufactured because of its delicate balance and fine accuracy at 1,000 yards. The full fifty-one-and-a-half inches of steel and walnut cleared the sheath. The man smiled, as he always did when admiring perfection. Two years ago, he had participated at the Creedmoor target range on Long Island in a world-class long-range competition with this rifle. There, he and his team defeated the Irish Rifle Team. The following year, he competed again in a rematch in Dublin, Ireland. Once again, the Americans trounced the Irish and every other country's team as well. He and his team were renown as skilled riflemen, especially at distances of between 400 to 1,000 yards. The rifle he had chosen so carefully had served him well.

His team was heralded from coast to coast, and the Pinkerton Detective Agency had identified him from newspaper photographs. He felt reasonably sure he was being followed in New York upon their return from Dublin. Able to shake his pursuers, he bide a farewell to his team members and once again disappeared.

He looked around at the gray-brown canyon walls towering above him. He turned and faced west toward the Rio Grande River and the narrowing valley leading to El Paso. The sun would set in two hours, creating a glare on the silver-bladed front sight, producing a slight complication. He glanced to the slate shelf overhanging the distant valley below. Several loose piles of rocks and boulders made a perfect area for sighting in the massive bullet-flinging machine, as he thought of it. He carried the rifle in his right hand. He hoisted it several inches a few times to feel the ten pounds of weight. Then he kneeled and peered over the rocky precipice he had chosen, observing the height of the mountain. The shadows of the mountain peaks falling on the valley below, coupled with the angle of the setting sun, indicated the approximate height of his position. With his knowledge of right angles, he ascertained his target was just barely less than 1,000 yards. He ran a greased rag over the satin-oiled finished walnut stock and checkered pistol grip. Flipping up the micrometered, tang-mounted rear sight, he made minuscule adjustments for windage and elevation. He calibrated the sight for the known loss of accuracy with his high elevation. Then he shifted, just slightly, the lateral movement of the Vernier-elevated sighting system ensuring his fine-tuning coincided with the drift adjustable front sight he had already set. Fixing the rear, tang-mounted sight higher than the front sight, he judicially took into account the gravitation pull on the bullet while it slipped downrange through the resisting wind.

Seeing the tiny, white-covered wagon in the far distance, he knew he had been too late. If he had known of travelers coming from the north, he would have provided safe passage. El Paso needed more families and less of the criminal element to grow as a community. He was there to help that growth. He grimaced at the thought of the carnage surrounding the stranded wagon. How long ago had it happened? Two hours? Maybe less? As time permitted, he purposely traversed the mountain paths to assist weary travelers in reaching El Paso. As was often the case, he was aware they were coming. He was there to ensure their safe journey. Unfortunately, he was not aware of these incoming travelers and was not able to protect them.

He peered through the rear sight, lining up the front sight in the direction of the wagon. Only a trained eye could distinguish the taper of the barrel, from 1.10 inch at the breech to the .99-inch muzzle. He placed the flat butt of the walnut stock against his right shoulder. With the hammer half-cocked, he extended the lever mechanism downward, opening the breech. From his cartridge belt, he removed a .44-90 caliber metallic cartridge containing a 520-grain lead bullet and inserted it fully into the chamber. Slowly returning the lever and closing the action, he fully cocked the hammer. He felt the double set triggers with his right forefinger. He coiled his finger around the rear trigger and exerted precisely sixteen pounds of pull, setting the front hair trigger to just under two pounds. Resighting his point of aim one last time, he slowly and deliberately squeezed the front trigger. The hammer struck the center primer containing the fulminate, which detonated the powder charge. This sent the massive bullet down the muzzle, exiting at a velocity of 1,770 feet per second. It provided a small burst of recoil, which was not punishing to him at all.

* * * *

White Eagle stared at the white man and young boy. Arrows penetrated the bloated, bleached bodies disrobed of clothing. His mind was no longer sharp as it had once been. Old age, lack of food and water, and a complacency that comes to one knowing he is dying muddies the mind. Yet, his sense of hearing and smell had not failed him. The smell of death hung in the air. And he sensed it was not the death of the white man. His stout pony stirred at the same instant he had discerned it. White Eagle turned his head to face east toward the rocky mountain peaks. He cocked his head to one side, listening. He had heard a sound, a faint glimmer of a noise similar to a bullet being discharged. The pony whinnied and bobbed its head as the speeding bullet struck White Eagle in the center of his forehead, exited the back of his skull, and branded the incident on the white canvas covering of the wagon. A painted mural depicting the many hues of red, from the faintest to the most brilliant, stained the canvas.

* * * *

The man on the hillside slowly lowered the front sights of the Sharps rifle. Methodically wiping the black powder from the muzzle, he returned the rifle to its sheath.

* * * *

That evening, a light rain covered the southern plains of New Mexico and the area around West Texas, including El Paso.

CHAPTER 6

Stetson rode her appaloosa hard to reach the rendezvous point before nightfall. She was certain Kincaid would lose the Kiowa warriors and arrive within the next hour. She permitted Sweetwater to forage freely, knowing the immediate area was safe from harm. She contemplated the old sod house in which they had agreed to meet and the surrounding countryside. She recalled the legend Kincaid had told of the three Eastern women, the Cook sisters, who had become pioneers and successfully made a home in this loneliness.

No one knew what became of the women. Joan Louise, Dorothy, and their younger stepsister, Madeline, had arrived in New Mexico from the New Hampshire region. Prosperity came to the three women at Cook's Corner, as the area became known throughout the territory. Their trading post thrived. Trappers and hunters could always rely on a cup of hot soup, warm biscuits, and a hearty meal that would fill their bellies. The women traded the buffalo hides and pelts of beaver they received for the shelter and food they supplied for provisions coming from Santa Fe. The cavalry often stopped to refresh their horses. Their small tents could often be found dotting the meadows surrounding the sod house.

Even though the war with the Indians had raged for years in the New Mexico Territory, the Apaches had also garnered respect for the three enterprising women. The warring tribes allegedly traded with the white women. However, the white man's inability to keep his promises with the Plains Indians eventually caused the rivers to flow with blood again. Joan, Dorothy, and Madeline could not escape the Indians rage and vengeance. When Cochise and more than 800 Chiricahua warriors attacked the Southwest with unparalleled fervor, their road of retribution took them to the solitary outpost of Cook's Corner.

Some people said the women had been captured, taken to Mexico, and forced to work at hard labor in the fields near La Hunta, Mexico, east of the Sierra Madre Mountains. Some said they went back home to care for Madeline, the youngest sister, who lost her mind after the Apache abducted her daughter. Others alleged the three headed for California and opened the most prominent, successful restaurant and hotel in San Francisco.

Stetson felt their strong presence dominating the old sod house. Both the Apache and white man had revered the sisters. She felt a sudden chill in the air. Just as quickly, she felt silly for believing in ghosts. At the same time, she felt homesick. She missed her three sisters and brother living in Pittsburgh. She remembered what Kincaid had told her about the Apache's romantic version of the women's fate. The Apache believed the Great Spirit loved the three women. In admiration, he asked them to become stars in the evening sky, forming a constellation that would provide an unwavering guidepost and navigation aid for those timid souls lost in the desert wilderness. She preferred the Indians' romantic version of their fate and knew she'd never see the night sky the same way again.

Late that afternoon, the echo of a single gunshot reverberating off the canyon walls startled Stetson. Leaping from her chair, she ran to the open door. Was it Kincaid? It was beginning to get dark, and he was late. Had he outrun the youthful Kiowa bucks? She hated when she worried, and she often worried about him. Shortly after hearing the gunshot, a soft rain began falling. There hadn't been a cloud in the sky to forewarn of an impeding shower. Stetson thought it was curious. It had been many months since it had rained, and the desert quickly absorbed the welcomed precipitation.

Well into the evening, Stetson detected a sound outside. Cautiously peering outside through the rain, she spotted Kincaid dismount his black stallion. Her heart skipped a beat, and she could not prevent the smile that stretched across her face.

Needing to hear his voice, she opened the door and anxiously cried, "Hey, you hungry?"

Kincaid, sopping wet, withdrew his Winchester from its leather sheath and tramped toward the old sod house. Peering from under the brim of his hat, his blue eyes glistened upon seeing her. He stepped inside and embraced her, holding her for a long moment.

Over the warm fire glowing in the sod house's fireplace, Stetson reheated the supper she had prepared earlier while Kincaid unsaddled his stallion. After feeding both horses and ensuring they were secure in the barn, Kincaid reentered the sod house. Stetson took off his hat and wet slicker and hung them to dry. Kincaid placed his Winchester against the wall near the door, removed his gun belt, and placed it on the table near the fireplace. He then ran his fingers through his thick, dark brown hair.

"Rain came up all of a sudden, didn't it? Guess the weather in New Mexico is as unpredictable as in Texas," he said as he stood near the fireplace, warming his hands over the coals. She put a ladle of beans on a tin plate.

"You hear a gunshot a while back? Single-shot, large-caliber rifle from the sound of it," he asked.

"I worried about you," she walked over and put her hand on his arm. He smiled and brought her close to him. She looked up at the man she loved and returned his smile. She chose not to tell him about the three Kiowa who had surprised her. He'd have been disappointed in himself if he had known he'd left her in danger, although he'd be plenty proud of the way she protected herself.

"I like it when you worry about me." His eyes flickered with humor.

She placed her head against his chest and hugged him. She could never explain why she had followed this man to this forbidden country full of soldiers, Indians, thieves, prostitutes, and hate. She just loved him. She followed her heart, like her mother had told her. And she hadn't regretted a day.

CHAPTER 7

Thirty miles north of El Paso, by an outcropping of shale near the base of the Jornada Del Muerto Mountains, Kincaid and Stetson sat motionless on their mounts. Twenty-five yards west, beside the Rio Grande River, rested a Conestoga wagon. Kincaid's senses were fixed on the surrounding area. Rustling wind and the sounds of the river babbling over the moss-covered rocks were clear. Birds feeding their young in nests securely lodged in the mountain crevices were audible along with the sounds of small animals scurrying for foliage, preparing their dens for the winter that would soon be upon them.

The towering, snowcapped mountains pierced the September morning moon as it hovered over the western horizon. The eastern sun peeked through the mountain passes, glowing like a copper penny through incandescent glass. Its beams streaked through the cool air. Palo Verde trees and odd rock formations created haunting shadows. A pale fog rose from the shallow Rio Grande River, spreading at tree level over the area. An eagle soared overhead. Yet, the previous evening's rain hadn't washed away the stench of death.

Kincaid and Stetson slowly approached the wagon. Twenty feet from the wagon, Kincaid held up his hand, signaling a stop. They sat stationary, watching and listening. In the open, they were vulnerable. Dismounting, Kincaid's tacit expression implied she should remain mounted. He crouched next to the black stallion. Three corpses were near the wagon. Two were stripped of clothing and were bloated. A multitude of arrows protruded from their white skin. The other corpse was an Apache.

Kincaid walked closer. Within ten feet of the bodies, Kincaid knelt to study the ground. The tracks depicted recent disturbance from many horses. Near the bodies and the rear of the wagon were human tracks. In front of the wagon were six dead oxen.

He motioned for Stetson to dismount and come forward. She left Sweetwater with the black stallion. Approaching, she felt nauseous. Not accustomed to death's subtle nuances, the foul odor made her stagger.

Viewing the bodies more distinctly, she saw the mutilation of the two white males. Closing her eyes, she turned in the opposite direction, holding her bandanna to her nose and mouth. She saw Kincaid peering at her from his crouched position.

"Sorry," she mouthed silently. He shook his head knowingly.

Walking closer to him, she whispered, "Indians?" She didn't know why she whispered. Kincaid stood as his eyes studied the ground.

"No, not Indians," he whispered back.

"But the arrows…" Her words trailed off as Kincaid knelt down again, tugging on her hand to kneel beside him. She squatted, balancing herself on the balls of her feet.

"See here?" He motioned to the tracks partially erased by the evening rain. "See these horse tracks?"

She shook her head, but she didn't understand.

"Indians don't shoe their horses," he explained.

"But," she tried interrupting, but he continued.

"Look here, these are human tracks. Some wearing moccasins, but most were wearing boots. See the heel imprint, here and here." He drew the outline of one with his finger. "See the large rowel imprint behind these heel markings? Spurs, Stetson. Indians don't wear spurs."

She followed Kincaid as he moved closer to the bodies that were disfigured beyond recognition. She closed her eyes. She felt tears starting to swell.

"Indians mutilate their enemies. It's their custom to send those they've killed to the afterlife disfigured. It's easier for them to identify sworn enemies in the afterworld. It's part of their beliefs," he explained.

Kincaid scrutinized the bodies. "Someone knows a lot about Indian mutilations," he whispered.

She watched him instead of the grotesque bodies. She studied his strong, unshaven jaw as he spoke about the things he knew so much about, the all-knowing tracker, Civil War hero, Indian fighter, and deputy of so many cattle towns. Surrounded by death, he still fascinated her. She watched his tall-framed, broad-shouldered physique as he studied the bodies. The perspiration-stained, five-inch, flat-crowned, wide brim hat covered his long, brown hair. She mused about the previous evening when they held each other close. Their bodies warmed each other as they listened to the rain descend upon the sod house. She remembered holding him close as he twitched and trembled in his sleep, knowing he was once again revisiting the nightmares of his past and the war.

"Each tribe has characteristic markings. These markings make no sense. These aren't from any Southwestern tribe."

Closing her eyes briefly, she forced herself to pay attention to his words in order to concentrate on the death that had enveloped her world. She watched him curiously.

"Northern Plains Indians," he said.

He motioned to the larger corpse. "See that one? The thighs are slashed to the bone."

She listened, choosing not to look at the cadaver.

"These markings are from the Sioux, the Ogallala and Hunkpapa. They're north of the Platte River. And this other one with its hands cut off…" He pointed to the smaller body. She looked.

"Almost a child," she thought, "probably the son of the dead man."

"Cheyenne markings. They differ from the Sioux in how they mutilate," he continued.

"And there," he pointed back to the larger, more bloated body with several arrows imbedded in the chest. "Those arrows…Navajo and Ute arrows are about two-and-a-half feet in length, like those."

"Apache, Comanche, and Cheyenne arrows are about three inches longer, like those," he pointed to the small boy. Kincaid was shaking his head, annoyed. "Everyone knows this."

"Only someone like you that has lived with this sort of thing would know what you're talking about," she corrected him, speaking through her bandanna. "Don't you see? The town will know Indians did this terrible thing. They won't care what tribe."

He knew she was right. "The local Apache will be blamed for killing these people." He looked at her as she spoke. "If Indians didn't do this, who did?"

Kincaid's eyes continued searching the area for additional clues. "Mexicans."

"Why would you say that?"

"Those horse tracks. Mexicans shod their horses with a heavier shoe than we do. Mexican boots made those deep, wide heel marks in the soil. American boot heels are narrower. Those rowels are large, similar to a *vaquero* spur. See those oxen? The Indians are starving in these parts. They'd have butchered 'em and taken the meat back to their village." He took a few steps toward the corpses.

"This dead Indian is an Apache medicine man. The markings on his clothing indicate he was a revered holy man. He wouldn't have killed these people." Kincaid looked down at the prone Apache. A bullet hole was centered perfectly in the middle of his forehead, just above the bridge of his eyes.

Kincaid noticed the bullet hole in the wagon's canvas covering. The rain had muted the bloodstain to a light pink color. Kincaid looked toward the direction the bullet must have traveled. Silently measuring the distance, a peculiar expression covered his face.

"Wonder why Mexicans would've killed these settlers and make it look like the work of Indians," he said aloud.

As he spoke, Stetson walked toward the rear of the wagon. She screamed. Kincaid ran toward her as his hand gripped his holstered revolver.

"Oh God…" Stetson buried her face in Kincaid's chest.

A woman lay in the wagon. She had also been disfigured. Her wrists were bound with leather strapping and tied to the wagon's interior. Kincaid embraced Stetson, holding her as she silently sobbed.

Regaining her composure, Stetson freed herself from Kincaid and cut the strapping with her knife. "We have to bury them."

He nodded in agreement.

Kincaid pulled the body from the wagon while Stetson looked for a family name for a marker. She shuffled through the Anderson's belongings in the wagon while Kincaid sought firmer soil in which to dig the four graves.

"Ellsworth!" Kneeling in front of an old, wooden chest, Stetson held a small doll.

"There was a small girl with this family." Her fingers followed the outline of the name carved into the chest. "Katy Marie."

"Did you see a young girl's body out there?"

He shook his head that he hadn't.

"Would the Mexicans have taken her?"

Kincaid recalled a time not long ago. A black-hearted Mexican insurgent named de la Caza had a reputation of capturing little American and Apache girls. The young girls were never heard from again, and their fates were forever lost.

"Maybe she wandered off," he said, knowing he hadn't seen any small footprints wandering from the area.

Kincaid had finished digging the graves when a herd of mule-eared deer darted from the cottonwood thicket behind him, running toward the eastern granite mountain. He froze, looking around his position. A cloud of dust on the distant western horizon was barely visible.

"Stetson, mount!" His urgency was a call to action, and Stetson immediately mounted Sweetwater.

"What is it?" she questioned as Kincaid threw his leg over the saddle. He nodded in the direction of the approaching cloud. Stetson looked west and saw the hurricane of dirt the thundering hooves created. Painted ponies and Apache warriors in full war regalia became clear.

Stetson grabbed for her rifle. Kincaid put out his hand to stop her.

"Face them," he commanded. They moved to meet the oncoming warriors.

The Apache, with their strong-willed expressions astride muscular ponies, were mesmerizing to Stetson. They swept down the hillside and crossed the narrower part of the river. The turbulent water splashed high as horseflesh parted the stream. Kincaid stood his ground, not moving a muscle and not changing his expression as the Apache's charged toward them. Fifteen feet from them, the Indians halted.

The obvious leader of the warriors was mounted on a pinto with many scenes painted on him. Horseshoes indicated the theft of many horses. Lightning rods denoted many victories against their enemies. The Apache leader's upper face was painted black. A thin, white line ran across his high cheekbones and the bridge of his nose, delineating the dark war paint from his own smooth, dark complexion. Leather moccasins covered his feet. His muscular thighs were bare, glistening with sweat from the morning ride. A buckskin breechcloth covering both front and rear was tied at his waist. He wore a blue waistcoat of a military officer; the military insignia was on the shoulders. Unbuttoned, it revealed well-defined pectoral muscles. A red neckerchief was wrapped around his forehead. His raven hair fell past his shoulders. The Apache gazed at Kincaid with coal black, passionless eyes. The other Indians, similarly dressed except for the blue waistcoat, guarded the area.

A long silence followed. Neither Kincaid nor Blue Dog uttered a word. Blue Dogs' eyes drifted several times toward Stetson. Her blonde hair hung from beneath her hat and lightly touched her shoulders. Finally, Blue Dog broke the silence, speaking in Apache tongue. Pointing several times to the bodies of the dead and back to his band, Stetson correctly assumed the Indian was disclaiming responsibility for the deaths. Not surprisingly, she heard Kincaid speak to the Indian leader in Apache, using both words and sign language to indicate he believed the Apache were not responsible. Blue Dog explained he kept his promise to Kincaid from years earlier. Only those who brought harm to the Apache would die.

As the two men spoke, other Indians dismounted and collected the body of the old medicine man. They placed his body on a travois and walked the pony toward the rear of their war party.

Blue Dog inquired about Stetson, asking Kincaid if she was his woman. A large smile crossed Kincaid's face. He indicated she was indeed his woman, putting off any thoughts Blue Dog had of bartering for her.

"You are well, my friend?" Blue Dog asked.

"Yes. And your family? They are well, too?"

Blue Dog nodded. "My daughter asks about you. She is older now and curious about the man who risked his life to save her. Were she not so young and had you not a woman of your own, my people would receive much joy from such a joining."

"And you?"

Blue Dog grimaced. "Yes, I have a woman also. She is not as beautiful as Yellow Hair." Blue Dog motioned toward Stetson. "She is an Apache. Apache women…" He sighed as his voice trailed. Then he laughed. Kincaid laughed, too.

"It is good to see you again, my friend."

"It is good to see you," Kincaid responded.

Kincaid and Blue Dog nudged their horses toward one another. They leaned forward and grasped the other's right forearm, indicating to all present that a bond remained between two friends. The Apache warriors then turned and moved away, taking the body of the holy man with them.

Kincaid finished burying the three Anderson bodies. He made three crosses and shoved them in the damp soil at the head of each lump of ground. Kincaid took off his hat. Standing next to him, Stetson took his hand and held it. They both bowed their heads.

Not used to praying, Kincaid said a silent prayer, one his mother had taught him as a young boy. He hadn't attended church as his mother had wanted, but he could visualize his mother kneeling and saying her prayers every evening.

Kincaid busied himself, packing any belongings of the Anderson's he found useful. Stetson placed the small, raggedy doll belonging to Katy Marie she had removed from the chest in her saddlebag. Mounting their horses, they took one last look at the three graves and then galloped south toward El Paso.

Chapter 8

On a wandering route beyond El Paso, south of the Rio Grande River, lay the treacherous Tres Castillos Mountains. Past its towering peaks, red cliffs, and cacti, the once legendary mission called Condeza Barajas, now decayed and crumbling, was at the end of a dead-end mountain pass.

One hundred years ago, the basilica withstood the onslaught of Spanish overlords during Mexico's fight for independence. The narrow pass became *El Valle del Diablo* (The Devil's Valley) when 5,000 Spaniards met death attempting to squash the Mexican revolt against Spain. The mission now stood in ruins, ravaged by the blistering sun and swift, scorching winds that race through the canyons. Superstitious Tarahumara Indians purposely avoided the area. They routed their sheep from the region because they believed the ghosts of Spaniards roamed the mission's perimeter.

Juan Rodriquez Felipe de la Caza stood inside one of the dilapidated buildings surrounding the mission. He was hunched over a wooden table studying the multitude of maps and charts. His long fingers searched for a detailed diagram of southern Texas. Agitated, he slid and pushed the collection of blueprints across the tabletop, continuously glancing at the clock hanging on the cracked adobe wall above the fireplace. It was fifteen minutes after seven in the morning. It was fifteen minutes beyond the time of the scheduled execution. Watching the minutes tick away swelled his anger. It was difficult controlling 212 maniacal murderers itching for a war, and those he trusted to supervise these unruly men continued to fail him.

He glanced again at the clock. Half past seven.

"Mother of Jesus," he thought.

He tossed a chart in the corner of the room. On the walls around him hung the many projections of the attack. Many more were scattered around the floor. Walking toward the door, he caught his reflection in the full-length mirror.

He was slouching. His shoulders were bent forward.

"I'm tired," he mumbled to himself.

He stood more erect, throwing his shoulders back. He stared at his tall, slender frame. He was thin with skin not near as dark as the typical *mestizos* (a Mexican of mixed blood), which he was forever thankful. His neck tapered into a strong, competent chin covered with a well-trimmed black goatee. Unlike those around him, he had always taken methodical care in his grooming. The goatee and mustache met, followed the firm contours of his jawline, and ran up into his sideburns. His nose was not flat and wide like Carlos Flores', Miguel Ignacio's, or the others. His was slender and angular, the nose of an aristocrat. A high forehead offset his dark, brooding eyes. A thin widow's peak of black hair swept straight back and was trimmed precisely. His French and Spanish heritage was obvious. He was a *criollos* (of Spanish ancestry born in Mexico). He was proud of his heritage and appearance. It wasn't because women were attracted to him, which they were many times over. It was because his looks set him apart from the others. He did not look like a gringo, but he did not look Mexican either. As a result, he felt special. He was different in a way that pleased him, the women, and his superiors in Mexico City. He knew the preferential treatment afforded him was partially due to his looks. Those who disliked him—and there were many—called him egotistical. His impeccable clothing only abetted those who criticized him. His knee-high black boots invariably enjoyed a flawless high gloss. His skintight, beige riding pants, tucked into his boots, was topped with a red, satin sash tightly cinched at the waist. The blue military waistcoat was custom fit, made by the finest tailors in Tlaxcala, Mexico. He was a fearless leader and a loyalist to his superiors and the men who chose to follow him. If it had not been true, he would be considered a vainglorious buffoon.

De la Caza stepped outside and stood on the wooden porch. With his two hands supporting him on the railing, he inhaled deeply, enjoying the clean, damp air that came with the previous evening's light rain. His chest expanded. Slowly, he allowed the air to escape his lungs, the faint cloud of exhalation rising from his nostrils.

He examined the grounds and buildings of the old church. It was in ruins when he had discovered it more than a year ago. It was withered with rot. Six buildings formed a perimeter around the mission. Fortress walls were never necessary because the surrounding mountains were a shield of invulnerability. The holy stronghold had been strategically built far from the cascading boulders so an adversary's arrows and bullets could never reach them. More than 700 yards clearance, from the mission to the emergence of the rising mountain, guaranteed no enemy could approach without exposing themselves. They could not position themselves along the mountain face and target those within the mission's confines. The distance was too great. Every boulder and plant had been removed within the clearance. The buildings stood in the open. Two officer's buildings were on the west, horse corrals were on the east, and the enlisted men's quarters framed the southern end of the square. The entrance faced north.

"The formality of decorative wrought iron gates had been foolish," he thought, "because they could easily be walked around." The mission was impenetrable from the south, west, and east with accessibility only from the north, directly from the mouth of the mountain pass.

The clock struck at precisely half past seven. Angered, de la Caza walked into the open courtyard and stood with his hands on his hips. He yelled for Carlos Flores, one of his first lieutenants. Flores could be an uncommunicative man, offish and sloppy in his appearance, but the men liked him. For that, de la Caza could not buy. Flores normally followed orders well and was more capable than he let on. It was difficult finding good men willing to do an acceptable job.

"Carlos, come here, now! Hurry before I find you and cut off your balls!"

Momentarily, a much smaller man than de la Caza, with a rotund figure, appeared in the doorway of the officer's quarters.

"*Si*, *El Commandante*, I am coming!" Sluggishly, he ran into the courtyard, his ill-fitting, rumpled uniform slowing him down. Other soldiers began filling the courtyard.

"*Si*, I am here." Flores didn't dare look directly at de la Caza. He stood looking at the ground, gripping his sombrero that he always removed when addressing de la Caza.

De la Caza slowly, smoothly turned. He was as graceful as a flamingo dancer. His arms were outstretched to the side, and his palms were up in a quizzical gesture. His eyes scanned the buildings, their windows and doorways, to ensure his audience was assembling. He came to an abrupt halt before Carlos and stared at his lieutenant.

"Carlos, the prisoner?"

Carlos turned crimson. "*Que*?"

"The prisoner!" Two hundred men heard the deep resonance of de la Caza.

"I demand to know where he is!" de la Caza again turned to his audience.

"*El Commandante*, he is in the stable." Carlos' voice was frail, just above a whisper.

"The stable? The coward is hiding in the stable?" de la Caza bellowed, talking more to the crowd than to Carlos. The grandstanding drew the men closer.

"Bring him here, Carlos. Bring him here, now!"

"*Si, El Commandante*!"

De la Caza stood with his hands on his hips, contemplating the crowd and impatiently tapping his foot as Carlos ran to the stables.

"*Muy bien*," he thought, just as he had wanted.

Carlos wearily returned to the center of the gathered mob. Behind Flores strolled Francisco Rojas. His head was lowered, and his eyes were downcast, trying to dodge their leader's gaze.

"Tie his hands." The order was succinct, and Carlos dutifully obeyed.

"*Amigos*!" de la Caza had everyone's full attention.

"This soldier…No!" His voice boomed in the cool morning air. "This man is no longer a soldier. He is not one of us! He does not follow orders! He is a coward, a traitor, and a drunk! Against my direct orders, he rode into *Tejas*, into El Paso, and was arrested and jailed for shooting and killing a gringo!" de la Caza walked around Francisco, whose head remained slumped. His chin rested on his chest.

"The very cause we have sacrificed for so long is now in jeopardy."

The mob was silent, motionless. No voice rose to support his allegations. Rojas was one of them. To them, his weakness for the bottle was not a crime. But the mob knew his capture by the gringos would be the cause of his death. They knew challenging de la Caza would also be a death sentence. They knew this for certain.

"His punishment is death!" There was silence in the courtyard. Only the buzzing of flies could be heard.

"*Amigos*, it is what we agreed when we accepted this duty. This can be a very ugly business," de la Caza implored, wanting them to understand. Their task was more important than any one life. De la Caza stared at Francisco Rojas. With an outstretched hand, de la Caza grasped the hair of Rojas and lifted his head so their eyes could meet.

"You are a coward and a traitor. May your mother spit on your grave!"

Carlos stepped forward. "*El Commandante*."

De la Caza spun toward the voice of Carlos.

"*Si*, Carlos, speak up. Speak up for all to hear."

"*El Commandante*, the men do not want Francisco executed. He has done us no harm. He is our friend."

"*Que*? The men? I do not hear them Carlos. They must speak." Absolute quiet permeated the courtyard.

"Perhaps they are all cowards, huh, Carlos?" Several men began stepping forth in Rojas' defense when de la Caza grabbed the pistol from Carlos' waistband and cocked it. The men froze. In their momentary hesitation, they finalized the pronounced sentence of Rojas' death. Without hesitation, de la Caza swung the pistol around and placed the muzzle on Rojas' right temple.

Rojas' eyes did not flicker. He was a young man, but he was already an old solider. He bravely stared at de la Caza as the trigger was pulled. The sound of the shot reverberated across the courtyard and into the surrounding mountains. The men standing nearby were showered with blood. Rojas' body slumped to the ground. De la Caza turned toward Carlos. The pistol now pointed directly at the center of the little Mexican's forehead.

"*El Commandante, por favor.*" Carlos began visibly shaking.

The words of de la Caza broke the air and sent a shiver down the backs of every man. "Carlos, twenty lashes each for the execution squad. To the man. At noon today! Hesitate and they will also be executed." de la Caza tossed the still smoking pistol to Carlos, turned, and marched off. The faces of 200 men followed him as he reentered his quarters. Many cursed him under their breath.

"We should rush him and kill him," one of the men mumbled.

"No, it would be foolish. The *federales* would hunt us down like dogs," said another. The men began dispersing.

"Rider!" A posted sentry called. A lone rider rode through the rusted, wrought iron entry gates.

"Message for Juan Rodriquez Felipe de la Caza," he announced as the horse came to a sliding stop. One of the guards grabbed the reins of the horse as another reached for the message.

"No, it must be delivered personally," the rider demanded. "*Pronto*, it is very important!" he barked.

A guard pointed toward de la Caza's quarters.

"*Que*? Quickly, what have you got?"

The rider, waiting to be recognized and given permission to enter, walked toward de la Caza with the papers in his extended hand. De la Caza jerked the message away and briskly excused the messenger. Perusing the message quickly, a smile replaced his sneer. He slapped the papers in the palm of his other hand and laughed aloud. At the doorway, he called for Carlos. Within moments, his faithful lieutenant was by his side.

"Good news, Carlos. Quickly, to the jail."

The two men walked promptly across the courtyard toward the mission. Two guards, standing on either side of the church's entry, nodded as de la Caza and Carlos approached. Inside, they walked swiftly down the center aisle of pews and turned right toward the temporary jail erected within the rear.

"Open up! It is urgent!" de la Caza grunted at the guard standing near the locked doorway.

"*Si.*" Nervous, the guard fumbled with the lock. Pushing him aside, de la Caza unlocked it himself.

The prisoner sat on the far end of the canvas-covered bed in the cell's dimly lit corner. His feet were pulled up close to his buttocks. His arms were wrapped around his knees. He sat silently, watching a wounded fly limp across the soiled blanket. At the sound of the approaching men, his eyes moved upward. His gaze met theirs.

"*Buena días, mi amigo,*" de la Caza turned on the charm, knowing the surprise he brought would stun his prisoner.

"Have we been treating you kindly this morning?" de la Caza's smile broadened as he saw the fresh bruises on the man's face.

Pulling up a stool, de la Caza sat close to the bars of the cell. "*Amigo*, if you tell us who you are and why you were with Francisco Rojas in El Paso, we will treat you fairly. Now, slowly, your name. *Por favor, mi amigo.*"

The prisoner said nothing and only stared into the dark pupils of de la Caza. He knew the punishment would come in a few moments. It always did, like clockwork. First, there would be the friendly face and voice. Then there would be the questions, demands, and, finally, the beatings. After a week of being brutalized, he enjoyed tormenting his captors by denying them the information they wanted. If de la Caza knew who he was or the knowledge he had, the Mexicans would move up their attack on the United States. He was trained to take their abuse, even if it meant death. Knowing the reputation of de la Caza, it ultimately would mean his death. The game was to prolong the journey the devil had laid out for him.

"Silence, always silence. *Mi amigo*, do you not tire of this game? *Si*, it is merely a game. For you, me, and men like us, it is simply a game. And I have grown tired of it."

De la Caza brought out the papers and cleared his voice. "You, my friend, as we now know, are Jack Randal Wood, a United States treasury agent. You served bravely in the foolish Civil War of yours and have worked for President Grant for the last eight years." de la Caza glanced at the papers in his hands and continued, "You have been stationed in the Texas territory to observe any Mexican aggression or infringement by the Mexican government into the United States." de la Caza looked up from the papers. Jack's countenance remained blank.

De la Caza laughed aloud. "You are Jack Wood, *sí*? A spy in Mexico? In a Mexican jail? You are a dead man, Mr. Wood, unless you tell me what you have learned since coming to El Paso and what Rojas told you. It is your decision, my friend." de la Caza stood and stared at Wood. "Tell me what I ask and live, or continue your silence and die. It is very simple, no? Tomorrow, my friend, we will talk again. *Buenos días.*" de la Caza turned briskly and exited the jail.

Inside his office, de la Caza spoke seriously to Carlos. "My friend, we begin our assault on *Tejas* in three weeks. At our departure, we shall execute the gringo spy for all the men to see. Our men will rally with his bloody head on a lance leading us through the streets of El Paso. Come now, look at these charts." de la Caza pushed several maps aside and pulled out a detailed map of central and west Texas.

"Here…" He pointed at El Paso. "We turn and head toward Dallas."

His finger followed the contours of the map, through the mountainous terrain of the Sacramento Mountains, across the Pecos River, and over the barren wastelands of the Callahan Divide.

"We will camp here…" de la Caza pointed to the town of Odessa. "After killing every man and every boy over the age of twelve." The corner of his mouth snarled.

"And here…" he pointed to a spot west of the Brazos River. "We enter and destroy Dallas. Then our demands will be heard by the *Americanos.*"

De la Caza looked away from the map and stared out the window. "Carlos, we must be swift in our endeavors, you understand? *¿usted entiende?*" Carlos nodded his understanding.

"Our killing must be unmerciful and quick. Talk to the men, Carlos. Make them understand."

De La Caza looked at the map again. "Others will join us. Throughout *Tejas,* they will join us. We will be 2,000 strong when we reach Dallas. We will expel the gringos forever, and *Tejas* will once again belong to Mexico!"

CHAPTER 9

Obscured by the evening fires' dense smoke, the Apache camped along the southern edge of the Pyramid Mountains in southwestern New Mexico. The warriors crossed the small stream and entered their encampment, carrying their shaman's body. Then, the village grasped the previous evening's rain was the prophecy of their august healer. Women wept silently, and the children grew quiet. The demise of the exalted medicine man was grave, and the warriors would not tolerate any impertinence. Even the many hunting dogs roaming the camp perceived the mournful mood and fell tranquil.

With composed gloominess, the women prepared the body for its final journey to the Great Unknown. Once cleansed and purified, the body was wrapped tightly in many blankets and then carefully elevated to the four-legged scaffold that stood ten feet in the air. The body was placed there, surrounded by items he cherished for use in the afterlife. The Apache believed his was a purposeful death because the rain refreshed their spirits and promised the Great Spirit had not forsaken them.

Knives were sharpened, bows were restrung, arrows were made, and firearms were loaded as the warriors prepared for war. An unknown enemy had perpetuated the killings and mutilations of white settlers, yet the United States Army blamed the Indians, specifically the Apache, and, more pointedly, Blue Dog and his Mimbreno tribe. Yet, Blue Dog had been true to his word for more than four years. His promise to the young white eyes, the *pinda lick-o-yi* who risked his life to rescue his infant daughter, had been sacred to the tribe. But the soldiers continued to hunt them with hatred and vengeance in their blood.

The shaman had advised Blue Dog to look south, across the border into Mexico. Many in Mexico wanted the Apache dead, obliterated from the face of the earth. The Mexicans paid heavily for the scalps of the Apache, whether it was from a warrior, woman, or child. A bounty of twenty-five dollars for a child's scalp, fifty dollars for a squaw's scalp, and upward of two hundred and fifty dollars for an Apache warrior's scalp was posted. The Mexican and Apache had warred for many years. The shaman had counseled that the Mexicans brought the United States government's wrath to the Apache.

Warriors danced the "dance of death" around the center campfire, now ablaze against an autumn moon. With faces painted to scare the most deadly of enemy and bodies stripped naked, they heaved their weapons high over their heads. Engrossed in their dance, their bodies twisted and contorted. Their feet rapidly moved in cadence to the mellifluous music. Their voices wailed with the intonation of bravado.

"Death to the Mexicans, death to the United States Army, death to all who would harm us."

Blue Dog again ascended the mountain, seeking answers to questions that were beyond his comprehension. Building a small fire in one of the larger crevices created from the timeless erosion of water dripping from the overhead ledge, he removed his clothing. He was thankful the fire kept him warm from the evening's chill. He scooped up a muddy mixture of paint, water, and buffalo feces; stretched his arms overhead; and offered the mixture to the night sky, filled with the stars of so many Apache souls. His mantra offered himself to the Great Spirit as a sacrifice so his people may live peacefully in the barren plains they called home. He prayed for the return of the limitless herds of bison and for his people to be victorious in the battles still facing them.

Blue Dog smeared the foul concoction on his calves and thighs. The icy coolness on his skin felt righteous and braced him against the increasingly frigid mountain air. He then spread his arms and shoulders with the odorous mixture. He continued over his buttocks and finished with his broad pectorals. He stood facing west, facing the darkness where the sun sets. In the west, the thunder and lightening originate. The west provides true power, the power to understand, protect, and defend. He raised his arms until they were perpendicular to the ground. His palms faced forward, and he faced the northwestern wind. Blue Dog closed his eyes and prayed for the power to defend and protect his people from those who would harm them as well as guide him in victorious battle. He then prayed for his people's understanding that their way of life was changed forever and nothing could stop the white man.

He turned toward the east. From this direction, each new day comes into the world. It is the place of illumination and all beginnings. It is the direction of renewal, innocence, spontaneity, joy, and uncritical acceptance of others. From this direction, courage is born, and truthfulness begins. It is the direction of childhood and playfulness along with guidance and leadership. Blue Dog prayed their children and their children's children would experience the joy and happiness of childhood as he had experienced at the feet of his father and mother. Again, he prayed for the Great Spirit's guidance.

Blue Dog raised the breastplate made of buffalo bone whittled by the chiefs before him, sinew from the antelope that runs swiftly across the plains, and brass beads brought from the Spanish across the seas from another world. He raised the breastplate to the evening sky and offered it as a gift to the Great Spirit. He cried out for the soul of the tribe's medicine man because he had blessed the breastplate and made it sacred, forging a warrior's shield of protection from magic. Blue Dog tied the leather thongs around his neck, allowing the breastplate to cover his chest. He prayed the breastplate would protect him in battle so he may return to his tribe and his nine-year-old daughter once this holy war had ended. He prayed the breastplate would give him the strength of the buffalo, the swiftness of the antelope, and the same fervent hatred for his enemy that the Spanish had carried against the Indian.

* * * *

Miguel Ignacio, standing close to his horse for warmth, shivered as the evening's rain soaked through his poncho and clothing. Thick, ominous clouds warned him that the storm passing through would continue for several more hours. Ignacio glanced back at the fifty men who had followed him across the border into the United States. Tired and weary from their journey as well as cold and miserable from the unanticipated downpour, they stood near their ponies trying to shield themselves from the cold. Winter was fast approaching, and flash floods through the canyons and shallow creeks that dotted the countryside was common this time of year. Without warning, a wall of water that had grown in intensity from miles away could crash around a bend and swallow everything in its path. The dry riverbed where they hid, its tall mesquite trees hiding them from the nearby soldiers, was prone to such flooding.

Ignacio knew they needed to move soon. The rain and thunder would mask the sounds of one, maybe two, men at a time. But it would take until morning for them to evade the United States soldiers and cross back into Mexico one by one. Fearing flooding, the downpour would not permit them to hide continuously in one spot for long. The ground was covered with rocks, scrubs, and dried wood. A single sound from a misplaced foot or a hoof cracking a dead timber would signal the soldiers that those they hunted were in the vicinity.

Unfortunately, he could not trust one man among these men. Not one man was honorable to carry the message to de la Caza that another foray into the United States had been completed successfully. Any of these men, if unwatched, would run to escape the clutches of de la Caza and a mission many believed was suicidal. The cowards would run, most likely to the nearest cantina to drown their fears and seek solace from the first prostitute they encountered. They would surely tell their tale and be captured, just as Francisco Rojas had been captured. They would talk to save their foolish souls from a day or two in jail. They would willingly tell their captors everything. In so doing, they would destroy Mexico's ambitions of taking back Texas for herself. They would destroy the years of planning, the years of penetrating the Texas and New Mexico borders to spy on the Yankee dogs, and the years of inciting havoc across the countryside and instilling fear in the hearts of the American people.

"No," Ignacio thought to himself, "I cannot allow a few men at a time to escape and disappear into the cold night." They would stick together in mass, even if it meant death from a flash flood or capture at the hands of the enemy.

Ignacio waited another two hours and then passed the word to mount. Leaning forward from the saddle, he stroked his horse's neck. Spurring her slightly, they moved forward slowly, the ever-alert Ignacio watching the jagged horizon for signs of soldiers. He would prefer engaging the enemy and cutting them to ribbons. Two hundred United States Army soldiers were no match for them. But the secrecy of their mission was far more important than drawing blood from the Americans too quickly. He, de la Caza, and their trained mercenaries would soon draw the blood of countless *Americanos.* The blood would flow deeply, and American masochism would be put to shame. The thought of killing hundreds of Texans while taking back what was rightfully theirs brought him internal warmth that thwarted the frigid cold. Another glance to the rear confirmed his men were mounted and following close behind.

Ignacio's eyes fell on the little girl who rode with Enrique, sitting just behind him.

"de la Caza will be thrilled with such a treasure," he thought.

It was unfortunate they happened upon the wagon and its occupants. There could be no witnesses, and they were forced to kill anyone seeing fifty Mexicans dressed as Apache warriors. The men had been trained well, and the deaths of the settlers would appear as if Apaches butchered them, perpetuating the American's fear of the Apaches. Once again, the soldiers would be called upon to hunt the Indians who had killed and mutilated a harmless family. De la Caza's ingenious plan continued to work. The Apache was hunted and killed for crimes they did not commit. Hatred and fear of the Apache escalated, and the United States Army was forced to pursue them. The countryside was paralyzed with fear of the Indian. Families stayed on their homesteads, making it easier to prey upon them. Towns were deserted by dusk, making them vulnerable to attack. Soldiers, away to hunt Apache, were unable to protect the inhabitants.

While the Apache and Americans warred against one another, Mexico would stealthy steal Texas. Ignacio's upper lip curled into a smile, and his nostrils flared. Revenge for his mother country would be sweet; victory would be even sweeter. Time was drawing near.

Miguel Ignacio and his men silently crossed the border into Mexico and headed south toward Condeza Barajas.

CHAPTER 10

Lieutenant Seth Woodrow wormed his way through the exquisitely dressed mass of people. The Washington, DC, parties had continued unabated since the territory of Colorado had recently been admitted to the Union, becoming the nation's thirty-eighth state. With the upcoming presidential election, the three electoral votes assigned the new state would be critical to President Grant if he sought an unprecedented third term.

The deafening conversations of the copious gathering, numbering more than 1500 of societies celebrated and prosperous well-to-do, distinguished politicians, and the army's eminent top military bureaucrats, drowned out the military brass band. Squeezing past tuxedo-clad gentlemen, military-dressed officers, and well-dressed ladies flaunting the most current, off-the-shoulder, European designs, and richly ornate ball gowns straight from the pages of *Harper's Bazaar*, Lieutenant Woodrow scrutinized the numerous faces while looking for Captain Jonah Walsh.

"Excuse me, ma'am. Excuse me, please." Lieutenant Woodrow, in his early twenties and a recent graduate of West Point, chivalrously elbowed his way to the north side of the immense ballroom. Five colossal, crystal chandeliers illuminated the concert hall. He recognized many of the prominent faces in government, both Democratic and Republican.

"Of course," he thought, "they're here to solicit votes for their causes and press the flesh of those who could benefit their party the most."

Lieutenant Woodrow would have enjoyed lingering for the remainder of the evening and observing this most dazzling display of the elite fraternize with one another. Unfortunately, working as an aide to the president was a full-time occupation.

"Captain Walsh!"

Hearing his name, Jonah Walsh turned toward the youthful lieutenant.

"Hello, Seth. My, my. You're an amazing young man, lieutenant. No matter where I may hide, you always seem to find me." Jonah smiled and took another sip of bourbon from a flask. Woodrow offered Walsh a white, folded message.

"Thank you, Seth, as always." Jonah jokingly bowed at the waist toward the lieutenant, accepted the note with a white-gloved hand, unfolded it, and read the encrypted message, already having guessed the communication.

"I'll be along, Seth." Jonah nodded to the lieutenant and then turned to the small clique encircling his date and him. Laughter and small talk quickly resumed after the interruption. Catherine observed Jonah pull his silver pocket watch from his tuxedo vest, glance at the time, pensively close the watch, and then return it to the vest pocket. Jonah noticed her glancing in his direction.

"Sorry, my dear. Duty calls," he said as he brought her right hand to his lips and pressed firmly against her cool flesh. Their group barely noticed Captain Jonah Walsh excuse himself and saunter toward the exit on the opposite side of the ballroom.

Moving through the crowd, he looked back at Catherine. Once again, she had their small party of friends captivated while she laughed and threw back her head, displaying the smooth texture of her neck. The tight, white tulle and green *poult-de-soie* gown displayed her bountiful cleavage and accentuated her small waist. He thought how this crowd and their intimate friends would be shocked—and humored as well—to know she was a double agent for the United States government. He had known beautiful women before, but he had never felt this way about one before. He had tried figuring it out and putting a name to it. At the thought of her, he was enchanted, bewitched, confused, and sometimes even nauseous. He loved her. Worse yet, she knew it, giving her power over him he had never allowed a woman before. Yet, she hadn't taken advantage of her uncommon influence. He loved her even more for that. Theirs was a dangerous business. For the first time in his life, he worried about someone other than himself and apprehensive about the risks she took for their government.

Jonah exited the Grand Terrace Hotel located on Seventh Street, just a block west of the National Hotel on Sixth Street where John Wilkes Booth had stayed eleven years ago. Walsh thought about the assassination of Lincoln often, even after all these years. It depressed him, and he chose to think of something else. Standing on the steps of the hotel, he smelled the recent rain and noticed the damp ground and the moisture clinging to the landscape. He inhaled deeply. His chest expanded, and he took in the aromas. He loved this time of year in the city, just before winter unleashed its blanket of snow and cold. The leaves were turning their brilliant colors of rust, reds, oranges, and yellows and were dropping to the ground as brown, curled remnants. A light wind scattered the grounded leaves over the manicured lawns. He took the steps, two at a time, down toward the street to the waiting black carriage, the *brougham*, as the Victorian snobbism called it, which had recently been retrofitted with the newly invented solid rubber tires.

Jonah nodded at Phineas, his customary driver who was dressed in a black rainproof overcoat and black top hat and was perched on an open seat in front, as he climbed inside. Phineas shook the reins to the solitary horse. Jonah leaned back, relaxed, removed his gloves, loosened the white satin bow tie, and unbuttoned the stiff tuxedo collar.

The city's gaslights promenaded by the *brougham's* window. The flickering lights cast shadows on the soggy streets. A midnight summons was not unusual from President Grant. Few knew of these select advisors to the president. Facetiously calling themselves the Shadow Cabinet, they habitually met late at night or early mornings. The omnipotence and influence they enjoyed with the president was as effective as Congress or any member of the Cabinet. Although not elected officials, nor sanctioned by Congress, the president had personally chosen the team for its knowledge and trust. Its multitasked purpose was to advise the president on national and international topics, ensure the viability of the presidency, and candidly offer opinions on the gravest of issues.

The powerful men behind Washington, DC, knew that undreamed of wealth lay in the growth of the West, the expansion of the railway system, and the development of large industry. Many men had abandoned scruples to get rich quickly. As a result, corruption ran amok within the government, and the president's second administration had become scandalous. The president trusted those who ultimately betrayed him. Fortunately, he had the wisdom to organize a select few he trusted who were without political aspirations or personal agendas.

Jonah thought about his selection on the team. As a cavalry captain with the Department of the Cumberland under Major General William Starke Rosecrans, he found himself rubbing elbows with Grant throughout the war. Grant liked and trusted him, and he finally transferred him to his command, using his abilities as a military tactician for the reminder of the war.

At war's end, the first challenge of national reconstruction was rebuilding America's economy and financial stability. Counterfeiting had become a threat to the soundness and strength of the nation. Safeguarding the currency became a priority. Just days after the surrender at Appomattox, President Lincoln signed a bill authorizing the Treasury Department to hire agents to investigate counterfeiting. That very evening, President Lincoln, while attending a performance of *Our American Cousin* at Ford's Theater, was assassinated. After the assassination, Walsh was assigned as an agent to the Treasury Department. Since that day, Treasury Department agents assumed a grander mission. In the years since, the authority given to agents had broadened. Now, as deputy assistant of the Treasury Department and supervisor of field operations who oversaw the department's secret service agents, he counseled and advised the president of the United States as part of this quasi-secret committee.

The carriage made its way northwest on Pennsylvania Avenue. Walsh remembered the Union Army's grand review in May 1865 on the street. The entire area was swathed in black, mourning crepe to honor Lincoln. Walsh contemplated the prosperity of the city's postwar years, which embodied conspicuous consumption and Victorian hypocrisy. Sighing, he slouched against the black leather seat. His normally fit physique showed signs of the good life. Patting his stomach, he felt the additional inches added since he came to Washington. He longed for an assignment in the West, preferably Texas or the newer state, Colorado. He planned to appeal for such an appointment with President Grant after the election.

The carriage drove by Kirkwood House on the corner of Pennsylvania Avenue and Twelfth Street, once the residence of Vice President Andrew Johnson. They passed the Willard Hotel on the corner of Fourteenth Street, where Grant habitually visited, sitting in the lobby and unwittingly jeopardizing his own judgment while smoking a few cigars and guilelessly allowing unprincipled individuals to influence him with their questionable, dishonest opinions. The Shadow Cabinet had strongly suggested he cease his visitations, and Grant obligingly agreed. The driver turned right on Fifteenth Street, passing in front of the Treasury Department and the State Department, where Jonah now spent the majority of his waking hours.

As the carriage turned left on G Street, Walsh had a direct view across the street of the charming brick home across from Lafayette Park and the White House where Lincoln's Secretary of State William Seward once resided. At this house on the night of Lincoln's assassination, an attempt had been made on Seward's life.

Walsh pondered the calamity of that evening. If his department had been established, would they have anticipated and averted the assassin's bullet for Lincoln and the attempt on Seward's life? Would they have thought to have agents stationed around the government's power structure? It was a hellish nightmare that continued to disturb him. Even now, his thoughts were haunted. Could an assassination attempt be made on Grant as he considered a run for a third term? Ever vigil, Walsh never truly relaxed.

Past Seward's residence, they approached his destination. The glare of gaslights bounced off the magnificent structure's white, painted sandstone. Approaching the north side of the building, which served as the main entrance, Walsh studied the three-story building with its colonial portico and two-story Ionic columns. He knew the south side was similar in appearance with its semicircle of mighty pillars. The building was once called the Executive Mansion or President's Palace. Since the time of President James Monroe, when the British burned the building during the War of 1812 and Monroe had it painted with a coat of white paint to cover the fire's scorch marks, people called it, appropriately, the White House. More than his position or the politics, Walsh's love of the history of this house and the Capitol kept him there.

Entering the circular drive, Walsh saw the old elms that were originally planted during President James Madison's administration and the extensive ornamental plantings authorized by President Andrew Jackson. Covering more than fifteen acres, the grounds were aesthetically landscaped with trees, shrubs, and flowerbeds. Coming to a stop, Walsh exited the carriage and briskly walked toward the front entrance. An armed military sentry nodded recognition and opened the door for him. Walsh knew the clandestine meeting would be held on the second floor, in the room now called the Lincoln Room, once the official study of Abraham Lincoln.

Walsh walked past the East Room. It had been decorated as many times as there had been presidents. Under Grant, the room had been remodeled to reflect the luxuriant, elaborate, and ornamental period of the Gilded Age. To Walsh, it reminded him of a resplendent, glittering, grand salon on one of the steamboats he had traveled on the Mississippi River just after the war. Walsh passed the Red Room and winked in jest at the immense portrait of the Grant family.

Climbing the stairs, Walsh followed the thick cigar smoke. Hesitating for an instant, he entered the room. "Good evening, gentlemen," Walsh announced as he entered the small study located in the southeast corner of the mansion.

"Good evening, Walsh."

"Evenin', Jonah."

"Hello, captain."

Pleasant salutations were uttered as Walsh joined them. The cigar smoke was dense. Grant had been known to smoke twenty or more a day.

"Please, Jonah, take a seat," President Grant beckoned, motioning at the couch with his left arm.

Walsh nodded to the president as he moved toward his appointed seat. The small, brick fireplace to his left had a fire not attended to and was slowing burning out. The red embers were glowing and occasionally popping. A window behind Grant was partially opened at the top, permitting the accumulating cigar smoke to escape.

Grant sat at the small nondescript desk that had belonged to the sixteenth president. In this room, President Lincoln had read stories to his son, Todd. Several small chairs, the legs cut short to accommodate the ladies' crinoline, bell-shaped hoopskirts of Lincoln's era, were situated in a semicircle facing the president. Walsh took his familiar seat on the couch.

"Gentlemen, it has been several weeks since we last met, and I apologize for that," John Gilmore, undersecretary of the War Department, said, starting the discussions. Dressed in a black tuxedo he had also been summoned from the celebrations. Unlike Walsh, his tie remained perfectly tied, and his vest was buttoned. Gilmore, a Yale graduate from the class of 1869, had taken command of the department in March after the House of Representatives had impeached Secretary of War William Belknap for receiving bribes in exchange for the sale of trading posts in Indian Territory. At twenty-eight years of age, he was the youngest of the advisors sitting before the president.

Gilmore continued, "Several situations in the Southwest have recently arisen that could negatively impact the upcoming election. This evening, the area under discussion is the New Mexico Territory." Gilmore glanced in Walsh's direction, smiling. "Fortunately, Captain Walsh is an expert in that geographic area. Walsh, perhaps you can relay the latest information you have for us before I go on."

Gilmore was competitive by nature. He was extremely protective of his knowledge and how he gathered it. Everyone in the room knew he disliked Walsh. He was jealous of the close relationship and trust that had developed between Walsh and President Grant since the war years. For Gilmore, sharing information with Walsh was similar to playing poker. He neither showed his hand nor allowed his face to be read. Gilmore smiled at his nemesis while running a hand through his wavy, light brown hair.

Walsh had not expected Gilmore to immediately turn the meeting over to him. He immediately knew Gilmore had hoped to catch him off guard. However, he was well-prepared.

"It's been five days since I've heard from our agent in the area. It's not like Jack Wood to not report in. I presume he's in trouble. However, his last communiqué indicated he had found thousands of counterfeit dollars being distributed in New Mexico and the border towns of southern and West Texas."

"Any idea where the money's coming from?" Charles Theodore Gifford, a close friend to the president and solid critic of the administration, questioned. His credentials as past superintendent of Washington College in Lexington, Virginia, cast him in a grander mold than most men. The gray in his hair and mustache gave him a distinguished presence, belying his age of forty-five.

"Mexico." Walsh glanced at the president. If Mexico was up to something, the deterioration of that relationship would hurt Grant's renomination.

"Jonah, are you sure? Do you have any positive proof?" Grant sat with his elbows on the small desk. His bearded face was cupped in his hands, and a quizzical countenance was on his face. Walsh stared at the president, a man he admired. He knew, as everyone in the room knew, Grant had been against the Mexican-American War, believing it an unjust invasion by the United States against a smaller power. Yet, Grant served his country well, having been decorated for bravery at Monterrey, Cerro Gordo, Molino del Rey, and Chapultepec.

"No, sir. No positive proof yet. I've been waiting to hear from Wood. He feels strongly that Mexico is up to something and was investigating the area surrounding El Paso. No, Mr. President. Nothing is certain at this time."

Gilmore glanced around the room. "So, Walsh, Mexico may be toying with the United States, but you're not sure. They may be undermining the very financial stability of our government with counterfeit currency, but you have no verifiable evidence. Thank you for that bit of information."

Walsh glanced at John Gilmore. "You pompous ass," he thought.

"John, damnit, I expect…No…I bloody well demand that all of you do your utmost to work as a team here. You understand me, John?" Grant earned a reputation as the "Slumbering Giant" and easily threw his weight around when necessary. Gilmore nodded his comprehension.

"Gentlemen," Professor Carl Upridge interjected. Upridge was another close friend to the president, having earned his place among them with his scholarly wisdom on every conceivable subject. An author and lecturer, his wealth of knowledge never surprised those in the room. Yet, it was overwhelming to everyone outside this group. He pushed his round, wire-rimmed glasses onto the bridge of his nose, straightened his bow tie for the hundredth time, and rustled through some papers in his lap.

"Speaking of the Southwest, I believe an Indian by the name of Blue Dog and his warriors have refused to return to the San Carlos Reservation. Our local newspapers say he is creating havoc among the settlers in the New Mexico area. Have you any information regarding this Indian, Walsh?" Everyone appreciated Upridge's attempt to bring the meeting to order.

"Yes, thank you, Carl. His Apache name is *Gy-tho-puiua*, meaning 'One Who Sees Far.' He's a leader of the Mimbreno Apache tribe. Doubt if he's creating havoc, professor. He pledged several years ago to leave the 'white eyes' alone. He only attacks the United States Army when provoked."

"Why do they call him Blue Dog? These Indians names can be quite laughable at times." Alexander Stewart, the tall, well-read secretary of the treasury, had never ventured West. He had been a New York merchant until Grant appointed him secretary of the treasury during the early years of his first administration. When Grant was informed his appointment was not legal, Grant, to everyone's dismay, made his faux pas worse by asking the law be disregarded.

"Well, Mr. Secretary, the soldiers don't laugh when they hear his name or spot him and his well-armed warriors, sir. He's usually seen wearing a soldier's blue coat, preferring an officer's coat, with the polished medals and buttons. He makes sure the coat carries the bloodstains of the man he has killed. He trades coats often, giving him great medicine and power with his people." Walsh, more formal with his supervisor than the others, was almost nonchalant in his reply.

"Major Weldon Cavendish and 253 men of the Sixth Cavalry were attacked this week by your Blue Dog, Walsh." Gilmore was having difficulty heeding Grant's admonition. The edge and tone in his voice was noticeable. He knew Grant and Walsh sympathized with the red devils. His personal belief, siding with the public, was that the only solution to the Indian problem was their eradication.

"Any survivors?" Walsh asked, picking up on Gilmore's continuing tone with him.

The professor cleared his throat and answered the question. "Surprisingly, Cavendish and 190 of his men were left to die in the desert. Luckily, they made it back to their fort, but not without witnessing the mutilation and scalping of their fellow men, most of which were half-alive while the heathens butchered them."

"I suspect Blue Dog let those soldiers live," Walsh responded. "My guess is they could have easily finished them off or prevented them from returning to their fort. Or they could've let them die from lack of water in that desert. No, Blue Dog allowed those men to live to send the fort's garrison and the survivors a very clear message. I promise you. Next time we send out the cavalry, the slightest sound will make our soldiers wet their pants. It sounds as if Blue Dog has the upper hand over the entire area." Walsh had read a mountain of briefs about Blue Dog and his renegade tribe and believed he could guess the Apache leader's every motive.

"Christ!" Grant was trying to maintain a promise he had made to his wife about controlling his temper and cursing.

"Ever since Custer and his men were slaughtered, the public has been outraged with these Indians. The word in Washington is that the public is demanding revenge." Grant ran a hand through his dark hair while glancing at each of the men occupying the small room. He stroked his beard. "We think we've got a potential problem with Mexico, and we can't control an Apache uprising in New Mexico." Grant glared at no one in particular.

The room was silent as Grant weighed alternatives. Professor Upridge glanced through his files and adjusted his tie. Gilmore stared out the window while Grant stared at his desk. Gifford and Stewart whispered to one another. Walsh cursed silently about Jack Wood. Where was he? Was he safe, or had he fallen into a trap set by the Mexicans? He knew Jack believed Mexico was intentionally allowing counterfeit money to come across the border. What Jack couldn't answer was why. What was Mexico thinking? He wished he could travel to El Paso to find the answer and Jack, but the president needed him in Washington.

"Walsh!" When it was serious, the president always called him Walsh instead of Jonah.

"Sir!" Walsh stood halfway.

"The president turning to me first was much better than turning to Gilmore," he thought.

"I need more information about Mexico and those counterfeit bills. Damnit, if Mexico wants a fight, we'll gladly indulge them. If those sons of bitches want to screw with us, we'll send 'em a message they'll never forget!" Grant didn't realize his remark had just broken his promise to his wife.

The room was charged with energy. The men leaned forward in their seats. Their forearms rested on their thighs as they listened intently to one of the greatest military leaders the country had ever produced.

"Get me information, Walsh. Information I can use. I don't care how you get it, just get it. Tell me what Mexico is doing and what they're thinking." Grant jabbed his cigar in the air as he talked.

Grant turned to his undersecretary. "The Indian situation is your problem, Gilmore. For Christ sake, you're the goddamned undersecretary of war. If need be, send in Sherman. He'll burn 'em to the ground like Atlanta," Grant gave a belly laugh and then paused. "Okay, hold on Billy Sherman, Gilmore. He'd sure as hell get in the thick of it."

Grant's military success lay in his energy and determination. The oldest of six children, son of an Ohio tanner and farmer and a religious mother, Ulysses Simpson Grant, commander in chief of the Union Army and president of the United States since 1869, had come alive for the first time in a long time.

Grant, having calmed down, continued, "Professor Upridge, assist Walsh as much as possible in gathering information about the counterfeiting issue."

Grant turned to his treasury secretary. "Stewart, put out the word to the military along the Texas and New Mexico borders to be on the lookout for counterfeit money when in town. Maybe we can help Walsh's field operative." Grant turned from the desk and stared out the window into the night.

The men stood and shook hands with the president and one another. Gilmore stood by the doorway as Walsh slid by. Gilmore smiled. Walsh returned the smile. Walsh theorized a chess game was happening between the two of them for some reason. If he hadn't had to get back to his apartment, he would have talked with Gilmore. The situation between the two of them had escalated the last several meetings, and he would like to know why. Tonight was not the night.

Excusing themselves from the room, Upridge walked the hallway next to Walsh. "I'll see what I can find on the situation. Will let you know as soon as possible, all right?"

"Thanks Carl, I appreciate your help. Talk to ya in a couple of days."

Grant pulled his friend Gifford to one side as he exited the Lincoln Room. "Ted, if possible, I'd like for you to come by within the next few days."

"That would be fine, Mr. President. Let me check my calendar. I'll schedule an appointment as soon as possible."

Grant nodded in agreement.

*   *   *   *

"How was your meeting this evening with the president?" Catherine lay in bed next to Walsh and ran her forefinger down the center of his chest. Walsh lay on his back, the sheet covering him from the waist down.

"Fine. Nothing important."

"You always say that."

"Uh-huh." Walsh focused on the counterfeit money passing from Mexico into the United States. He worried about Jack Wood, one of his most competent field agents. Jack had never missed his biweekly contact with him. Walsh feared the worst about Wood. There was no other explanation. Jack was certain the money was coming from Mexico and the Mexican government condoned the action. In El Paso, Jack was trying to find out why the money was pouring in from south of the border. What were the Mexicans up to? Walsh needed to find out in a hurry. He mentally ran through a list of possible options of how to get the information he needed.

"Are you ignoring me, mister?" Catherine giggled and stuck her finger in Jonah's mouth. He slowly pulled her finger out.

"How could any man ignore you, my dear?" Walsh pulled up the sheet and gazed at her naked body.

"I try having a conversation with you, and you tell me a midnight meeting with the president was nothing important. Don't you want to talk about it?"

"Yes, I do. But not with a double agent," he joked.

"I'm working on your side, silly."

"This week."

She punched him hard in the arm. He grabbed her and rolled over on her.

"Again?" she asked.

He pulled the sheet over their heads. His lips came down softly on hers.

Chapter 11

"Morning, Jim."

"Morning, Bill."

Bill Sinclair smiled briefly at his friend as he strolled through the Texas Ranger office in Waco, Texas.

"Busy morning?"

"Same as any, I guess," Jim replied.

Bill felt some compassion for Jim Bison. The man who had once been called a "raging bull" by fellow Texas Rangers during the Indian uprisings in the late 1860s was all but forgotten now. Bill had watched Jim sit behind a desk for nearly three years, shifting through wanted posters, shuffling paperwork, and assigning duties to others he could perform better himself.

"Going through some wanted posters?"

It had become difficult to have even a middling conversation with the man who once ruled Company C with an iron fist. Company C had been the model for all Rangers. Tough and determined as its leader, Company C had been feared by hostile Indians and outlaws throughout southwestern and central Texas. Once Captain Jim Bison was on their trail, outlaws either surrendered or left the country. Indians revered the man they called "White Buffalo" for his tracking abilities, fighting tenacity, and honesty. The oldest member of the famed Texas Rangers, Bison was relegated to a desk job after being severely wounded during an Indian pursuit near Big Canyon Creek. If it hadn't been for Bison, fifteen Rangers would have been massacred. His heroics saved their lives, but it sentenced him to a monotonous, paper-pushing job that, in his own words, made him feel as dumb as a box of rocks.

"The only pleasure I get nowadays is knowing when one of these sons of bitches has been brought in by a Ranger." Bison forced a smile.

"It's been quiet the last few weeks, Jim. Maybe Texas is becoming civilized."

"Texas won't ever become civilized. It'll take years and plenty of Rangers before that happens." Bison wadded up several posters and threw them in the basket. "Damnit," he remarked as he missed the basket.

"You okay?" Bill asked.

"Yeah. Shoulder hurting last couple days." Bison referred to his right shoulder that took a Comanche arrow fired by Chief Stalking Moon during the Big Canyon Creek fight. Most men wouldn't have survived such a wound. The arrow had been driven so deep. That gave Bison big medicine with the Indians. The Comanche's admiration for Bison charging them with an arrow imbedded in his shoulder, the quivers bobbing with every stride of his horse, sanctioned their retreat with honor. Bison's right arm never healed properly and occasionally flared up.

"Anything I can do, Jim?"

"Naw. It hurting means something's about to happen."

"No kidding? You've never told me that before."

"It ain't hurt in a couple years."

"Good or bad?"

"Huh?"

"The something that's going to happen. Is it usually good or bad?"

Bison shrugged his shoulders. "Never been able to figure it out. Just something out of the ordinary usually happens."

"Don't know if I'd want to know something like that."

"Beats sitting around all day, thumbing through papers."

"When that something happens, you let me know." Bill walked into his office. He enjoyed pushing paperwork as opposed to the daily grind of taking care of a horse, riding in terrible weather, sleeping on the ground, and worrying if some outlaw or crazed kid was out to make a name for himself for shooting a Texas Ranger.

"Captain Jim Bison?"

Bison looked up from his mindless doodling. "Yep."

"Letter for you, sir," the messenger said as he entered the office.

"Thanks," Bison said as he reached for the letter.

"You'll have to sign for it, sir."

"I've never had to sign for something before."

"It's from the governor's office. Official business. Sorry, sir." The messenger handed Bison the form to sign. Signing and returning the form, Bison took the letter, threw it on a pile of unfinished paperwork on his desk, and went back to doodling.

"Open the letter, will ya?" Bill peered around his office door. "For Christ's sake, it's from the governor."

Jim knuckled his white, walrus moustache and then curled the Imperial under his lower lip, creating a tight tip on the end of the white hairs. Eyeing the letter, Bison sighed and picked it up. It was simply addressed "Captain Jim Bison, Texas Rangers, Company C." The return address was the governor's in Austin. Flipping it over, Bison saw the governor's wax seal. Bison slowly opened it and read the contents.

"What does it say?"

"Not much."

Bill walked over and stood before Bison's desk.

"Just says the governor requests the honor of my presence."

"That's all?"

"Yep." Bison folded the letter and put it in his rear pants pocket.

"You best be going, Jim. Austin is a two-day ride. I'll cover for you here."

"You do that Bill. Just keep pushing them papers 'til I get back."

Bison hadn't seen Governor Randolph Crittenden for a few years. There was a time when they called each other friends. That was when Bison was heralded as the heroic Texas Ranger and when people couldn't read enough about his exploits in the newspaper. It was wise for any politician to court favor with the famous "Texas Terror," as the journalists had christened him. Jim had even campaigned for Crittenden. Now in his second term, the governor no longer needed the friendship of an old, stubborn, recalcitrant Ranger, a man bitter over losing the full use of his right arm. The governor had recommended the office job for Bison. If it hadn't been for the governor, Bison would have lost his authority over Company C and his job. Unbeknown to Bison, the governor had traded favors for his friend. They had not spoken to one another since.

Bison reached Austin the afternoon of the second day. He rode directly to the governor's mansion. A sentry took his horse, and Bison casually climbed the stairs to the front door. The doorman showed him inside, to a seat where he could wait until called. Momentarily another man appeared.

"Captain Bison, sir?" the manservant inquired.

Jim looked up from his seat. "Yeah?"

"The governor will see you now."

Jim followed the servant upstairs and down a long hallway. Entering the office, Jim caught a glimpse of Governor Crittenden over the servant's shoulder. The governor had aged over the years. The thick, black hair was now thin and gray. His face was weathered. Deep lines circled eyes that disappeared into large, dark shadows. His nose was a blood-gorged proboscis beak, upon which sat thin, wire-rimmed reading glasses. His bleached, blatted coloring was of a man who rarely saw the outdoors. He was formally attired in a matching three-piece suit; white, high-collared shirt; and black tie.

Looking up from his desk, the governor smiled and rose. "Jim, Jim, please come in." The governor carried himself erect, towering over Bison's five-foot-eight-inch frame.

The servant excused himself as Jim approached the desk, reached across, and shook the governor's hand.

"Governor."

"Jim. Please, take a seat." The governor motioned toward a plush, upholstered, high-back chair.

"You look good."

"Thanks, governor."

The governor peered over his glasses. "It's been a long time. Too long. I hope any misgivings you may have harbored have long since subsided."

Bison took his chair and stared at the governor. "They have, governor."

"Good, I'm glad to hear it."

"Your message said it was urgent," Jim wasn't good at pleasantries.

"Yes, it did. Thank you for arriving quickly." The governor pulled an envelope from the top drawer of his desk.

"Jim, we apparently had a little mishap around El Paso."

"Mishap?" Jim thought it was politician talk.

"Uh-huh. I've been asked to have a few Rangers look around the area."

"What would Rangers be looking for?"

"An agent. An agent from Washington's Treasury Department. Seems he's missing."

"He lost or something?"

"Or something, yes. Perhaps kidnapped. No one knows. An agent assigned to the area hasn't been heard from for about a week or so. Someone higher up thinks it's important enough to investigate."

"Higher up? Not you?"

"No. Much higher."

"Gonna keep me guessing?"

"President of the United States."

Bison let out an audible whistle. "Sounds important."

"Very. Classified information. Top secret."

"Why me? I was put out to pasture long ago."

The governor flinched. He knew Jim blamed him for pulling him from active duty. Yet, what Jim didn't know and what he would never tell him was that, after losing partial movement of his right arm, there were those in the capital who would have allowed Jim to fade into obscurity. Jim had been too good of a leader and too good of a friend for the governor to allow that to happen. At least Jim had a steady income and would qualify for a government pension in a few years. It was the least he could do for a friend.

"Jim, you're a good man, probably the best Ranger in the force. Trustful, determined, committed. You're just what they want."

"Who they?"

"The folks in Washington, DC."

"And you?"

"They didn't ask me, Jim. If they had, you would have received a glowing recommendation. I hope you know that."

"The president asked for me?"

"By and by. You know a Captain Jonah Walsh?"

Bison's face lit up, and a smile crossed his face for the first time since he had arrived in Austin. "Yeah, I know him."

"He recommended you—and only you—to the president. My orders come from the president. And he wants you." The governor wished he could say it was he who had made the recommendation because he believed Jim was worth more than a battalion of Rangers any day.

"Okay. What do they need from me?"

The governor was pleased the fiery Irishman had accepted the assignment. The governor then outlined what Captain Jonah Walsh had suggested.

* * * *

Bison's two-day ride back to Waco turned into a one-day hard ride. Jim climbed the stairs two at a time, ran to his desk, and began writing. He hummed as he worked.

"Well, look at you, Mr. Chipper."

"Hey, Bill!" Bison briefly looked up and smiled at his friend.

"What's up?"

"I'm back in business."

"Governor give you a job?"

"Sort of."

"Guess that something you were talking about happened. Wish I could go."

"Wish you could too, Bill," Jim cut him off. "But not this time. Thanks."

Bill smiled. He had no desire to ride off into the dusty sunset after outlaws or Indians. "When will you get back?"

"Couple weeks. Probably sooner," Jim said as he finished signing several letters and stuffing and licking the envelopes. "Gotta mail these. I'll be back."

Bison walked out the office. Bill was pleased to see the old Jim Bison back.

CHAPTER 12

Jake Johnson wore his Sunday best. He had put an iron to his sack coat the night before, pressed his pants, and polished his boots. His borrowed white shirt was snug in the shoulders and was a little short in the sleeves. His string tie hung crooked. But his smile obscured any untidiness in his clothing. Jake knocked on the door to the house. His excitement level was about to burst.

The door opened.

"Afternoon, Mrs. Place," Jake said ever so gently to the mistress of the house. In her mid-eighties, Virginia Place looked fifteen years younger. She had spunk and a twinkle in her blue eyes. Her graying hair was meticulously combed and was tied into a bun on the back of her head.

"Good afternoon, Jake. She's almost ready. Please come in." Her voice was coarse and gravelly with age. She held the wood-framed screen door open as Jake politely slid by her.

The cottage was decorous in its simplicity. The tiny living room was comfortable with two chairs and a couch slightly angled toward the fireplace to take advantage of the warmth during the winter while offering a conversational air. A handmade oval rug, on which the furniture sat, covered the wooden floors.

Mrs. Place closed the screen door, leaving the front door open to permit the light September breeze to cool the musty house.

"Have a seat in the parlor, Jake. Charlotte will be here shortly."

"Thank you, ma'am." Jake sat in one of the chairs. The other chair, a rocker, was a favorite of Mrs. Place.

"Would you like some iced tea, Jake? Made some fresh this morning."

"Thank you, ma'am." Jake sat upright with the fingers of his hands patiently intertwined. His nervousness was obvious. Mrs. Place excused herself and went to the kitchen.

"Here we are." Mrs. Place brought two glasses of tea on a copper-covered tray. She offered Jake the tray, and he took a glass. The glass was cool to the touch.

"Thank you, ma'am."

Mrs. Place liked Jake. He had been polite since the first time she had met him. He had a good disposition, was easy to talk with, and was, in her estimation, a very good-looking man. At twenty-one years of age, his short, light brown hair had begun receding, if only a little. It detracted little from his sparkling eyes and large smile. She believed he was the first man she had ever met who did not have one mean-spirited bone in his body, so very much unlike her Tubbs, who had died eight years ago. Her husband of forty-three years was the typical man with his inferiority complex and sudden bursts of meanness. He was usually argumentative, always trying to prove he was right, even when everyone knew he wasn't. He had never hit her, even though, on occasions, especially when they were first married, he had threatened to. No, Jake was the quintessential Victorian gentleman. She could sense a strong masculine side, maybe even a mean side. After all, he had been a Texas Ranger for three years. His reputation within the community of Jasper was firm but fair. He did not show any fear in the pursuit of outlaws and cattle rustlers. She had heard whispers about how he single-handedly brought in the Pitchard gang. They were shot up pretty bad. Jake rode into town while leading all four outlaws tied to their saddles. Some said he should have killed them for robbing the bank, wounding the teller, and killing an innocent bystander. She believed Jake had shown compassion and restraint in bringing them to justice.

"Awfully hot, ain't it, ma'am?" Jake admired the woman, but his shyness prevented him from making small talk.

"Yes, it is. The breeze isn't helping much today, I'm afraid. But the tea sure does taste good, don't it?"

"Yes, ma'am, it surely does." He liked her slight southern Texas accent. She originally hailed from Nova Scotia, but she came to the United States during the Civil War to care for her granddaughter. She and Tubbs made a good home for the young girl, ensuring she went to school, studied, and was greatly loved. After Tubbs passed away, she made her living by ironing and doing laundry.

"Afternoon, Jake," Charlotte said as she entered the parlor. To Jake, she was the prettiest thing he had ever seen. Her white chiffon dress flowed as she approached him. Her smile was radiant. Her black hair looked wet, as if she had just washed it and it hadn't fully dried. She wore a hint of makeup, hoping her grandmother wouldn't notice.

"She's as graceful as a ballerina," Jake thought. Then he smiled. He'd never seen a ballerina, but one would surely glide across a stage as smoothly as Charlotte glided across the parlor floor.

Jake jumped up, nearly spilling his tea. He smiled at Mrs. Place for his clumsiness, and she returned the smile while noticing her granddaughter's touch of makeup. It reminded her of Tubbs courting her so many years ago. She beamed at Charlotte, the love of her life.

"Charlotte, you look…Well, you look…" Jake was at a loss for words again.

"Thank you, Jake." Charlotte loved his taciturn ways.

"Grandmama, Jake and I will be sitting on the porch."

"That's quite all right, dear."

"That is…Hmm…If you'd like to join us, ma'am?"

"Oh, that's quite all right. You two enjoy yourselves. I have some needlepoint to finish."

"Always the gentleman, that Jake," Mrs. Place thought and smiled.

"Yes, ma'am." Jake liked the companionship of Charlotte's grandmother, even though what he had to say to Charlotte needed to be said to her alone.

Taking her seat on the whitewashed, wooden swing, Charlotte patted the seat next to her, indicating she wanted Jake to sit next to her.

"This is a pleasant surprise, Jake. It's very few Sundays we have together, what with church, Grandmama, and your responsibilities. I have so been looking forward to today since you asked me last Thursday."

Jake sat beside her. He couldn't believe someone so lovely would be interested in him. He had girlfriends before, but he never had one so lively or intelligent or one who showed such a keen interest in him. He liked that she liked him so much. He was puzzled that she liked the idea of him being a Texas Ranger. He didn't make much money. He could make more tending store in town. His duties were usually hazardous and took him away from home for days and weeks at a time. Yet, unlike the other girls he'd known, she graciously accepted him on his terms. Over the last eighteen months since they first met, she had never broached the subject of changing him or changing what he did for a living.

"Well, it just don't seem right. You sitting here on a pretty Sunday afternoon and me off doing chores. Thought it'd be fun spending time with you."

Charlotte blushed. She worshipped Jake. He was always flattering her, being chivalrous, and trying to say the things he felt she wanted to hear. It pleased her immensely just knowing he was always trying to please her.

"Want to walk to town?" she asked.

"Sure."

"Grandmama, Jake and I are going into town. Need anything?" Charlotte asked as she poked her head inside the house.

"No, honey. Have a good time. Supper's on at four. Be sure to invite Jake."

They walked several blocks into downtown Jasper while holding hands. In Jasper, no building was more than two stories tall. Every building had a Victorian-style facade painted in bright, pastel colors. Maple trees lined Main Street. Picturesque, Jasper was a thriving community of 5,000 people with two banks, two general stores, a Protestant and Catholic church, three saloons, one doctor, three stables, and a newspaper that also circulated in several outlying towns.

Looking through a window of one of the closed stores, Jake turned to Charlotte.

"I got a letter the other day."

"Oh, from whom?" She turned toward him, looked up into his brown eyes, and smiled.

"A friend of mine. Another Texas Ranger."

"Is he coming to town? I would just love to meet one of your Ranger friends."

"No, he ain't coming here. He wants me to meet up with him."

"Another exciting assignment?"

He smiled. She was always thrilled about his assignments, even though she never knew where he was going or what he was asked to do.

"Maybe so. Don't rightly know yet. Haven't seen or heard from him in a couple years."

"Couple years? Wonder why he'd contact you now?"

"Like I said, he's a good friend, even if we haven't seen each other. Guess it's a bond or something, especially since I'm alive today because of the captain."

"Really?"

"Uh-oh," Jake thought, "here it comes."

"He saved your life?"

"Yeah, mine and more than a dozen other Rangers to boot."

"Please tell me about it, Jake. I would love to hear about it."

He took a deep breath. "Well, let's walk, too. Hate to just stand here." The two continued to hold hands and crossed the dusty street. Jake began his story. "It was about three years ago or so."

"When you first became a Ranger?"

"Uh-huh, about that time. The Comanches were raiding over in West Texas, around San Angelo. We were assigned to rid the area of them until the Army got there. We rode out that way for about three days. On the fourth day, we came across a trail, figured it was Comanches, and took the trail for the next two days. We followed it into a canyon." Jake momentarily stopped his story. His right hand began twitching.

"Jake, honey?" Charlotte held his hand steady.

"It's okay. We were stupid. Just plain stupid," he repeated to himself.

"Them Injuns were leading us into a trap. I reckon they had been tailing us before we found their trail."

Charlotte nodded her head to indicate she was listening. They stopped walking.

"Jeez, Charlotte, next thing I remember was the sky full of arrows. Two Rangers were hit. We jumped off our horses and pulled the wounded to safety behind some boulders. The Comanche were everywhere. They were shooting rifles, too. Thank God, they weren't much good though."

Jake's hand and arm continued shaking. Charlotte motioned for them to sit on a bench in front of one of the stores. "All day long, they kept coming. We held them off best we could. They got close, too. Another Ranger was hit. Every time we tried looking over our breastwork of boulders, they'd get one of us. Ran off our horses. Had no water, and it was hotter than blazes." Jake took another deep breath. "Thought we were done for. We all did. Ammo was running low, and it was getting' dark."

"That's good. Indians don't fight at night, right?"

"Don't think them Comanche ever heard that saying. All night long, they kept coming. They were trying to count coup on us. Couple Injuns ran right through our group during the night, yelling and shrieking. Gives me the willies to even think about it. We couldn't shoot at 'em for fear of hitting one of us."

"Next morning, we're talking about sending for help. Everyone knew it would be suicide. But it was better than doing nothing and dying." Jake hesitated and then continued.

"Three Rangers were picked to go. I was one because, as the youngest, everyone figured I'd run pretty fast. We were deciding the direction we'd run when the Comanches made a hard charge at us. We spent most of our ammo then. The three of us heading out didn't figure we'd make it. Those staying behind knew they wouldn't make it either." Jake's arm visibly trembled.

"Me and the other two was starting to go when we heard the most god-awful scream. Thought they'd hit one of us. We were looking at each other, wondering if one of us was hit. Then there was another scream. Mother, Jesus of God. We saw a pony tear through the canyon."

Jake looked at Charlotte, and a tear formed in his eye.

"Yes, honey?" she asked.

"It was him."

She waited, and he said nothing. "Who?"

"Captain Jim Bison. He was all by himself, riding hard and shooting that Winchester of his faster than I could spit. He hit a few of them Injuns, too, at a full gallop. It was a sight to behold."

"Well, those Injuns got the fear of God in 'em. Probably thought a crazy man was after them. He was yelling and screaming something fierce. I was told later that, during the war, it was called a rebel yell. Scared the bejesus out of those Comanches and me, too."

"The Injuns grouped at the end of the canyon. The captain pulled his horse around, facing 'em from the other end of the canyon. We put our last rounds in our rifles, figuring those Comanches were going to charge the captain and we were going to get as many as our ammo would allow."

Jake laughed, and his shivering became shallow.

"Son of a bitch…" He looked at her. "Oh, Charlotte, I'm sorry to be saying that."

"No, no. It's okay. Please, go on."

"We're all trying to get a good aim when that crazy Captain Bison charges them! He does! He charges them Injuns head-on. The chief, or what we figured to be the chief because of his headdress, moves forward on his paint, out in front of the others, and fires an arrow at the captain. It sailed awfully high in the air. We're all staring at it when it hits the captain in the shoulder. It hit him hard and went in deep. We knew he was a goner. The captain pulled the horse's reins and slid to a stop. It was like he was moving very slow. The captain dropped his rifle, and we stood up to shoot them Injuns. It was a standoff. The Injuns on one side of the canyon and the captain on the other."

"Then what, Jake?"

"We couldn't believe it. He goes and does it again."

"What does he do?"

"He charges them. At a full gallop, both pistols blazing and screaming that rebel yell again. Oh, the sound of it. I can still close my eyes and hear it. He's heading right at them. You know what, Charlotte?

She shakes her head.

"They run. Them Comanches turn tail. The captain is yelling. We're yelling."

"He saved our lives that day. I'll be beholding to the man forever."

"He sent you that letter?"

"Yeah. And I gotta go. I'd follow that man into hell, if need be."

"I understand."

"I appreciate it. I really do, ya know?" He squeezed her hand.

"Do you know where to meet up with him?"

"Whispering Pines."

"That's a long ride."

"Yeah, but worth it just to see the old captain again."

"You think it might be dangerous, Jake?" She had never asked the question before.

Jake shrugged his shoulders. "Figure it might be. The captain is a fighting man. When a job looks tough, they usually call for him. I'm suspecting it might be."

"I'll bet you're pretty tough yourself." She smiled nervously.

"Reckon. Pleased the captain would ask me. Very pleased."

"Then so am I," Charlotte said very confidently and proudly.

"That's why I wanted to see you today."

"To tell me good-bye?"

"Yes. And to ask if you'll wait for me."

"Why, Jake Johnson, whatever do you mean? You've never asked me that, and you've gone away before."

"I'm guessing this is serious business. I'm guessing I'm looking at the best thing that ever happened to me when I look at you. Well, I…" Jake didn't continue.

"Yes, Jake. Of course, I will wait for you."

"Until forever," she then thought to herself.

"Grandmama wants you to come to dinner tonight. We'll make some extra for the ride."

Jake's shaking ceased. They stood and headed toward Charlotte Place's home.

Chapter 13

"Who the hell named this town Whispering Pines?"

The batwing saloon doors burst open, and the doors were nearly torn from their hinges. Standing in the entry to Henry's Saloon was Bill Scrimshaw, a big, beefy man carrying a Winchester in his right hand. From head to toe, he was covered with the red and brown grit of the land. The early morning sun exploded through the door, making it difficult for anyone in the bar to see anything besides Scrimshaw's immense silhouette.

"There's not a damn tree anywhere near here for thirty miles."

Scrimshaw scrunched up his eyes to peer inside the dark, small, one-room saloon. Through sifting dust dancing on sunbeams, he saw several round tables in the center of the room for poker players. The back wall was empty. To his left, he saw a twenty-foot, cheap, pine bar. The back bar consisted of one square mirror surrounded by several bottles of different grade whiskey. Only two men were in the bar; the bartender and another man standing at the bar. Scrimshaw walked over to the bar and leaned his rifle against it.

"Three bottles," Scrimshaw demanded.

The barkeep's eyebrows rose at the large order.

"Wrap two up for the saddlebags. Hand over the other." Scrimshaw leaned against the bar, ran a hand over his week-old unshaven stubble, and faced the smaller man standing next to him.

"You live in this sinkhole?"

"Nope." The man continued looking at his coffee mug, even though he hadn't missed the big man's entrance or the .44-40 caliber Smith and Wesson holstered on his right hip. Scrimshaw wore weathered shotgun chaps and smelled of cow dung. His breath was worse.

"Work around here?"

"Nope," the man answered.

Scrimshaw immediately disliked the man. The man hadn't looked in his direction once. Scrimshaw sized him up. He was a much smaller man. He was less than six feet and thin with a narrow waist. He wore a cross-draw rig holstering a Colt and spurs. Scrimshaw licked his cracked lips and leaned closer. The man had a small scar on his left cheek and sported a well-trimmed, dark brown mustache.

With a soiled towel, the barkeep wiped the dust from the bar top where Scrimshaw stood. He set an open bottle in front of him and then set the other two bottles on the bar, both wrapped in newspaper.

"Twenty dollars, mister."

"Twenty dollars?"

"Yes, sir. Twenty dollars."

"My ass."

The barkeep stared at Scrimshaw and fingered a shotgun located behind the bar, just in front and beneath where Scrimshaw stood.

"If you ain't got the money…"

Scrimshaw reached over and slapped the barkeep. "Don't sass me." He reached in his pocket and pulled out several twenty-dollar gold pieces and threw them on the bar. He placed a thick, callused index finger on one and slid it toward the barkeep. "Twenty dollars," he said.

The man next to Scrimshaw watched everything from the reflection in the mirror. His jaw tensed when the bartender was slapped. Scrimshaw saw the man looking at him in the mirror.

"Got a problem, mister?" Scrimshaw turned and focused his attention on the man next to him. He moved closer.

The man next to him said nothing.

"Son of a bitch. Don't talk much, do ya?" Before the man could reply, Scrimshaw said, "And don't go saying nope again. You're starting to piss me off."

The man stood erect and turned to face Scrimshaw.

"I do have a problem…with you."

Scrimshaw put his hands on his hips with his right hand near the pistol grip. "That so?"

"You been passing counterfeit gold eagles long?"

"What?"

The man reached over and picked up one of the twenty-dollar gold pieces from the bar. "This, mister, is counterfeit."

Scrimshaw looked at the gold piece held between the man's thumb and index finger. "How can you tell?"

The man slowly pulled a knife from his belt and scratched the gold piece. "A gold piece is solid. This one ain't." He offered the scratched piece to Scrimshaw, who took it and rolled it between his fingers. The scratched area was silver beneath.

"Where'd you get them, mister?" The man had heard rumors that counterfeit money had been floating up from Mexico in large quantities. This could be confirmation of the rumor.

"San Antonio. At the Hundred and One on East Second Street." Scrimshaw was seething with anger. It was crystal clear where he had gotten the money. He had been playing poker all night with a table of Mexicans and winning.

"San Antonio, huh? How long ago?"

"Couple weeks. Look, mister, you're asking a lot of questions for someone who had no interest in talking to me a minute ago. What's this to you anyhow?"

The man moved his coat to expose a Texas Ranger badge on his vest. "Name's JJ Bost, Texas Ranger."

Scrimshaw's hand dropped to his revolver. "I ain't done nothing wrong here. I must've got hoodwinked from some greasers down San Anton way."

The Texas Ranger reached over and took the other gold eagles from the bar. "You got anymore of these?"

Scrimshaw tensed. The bartender reached over and took the three whiskey bottles from the bar, breaking Scrimshaw's concentration on the Texas Ranger.

"You son of a..." Scrimshaw went for his gun. The Ranger drew his and whipped the barrel across Scrimshaw's skull. The big, burly man swayed. He gripped the edge of the bar to steady himself and then toppled to the wooden floor.

JJ turned, walked toward the back of the saloon, and sat down. He looked at his pocket watch. Jim Bison would arrive soon. Perhaps then he'd find out why they were heading to El Paso.

CHAPTER 14

Tex removed his hat. With the stained bandanna tied around his neck, he mopped the sweat and dirt from his brow and thinning white hair.

"It's god-awful hot for September," he thought.

He played out the braided rawhide lariat, grasping both the main line and loop in his right hand while holding the coiled rope in his left. The quarter horse moved as far away from him as the corral would permit.

"C'mon, Petey," Tex said aloud. Taking a few steps closer, he began twirling the rope overhead. The horse snorted. Instinctively, Tex let the rope go. Again, the horse moved. The rope fell limp to the ground for a third time. Exasperated, Tex walked to the corral fence and sat on the bottom rung.

"I'm getting too old for this," he thought.

"There he is," commented Captain Jim Bison as they rode across the ranch. "Hold up here for a minute."

Bison dismounted, and the others followed. Tying their horses at the cabin's hitching post, they sat on the porch while watching Tex.

"That's one hell of a cowboy, boys," Bison remarked.

"What I've heard, one hell of a Texas Ranger, too," JJ interjected.

"Kinda old, ain't he?" Jake innocently asked as he watched the sixty-four-year-old Ranger.

"Yeah, he's that, but you'd never know it," Bison responded, somewhat defensively. Tex carried his tall, six-foot-two-inch lanky frame erect. He was still strong and agile, and his aim, which he practiced weekly, was as true as ever.

"How come he ain't a Ranger no more?" Johnson asked.

"Rangers like 'em young. Like you, Jake. They put the older ones, like me and Tex, out to pasture," Bison laconically replied.

Standing, Tex went through the same methodical process with the rope. He was a little slower the fourth time as the heat began wearing him down. He spoke softly to his horse of fifteen years, attempting to coach him closer.

"Damnit, Petey," Tex said. Another thrown loop fell short. "Oughta just shoot ya, dang it." Wiping the sweat from his eyes, he flexed and rubbed his fingers. The arthritis was acting up, and his feet and back hurt.

"Tex is a decorated hero, Jake. Fought with Bobby Lee in the Mexican War. Promoted to colonel. Decorated for valor." Bison pulled off his hat, pulled out a bandanna, and wiped the sweat from around the interior sweatband. "When the Civil War started, he chose to fight for Texas. Texas is in his heart and in his blood. He was there beside Lee at Appomattox."

"Damn Yankees," JJ commented.

"What happened?" Jake queried.

"After the war, he came home." Bison hesitated, thinking about his own family and how similar his story was to Tex's. "Both his boys had died. Comanche destroyed his ranch. Wife died from cholera a year later. He was a lost soul. He was a cowboy for a few years. When the Rangers reorganized, he joined up."

JJ leaned against the porch's railing, adding, "Had a hand in clearing out the Comanche in Texas, he hated 'em so. Rode with Leander McNelly along the Nueces Strip. One day, he got assigned a desk job in Waco, like Jim here. Smart, old codger. He turned it down and came home."

"Got leadership written all over him, but the Rangers was promoting the young ones, Jake," Bison concluded.

"Heard tell he pissed off some folks higher up," JJ added.

"Yeah, Tex can be stubborn. Damn stubborn. Got a good heart and a good head, too. But stubborn, ya know? Texas stubborn. Worst kind. Worse than a mule. Always been a loner. Goes his own way. Rides his own path."

"He gonna join us?" Jake asked.

"Hope so. He's a man you can trust, and he can shoot straight."

"Whoa there!" With his last throw, Tex lassoed the obstinate horse, pulled hard on the rope, and tightened the loop around his neck. He walked slowly toward the horse, speaking softly with each step.

"That's a boy. Easy does it. C'mon, Petey, it's me. I won't hurt ya. Calm down. That's it. Yeah, that's it." Tex stroked the horse's neck.

"You're getting old," he thought, "but, like me, you have a few good years left."

"C'mon, boy, let's get you in the barn." Tex turned to lead the horse when he saw the men on his porch.

"Who goes there?" Tex adjusted his oval glasses.

"Huh?" His hearing had been failing him over the last few years. He wasn't certain if they'd answered.

Bison, Jake, and JJ walked toward the corral. When Tex saw his friend Bison, he let out the old rebel yell and smiled. His white mustache stretched across his weathered face. Tex tied Petey to the fence and stepped through the rungs as the three Rangers approached.

"My God! It's good to see you, Jim." Tex reached out and grabbed his friend's hand, pumping it.

"How the hell are ya, Tex?" Jim asked. "Jesus, you're getting old." Bison noticed how weathered the face was of the man who all the women in the county once chased.

Tex's smile was infectious. "Same as you, Jim. Getting old. You still got more hair than me though," Tex joked. Both men had receding hairlines, even though Bison's was much thicker and not as white.

"Tex, this here is Jake Johnson and JJ Bost, fellow Rangers."

"Let's go into the house for some lemonade," Tex offered.

"What about your horse, Tex?" Jake asked, pointing toward the corral. They turned to see that Petey had loosened the rope and had moved back deeper in the corral.

"Oh, that dang horse will be the death of me. Forget him. Come into the house."

After talking about old times, Bison got down to business. "Tex. Had a chance to visit a spell with the governor the other day. He asked me to look into a problem in El Paso."

Tex nodded his head to continue.

"Counterfeit money is coming across the border. An agent from Washington is missing in El Paso. He seemed to think Mexico is up to something. He was snooping around and disappeared. Probably got dry gulched. No doubt by Mexicans."

"You boys heading to El Paso?"

"Yep."

"You want company?"

"Yeah. I was asked to put together a team and find out what happened to this agent. Name of Jack Wood. Wanna go?"

Tex looked around at the three Rangers and broke into a large smile. "Just us four?"

"No, a couple more Rangers will join us on the trail."

"You and I are a couple of old farts. Eyesight shot. Hearing ain't too good either. Jake's kinda young. No offense, Jake." Jake shook his head, indicating he hadn't taken any offense. "Do the folks in Washington know who you're asking?"

"Up to me, Tex. I only ask the best men. You know me well enough to give me that. What I want to know is if you have a mind to join us, old farts or not?"

"Bunch of old coots like us? Hell yeah, I'll go. We'll surely find that Jack Wood."

Bison felt a huge sigh of relief.

"By the way, Jim," Tex asked. "That Wood fella. He ain't a Yankee, is he?"

CHAPTER 15

"Boys, about time for a song." Sitting on a log positioned around the campfire, Justus faced the four men captured during the day. "Anyone got a favorite?"

Wanted for holding up the First National Bank in Sterling City, Texas, a posse of twelve citizens led by Texas Ranger Justus Strummin had dogged the four men for two days. During the robbery, a small boy peering in the bank's window alerted the town. Fleeing the bank, shots rang out from the local citizens, and the robbers returned their fire. Galloping away from the melee, they rode near the town's school. Several children in the playground had been wounded. Some were seriously hurt.

Eighteen hours after the holdup, the thieves were surrounded near Devil's River on the Val Verde Plateau. They surrendered easily.

"Ranger, don't mind the romantic fire. Don't mind that full moon overhead. But don't go singing no fancy love ballad. One of these ugly boys might take a liking to me," one of the robbers, Nick, commented and gave a belly laugh.

"How about I untie you boys? Let you dance a few numbers? You'd like that, wouldn't ya?" Justus returned the laugh.

"Justus, why you got to sing to 'em?" asked Deputy Sheriff Lou Ester.

"Lou, I got me a captured audience." Justus laughed at his own joke. "Go curl up in your bedroll like the others. Leave me be for awhile."

"Listen up, boys." Justus turned his attention back to the four fugitives. "I gotta tell ya, Justus Strummin is my…stage name. After a few more years of being a Ranger, I'm going to travel, visit them big, fancy cities like Chicago and New York, and let those folks hear some real cowboy music."

"Why wait Justus? Why don't you head out before you get too old?" Nick suggested.

"Yeah, like tonight?" one of the other robbers proposed. All four laughed.

"You dirtbags," said Will Summers, another posse man, who kicked dirt at the four. "You think robbing a bank is funny? Honest people have to pay for filth like you!" Summers turned and walked off.

"Rider coming in!"

A deputy from town rode into camp. Tying his horse to a nearby tree, he walked over to warm himself near the fire.

"Got news from town. Justus, you best wake the boys."

Justus laid his mandolin down and woke the others. They gathered around the campfire.

"Evening, men. Just came from town. I've got some sad news." He glanced at the four robbers. "All in all, four children were wounded. You probably already know that much. Late this afternoon, little Jenny Waters died." He glanced again at the four men, who were now wanted for murder. Jenny Waters, the daughter of the grocery store owner, was only seven years old.

"Should have killed them when we had the chance," one of the posse men said.

They stared at each other. "We can string them up here and now."

"Hold on, Johnny," Justus replied. "These men deserve a fair trial."

"A trial? What for? They robbed the bank. They've already admitted it. They killed little Jenny Waters. Why waste time and money on a trial? Folks won't acquit them."

"It's our job to bring them in."

"Justus, hold on and listen. Makes no sense to drag these killers to town. Our job sometimes has got to be judge, jury, and executioner. We've all had to do it from time to time."

"It ain't right. It's all I'm saying."

"You'd hang 'em if they stole somebody's horse, wouldn't you?"

Justus hung his head low. Three months ago, he and several of the same men in the posse had hung a horse thief. Justus nodded. Yes, he would hang a horse thief.

"Somebody killing little Jenny Waters got anymore rights than a horse thief, Justus?"

Justus looked at the others and knew they were right. "Boys, do me this one favor. Let's take 'em back to town. I'm sick and tired of hanging men. Let someone else do it."

"Maybe Jenny's ma or pa? You want them to set eyes on these killers? They're already grieving. You want them to go through all of that?"

"Look, boys, all I want is what's right. If these boys need hanging, let a jury decide."

A posse member struck Justus from behind. That evening, the posse unanimously decided to hang the murderers. Dragged to a tall oak tree and mounted on their horses, a noose was placed around their necks. The four were hung.

The posse placed Justus in his bedroll. The deputy from town took a telegram from his jacket and placed it inside Justus' shirt. They then rode back to town.

Justus stirred the next morning, rubbed his head, and cursed under his breath. Sitting up, he stared at the dying embers of the campfire. He saw they had left him. Disappointed, he hoped they came to their senses and took the prisoners back to town. He knelt down, tied up his bedroll, and then ambled to his horse. He threw a saddle blanket and saddle on her, tied the bedroll behind the cantle, and then tied the mandolin atop the bedroll. He tightened the cinch one more time, placed his foot in the stirrup, and threw his right leg over the saddle. Swinging his horse around toward town, he noticed a movement in the woods. With a nudge of his spurs, he guided his horse toward the movement. His hand rested on his revolver.

Then he saw the four bodies swinging in the breeze. Holding his stomach, he felt the telegram. It was from Captain Jim Bison, an old friend and Ranger he had ridden with almost seven years earlier. Bison was requesting his presence in El Paso on urgent business. Bison had always been a fair man. He was tough-minded, but he was always fair.

Justus didn't believe the hanging was right or the four men had shot any of the children during the holdup. The town's citizens, firing randomly at the escaping men, had unintentionally hit the children in the playground. What happened to these men wasn't right. He needed a change. Perhaps riding with Bison was the answer. It was at least a good enough answer for the time being.

Justus turned his horse around and spurred her toward El Paso.

CHAPTER 16

Bison, Jake, JJ, and Tex headed west, toward the Pecos River.

Tex, the loner, rode thirty yards to the group's right, as if they were driving cattle. Bison rode point, Jake and JJ rode drag, and Tex rode swing. Only the cattle were missing.

At Coyote Draw on the Pecos River, Bison let his horse drink. The others followed, lingering around the river while allowing their horses to rest and dusting themselves off from the relentless Texas dirt.

"I'm gonna cross here to take a look up ahead," Bison told the group.

"Want some company?" Jake asked.

"Yeah, sure."

The two men crossed the shallow river and rode for some distance.

"Hold up Jake." Bison sat motionless and stared in the distance. Along a tributary of the Pecos, shadowed by the Guadalupe Peaks, a solitary teepee sat with smoke rising from its peak.

"Let's pay a visit," Bison said.

Jake leaned forward in his saddle. "Someone you know?"

"Think so. Let's take a look."

The two rode toward the teepee. Looking for anything unusual, Jake watched the tree line at the foot of the cliffs and the river meandering northwest. Bison stopped thirty feet short of the teepee. The only sound was the blowing wind.

"Hello!" Bison's voice echoed off the granite boulders and the grass-filled valley.

"Hello!" he attempted again to get a reply. Jake slid from the saddle with a carbine in his right hand. He walked cautiously toward the open flap of the teepee, crouched, and peered inside.

Jake circled around the teepee, stopping at the open flap. "No one here, Jim."

"You sure?"

Jake rolled his eyes. He had just walked around the teepee and looked inside. "Yeah, I'm sure."

Suddenly, Jake was grabbed from behind in a bear hug around the shoulders and chest and was jerked off his feet. Jake fell with a loud grunt and rolled on his back while trying to bring up his carbine. A knee on his chest shoved him to the ground as a knife blade twinkled in the afternoon sun. Jake yelled out. The knife was inches from his face.

Bison started laughing. "Let 'em up," he called out, trying to stifle his laughter.

Bison slid off his horse and walked to Jake. Reaching down, he grabbed Jake's hand and jerked him to his feet.

"You might be a hell of a Ranger, but you're not much of an Indian fighter," Bison smiled and turned to the man who had felled Jake.

"I've seen you do that fifty times, and I still can't believe my eyes," Bison reached out and gave the tall man a hug. Jake dusted himself off and looked at the Indian. He was tall, well over six feet, with long, black hair braided in back and tied off in a ponytail. He wore buckskin from head to foot. His jacket was heavily fringed and beaded. His knife sheath and moccasins were also thickly embroidered with beads. His large chest cavity protruded well beyond his waist and was solid, as were his enormous shoulders and arms. He looked as if he could wrestle a buffalo.

"Jake, meet a good friend of mine, Isaac Roberts. Isaac, this here is Texas Ranger Jake Johnson." They shook hands.

"You an Indian?" Jake asked.

"Half. Part-Sioux, from my mother's side," the half-breed smiled.

"You live out here all alone?"

"Didn't use to. Indians killed my family. I camp here for the winter."

"For the winter? It's as cold as a witch's tit here in the winter. I could think of better places to hole up. And your family? Killed by Indians? But you're half?" Jake was overly inquisitive about the man who had tricked him.

"I like the area. My wife liked the area. It's why I come back. Mountains block the northern winds, plenty of water from the Pecos, and the game come out of the mountains during the winter to forage." Roberts shrugged. "I like it here."

Jake nodded. "What happened to your family?"

"Comanche raided my wife's village. Killed everyone, including my wife and daughter, couple years back."

"I'm sorry, Isaac."

"Jake, his Indian name is Crowhorse. I think he prefers to go by that name. That still the case?" Bison asked.

"Yes, my friend. I prefer my given Indian name. Some call me Comanche Killer."

"Oh?" Jake asked.

"To avenge my wife and daughter's death, I took an oath to kill those who killed her and her family."

"Why the name Crowhorse?"

"A long story. Please, come inside. Let us eat. It's getting late in the day."

"Crowhorse, other Rangers are waiting for us at Coyote Draw."

"Bring them here to camp. The days grow shorter now, and here is a good place to rest 'til tomorrow."

"Jake, I'll get the men."

"No, that's okay, Jim. I'll get 'em," Johnson said, worried the big half-breed might play other tricks on him.

* * * *

"I'm telling you. He came out of nowhere. I walked the entire perimeter of that teepee. He wasn't inside or outside," Jake told Tex and JJ as they rode toward the camp.

"Came out of nowhere, huh, Jake?"

"Hate Injuns. He ain't riding with us, is he?" Tex asked.

"No, he's just a friend of Bison's. But it'll be a good place to camp."

"All right, just as long as no Injun rides with us," Tex concluded.

* * * *

"We'll bed down here for the night," Bison addressed the Rangers as they dismounted. Crowhorse emerged from the teepee. His appearance startled the Rangers. He was as Jake described—large facial features, strong jaw, wide nostrils, scarring on both cheeks, and large, round eyes that drilled straight through the man he was looking at.

"Make yourselves comfortable. It'll be dark soon. Tonight we feast on venison."

"Venison?" Jake exclaimed, slapping his stomach. "Sounds great!"

The campfire crackled while the meat slowly cooked. Occasionally, Bison or one of the others would rotate the meat to cook it evenly.

"Before we eat, I ask everyone to come inside. It is customary to pass the pipe among friends before they eat."

The Rangers had seen teepees before, but they had never seen a teepee like this. Although similar in size to others from the outside, it was cavernous on the inside. Twelve men could easily sit around the center fire. Items that evoked special memories to its occupant hung from the lodge poles. Fringed shirts, knives, and painted shields of various sizes decorated the buffalo hide walls.

"Crowhorse, what are those?" Jake asked.

"Scalps," Crowhorse replied.

"Scalps? Must be twenty or thirty," JJ exclaimed.

"Fifty-one," Crowhorse corrected him.

"White men?" Tex asked angrily.

"No. Comanche." Crowhorse smiled without offering an explanation.

"Some look fresh," Bison commented.

"Yes," Crowhorse admitted. "Few Comanche come this far into Texas anymore. Texans have driven them northward." Tex smiled at the remark. "Occasionally, one or two will fall within my grasp. When they do…" Crowhorse broke a twig.

Perhaps it was gorging on venison or smoking the pipe, but Jake became sick later that night and vomited all he had eaten. He good-naturedly took the ribbing from the other Rangers.

At the crack of dawn, Tex was stoking the fire and cooking bacon, biscuits, and strong coffee. The Rangers packed their gear, itching to go. They estimated they would arrive in El Paso by dusk.

"Much obliged by your hospitality." Bison proffered Crowhorse his hand.

"You and your men are welcome anytime."

"Just a thought. You interested in going to El Paso for a few days?"

"Don't expect your boys would appreciate my presence, being a half-breed and all."

"We might need the help. El Paso is a dangerous town. You could ask questions of certain people who wouldn't give one of us the time of day. Pays same as a Ranger."

"Hmm, pay? I like that. If it's okay with the others, I'll go along for a few days."

*   *   *   *

"I don't want any thieving Injun on the trail with us, Jim." Tex was getting excitable. The men stood among their horses. Away from Crowhorse, they were arguing.

"Tex, he ain't an Injun, and he ain't a thief."

"He's a half-breed and a man who enjoys scalping, for Christ's sake," Tex said.

"JJ, Jake, say something. Tex, the rest of the boys are okay with the idea."

"Tex, he only scalps Comanche. I thought you hated 'em?" JJ said.

"This trip ain't all it's cracked up to be, Jim. First, we bring along that youngster. Now, Jake, don't get me wrong. You're young and inexperienced, and I've noticed your hand trembles at times. That worries me. Jim, that shoulder of yours might get us all in trouble if and when the fighting starts."

"Yeah? You can't see worth a damn, can't hear shit, got arthritis in your hands, and keep to yourself too much." Bison was exasperated with Tex.

"He goes. I stay."

"Damnit, Tex. You gave me your word. I'm counting on you and everyone here. We got serious business ahead of us, government business. I betcha that everyone, including the president of the USA, knows we're heading to El Paso to help."

"Old Useless? Another damn Yankee," Tex grunted.

"Tex, we're burning daylight here. You stubborn, old goat, you're going. And that's an order. And you will get along with the Injun. Er, Crowhorse. Got me?"

"Can't order me. I'm not a Ranger anymore."

"Bet you two bits you got your star in those saddlebags. Right?"

Tex hesitated. "Well, yeah."

"You're a Ranger, all right. Once a Ranger, always a Ranger. Maybe a disagreeable, old curmudgeon, but you're a Ranger nonetheless." Bison turned to the others. "Let's mount." He turned back toward Tex. "You ride swing. Like always, okay?"

Tex looked at his friend and shrugged. "Okay."

"Crowhorse. Mount up! You ride with us!" Bison, pleased with himself, called out.

During the ride, Tex learned about Crowhorse. Bison would drift over and talk to Tex, telling him what he knew about the half-breed. Isaac Roberts was the son of a famous mountain man who had taken a Sioux for a wife. Insisting Isaac attend school back east, his father sent the boy to live with family in New Jersey. Upon news of his father's death, Isaac, at the age of thirteen, joined a wagon train and headed west along the Santa Fe Trail. One day, Sioux attacked the train. The men were killed. The women and children were placed in different Sioux tribes as slaves. The family who took in Isaac brought him up as a Sioux. They never believed he was half-Sioux. On his sixteenth birthday, he proved himself to be a warrior when he invaded a Crow camp and captured their ponies. His tribe's elders bestowed his Indian name on him. He married the chief's daughter, and they had a daughter. Ten years later, Comanche attacked his village while he and the other warriors hunted buffalo. Crowhorse's life changed to one of revenge. He didn't have a home. The whites looked upon him as an Indian, and the Sioux blamed him for the deaths of the Sioux, saying the presence of a white man living among them had brought death to their loved ones. He was more a loner than Tex. Tex understood Crowhorse's withdrawal from society. It wasn't any different from his own exile to his ranch to be by himself. Tex knew the sadness from losing one's family, and he unquestionably grasped Crowhorse's hatred of the Comanche. Tex gradually released his animosity toward Crowhorse. He continued riding alone and didn't say a word to Crowhorse the entire trip to El Paso.

Nevertheless, he understood the heart of the man.

CHAPTER 17

Kincaid and Stetson reached the outskirts of El Paso as the metallic sun dipped beyond the expansive vista. Located at the southern tip of the San Andres Mountain range, west of the 6,700-foot Hueco plateau, the town of mud and adobe was a lawless, but God-fearing, community with a population of 300 Anglo residents and more than 2,000 men, women, and children of Mexican heritage.

The streets ran north and south. Auxiliary streets branched off east and west every thirty to forty yards. The sheriff's office was located on San Antonio Street, in the northern section of town. Kincaid had rehearsed the strategy several times. Tying the stallion and appaloosa at the hitching post in front of the sheriff's office, Kincaid and Stetson entered the sheriff's office.

"Sheriff Perry?" Kincaid saw the old man sitting behind the rolltop desk against the right side of the room. The old man swiveled in his chair and leaned back while contemplating the two strangers.

"Who's asking?" The old man's voice was scratchy.

"Kincaid. Ellsworth Kincaid." Kincaid saw the deputy sheriff badge on the old man's wool vest. His gray hair and matching mustache twisted into a handlebar was a surprise. Kincaid thought Sheriff Perry was a younger man.

"What's your business here, Mr. Kincaid?" The old man placed his bifocals on the bridge of his nose to better see the twosome standing in his office.

"I have instructions to meet Sheriff Perry and relieve him of a prisoner, a Mister Jack Wood. I'm taking him back to San Antonio for trial." It sounded good when he rehearsed it, but it sounded like an out-and-out lie saying it.

The deputy snickered. "Why would I relinquish a prisoner to you?"

Nervously rocking in the chair, the deputy glanced at the double-barreled shotgun hanging over the entry to the cellblock.

"That Kincaid fella looks fast with a gun," the old man thought. He wisely decided he'd be dead before he ever reached it. And that woman? It was hard enough not staring at her. She was pretty as a little red wagon.

"If I was only twenty years younger...well...maybe thirty years younger," he thought. He theorized she was probably fast with a six-shooter, too.

"You Sheriff Perry?" Kincaid hadn't dreamed of running into an old geezer.

"Sorry, sonny, you're about a week late." Annoyed, the deputy rotated back toward the desk. The chair creaked with the movement.

"The nerve of some people. Relinquish a prisoner to an unknown cowboy. They must think me a fool," he thought.

Stetson stepped forward. "Sheriff, is Jack Wood your prisoner?"

"Nope. About a week late for him, too." The deputy examined several wanted posters piled on the desk.

"That Kincaid fella. Something about him. Name sounds familiar. Could swear I'd heard it before," he thought. "Just can't recall where."

Kincaid walked over and stood behind the deputy. "I need to know where Sheriff Perry might be. Can you help us?" Kincaid was insistent, yet soft. He didn't want to be inconsiderate to the old man.

"Young man..." The old man turned in his chair and removed his glasses. "Sheriff Perry was the best darn man to ever wear a badge here in El Paso." The old man stood to face the man and woman asking so many questions. He unconsciously wiped his nose with the sleeve of his right arm.

The old man continued, "He was a solid friend, one you could trust. Knew him for nearly ten years. He was fair and honorable, even to the filth that came to town. He never lynched a one of 'em, and plenty needed hanging." The old man would have gone on the rest of the evening. Kincaid interrupted.

"Perry's cousin, Sheriff Overly in Lubbock, is a friend of mine. He asked me to look Perry up and discuss the circumstances surrounding Jack Wood's imprisonment. He sent a telegraph to Perry regarding my coming." Perhaps a clear, simple explanation would coax the old man to make his point.

"Well, son, they killed him. Murdered him in cold blood. If I was a younger man, those greasers would have paid with their own lives." The old man sat down in the swivel chair.

"Who was killed? Jack Wood? Sheriff Perry?" Stetson's compassionate voice relaxed the old man's composure.

"John Perry." The old man's eyes glassed over.

Kincaid walked toward the entry to the cellblock and opened the door. Using the arms of the chair to steady himself, the old man stood again.

"You won't find your friend in there, sonny." The old man smirked. He suspected Kincaid was a friend of the prisoner. He might be getting old, but he was no man's fool. He knew Kincaid wasn't a very good liar. He didn't take a liking to those who were. The old man liked the young woman. He wasn't sure yet about the man. They seemed good people. Why were they after that murderer Wood?

Kincaid sat in a chair and motioned for Stetson to do the same. It was going to be a long night.

The sheriff shared a tepid pot of black coffee with his two visitors and began telling his tale after warming up to the couple.

"Jack Wood was a prisoner here. Shared a cell with another man, a Mex." The old man stirred his coffee. "I arrested 'em both for murdering the deputy sheriff. They apparently tried robbing one of the gamblers from Rosita's Cantina. That's how the drover told his side of things. The deputy witnessed the robbery in progress, pulled his gun, and asked the Mex and Wood to put their hands in the air. Next thing, the Mex pulls his gun and kills the deputy. I was just rounding the corner when I heard the shots and saw Wood bending over the deputy's body. I arrested the two of 'em and marched them here. Sheriff Perry was home with his wife and children that night."

"Next morning, Sheriff Perry came in and listened to my story. He spoke with the prisoners for about an hour. He wasn't convinced of Wood's involvement in the murder, but the Mex made Perry nervous."

"Perry had to make his rounds. About twenty Mexicans galloped into town and headed straight for the jail. Perry stops them and asks what they want. Without a blink of an eye, those sons of bitches shoot him. They riddled him. He was dead before he hit the ground. They released the Mex and Wood. I saw the whole thing from across the street." The old man looked at the floor and then looked back at Kincaid and Stetson. "I was scared. Ain't afraid to admit it."

"Now it's just me. No sheriff in town and no deputy sheriff. Just an old goat like me upholding the law."

"Samuel, you know where they took Wood?" They learned the old man was Samuel Marsh. He was raised in Kansas and traveled to Texas during the war. He couldn't get a job. Sheriff Perry took a liking to him and made him a deputy. He gave him a monthly income and a roof over his head. He did odd jobs and kept the jailhouse clean. The gun on his hip wasn't loaded. Even if it was, he admitted he didn't know how to use it properly.

"Don't rightly know. If I had to guess, I'd look for your friend south of the border, beyond the Rio Grande, in a place called Condeza Barajas. I heard one of them Mex mention a place while rescuing their friend. But I ain't sure." Marsh ran a hand dotted with old age spots over a two-day growth of beard.

"Wait one minute! I might know where you could find out." Samuel scratched his stubble. "The reverend knows everything that's fit to know." Samuel winked at Stetson. "And probably a few things that ain't fit to know either."

"Where might we find the reverend?" Kincaid was anxious to find his friend.

"Down at the mission, south side of town. He holds Mass practically every evening. More than a few souls need saving in this town. Greasers love him. If not for him, they'd be starving. Ask for Father O'Brien. If anyone knows what happened to your friend, he surely would."

Kincaid and Stetson proceeded down San Antonio Street and then turned southwest on Kansas Street. The three-story adobe church located in the southwestern end of town, the first mission in Texas, was founded to civilize and Christianize the Tigua Indians.

The mission was discernible by a large bell tower on the left rear of the structure. The spire was crowned with a silver dome whose peak held the Holy Cross. The setting sun and amber sky provided a somber framework for God's house of worship. The large structure, square in shape, had an imposing façade that included a wooden double door, a large circular window directly above the door, and a chiseled alabaster statute of Saint Anthony holding a small child in his left arm at the pinnacle of the building. The adobe had been recently whitewashed. The grounds were flawlessly manicured, and the graveyard, located to the right of the structure, was faithfully cared for.

The church's congregation was departing the last Mass for the evening. Father O'Brien, positioned at the mission's double door entry, shook hands, and made small talk with the exiting assembly. Kincaid froze. Stetson looked at him quizzically. Kincaid took two steps back and leaned against a building that partially blocked his view of the mission. He knelt as if he was hiding.

"Ellsworth? You all right?" Stetson was baffled. Kincaid behaved as if he had seen a ghost.

"It's him," Kincaid exclaimed as he scrutinized the priest. The black robe and white collar couldn't disguise the muscular silhouette of one of the great Texas Rangers.

"Ellsworth, who are you talking about?" Stetson glanced back and forth from Kincaid to the mission.

"Is it Father O'Brien? Do you know him?"

"Thought he was dead. Holy Mother of Christ." Kincaid studied the Catholic priest. He was about five foot eight with wavy hair, now graying and receding. He had strong hands and a thick, muscular neck.

"Stetson, watch how he moves. Graceful, not like you or me or even a priest. He's more like a trained boxer."

"Okay, fine. Don't tell me what you're talking about. I'll just go over, introduce myself to Father O'Brien, and tell him a strange man is staring at him."

"Wait, don't do that. Let's watch and make sure," Kincaid whispered. Stetson stepped back and complied.

William E. O'Brien rejoined the Texas Rangers at the conclusion of the Civil War after he relinquished his commission as a colonel in the Confederate States of America. Texas was home, and she would need an abundance of help withstanding the inevitability that lay ahead of her as carpetbaggers, rustlers, murderers, and thieves made their way to the great open spaces of the Texas frontier. During the war, O'Brien had quickly established a reputation as a stern, but compassionate, leader. He was as quick and true with his pistols as he was with his fists. A well-qualified boxer before the war, he became the Confederate champion boxer four years running, from 1861 through 1864. He retired the championship undefeated. After the war, Northerners offered him a small fortune to fight professionally in New York, but O'Brien returned home to Texas. As a Texas Ranger, his name was known from Brownsville to Amarillo as well as from Beaumont to Odessa. He was hailed a celebrated hero after single-handedly cleaning the town of Mineral Wells on the Brazos of Creed Culpepper and his gang. Eleven outlaws were dead, and one Texas Ranger was without a scratch. Referred to as "Wild Bill" O'Brien, the eastern journalists wrote about both his real and imagined exploits.

Bill's trouble started in San Angelo when he was reacquainted with Janice Clayton, who had spied for the Confederacy and had been a courier for Confederate President Jefferson Davis. Based on information supplied by her, a Confederate blockade runner sank a Union warship. Made an honorary captain, she became the most notorious and wanted female during the war. In San Angelo after the war, they saw one another as she boarded a stagecoach for Gonzales. Their brief encounter convinced her to stay in San Angelo for an extra day or two. She never left.

Janice then disappeared while attending an outdoor recital at San Angelo's town square. Having looked everywhere for her, a newspaper boy told Bill he had seen her at the home of Herschel Jacoby, a local cattle baron and potential candidate for governor of Texas. Bill immediately rushed to the stately two-story Greek Revival home.

"Hello, Bill." Boyd McCalvey, the local sheriff, slowly walked out onto the freshly whitewashed front porch. "Can I help ya?"

"Boyd, I'm looking for Janice Clayton. Have you seen her?" Bill took in the large home's surrounding area, including the yard and roof. Once a Texas Ranger, always a Texas Ranger. You never apologize for a vigilant eye, even when talking to the local law.

Boyd, with his hands crammed deep in his pockets, looked down at the freshly painted porch and mumbled, "Yeah, Bill. I've seen her."

"Can't hear you. You say you saw her?" Bill leaned closer to the white picket fence surrounding the front yard. Something wasn't right.

"Yeah, I've seen her. Now git." Boyd's voice was brusque and resolute.

"Git?" Bill put his wide, strong hands on his narrow hips. "If you've seen her, you tell me where she's at."

The upstairs bedroom door suddenly burst open. "Bill, help me!" She was crying with her clothes torn as she scrambled onto the portico. Three men charged out of the room, seized her, and dragged her back into the house.

Bill pointed his index finger at Boyd. "For the love of God, what's going on?" Bill clenched his jaw.

"She's got a price on her head. Two thousand dollars."

"That was during the War. It's over. Let her go."

"Can't do it, buddy boy. That reward's good. The money's mine. Now git, like I told you."

"I'm asking you as a friend. Let her go!"

Screams from the second story perforated the quiet, sunny afternoon.

Boyd yelled toward the front door. "Billy Ray, Bobby, Smithy."

Three self-assured gunmen wearing deputy badges strolled out the front door and stood near the porch railing, opposite Boyd.

"I mean business, Bill. One last time, git."

"What do you intend to do with her?"

"Going to hang her, Bill. Right after the boys have some fun with her, if you know what I mean." The three gunmen chuckled. "After all, the reward's dead or alive."

"Gentlemen, y'all know I'm a Texas Ranger. I don't recognize you or those badges on your chest. Let the woman go…peacefully."

Boyd nodded at the three deputies. The gunmen reached for their guns, but Bill's reputation, which many had only read about, became reality as his .44 caliber slugs collided with the three men. None of them fired a single round.

Kicking open the gate, Bill approached the house. Boyd dropped to his knees, held up his arms to shield his face, and cried, "Don't shoot me!"

Bill vaulted the three steps to the porch and bounced the still smoking gun barrel off Boyd's left temple, slapping him to the ground unconscious.

Bill kicked open the screen door to the house. There, another man armed with a shotgun and a badge on his chest stood. The man fired the shotgun from the hip, miraculously missing Bill and blowing a hole through the wall next to him. Bill fired at point-blank range, killing the deputy. The screams from upstairs continued. Bill bounded the staircase steps, three at a time. At the top of the staircase, Bill yelled for Janice. The first man who rushed out of the bedroom met Bill's right hook. Bill stepped into the room to meet the other two gunmen. He gave a quick jab with the right and followed with his left power punch. The closest man to him lay unconscious with a shattered jaw. As the other man pointed his weapon at Bill, Janice violently struck him in the head with a water pitcher. The house became silent. Bill held Janice close for one brief second. They escaped through the back entrance as the townspeople gathered on the front lawn. From that time on, Bill was a wanted fugitive for killing four deputies along with breaking one deputy's skull and another's jaw. Boyd swore he'd hunt them down and Bill would never live in peace. The bounty was raised to $10,000, dead or alive. The legendary "Wild Bill" O'Brien, famed Texas Ranger, disappeared without a trace.

"It's him." Kincaid looked at Stetson.

"He's the reason I joined the Rangers. As a boy, I idolized him, like so many other young boys. He was a real hero, not one of those fables they write about. They say Indians killed him. I never believed it. There he is, big as life. He's still a wanted fugitive."

"If he's wanted, will you take him in?" Stetson knew Ellsworth believed in the law, had fought for it, and was willing to die for it. Even though he was no longer a Ranger, she knew, if he came across a wanted fugitive, he wouldn't hesitate to honor the oath he had taken.

He considered his reply. "No. Not this time. The law was wrong. He was right. Let's go talk to him. Let's not scare him any, though I doubt that man scares at all. All the same, I intend for this to be a friendly discussion. Come on, let's go have a talk with Father "Wild Bill" O'Brien."

CHAPTER 18

Sitting astride their horses, the Rangers looked west across the flat terrain. A half-mile away, the gleaming setting sun bathed the small town of El Paso in a shower of orange light.

"We'll not go in as a group," Bison said. "We might draw too much attention."

Bison turned in his saddle. "Tex, you ride in with Crowhorse. JJ, you ride in with me and Jake."

"I'll go in alone," Tex interrupted.

Bison hoped the ride to El Paso would have changed Tex' mind regarding the half-breed. It apparently hadn't. He nodded in agreement.

"Listen up," Bison counseled, "stay in pairs. Take off those Ranger badges. There's no need to make folks nervous. Remember, our mission here is to find..."

"Jack Wood," they answered in unison.

"Don't go drawing any attention to yourselves," Bison added.

"Where do we rendezvous?" Jake queried.

"JJ, you know the town."

"The main street is San Antonio. There's a Mexican cantina with gambling, a real hurdy-gurdy. Ya can't miss it. It's the biggest place in town. Called Rosita's. A dozen Rangers could get lost in there. Watch yourselves. The women are rowdy, and so are the cowboys." He laughed. "And both want your money."

"Tex, wait about ten minutes and then follow. Crowhorse, you come in last. Jake, JJ, let's ride," Bison instructed.

Spurring their horses to a lope, the three Rangers headed for town.

* * * *

"Sheriff?" The three Rangers walked into the small, one-room building. Sitting at an old rolltop desk was a gaunt, grizzled old man with gray hair thinning faster than Bison's.

Samuel Marsh swiveled in his chair. "Acting deputy sheriff. For a while anyway. Can I help you boys?"

"Looking for someone. Thought you'd be the best person to ask."

"Ask away. I ain't got all day."

"Haven't got a description of the man. His name is Jack Wood."

"Friend of yours?" Marsh leaned over, spit a wad of chewing tobacco in a spittoon near the desk, and then wiped his chin with his sleeve. The drivel hit dead center of the copper tureen.

"Not rightly. Just looking for him."

Marsh mistrusted the man. First, the young man and woman were looking for Wood. Now three newcomers in town were looking for him.

"Not a coincidence," he thought.

"He ain't in town." Marsh turned back around in his chair to face the desk.

"He was here in town?"

The old man talked over his shoulder as he rifled through paperwork. "Yeah, a few days is all."

"You know where he went?"

The old man turned back to face Bison. "If he's not your friend, why you asking all these darn questions about 'em?"

Bison didn't have a choice except trusting the old codger.

"You got five seconds. Then I'll ask you kindly to leave."

Bison's voice lowered to above a whisper. "I'm a Texas Ranger."

"You got any papers proving that?"

Bison could feel his adrenaline surge. "Will a badge do?"

* * * *

"No Injuns, friend," said the tall, barrel-chested man in a black, brocaded vest and black tie. He stood in front of the swinging saloon doors, preventing Crowhorse from entering Rosita's Cantina.

Crowhorse looked at the man enforcing the saloon rules up and down and then grunted. He took a step closer, and the man placed his palm on the buckskin-clad breast to prevent entry. Crowhorse grasped the man's forearm and pulled it tight toward his chest, forcing the back of the man's hand to nearly touch his forearm.

"You're breaking my arm!" The man collapsed to his knees. Two other men from inside the saloon moved toward Crowhorse. Crowhorse's fringed pants leg swept out, tripping the man to the right. The third man pulled his revolver.

"Hold on there, mister." The cocking of the Walker Dragoon caused the man with the revolver to freeze.

"I'll take that," Tex said as he took a step up on the boardwalk toward the man with the revolver. Tex reached over, took the firearm, and tucked it in his trousers behind his gun belt. "Thanks."

"We don't serve Injuns here, mister. Saloon policy," the man on the ground said to the tall Texan.

Tex looked down at the man while holstering his cap-n-ball six-gun. "He ain't an Injun."

"The hell you say," said the other man, who was sprawled on the boardwalk.

Tex looked at Crowhorse. "You an Injun?"

"Half-breed."

"That settles it. He ain't no Injun." Tex walked through the saloon doors. The men on the ground quickly stood to block Crowhorse's entry. A small crowd inside was watching.

Crowhorse touched the knife on his beaded leather belt.

"You look like an Injun," said the man who had his revolver taken from Tex. "Smell like one, too."

"Believe this is yours," Tex said, pulling the revolver from his waistband. The man turned to retrieve his gun. Without hesitation, Tex buffaloed the man with his own revolver. The slap across his skull echoed into the saloon. The man pitched to the boardwalk unconscious.

"Look, he's a friend of mine," Tex said to the others and shrugged, fingering the grips of his Dragoons.

The two men deliberated. The man with the fancy vest nodded. "Okay."

Tex smiled and walked back into the saloon.

In perfect English, Crowhorse said, "I'd suggest removing your friend and taking him to a doctor."

The two men's eyes widened, nodded in agreement, and then stooped to get their friend. Crowhorse entered behind Tex.

"Wasn't necessary, Tex."

Tex took a seat at an empty poker table toward the center of the colossal room. "Afraid you might've killed 'em."

"It occurred to me."

"Remember what Bison said about not drawing attention to ourselves." Tex smiled, knowing they had drawn considerable attention to themselves.

"Don't think we did, do you?"

"Nope," Tex replied as every man in the saloon briefly glanced his way.

Crowhorse pulled a chair from the table and then hesitated.

"Sit," Tex directed. "Coffee's on you."

That evening, Justus Strummin entered the saloon and shook the rain from his hat. The weather was turning cold, and the rain fell as it only does in West Texas—in a torrential downpour. The dusty streets of El Paso appreciatively consumed the drench, turning itself into a quagmire of mud. Justus borrowed a towel from the bartender and cleaned his mandolin. Looking at the crowded saloon, he recognized Tex playing cards with a large Indian. Justus walked over.

"Tex!" Justus shouted over the discord of men gambling and drinking.

Tex waved him over and introduced Justus to Crowhorse. After shaking hands, Justus took a chair and sat down.

"Deal 'em," Justus deadpanned.

Tex reshuffled the deck. Maybe his luck would change with Justus sitting across from him. If they had actually been playing, he would have owed Crowhorse $200. Tex hated losing at anything.

"When did ya get into town?" Justus asked.

"Few hours ago," Tex responded.

"Bison with you?"

"Yeah…and a couple others. Any luck?" They whispered, fearing others might eavesdrop.

"Nothing. Been here two days. Any suggestions?"

"Wait for Bison."

As they scooped up the hand dealt them, Justus leaned over and volunteered to Crowhorse, "Justus ain't my real name."

"Sometimes it is necessary for men to go by different names," Crowhorse replied.

"Hell, Crowhorse ain't his real name either, Justus," Tex offered.

"That your stage name?" Justus asked.

"Huh?"

"Justus is my stage name. You see," Justus leaned over the table and whispered, "my real name is Jeffery, an awful-sounding name for a performer. I'm just asking if Crowhorse is your stage name."

"I'm not a performer, Justus. My given name is Isaac Roberts."

"Play cards, will ya? Crowhorse can tell you his life story some other time." Annoyed, Tex threw two cards down and dealt himself two more.

* * * *

Bison motioned to the center of the cantina. JJ and Jake followed through the throng of gamblers and prostitutes. They squeezed past hardened men with the entrenched foul smell of alcohol, tobacco, and filthiness associated with working the land.

"Boys," Bison acknowledged, pulling up a chair. "Any luck?"

"None whatsoever. And these cards stink," Tex threw his five cards in the center of the table.

"I fold." Justus raked his few remaining dollars into his hand. Bison introduced Jake and JJ to Justus.

Bison glanced at each man quizzically. Each man shook their heads negatively. Bison swallowed hard. He'd have to telegraph the governor and tell him what little he had learned about Jack from the old rascal of a deputy.

"Listen." Bison leaned in. "You boys stay together, at least two of you at all times. This town gives me the willies. And no drinking either."

"Anyone seen Billy Irons?" Bison then asked.

"Billy Irons? He invited along for the hunt?" Tex questioned.

"You invite all your friends on this foray?" Strummin asked.

"Just enough men to get the job done."

"With Billy, that makes six…No, seven, including me." Tex counted.

"Safety in numbers," Bison replied.

JJ walked over to the table with enough food for everyone. "Chow down, girls," he whimsically commented.

Playing cards, Tex elbowed Bison. "You say we shouldn't be drinking?"

"Yeah. Think it's best, Tex."

"Well, here comes Irons. Don't think he got the word."

Billy Irons slowly ambled down the staircase in the rear of the gambling house, leaning on the banister as if his lanky frame weighed five times its weight. Irons noticed Bison midway down his descent. A big smile crossed his face. A cigarette dangled in the corner of his lips. He waved unpretentiously at Bison, as if he had just seen his best friend. There had been a time after the Civil War when Bison and Irons were best friends. Both had drifted to Texas to scout, herd cattle, and do the odd assortment of jobs small towns offered. Irons and Bison scouted for Custer during the general's short stay in Texas.

When Custer was transferred, Irons and Bison stayed to hunt buffalo in Texas' panhandle. On the plains, Irons became a teller of tales. Wherever Irons planted his bedroll, buffalo hunters gathered to hear his long-winded yarns. With the reorganization of the Texas Rangers, both men joined Company C. Bison was soon promoted to captain, and Irons was reassigned to Company A. The two men lost contact with one another. Irons fell out of favor with the Rangers due to excessive drinking and womanizing. Caught in bed with Company A's commanding officer's wife, Irons was banished to mundane paperwork. It wasn't until Bison was assigned his desk job in Waco that he understood Irons' misery. Bison discovered that fighting men die many deaths when exiled from the profession they love. He had thought of Irons first when the governor enlisted his aid. Watching Irons stumble down the staircase in a drunken stupor put immeasurable doubt in Bison's mind. Bison shook his head. Enlisting Irons for duty in El Paso might be both their undoing. Despite their mixed bag of personalities, the other Rangers had not disappointed him.

"Good seeing you boys," Irons said as he leisurely shuffled over to the Rangers. The men returned his acknowledgement.

"Billy," Bison snapped. "Take a seat."

Irons sat next to Bison. He was intoxicated.

"You been drinking?" Bison asked.

Irons nodded.

"How long you've been here?"

"Week. Er, short of a week. Three days."

"Drunk the entire time?" Bison was seething.

"Most of the summer. I quit, but I started back up yesterday."

"What's going on Billy?"

"Hear about Custer?" Irons referred to the battle in June at the Little Big Horn River in Montana where Indians wiped out Custer and five troops of the Seventh Cavalry.

"Yeah, the whole country has. Old news."

"Old news? Just because you hated him doesn't make it right."

"That why you been drinking, Billy? Because Custer put his ass where it didn't belong?"

"I was supposed to be with him that day, you know? He asked me to scout for him up along the Big Horn. But I ain't a scout no more. Haven't scouted for years. I'm a Ranger doing the paper shuffle. Like you, or so I hear."

"Because of Custer you took a drink or two?"

"Nah, I quit. Then I hear about ol' Bill and started up again." Irons' reference was to Bill Hickok, a mutual friend assassinated in Deadwood in August, six weeks after Custer was killed. Hickok, Bison, and Irons had become friends when they scouted for the Sixth Cavalry in 1867.

"Seems everyone's dying. I quit…until I got here."

"Someone else die?"

"We're about to. That's how I see things."

"Come again?"

Irons lowered his voice. The other Rangers leaned in to listen. "I found Wood."

"You found him?" Tex asked.

"You boys don't know him. I rode with 'em in the war. I could find him anywhere."

"Where's he at, Billy?" Based on the account the old deputy sheriff gave, Bison suspected Jack was dead. Bison knew he had been taken by Mexican guerillas south of the border. He hadn't seen fit to tell the others until he parlayed with the governor.

"Condeza Barajas," Billy whispered. His eyes were as wide as a saucer.

"Where the blazes is that?" Justus asked. Bison leaned in closer. Irons knew more than he had ascertained from the old deputy.

"You don't want to know. We ride down there, and we'll get ourselves killed. That's why I'm drinking again."

"Condeza Barajas. Old Mexico," Bison stated flatly.

"Yep," Irons said.

"We going to Mexico, Jim?" JJ asked.

"That ain't the half of it," Irons continued, ignoring JJ's question. "Those Mexs who got Wood belong to a gang run by some nut name of Juan something or other. A couple hundred are running around loose around Condeza Barajas."

"Find out what's going on?" Justus asked.

"No one's talking. Mexs in town keep to themselves. I think it's some kind of revolution."

"Let's discuss this later," Bison worried others would learn they were Rangers.

"If we go down there, those greasers will cut us up. Wood ain't got a chance down there. If we go, we don't either," Irons remarked.

"Billy, I need to talk to you later about…"

"My drinking?"

"Yeah."

"Now you and the boys are here, I'm done. Swear it."

"Billy, I'll hold you to your word on that. You did good on Wood," Bison added. He shouldn't have doubted his old friend. Billy found Jack, at least his whereabouts. The mission was accomplished. The question remaining was if they should enter Mexico to get Wood. The governor had been very precise about the issue. Under no circumstances, they were not to cross the border with a military coup happening. After Benito Juarez's death, an ambitious army general was overthrowing the existing bureaucracy. Porfirio Diaz was trying to make himself president and dictator of the country. Moreover, his victory was at hand. Diaz declared he'd execute anyone found crossing into Mexico without proper documents, and he'd consider it an act of war if the United States Army or any law enforcement agency crossed the border. Only Washington had authority to send them across the border.

CHAPTER 19

"Father...Father O'Brien?" Kincaid leaped the church's two steps leading to the double door entry.

Father O'Brien was closing the large wooden doors when he heard his name. Turning, he saw a young man in his late twenties or early thirties through the narrowing gap created by the closing doors. O'Brien's adrenaline pulsated. The fugitive instinct to fight or flee seized him. The young man was tall and lean with the telltale tan under the wide-brimmed hat that spoke of a man who had seen many miles in the saddle. He wore a brace of forty-five caliber Colts affixed with Ivory grips. The right revolver rode high on his right hip; the left was carried in the popular cross-draw fashion of a horseman. A brief glimpse of a possible adversary by a trained eye of a Texas Ranger gave many clues. O'Brien suspected he was looking at a lawman. The absence of a badge on the man belied his gut instincts. O'Brien's eyes narrowed as the fleeting thought of running away subsided. The man calling his name looked serious, but his voice was not threatening.

A woman stood behind the man. Her blonde hair cascaded beneath her hat, and her penetrating emerald green eyes were fixed on him. Her skin was smooth and silky, unmarred by the blistering sun.

"She's absolutely stunning," O'Brien thought. She had a self-confident air that he liked in a woman. O'Brien couldn't imagine what she was doing in El Paso. Her inviting, warm smile permitted him to relax. He surmised she could be a handful, but that didn't appear to be her or her companion's intent.

O'Brien greeted his guests. "Yes, my son?"

O'Brien openly smiled. His muscular neck tensed involuntarily, and his broad frame filled the gap between the opened doors. Stetson stood to Kincaid's right, wondering if either man would acknowledge the other as a Texas Ranger. Knowing to do so would put both men in a precarious position. As a fugitive, O'Brien would probably fight, and his large hands and callused knuckles foretold the outcome of a fistfight between the two. Kincaid would be obligated to take the wanted man in. The law was uncompromising, and Kincaid believed in the law uncompromisingly.

Father O'Brien broke the silence, "How may I help you?"

Kincaid was certain he was starring at "Wild Bill" O'Brien. The two vertical scars on his upper lip proved conclusively what had only been a strong hunch. The small scars, faded with time, had been earned in an unarmed duel to the death with a Comanche chief. Desperate to save the lives of his fellow Rangers, O'Brien had challenged the leader of the fiercest warriors on the Texas frontier to a duel. The chief readily obliged. With both ends of a six-foot length of leather rawhide strapped to each man's right wrist, the two men fought hand-to-hand for thirty minutes—without any weapons. O'Brien fought to save his life and the lives of the ten Rangers who had found themselves surrounded by 100 Comanche warriors. The chief fought for honor. O'Brien was a great Indian fighter. Vanquishing such a formidable foe would be big medicine for the chief. Weary from combat, they found themselves on their knees facing one another after thirty minutes. Suddenly, the chief thrust his head forward. He bit into O'Brien's upper lip, piercing the soft membrane. The chief jerked away with blood smeared on both men's faces. With the same suddenness, O'Brien lunged forward and took the chief's upper lip between his teeth. Clamping down tight, O'Brien yanked back and took the upper lip with him. The warriors stood in disbelief. Moments passed. The chief smiled, exposing his bloody gums. O'Brien removed the crimson lip from his teeth and offered it to the chief. The chief accepted the gift and offered his hand, a symbol of peace. The legend of "Wild Bill" O'Brien grew another notch.

"I need to ask you about an area called Condeza Barajas."

O'Brien's muscles tensed again upon hearing the name. They followed him into the church and down the center aisle between the wooden pews. They passed stained glass windows depicting the fourteen stations of Christ. At the altar, where an enormous hand-carved wooden crucifix loomed, O'Brien turned right and led them to a small antechamber that served as his living quarters.

*　　*　　*　　*

"Condeza Barajas is a very bad place." O'Brien fed a few logs into the fire. A look of disapproval covered his countenance.

"A friend of mine, Jack Wood, is supposedly being held down there. I intend to get him out." Kincaid spoke with the convictions of a man sure of himself.

"Well, son, I wouldn't advise going down there."

"How far is it?" Stetson asked.

"Day, maybe day-and-a-half ride, if you're going straight at it, which I wouldn't advise."

"What's down there?" Kincaid asked.

"Some badass Mexs." O'Brien looked upward, closed his eyes as if in prayer, and silently apologized to God for swearing.

"Listen, you two alone in Condeza Barajas is suicide. I've heard they got an American down there. May just be your friend. Bunch of 'em rode into town about a week ago, killed the sheriff, and rescued one of their own from our friendly jail. They took a gringo with them."

"Can you get us in there?" Kincaid was unrelenting on his quest.

O'Brien moved to a hutch and pulled open a drawer. He withdrew a rolled map, unraveled it, and placed it on the table.

"We're here," O'Brien pointed to a dot on the map representing El Paso. "And here..." O'Brien placed his finger at the end of a mountainous pass south of El Paso, "is Condeza Barajas."

"How do we get in?" Stetson queried.

O'Brien looked at her. "I wouldn't suggest you even consider it, young lady."

Stetson looked into O'Brien's eyes. "He goes; I go. I'm very capable."

"No doubt you are, miss. If those Mexs get their filthy hands on a beauty like you, believe me, if there's a hell on earth, you'd have found it in Condeza Barajas."

"She stays. Now, how do I get in?" Kincaid could feel Stetson's glare bore into him. He chose not to look at her.

While the thunder and rain encircled El Paso, Kincaid and O'Brien studied the map in detail. The pass leading to the old mission appeared impenetrable. O'Brien's knowledge of the area was surprising as he pointed out sentries' posts along the passageway and informed them about Juan Rodriquez Felipe de la Caza.

"If you're intent on rescuing your friend, I'd suggest asking the Texas Rangers for help, son." O'Brien looked up from the map to watch Kincaid's expression. It didn't change.

"Texas Rangers? Where'd I find any Rangers in a town like this?"

"Rosita's Cantina. About half-dozen or so are in town. Hear they're asking questions similar to yours."

"About Condeza Barajas?"

"About your friend Wood. Rumor has it anyway."

Kincaid glanced at Stetson. The quizzical expressions on both faces told O'Brien what he had hoped. Kincaid wasn't a lawman, and he wasn't there to arrest him.

"Excuse me, I've interrupted y'all."

All three turned toward the soft voice. Standing in the doorway, wearing a white habit, was a Catholic sister. She had a rosary in her hand. A sizable crucifix hung from a chain around her neck. Her angelic face had aged over the years, yet her smile was welcoming.

"Ah, sister, come in. Meet our new friends." Father O'Brien stood and motioned for the sister to enter the room.

"Ellsworth, Stetson, this is Sister Marcella Gonzales from Nogales," O'Brien said as the nun stepped into the room. The light from the fireplace and the three candles on the table graced her entry.

"My pleasure," she said softly.

"Sister Gonzales has assisted me in making the church a domicile for homeless children," O'Brien explained, "and she has done a wonderful job."

"Sister, it's nice to meet you, but excuse my rudeness. Father, where is this Rosita's Cantina?" Kincaid was anxious to leave.

"Yes, of course, you must be going. Head two blocks east, turn north, and go about another block. It's a nasty part of town."

Stetson and Kincaid said good-bye and then headed toward a rear door.

Lightning snaked across the pitch-black sky. The rain fell hard, and thunder roared in the distance. The streets of El Paso turned to muddy ooze. The two hurried toward the cantina.

"I was right, Stetson. That was Wild Bill O'Brien. He's about sixty-five or so, but he looks as if he could retain a boxing championship." Stetson nodded in agreement as they quickly walked the wooden boardwalk, attempting to stay under the few storefront overhangs that provided protection from the downpour.

"That Sister Marcella Gonzales? That's Janice Clayton. Both disappeared about six years ago." His voice rose with the crackling of thunder. "If those Rangers at the cantina find out about the good padre, there'll be hell to pay."

"I've never seen you so taken before," Stetson shouted over the thunderclap.

"He was a hero of mine a long time ago. That's all."

CHAPTER 20

By dusk, the streets of El Paso were deserted, and it wasn't from the torrential shower. It was from fear—fear of the Apache. Rumors quickly spread that the red devils had butchered a family on its way to El Paso. The entire countryside knew the Apache did not fear any white man and did not have any respect for armed or unarmed citizens who walked the civilized streets of the white man's town. The Apache attacked without warning, mutilating women and children. The citizen's apprehension was exacerbated when a gang of Mexicans entered town within the week and liberated a prisoner and killed a respected sheriff in cold blood. With the mistaken feeling of security, inhabitants of El Paso kept to their homes after dark. Local businesses closed when their customers went home, leaving El Paso appearing abandoned. The few establishments remaining open catered to a constituency of the population who no longer feared for their lives, including men and women who lived on the edge and expected death around every corner. They were an assorted coterie of cowboys, gamblers, outlaws, carpetbaggers, vagabonds, and prostitutes. Finding themselves in El Paso, many believed they had already found hell. The others were saloon and cantina owners along with madams and card sharks catering their nefarious trade to those willing to pay a price for it. El Paso may have had only one Catholic church, but it proudly offered fifteen saloons and twenty whorehouses.

Juanita Rosita Del Rio owned the finest saloon and parlor house in El Paso, located in the center of its filth and decadence. Among the six blocks of adobe storefronts and wood shacks that sanctioned El Paso a town stood a three-story structure with an ostentatious sign proclaiming "Rosita's Cantina." The cantina had demonstrated itself to have the finest in liquors, entertainment, gambling, and prostitutes.

Juanita, born Juanita Hernandaz Guadalupe Espinoza Smith, was born and raised in the small coastal town of Coatzacoalcos, near the Yucatan Peninsula, facing the Gulf of Campeche. A *mestizos*, a mixed breed of Anglo and Indian, her father was an American merchant seaman who had fought for Mexico's independence and had fallen in love with her mother, a beautiful Zapotec Indian maiden named Rosita. Her parent's brief passion was a sad but romantic story, as Juanita told it. Her father was killed during the Mexican-American War, leaving his family penniless.

Poverty was all she and her family knew. Forced to sell her body at a young age to provide food for her mother and five siblings, Juanita, beautiful like her mother, quickly discovered the power she had over men. Juanita's gift of lovemaking was like no other, and men clamored for her, willing to pay dearly for her gift. They traveled far—from Mexico City, Veracruz, and Manzanillo—to spend just one evening in her arms. She fell in love with and married Don Vertullo Del Rio, a cattleman with a hacienda near Piedras Negras on the Texas border. They planned to breed longhorn cattle and a horde of children. Three years later, Apaches ambushed and killed Don Vertullo and thirty cattle ranchers attempting to protect their herds. Her life of prostitution began the day the ranch was foreclosed upon. Saving every dollar she earned, she swore she'd strip herself of the destitution that plagued her. El Paso became her salvation. There, Texans had money and coveted sex. Within her first year, she bought her first parlor house. After becoming the madam and proprietor, she eschewed sexual relationships, swearing never to touch a man again or have one touch her. It was a vow she broke time and again. Three years later, she built "Rosita's Cantina," named after her beloved mother. Life had never been so good since she had lost Don Vertullo.

The uproar from the entertainment and gambling was the loudest on San Antonio Street. Lights shined brightly through the windows of the saloons dotting the street. The size of Rosita's Cantina distinguished it from the other buildings, as it dwarfed the two-story building next to it, the Overland Stage office located on the corner of El Paso Street and Overland Street.

Walking under a framed portrait of a tiger, indicating the popular game of faro was offered within, Kincaid and Stetson pushed through the swinging batwing doors of Rosita's Cantina and entered a massive room filled with the thick haze of shifting dust mixed with cigar and cigarette smoke. To their left was a massive mahogany bar, the finest cabinetry from the Brunswick Company of

Chicago. Shined to a high gloss, it had a brass foot banister running its entire forty-foot length. Brass spittoons interspersed it. Centered among the liquor cabinets covering the wall behind the bar was a huge, gold-framed, ornate, baroque mirror. According to the handwritten sign hanging on its top left corner, it was imported from France. Rosita's Cantina was the best gaming and parlor house in a thousand-mile radius.

The gambling tables were bustling. Roulette, craps, monte, blackjack, lanterloo, and chuck-a-luck were the prime temptations for the gamblers toward the far right of the room. Nearer the entry, five-card stud was the name of the game. Faro was the main attraction in the center of the room. At the rear of the room was a half-spherical stage, bordered on either side by floor-to-ceiling burgundy drapes laced with gold trim. A lively cancan was in progress.

Kincaid and Stetson stood at the bar and watched the populated saloon. Kincaid pointed to the poker table nearest a faro game in the center of the room. The Texas Rangers Father O'Brien had mentioned sat at the table. Kincaid knew each personally and their illustrious reputations.

"Drink?" The corpselike thinness of the bartender startled Stetson. He was an old man with silver hair, wire spectacles, and deep creases around his eyes and mouth. His pale complexion was indicative of someone that rarely, if ever, ventured outdoors. He was fashionably dressed in a paisley silk, brocaded vest; a gold string tie; and gold nugget cuff links on his stiff, white, French cuffs.

"Coffee, black. The lady, too."

"That'll be two bits." The bartender sat the hot mugs down in front of the couple. Stetson sipped the coffee and sniffed the favorable aroma, pleasantly surprised to find Arbuckle's Ariosa Coffee in such a godforsaken town. She crinkled her nose at the hint of peppermint in the mug, a trademark of Arbuckle's. Kincaid stared in the mirror behind the bar, watching the Rangers.

Captain Jim Bison, with the yellowish-white handlebar moustache and Imperial below his lower lip, was wearing a wide-brimmed, silver belly hat with a Montana peak creased in the crown. Although slight of build, Bison could be a very tough hombre. An old shoulder wound forced him to a desk job. Instrumental in cleaning out the outlaws and vigilantes in Laredo and Brownsville, he was undoubtedly the toughest and most demanding of Rangers.

"Men of his caliber could help me rescue Jack," Kincaid thought.

The man across from Bison, clad in buckskin and fringe, was Crowhorse, a half-breed Sioux Indian. He was as calm and gentle as a milked cow, yet he was a cold-blooded killer. He had single-handedly captured Black Claw, leader of a warring tribe of Comanche who had killed his wife and daughter, and took the scalps of nineteen other Comanche warriors who rode with the leader.

Jake Johnson, studying his cards, was the youngest of the Texas Rangers in the group, nicknamed "Shakey" Jake because of a nervous affliction. Kincaid noticed his hands still trembled. He had been responsible for the area east of the Trinity River, the "safest place to live," according to the people who praised Jake.

Standing off to one side, quietly thumbing a mandolin was Justus Strummin. Kincaid always enjoyed Justus' company. After a hard day on the trail, when the tenseness wallpapered the air, Justus would strum that strange instrument and sing a tune. Soon, everyone on the trail forgot his woes.

The tall Texan standing near the stage, ignoring the others and watching the cancan girls, was Tex, the oldest in the group. Kincaid smiled. He watched Tex clap his hands and stomp his feet in harmony with the music while the onstage women flirted with him. Tex hated most men sympathetic to the Northern cause. How they became friends was still a mystery. Tex had become a legend in his own time. He was another man Kincaid would want on his side in a gunfight.

Finally, JJ Bost was looking at his cards and placing his bet. In his early thirties, he was good-looking with dark brown hair combed and parted on the right. He sported a well-trimmed moustache. He was a natural man hunter and fighter.

They had all been colleagues of Bison's at one time or another. Kincaid looked around. If Bison and the Rangers were involved, Billy Irons would be somewhere in the vicinity. Glancing around the room, Kincaid saw long-legged Billy sluggishly progressing up the staircase. A smug expression was on his face, and a cigarette dangled from his lips. As usual, the lothario had his arms around two beautiful *señoras*. His evening was obviously just beginning. Kincaid laughed. It seemed like old times.

"Rosita, please. I love you. Open the door," a pining drunk cried at the top of the stairs of the third landing, pounding his fists on a bedroom door.

"Come out! I beg you!" the man pleaded.

Few of the cantina's patrons noticed his outcry. The disharmony of noise that was the hallmark of any gambling casino drowned his cries of love. Kincaid picked up the man's cries and glanced at the sound. Stetson saw Kincaid smiling and glanced in the same direction. She also stared at the drunkard.

Suddenly, the door burst open. An obese, fleshy woman with uncombed, tasseled black hair and arms as round as a man's thighs, dimpled with fat, stormed out of the room. As the man opened his arms to embrace her, the woman whacked him in the face with her fist, staggering him backward. The banister couldn't hold his weight, and he came crashing through it. He landed on his back in the middle of a faro table. The group at the table and in the immediate area looked upward and saw Juanita Rosita Del Rio standing at the top of the landing. Her hands were on her green velvet-covered hips, and she was staring at the man she had nearly killed.

"Pig!" she screamed.

The gamblers laughed and gave her a wave. With an insipid motion of her hand, she turned and reentered her room, slamming the door behind her.

"Who was that?" Kincaid queried the old bartender.

"The woman? That's the proprietor of this here establishment."

"Rosita?" Stetson asked.

"The same. A beaut, ain't she?"

"But the stories I've heard. She's the prettiest woman in all of Texas. Some call her the Texas Rose."

"Yes, ma'am, that was a few years back. But drinking, whoring, staying up all night, and running this business sure have taken its toll. She's more like a Texas Tumbleweed that's been through a Kansas twister." The bartender chuckled at his own remark as he turned to draw a beer for another patron.

Kincaid smiled and winked at Stetson. She returned his smile. By the twitch in his jawline and the narrowness of his eyes, she knew he was tense. She also knew, with the knowledge Father O'Brien gave him, he was anxious to get moving and help his friend. He motioned to the table of Rangers.

"C'mon, let's say howdy to some friends." Kincaid pushed off from the bar. Stetson quickly followed.

"Aces high, cowboy. Read 'em and weep," a gambler laughed as he leaned over and scooped up a pile of chips.

"I'll take two cards," said another from the next table.

"Last turn, gentlemen," a faro dealer announced to those that chose to "buck the tiger."

Kincaid and Stetson elbowed their way through the throng of roulette, poker, and faro tables toward the center of the room. The room was full of numerous sporting women. Some were attractive, and some were repulsive. All were trying to provide their services to the drunken cowboys.

In the background, the piano player started a medley of Stephen Foster hits, beginning with "Camptown Races." Bison smiled broadly as he noticed the two coming his way.

"I'll be. Would you look at this!"

The Rangers looked up from their game.

"Boys," Kincaid said stoically to the Rangers, showing none of the enthusiasm he held for them.

The Rangers acknowledged Kincaid.

"Have a seat, Ellsworth." Bison motioned to the empty chairs across from him. Kincaid pulled a chair out for Stetson and then for himself. Both sat next to young Jake. Bison reached across the table and shook Kincaid's hand, welcoming him.

"So, this must be your lady friend I've heard so much about." Stetson blushed.

"Jim, this is Stetson. Stetson, this is one of the best darn Texas Rangers you'll ever meet, Jim Bison." Stetson reached across the table and offered her hand, an unladylike gesture for the big, civilized cities in the East. Yet, it was one that produced an infectious smile from all the Rangers. Each man stood, nodded, offered his name, and shook her hand. They began talking to her at the same time, as if they had never been in the presence of an attractive woman. Catching themselves, they laughed nervously and then started another game of cards. They had taken to her instantly and were obviously smitten.

Kincaid noticed that not one of them wore his badge. "It's doubtlessly clever to be cautious in a lawless town unless provoked," he thought.

"What brings you to this hellhole?" Bison asked innocuously.

"Same as you. Looking for Jack Wood."

"Jack Wood?" Bison shrugged his shoulders.

Kincaid leaned forward, resting his forearms on the table. "I hear you and the boys have been asking questions about him. He was here in El Paso, got himself arrested, thrown in jail, and then got snatched by a bunch of Mexicans."

Bison shook his head pensively. "Don't know what you're talking about."

"He disappeared about a week ago. I know you've been asking questions."

"Me and the boys have been here a day, maybe two, at most." Bison glanced at the other Rangers for corroboration. Several of the others nodded in unison. Kincaid took a deep breath. He knew they were asking questions, but he couldn't divulge his source was Father O'Brien. They'd be forced to arrest him.

"Jim. I need your help. Jack, let's say a friend of mine, is being held south of the border in an old mission called Condeza Barajas."

"What do you propose?"

"Ride with me, and get him out."

Bison leaned forward to be heard when several cowboys began singing loudly as the piano player started another song.

"Ain't that simple. No gringo can just ride into Mexico, not with the Mexican military swarming over the countryside. Some army general named Porfirio Diaz has made himself president and dictator. All hell is breaking loose down there. It ain't safe."

"Tomorrow, I head for Condeza Barajas. Join me, Jim. It'll be like old times."

"We can't. Listen to me. It's suicide to cross the border. As Texas Rangers," Bison's voice softened to a whisper, "we have no jurisdiction down there."

"How many times you ride into Mexico after a wanted fugitive?"

Bison glanced at his cards. There had been too many times to count. If need be, a Ranger would follow an outlaw all the way to Mexico City. But this was different. Washington was pulling the strings.

Bison looked at his longtime ally. "We can't."

Kincaid stood and looked at the other Rangers.

"Any of you boys interested in tearing up Old Mexico with me?" They remained silent.

Jake and Kincaid had been friends before Jake joined the Rangers. He wanted to help, as did the others. "Listen to Bison. Wait a spell. We'll figure something out."

"Jake, I don't have time to wait."

Kincaid turned on his heels and worked his way toward the saloon doors. Stetson stood nervously, watching him go. She then turned her attention and anger toward the Rangers who had resumed their card game.

* * * *

"I cannot believe this! You men, you Rangers, are letting your friend ride into Mexico alone? He could be killed!" Stetson's voice started to rise above the saloon noise.

The Rangers hoped no one had heard her reference to the Texas Rangers.

"Sit down. Let me explain." Bison wanted to tell her about Jack Wood working for the government, about Washington wanting to know his whereabouts, and the counterfeit money coming in from Mexico. But he couldn't.

Bison exchanged glances with the other Rangers. "Stetson, we've got no authority in Mexico. A man named de la Caza has more than 200 well-armed killers worked into a frenzy down there. The odds are against us. It'd be like riding into hell." Bison glanced at his comrades. He knew he had said too much. He wanted to rationalize why they couldn't help Kincaid. Doing it without divulging Washington and the intricate mess he found himself in was difficult.

Stetson's face turned crimson. She looked around the table. Not one eye met hers. Their faces turned away, staring at the floor or into their coffee mugs or shuffling cards. Her words came out slowly and deliberately.

"Look at you! Texas Rangers, Indian fighters, buffalo hunters. Your exploits are legend. Guess the years have taken the edge off. Or maybe Kincaid lied to me about his adventures with you."

Bison and Jake motioned for her to lower her voice.

She continued. "Odds! From the stories I've heard, the odds are in your favor! The toughest hombres in Texas. That's a laugh! All lies. You're only as colorful as the best dime novelists can make you. That's it, isn't it?"

Her diatribe had reached a fever pitch. With the last word shouted so the entire saloon could hear her, she swiftly turned toward the saloon doors, bumping into a faro table. In anger, she grabbed the dealing box on the table, knocked over a rack of chips, and then tossed the box to the floor as the cards spilled to the ground.

She turned back toward the Rangers. "He won't ride into hell alone. Mark my words, gentlemen." She worked her way toward the exit.

Chapter 21

Catherine Webb lay perfectly still between the satin sheets. Positioned on her back in the hush of the night, her breathing was purposely slow and deliberate as she listened to the inhaling and exhaling of the man resting next to her. By the resonance of his breathing, she knew he was fast asleep. The effectiveness of the drug she had slipped him took longer than anticipated. She had come too close to making love to this fat, stinking, pig of a man. She shuddered at the thought of him groping her breasts as well as his fat, chubby fingers sliding up her thighs and squeezing her buttocks. She had used the same sedative on men before, but never a man as enormous and rotund as the monster laying alongside her now. She should have increased the dosage she had sprinkled in his glass of champagne while at dinner to ensure the efficacy of the narcotic. Unfortunately, an overdose brings on a sudden, inexplicable heart attack. Her mission tonight was to gather information that would be vital to the preservation of the United States, not kill the man. However, the thought of this particular man's death—a grotesque, arm thrashing, throat swelling, gasping for air death—brought a roguish smile to her full, red lips.

As a member of the United States government's Office of Intelligence, she had assignments whose objectives were to entice information from government dignitaries and heads of state from foreign countries. Her government simply assumed she slept with most, if not all, of her assignments to procure knowledge that had always proved invaluable to the United States' national security. However, she was too clever to allow herself to become a whore for national interest. She had never made love to one of her assignments, and she had never been tasked with a mission to exterminate an adversary. She knew the data she accumulated frequently led back to her source, embarrassed them, and often led to their deportation. She was aware, in rare cases, the foreign government executed the dignitary upon their return. Yet, she never felt any remorse for those men who may have died.

All played the dangerous game of international intrigue, spying on one another for profit and possible spoils of war. She never had an assignment that did not lead to conclusive evidence of another country's mistrust. An assignment or foreign country had never concluded she had been the leak of information or the cause of its demise. All of her assignments believed the two of them had made mad, passionate love for one delicious evening and they were the world's best lovers. Fortunately, the narcotic she slipped them always left them with a mild case of amnesia.

"Yes," she thought to herself, "I'm as good as one could get as a double agent."

Her head slowly rolled to her left. Her dark, wavy hair caressed her right cheek and shoulder. She stared at him. His Excellency Humberto Bernardino Bustrillos, the Mexican ambassador to the United States, unceremoniously lay on his back with his mouth wide open. His snoring could wake the neighbors, if any neighbors lived near the secluded three-story townhouse, just three blocks from the White House. The entire structure was leased to the Mexican government for the ambassador. His entourage of bodyguards, cooks, maids, and male servants occupied the entire home and was threefold what other foreign governments allowed their dignitaries.

Her mission to gather information and disappear into the night with a love note of fond gratitude would have been impossible with the other occupants in the house. Tonight, the entire household staff had been dismissed for the evening. During dinner, Catherine embarrassingly admitted to Humberto that she was a passionate lover and her screams of delight may be interpreted as screams of misfortune. She pointed out how embarrassed they would be if bodyguards burst into the bedroom during their ecstasy of lovemaking. The ambassador, choking on his meal while imagining such bliss, immediately sent word to his staff that they had the night off.

With each intake and exhalation of breath, the satin sheets heaved up and down rhythmically with the ambassador's massive belly. His large, dry lips stuck to his yellowish, gaping teeth. His face was covered with sweat, accentuating the chubby, pock-marked jowl and chin.

"The surface of the moon must certainly look like this," she thought. *Señor* Bustrillos was the ugliest man she had possibly ever seen in her life, and she had been within a hair's breadth of having sex with him.

"God," she thought, "the lab will have to make a stronger potion for me in the future."

She carefully slid her naked body between the satin sheets until her feet touched the floor. She paused and listened. His plump majesty didn't move. His obnoxious breathing continued laboriously. She stood deliberately. The cool air enveloped her body, creating unwelcome goose bumps. The street lamps outside dimly lit the second-story bedroom. Catherine painstakingly placed one foot in front of the other, ensuring each step was solid on the large Oriental rug covering the hardwood floor. The room was cluttered with antique furniture, end tables, chairs, and lamps. If she accidentally knocked something over, it would undoubtedly awaken him. With her luck, he would be amorous. Having seen him in his childlike sleep, she decided she would rather kill him than crawl back into bed with him.

She made her way toward the double doors that led to the study, which was just off the bedroom. She recollected, when they had first come into the bedroom that evening, it was toward her right. They had been laughing and holding one another, stripping off their clothes. He mentally visualized his studlike prowess; she wondered when the narcotic would take effect.

Her foot struck a small table, and several books wobbled. She reached for them and steadied them, cursing softly to herself. She held her breath, afraid to look back toward the bed. Again, the loud wheezing reaffirmed Bustrillos' slumber, and she began moving once more.

The coolness of the wooden floor confirmed she had reached the far side of the bedroom. The study doors were only two steps away. The streetlight grew dimmer as she moved away from the bedroom windows. She moved until the study's window shed some light. In another two steps, she touched another thick carpet.

"Hello, study," she said to herself as she carefully moved toward the desk.

No one could imagine the difficulty of moving through an unfamiliar darkened room full of fine furniture and delicate items unless they had personal experience. Bumping an object whose clatter could scream your whereabouts in a split second, leaving you without an explanation of why you were someplace you shouldn't be in the middle of the night, was her worst fear.

She hesitated. The gas streetlight barely cast its glow on the desk. She could scarcely see. She tiptoed around the desk, attempting to gain an ounce of light from outside. Her fingers moved the many papers and documents piled on the oak desk. She had no idea what she was looking for. Captain Walsh could not give her much information when he assigned her the case this morning. That's the way it usually was. If caught, she couldn't possibly divulge any classified information, even under torture.

She opened a desk drawer and then another. She pulled out several files and placed them on the desk. Facing the study's French doors, she raised her head to look through the glass panes. She stared for what felt like five minutes. She couldn't make out Bustrillos' silhouette. She listened, catching an occasional faint sound. She held her breath to make sure she wasn't listening to herself.

"Okay, it's him," she thought, "sleeping like a baby."

She focused her attention on the files, moving around the desk to improve the lighting condition. She came across a large manila envelope, sealed with the wax imprint of the Mexican government. Fishing around for something to open it, she found a letter opener with a four-inch blade. It was shaped like a miniature, medieval Spanish dagger. Nimbly opening the envelope, she studied the information.

"My God," she thought as she read the confidential information, "Walsh would find this extremely enlightening." She slid the documents back into the envelope. "Time to go," she thought. She was pleased she had found what Walsh seemed to want so badly.

She smiled at the thought of Captain Jonah Walsh. He recruited her during the summer of 1872, a little more than four years ago, when she worked as a secretary in the French Embassy. The French ambassador had kept Walsh waiting for hours. He flirted with her, and she flirted back. She politely refused his dinner invitation. She thought he was good-looking with a good sense of humor, and she began thinking twice about her refusal of dinner when the ambassador appeared. Walsh joined the ambassador in his office. She hoped Walsh would ask her again for dinner. She skipped lunch to wait for him. Her decision proved judicious. As Walsh left the office, he stopped and very courteously asked her again if she'd reconsider dinner. She hesitated for only a moment and then gladly accepted the invitation. Learning she spoke four languages, Walsh suggested she work for the American Consulate. Within six months and his urging, she was swept into the intrigue of the secret service. Their torrid affair, as she thought of it, was known to only a chosen few.

"Ah, *señorita.*" The fleshy, moist hand coiled around her stomach. She stiffened. Failing to check on his breathing, he caught her by complete surprise.

"My beautiful one, I missed you." Bustrillos brought her closer to him. Bent over the desk, she could feel his hairy stomach against the small of her back and buttocks. His right hand caressed her flat stomach as his left hand moved over her left breast. He cupped his hand there, softly massaging the nipple between the thumb and forefinger.

"Come back to bed, *mi amor.*" The ambassador began nibbling her earlobe when his eyes focused on the documents on the desk.

He murmured into her ear, "*¿Cuál es éste?* (What are you doing?)" Bustrillos' large hands brought her closer to him. She felt his breath on her neck.

"*¡Puta!* Whoring bitch spy!" His voice grew louder as his left hand moved from her breast to her neck.

"Tell me what you are doing here."

His grip around her throat tightened, and she began gagging. He pulled her upright until her back was fully against his chest. Her toes barely touched the floor. He shook her roughly as the narcotic began wearing off.

"*¡Dígame!* (Tell me!)" Humberto was confused. He tightened his grip on her. She was so beautiful. He had never been with such a gorgeous woman without paying for her first. Why was she doing this to him? Why?

"*¿Por qué?* (Why?)" he screamed. He had never felt so much anger toward a woman. Bending her down over the desk, he slammed her forehead against the oak desk. Again and again, he slammed her head.

Catherine gasped for air. His grip around her throat was cutting off oxygen. She was thrown forward. His forearm was buried into her stomach, forcing her to bend over the desk. The first blow to the head drew blood. She nearly lost consciousness after the second smashing of her skull. She was frantic. Her hands grabbed the desk to prevent him from hurdling her against it again. She was strong, but her strength against such a monster weakened by the second. She searched the desk for anything to throw at him or through the window to possibly attract attention. As she started blacking out, she felt the fat diplomat's erection against her buttocks.

"This son of a bitch," her dying thoughts raced, "is excited about killing me!" Her thoughts awoke everything she hated about men like him. Her fingers identified the letter opener. Seizing it, she plunged it into his left thigh.

"Ahhhhh! *¡Perra, puta!*" Bustrillos cried as the opener hit bone. His grip loosened. Moving swiftly, she twisted around to face him. She jerked the opener from the gaping, bleeding wound. His hands moved instantaneously. His left grabbed her hair at the back of her head, and his right moved between her breasts, reaching for her bruised neck. Catherine twisted—left and then right—and swung the opener, striking the intended target.

For a brief moment, they gazed at one another, nose to nose. His foul-smelling breath cascaded over her face. The diplomat's eyes rolled in their sockets. The blood dripped from the wound in his left temple. The opener throbbed in cadence with the diminishing pulse.

Dressing promptly, she left the townhouse after scribbling an encoded message. Walking through the fog-shrouded night down Thirteenth Street, she turned at the intersection of Thirteenth and G Street, heading away from the White House and the Treasury Department. At the next block, she turned south on Twelfth Street, zigzagging across town to determine if she was being followed. On the corner of Twelfth and F Street, she slipped the note into an opening in a wooden street lamppost. Hesitating only a moment, she continued south and hailed a cab on E Street.

An hour later, two nondescript men entered the townhouse of the Mexican ambassador. Hurrying up the flight of stairs to the second floor, they entered the bedroom down the hallway that overlooked the corner of Thirteen Street and New York Avenue.

They moved across the room to the study.

"Jesus!" the shorter of the two men pronounced. "What a mess!"

"We've got two hours until the staff gets here. Get busy," the taller man said as he moved toward the ambassador's corpse.

"It'll take both of us to move him, John. Clean up the place first. Then help me take him downstairs."

The smaller man nodded as he stooped to pick up the pile of papers thrown on the floor.

CHAPTER 22

The eighteenth president of the United States sat pensively in the Lincoln Room, patiently awaiting the arrival of his advisors. Checking the time with his pocket watch, he saw it was three minutes after midnight. He looked out the small window behind the oak desk, beyond the Potomac River, and stared at the wintry sky with its millions of flickering stars. He took another drag from his twentieth cigar for the day.

Grant seriously doubted a run for a third term would be successful. Those close to him attempted to boast his morale, pointing out, if he wasn't elected to another term now, another attempt in 1880 could be made with the support of the Republican Party. To run and be unsuccessful was unacceptable to him. Failing at any endeavor at this point in his life would be unbefitting. In his heart, he knew he had to choose whether to run for an unprecedented third term or stop the movement that favored him. Rumors circulated that the Democrats favored Samuel J. Tilden as their candidate, a strong consideration for his pulling out of the race. Tilden, a New York lawyer, had been instrumental in breaking up the corrupt politics in his state. A third party called the Greenback party, surfacing for the first time during this campaign, supported the issuance of large amounts of paper money, hoping it would bring back prosperity, especially to the farmer, by raising prices and making debts easier to pay. Their nomination, Peter Cooper, was an unknown, yet this party could split the votes. The Democrats, to Grant's dismay, had won a majority in the House of Representatives in the election of 1874. The likelihood of a Republican presidential win now didn't seem favorable. However, his loyalty to the party made him feel obligated to accept the nomination, and he believed the country shouldn't have to suffer both a Democratic House of Representatives and Democratic president. Grant wondered if the scandals during his administration prevented a successful run. His administration had been the subject of abuse and slander never equaled in political history. He ran a nervous hand through his hair. He had to make a decision that impacted the very fate of the nation, and he needed to make it quickly, before the Republican National Convention convened in Cincinnati.

Grant heard footsteps as the door to the study opened. His good friend, Charles Theodore Gifford, peered in.

"Mr. President?"

"Come in, Ted, please." Grant stood to welcome his friend. Gifford's six-foot-one-inch slender frame dwarfed Grant's five-foot-eight-inch, stout physique. Grant apologized for having canceled their earlier meeting, scheduled for three that afternoon, citing continued conflicts in his schedule and, laughingly, in his administration.

"Hiram, you look worried." Gifford called Grant by his given name. Few knew Ulysses was actually the president's middle name. Due to an error upon his appointment to West Point, Hiram Ulysses Grant became Ulysses Simpson Grant. Grant accepted the new name, preferring his mother's maiden name of Simpson, feeling it paid homage to a calm, quiet woman of great simplicity whom he loved and respected.

"My biggest undertaking as president has been to worry." Grant smiled at his confidante. Genuinely concerned for his friend, Ted returned the smile, detecting the enormous stress the president's face exhibited. For years, Gifford had known that Grant suffered bouts of depression.

"Ted, a straight answer to a straight question. Just between friends. No holds barred."

"Of course."

"How will the history books record my presidency?" Grant's blue eyes bore into Ted's, searching for the truth before the words were spoken.

Gifford weighed his answer for several moments. With deliberate inflexion, he responded, "The history books will show you're one of the greatest military leaders this country ever produced. A brilliant tactician and a leading strategic theorist. Hell, Hiram, you won the war, saving this country much hardship. You saved thousands of lives by bringing the war to a conclusion."

Grant smiled. "Just like you to skirt the question while putting a positive spin on it. Well done. You should have been a politician. Now, a simple reply to a simple question…as a friend."

Gifford turned in his chair to squarely face his friend. "There isn't a simple answer. And, you know the reply. Pick up the *New York Herald* or the *New York World.*"

Gifford hesitated, knowing the two publications were anti-Grant. He needed to add several pro-Grant newspapers. Otherwise, Grant would totally discount him.

"Or the *New York Times* or *Tribune.* My dear friend..." Ted looked stoically into Grant's expressionless face and vacant eyes. "Your administration has been fraught with scandal. Congressional members accepting financial favors to support bills aiding the Union Pacific Railroad...your Secretary of War, that little shit..."

"Belknap," Grant corrected.

"Yes, Belknap. He was investigated for selling army trading posts for personal gain. Heavy evidence showed that he collected more than $20,000 regarding the Fort Sill post." Gifford hesitated for a moment. Grant ran a nervous hand over his beard. Grant was not listening to anything new.

Gifford stood, walked to the fireplace, placed a hand on the mantle, and turned to face Grant. "By accepting Belknap's resignation, you protected him from criminal prosecution and impeachment proceedings for malfeasance in office. That had the appearance of presidential collusion and political manipulation."

Again, Gifford hesitated, glancing at the floor. Grant nodded for him to continue. "The newspapers violently criticized the Salary Bill of 1873, doubling yours and everyone's salary in Washington." Gifford caught himself counting off the offensive transgressions with each finger and stopped. He knew it was annoying, especially because he would run out of fingers.

"Our splendid postwar boom abruptly ended when the Republican Congress voted to end the coinage of silver. The House voted that all greenbacks produced during the war could be redeemed in gold. These decisions forced banks to fail in this country, Hiram. Factories closed. There was panic in the streets."

Grant lit his twenty-first cigar, and Gifford paused only momentarily. "European bankers withdrew their funds from American investments. The New York Stock Exchange closed, plunging us into a recession. Farmers went bust. Mortgages were foreclosed on. The Northern Pacific Railroad declared bankruptcy. As a result, the Democrats recently won a majority in Congress. Finally, the Internal Revenue Department's alleged stealing of excise taxes was another example of poor decision making and cover-up in this administration. Hiram, during your eight-year term, every single one of the executive offices has come under congressional investigation." Gifford looked at Grant.

Grant's weakness was trusting people who pretended to be his friends, but had hidden agendas. Gifford couldn't quite say to Grant that he feared disgrace and dishonesty had clouded his presidency. Although the man was personally honest, graft and corruption had undermined his presidency. The voting, naïve public never seemed to understand that military leadership and heroics rarely, if ever, equated to the capacities necessary to become an effective president.

"From one friend to another," Gifford ended while trying to smile.

Grant looked up from the desk. "From one friend to another. That's why I asked you. Thanks, Ted. You've taken a burden from my shoulders. A decision I have been wrestling with just became clearer."

Grant made a mental note to contact Roscoe Conkling, the leader of the Stalwart faction of the Republican Party and primary supporter of a third term, in the morning.

"Ted, perhaps it was my misfortune to be called to the office of chief executive without any previous political training. I never aspired to the presidency, and I have never quite forgiven myself for resigning the command of the army to accept it. Admittedly, I never had the ambition or the taste for political life."

A knock on the door interrupted the two friends. Alexander Stewart, the secretary of the treasury, led the group into the small room. The scholarly Professor Carl Upridge, Captain Jonah Walsh, and Undersecretary of War John Gilmore followed.

"Evening, gentlemen. Or, might I say, good morning," Grant was composed and contented. The quick chat with his friend had been brutal, but refreshing.

As the men took their familiar seats facing the small square desk at the back of the room, Gilmore glanced at Walsh, wondering the depth of information the deputy assistant of the Treasury Department had brought. Walsh represented all the men he had disdained his entire life.

"A hip shooter, smooth, calm, self-confident. No real depth to him," Gilmore thought. "Sure, Walsh is street-smart and the only man in the room with experience in the West besides Grant. Yet, he lacked the formal education that Washington, DC, and the government needed. The provincial country needed solid, erudite citizens to lead and develop it into a formidable nation. The time for cowboys had passed. Walsh, when stripped of his high-priced clothes and courtly manners, was merely a cowboy."

How such a man could hold the position he held in the government was beyond comprehension. Grant favored men like Walsh. For that, Gilmore mistrusted the president. Perhaps it would be best for the nation if Grant didn't run for a third term. He needed to give that idea more consideration.

"Mister Gilmore, you're up first." Grant broke Gilmore's introspection. Unruffled by the intrusion, Gilmore turned in his chair to face Grant.

"Mr. President, a thorough investigation into the Apache's recent activities in the southwestern states of Arizona, New Mexico, and Texas has been completed." Gilmore pulled several papers from his satchel.

"As we know, Blue Dog is a Mimbreno Indian. This tribal branch of the Apache calls the area between the Rio Grande and the Mogollon Mountains home. They are fiercely independent. Blue Dog has struck terror in every town and farm in the tristate area. His dog soldiers readily kill and mutilate every white man, woman, and child who crosses their path. Commerce has decreased in this area over the last five years due to this ignorant heathen. He and his warriors are personally responsible for the deaths of more than 350 people in the last four years. The army has attempted to track him down and bring him to justice, yet he continues to evade our troops. We believe he and his people are now hiding in the southern section of the Gallinas Mountains. As we speak, troops are canvassing the surrounding area to locate him and destroy both him and his village."

"Thanks, John. Well done. I only wish we could reach an amicable solution with this Blue Dog and his people." Grant had always sympathized with the Indians and their plight.

Grant glanced around the room. "Any questions, gentlemen?"

"Yes, sir. I have a question, but I first have a small correction." Walsh disliked Gilmore almost as much as Gilmore disliked him. He hated to display his displeasure of the man in front of this group of refined advisors.

"Then again," he thought to himself, "they all know my feelings."

"First, you refer to Blue Dog's warriors as dog soldiers."

Gilmore nodded in the affirmative.

"Dog soldiers is a term applied to certain warriors of the Northern Plains, specifically the Cheyenne. Sorry, John. I just want the facts straight, okay?"

Gilmore stared at Walsh in disbelief. Correcting him on such a minor issue was absurd. Yet, given a chance, Walsh could easily undermine him.

Walsh looked at Gilmore. "Now, John, what new information do you have?"

"What?" The right corner of Gilmore's mouth curved upward.

"We know about Blue Dog and his tribe. The information you provide is repetitive, John. Let me ask another way. You say he's killed more than 300 people? Who?"

"Who? Jesus, man, do you want names? Suffice it to say, he's a butcher."

"Blue Dog has killed. I'd be the last to deny it. But, if you'll look into it further, you'll find the people he fights are not unarmed American citizens. They're mostly Mexicans and the United States Army when they get close enough, which is too frequent."

"Do you have proof, Jonah?" Alexander Stewart was proud of his deputy assistant and the widespread knowledge of the West he brought to the table.

"Yes, sir. Our own military records prove Blue Dog only fights those who attempt to hurt him and his people. He doesn't war with the farmer, and he does not raid our towns. He hasn't for several years. There's no record of any innocent white man being killed by this Indian, or his immediate tribe, in the last four to five years."

"You speak as if you know him, Walsh." Stewart pursued the issue, giving Walsh the excuse to flaunt his knowledge in front of Gilmore. Stewart disliked the undersecretary of war as much as the others in the room.

Walsh leaned forward. "Personally? No, I don't. I respect him. As Gilmore said, Blue Dog has evaded our better-equipped army for years. How? He's probably one of the greatest military tacticians I've seen. He knows the art of war. He's a genius on the battlefield. No offense, Mr. President." Jonah smiled at the president. "He and his men can cross the desert without water. Hundreds can hide in the mountainous ravines without detection. The entire village can move under the watchful eyes of our scouts without notice. For the last fifty years, the Apaches have hated the Mexicans and have warred with them. The Mexican government has hunted and killed the Apache for even longer. We've just gotten in the way, and our policies against the Indians have become tantamount to total extermination." Walsh stopped before he got on a familiar soapbox. This wasn't the time to chastise the president and the government for wrongs against the Indians. The extermination policy was an issue he'd always wrestled with, and he would take it up again with the president at a more opportune time.

"Gentlemen, Blue Dog hasn't killed any innocent white people—only those inflicting harm on his nation. I might add that his kill ratio is more than fifteen to one against the United States Army. As the undersecretary of war, John, it should concern you that such an ignorant heathen, as you call him, with undernourished warriors can keep an upper hand over our boys." Walsh smiled at Gilmore, who returned the smile with a scowl.

Gilmore realized it wasn't the time to banter with Walsh on the Indian issue. No one in the room knew better than Gilmore that the soldiers fighting on the plains were poorly trained, inadequately fed, disappointingly equipped, ineptly led, and underpaid. He wasn't a military expert, but he clearly understood what they were up against. Gilmore was having difficulty holding his tongue.

"Cholera and smallpox kill more of our men than Indians, Walsh," Gilmore responded, if only perfunctory.

"Jonah."

Walsh looked at Grant, expecting to be scolded. "We may never find a solution to the Indian problem. I'd appreciate your insight on this matter at a later date. However, I believe you and the professor are here to address the counterfeiting issue."

"Yes, Mr. President. I believe everyone in the room will be surprised at our findings. Professor?" Jonah turned the discussion over to Carl Upridge.

Upridge straightened his bow tie for the hundredth time, a nervous habit. "Gentlemen, I'll allow Captain Walsh to discuss our findings on the counterfeit issue. We have knowledge concerning the Mexico matter, specifically the area south of El Paso." The professor fumbled with his documents as he spoke, arranging the papers in a particular order.

He continued. "Based on documents that fell in the hands of Captain Walsh from the Mexican Embassy..."

"Let me see those, professor," Grant interrupted the professor's presentation and reached over to accept the extended papers.

"Jonah, this wouldn't have anything to do with the disappearance of the Mexican ambassador, would it?" Grant studied the Mexican Embassy's emblem and letterhead on the stationary as he asked the question.

Walsh looked to his immediate supervisor, Alexander Stewart, for direction.

"Mr. President," Stewart asserted. "We're aware His Excellency Humberto Bernardino Bustillos has been reported missing. His disappearance is a mystery at the moment. The authorities are investigating. However, any involvement our field operatives may—or may not—have had with the Mexican ambassador or the Embassy would be considered classified information."

"I'm the president of the United States, Alex! Classified from me?"

"I'm afraid so, sir. Until the matter is resolved satisfactorily, this incident remains classified to all except a select few, sir. However, I feel fortunate that Captain Walsh was able to acquire information before the incident became classified."

"The old saying of 'what the old man doesn't know won't hurt him' was appropriate at the moment," Stewart thought.

Grant's eyes narrowed as he studied Walsh and Stewart.

"What the hell," he thought, "it'll all be someone else's headache in a few more months."

"Carry on, professor," Grant said.

"There appears to be a resurrection in the Mexican government's desire to gain control over Texas."

"We fought that war thirty years ago, professor." Gilmore was getting impatient with Upridge's slow, methodical ways.

"Yes, sir. That's true. But a *Señor* Porfirio Diaz, a very ambitious army general, is leading a revolt against the incumbents in office in Mexico. He has the support of the upper crust of Mexico. He's mistakenly viewed as a 'man of the people.' The people rally around many promises he's made. One of those promises is to retake Texas."

"Preposterous!" Gilmore knew this had to be pure conjecture from both Walsh and Upridge.

"Afraid not, John," Walsh was ready for Gilmore. "A small army is massing just south of El Paso. A revolutionary rogue is training roughly 200 well-equipped men. The leader's name is Juan Rodriquez Felipe de la Caza. His intent is to invade Texas via El Paso, turn toward the cities of Dallas and Fort Worth, and capture these two towns while destroying everything in their path. He'll march on Dallas like Sherman marched on Atlanta, burning everything that stands. The killing of Americans will be in the thousands."

Walsh paused for emphasis. He clearly had everyone's attention. "After destroying El Paso, a signal will be sent to other small bands of Mexican banditos gathering along the border. Upon hearing of de la Caza's success, they'll invade Texas. De la Caza's 200 men will swell into 1,000 within twenty-four hours of razing El Paso."

"With the population of Texas approximating two-thirds Mexican, many Mexican loyalists will join their ranks. Their number could swell to several hundred thousand," the professor added.

"Sounds suicidal to me, professor." Grant smiled the smile of a Union general who was hearing news of a breach in the line and knew he had the superiority to turn the enemy back.

Walsh continued. "The Mexicans have been in an uproar over the loss of Texas ever since they lost it to us. They're willing to die for this cause, a cause *Señor* Diaz has perpetuated."

"Gilmore, how long will it take to mobilize our troops against these Rebels?" Grant was thinking like the days of old. War was the only thing that ever aroused him.

"Mobilization? Mr. President, we have hardly more than a police force. Our troops have no experience in handling the problems of war mobilization and large-scale command."

"What's the strength of our military, Mr. Gilmore?"

"We currently have 25,000 men in uniform, sir."

Grant took a deep breath. Twenty-five thousand men? He thought back to the war. There were 65,000 Union volunteers with the outbreak of war in 1861. By the time he held the rank of commander in chief of the Union Army, more than 1.5 million troops were at his command. After the war and before his administration, Congress slashed the military budget in 1866, reducing the size of the army to 54,000 men. It was reduced again in 1874 to its current size. These few men were strung out over 2.5 million square miles, covering hundreds of forts between the Mississippi and Pacific Ocean. Given the great distances, communication was poor with them. Grant recalled the briefings, noting that perhaps 10,000 men were available to contend with the Indians. Grant leaned back in his chair and stared at the ceiling while watching the cloud of cigar smoke hover above him. Had his entire administration been a smoke screen?

Everyone in the room waited for Grant. Noticing the quietness of the room, he leaned forward in his chair. "Gentlemen, if Mexico should invade Texas, our only recourse, with many civilian lives at stake, would be to respond as I have in the past. I would ask Mexico for its unconditional surrender."

It didn't take a scholar of the Civil War to recall the afternoon of February 14, 1862. The Confederates held Fort Donaldson near Dover, Tennessee. Union gunboats on the Cumberland River were unsuccessful in their bombardment of the fort. Grant, trying to gain control of the Mississippi River and bisect the South, issued an ultimatum to the fort, "No terms except unconditional and immediate surrender." Confederate General Simon Buckner accepted and delivered more than 13,000 troops as prisoners. Grant championed the first major Union victory of the war. Grant's first two initials became synonymous with the words, and his nickname became "Unconditional Surrender Grant" during the war.

"Jonah, what's the motivation of this Juan Felipe…whatever his name is?" Grant asked in order to break the silence.

"His motivation, sir?" The question confused Walsh. Taking Texas back for the motherland was motivation enough.

"I've learned in battle that understanding an opponent's motivation could provide an edge for supremacy on the battlefield. Why would a man risk a suicidal attempt against the United States? Other than the obvious, for the sake of the homeland and government, which he unmistakably believes in, what motivates this man?"

"Ah, Mr. President, I may have something on that." Professor Upridge straightened his bow tie again and dug deeper in his briefcase. Pulling out another folder, he pushed his glasses, which had slid down the bridge of his nose, into place and quickly glanced at the folder.

"From what I can ascertain, his motivation is retribution, Mr. President." The professor cleared his throat. "de la Caza witnessed the execution of his mother and father at the hands of several hundred Texans back in 1847. His family owned a large ranchero, several thousand acres, which had been handed down in his family over many years. His family was quite prosperous. After the war with Mexico, Texans enacted their own form of eminent domain, taking the property of hundred of ranches owned by Mexico's upper crust. De la Caza's parents were lynched while the young boy watched. According to the records, he also had a sister. She was about five years old. The Texans took her with them. De la Caza swore revenge. He was only ten at the time. He promised those Texans he would hunt them down and kill them."

The professor sipped from a glass of water and then continued, "Surprisingly, or perhaps not so surprising, about nine years later, several of the men who had raided the de la Caza ranchero began disappearing. Their bodies were found with their heads decapitated. No one knows who killed them. And, no one knows what became of de la Caza's little sister."

A silence hung in the room, as each man dealt with his own reflections of the scene Professor Upridge so vividly described. The fireplace smoldered. The embers popped in the small room.

"What about the currency issue? What have you on that?" Gilmore no longer had the energy or desire to fight his nemesis on the Mexican issue.

"Thousands of dollars in counterfeit currency have come across our borders from Mexico. I have letters of confirmation between the Mexican Embassy in Washington and Mexico City that a plan to devalue our currency is underway. Goods and services paid by contraband currency will force small businesses and, ultimately, entire cities into bankruptcy. Another panic would develop along the border towns in Texas." No one had forgotten the resulting panic from Congress' recent decisions to honor all greenbacks produced during the war with gold redemption. It was a well-made point.

"I'm guessing that de la Caza intends to undermine the wealth of the very people who robbed him of his wealth. The American dollar would be rendered useless, at least in Texas. The Mexican peso would prevail as the stronger currency."

Walsh sat motionless. His forearms rested on his thighs, and he leaned toward the center of the room for everyone's attention. Those around him sat in a similar fashion, listening to every word.

The president broke the silence. "What do you recommend, Jonah?"

"I took the liberty several days ago of notifying the Texas Rangers via the governor of Texas. They'll scout the towns along the border. Of course, they're sworn to secrecy. I have my best Rangers in El Paso, sir, trying to find Jack Wood. Other than that, I'd recommend notifying the army posts. I see little reason to be out hunting Injuns with the Mexs breathing down our necks," Jonah Walsh spoke quietly, finishing his last sentence just above a whisper.

The president nodded approval and looked at Gilmore to acknowledge the command.

Gilmore took his cue. "Mr. President, I'll notify the forts on the Rio and along the southern Texas border as well as in Dallas."

"Isn't Fort Bliss just north of El Paso?" Gifford asked.

Gilmore glanced at the president and then responded. "It was closed to cut costs."

Grant stewed and then added, "Gilmore, contact Fort Davis, too."

"Yes, sir. Excellent. The Twenty-fourth, Twenty-fifth, and Forty-first Infantry Regiments and the Ninth and Tenth Cavalry would want into this fray." Gilmore referred to the black troops the Apache commonly called buffalo soldiers.

"Gilmore, also notify the army posts in New Mexico, specifically the Third Cavalry at Fort Crittenden and Fort Cummings with the Fourth Cavalry. It may be wise to also contact Fort Apache and Fort Bowie in Arizona, too. If de la Caza gets wind of our knowledge, he might change direction on us." Walsh still spoke in a whisper.

"I suggest no telegraph, gentleman," Gifford suggested. "Any eavesdropping may spoil our surprise."

"How long to get word to them via courier, Gilmore?" Grant asked.

"Two days, maybe three." Gilmore answered.

"It may be too late, but okay. Handle this pronto, Gilmore."

"Yes, sir, Mr. President."

"Gentlemen, secrecy is our bond. Tell no one. And Walsh..." The president turned his attention once again to his able confidante. "If you hear anything from Wood, notify us at once."

The men stood and shook hands. Gilmore's hands were soft and damp, as if he had been nervous during the briefings. Walsh smiled to himself.

Chapter 23

"No! Please, nooooo!" The woman's anguished screams filled the cramped shanty. Armed men filled the main room of the small, one-story, ramshackle cabin. The man dragging the woman across the wooden floor slapped her across the face with the back of his hand.

"Shut yo mouth, bitch!" His knuckles skipped across the bridge of her nose. A decisive snap was heard above the crackling fire that engulfed the entire rear wall of the place she and her family had called home for more than three decades.

"Son of a bitch!" The huge black man wrenched and flailed, breaking the grip of the three hooded men holding him.

With two large strides, he was across the small room, clutching the man who had hit his wife. With one powerful motion, he raised the man off the floor and threw him toward the rear of the cabin, near the inferno whose tongue licked the cabin's ceiling. The white robe covering the thrown man caught fire, and he began screaming. Several similarly dressed men raced to stomp out the burning white cloth.

A wooden rifle stock collided with the black man's skull. He turned to face the man who had swung the weapon and then collapsed.

"Grab 'em, boys. Git outta here. This place is going up fast," the white-robed man nearest the door exclaimed.

Three men dragged the unconscious black man from the cabin. The woman fought and screamed as she was also dragged into the dark of night.

"My children! Oh God, where are my children?" She shrieked as she stared back at the cabin nearly engulfed in flames.

Her husband, lying on the ground, the back of his head bloodied and bruised, raised himself up. One of his captors was raising his torch for another pulverizing blow when the black man vaulted forward and tackled him. The black man escaped several of the men's grasps. With disbelief, they watched the man run for the burning cabin, leap the wooden porch, and enter through the flames. His wife sobbed mercifully.

Smoke from the fire amassed overhead. A slight breeze carried the haze high over the forested area, giving the woods a serene feel. The twelve white-hooded men's torches added little to the illuminated area. The glow from the blaze enveloped the cabin and grew in intensity. Flames climbed into the night sky and rippled over the voluminous moon.

The woman and members of the Ku Klux Klan witnessed the ravenous fire devour the decrepit cabin. Suddenly, her husband emerged through the conflagration at the cabin door, carrying their three small children. Homer Gee descended the two steps from the smoking wooden porch and silently faced his antagonists. Kathy Gee opened her arms and accepted three-year-old Olivia from her husband, embracing her tightly. Five-year-old Mattie, covered with soot and coughing, scampered to her mother and hung on to her apron. Seven-year-old Wade stepped bravely toward the tallest of three men standing on either side of his mother and spat on him.

As one of the men swung his arm to strike the boy, the leader of the group shouted above the roaring blaze, "Grab the niggar, and tie 'em up!"

Bound and shackled, Homer was dragged to an open outcropping between the forested landscape. The torches lit the dense surroundings.

"Put him up on that horse," dictated one of the men, pointing to a gray roan.

Several others threw a rope over the limb of a tall oak and tied it off at the base of the tree. Cutting the rope manacles from around his ankles, a white-cloaked man threw Homer's right leg over the saddle.

"Let me do it," one of the men exclaimed as he placed the noose around Homer's neck. As the man tightened the noose, a voice from the shadows was distinctly heard.

"Deacon McQuire!"

"What the hell?" McQuire announced. "No names, damnit."

Deacon McQuire turned his rotund frame in the saddle, looking for the man who had broadcast his name. The Ku Klux Klan was a secret, quasi-military society of ex-Confederate veterans and other white Southerners opposing the Reconstruction government and giving freed blacks their rights. White robes were worn in reverence to the "ghosts of dead Rebel soldiers." Under the strictest of orders, members were to never divulge their real identities. McQuire scanned the hooded figures illuminated by the glowing torches.

"Over here, Deacon," a solitary man advanced from the tree line and into the periphery of dangerous men. A long, gray duster hung down to his spurs, the right flap pulled back to expose an ivory-handled Colt .45. Deacon stared him, attempting to recognize the man who unmistakably knew him.

"What's your business here, mister?" McQuire hadn't the time to contemplate the man's identity.

"I'll ask the same of you and your men, Deacon." The voice was steady for a man facing down twelve, heavily armed men.

"We're having what you'd call a necktie social. We intend to hang this niggar tonight. Tonight and every night this month, we're gonna hang a niggar until this kind of filth leaves town." McQuire's eyes bored holes into the steadfast stranger.

"That man is a friend of mine. Untie him, slowly now." The stranger was resolute.

"You ain't the law in these parts," another white-hooded man bellowed.

"That you, Mack?" The stranger obviously knew these Klan members, at least Deacon McQuire and his eldest son, Mack. The others started feeling anxious.

"Get on with it, McQuire. Hang this son of a bitch so we can get outta here," a faceless voice announced.

The stranger threw open the duster, exposing a badge. "See this badge, boys? United States Deputy Marshal. Take off that noose...Now! I won't ask again!"

"Go ahead, jerk that six-gun, marshal. You can't take us all," Mack McQuire challenged.

"Jack, you in place?" The stranger's voice carried over the heads of the twelve saddled men.

"Yeah!" Jack Wood calmly announced. "Got a bead on the fat one, Kincaid!" The comment left open exactly whom the man behind them had his gun sights fixed on.

"Your call, Mack."

"Christ," Deacon McQuire said to his son. "It's that son of a bitch Ellsworth Kincaid." Deacon and his son remembered Kincaid too well, having fought against him several times during the war. "That damn Union Cavalry Officer, remember?" Deacon asked his son. For a man who hadn't had a drink in years, Deacon McQuire suddenly felt stone-cold sober.

One of the men next to Homer Gee made a slight movement. Kincaid drew his Colt before anyone saw he had moved.

"Let's not be careless," Kincaid said, not taking his eyes off Deacon.

Mack broke the stillness. "I know you, Kincaid. Not afraid of you or any other Yankee either." Mack's ears flattened against his head when he heard a rifle behind him chamber a round.

"Okay, boys. Let's end it. Drop your hardware, or commence fighting." Kincaid drew his second Colt and started walking toward Homer. Both guns were aimed at Deacon McQuire.

"Cut him loose," Kincaid dictated.

McQuire pulled his hood off and nodded at the man to obey.

"You ain't seen the last of me, Kincaid. I swear." Deacon ran a hand over his graying beard. The others slowly and decidedly dropped their guns to the ground. Mack removed his hood, displaying the gashing scar that ran from under his left eye, cut across his left cheekbone, and ended abruptly at the corner of his upper left lip. Mack's left hand instinctively touched the wound that had left him disfigured as he gazed at Kincaid, the cavalry officer whose slashing saber cut across his face during the war. Mack emitted a low groan filled with hatred.

"You can always find me at the Hays House over in Council Grove if you get the urge," Kincaid replied to Deacon as a hooded man cut the rope around Homer's wrists and then loosened the noose.

"Until then, Deacon, I'll expect you and your boys to rebuild that cabin you burnt down tonight. Starting tomorrow morning. Any other hangings or killings around these parts will force me to hunt every last one of you men down, whether you had anything to do with it or not. Understand? Keep things peaceful around here, from here on out. You understand me, McQuire?"

Angrily, McQuire and the others nodded in the affirmative.

* * * *

Anger, when kindled, was not an emotion she easily smothered. Stetson stood on the boardwalk outside the cantina, no longer hearing the dissonance of the saloon's liveliness behind her. She could only hear the blood vibrating in her ears.

"Damn them," she thought. "How could good friends ignore a request for help?"

She knew Kincaid would start early and would want his rest for the task that lay ahead. She had gotten to know him well over the last year.

"He's probably cleaning his pistols and rifle at this very moment," she thought.

Sometimes, he took life too seriously. Yet, he had softened his approach to life in the short time she had ridden with him. He was a good man. Except her father, she didn't know a finer one. He wasn't as refined and consummate as her father, but Kincaid's life on the Western frontier had been so much different than her father's life. Their struggles were the same. Both were lone men in a competitive world, fighting for their inch of turf the best way they knew how. But the perils were different. While her father used skills to exist in the new industrial age, Kincaid used skills most men in the East had never honed. She had never met their equal. Neither man had a formal education as she had been given. Yet, they were the most educated men she knew. Both were good-natured with a sincere compassion for their fellow man. Both were excellent with animals, especially with horses they loved so much. Both were hardworking and always focused. Her mother had often told her how lucky she had been to find such a loving and caring man as her Andrew. Her mother understood, as only a mother could, when she found herself terribly torn and confused between the life she loved with her family and the life she knew she wanted with Kincaid.

Very chauvinistic, like most men, she knew he'd resist her coming along. More than anything, danger brought it out of him. She had proven her worth to him on many occasions, but he wouldn't change. She liked that in him. In fact, she liked everything about him. Stetson smiled. Like her mother, she was a very lucky woman.

Stetson crossed the dim street toward the hotel. Hearing a noise, she turned, but she did not see anyone. She heard another noise. She moved to the boardwalk, near where the noise was coming from. Again, she heard the noise. Thinking she saw a movement down the alley, between the saloon and the general store, she drew her nickel-plated Colt.

"Come out with your hands up!" Her voice was husky, sounding like a man's. She swallowed and did not see a thing. Then she heard another noise.

"Come out or I'll shoot!" Her voice had strength. Cocking the Colt crystallized the command.

"Don't shoot, missy. Please don't shoot!"

Stetson took a step back as the immense black man slowly moved out of the shadows. He appeared seven feet tall, or so it seemed. Shadows can play tricks, especially when one's eyes haven't become accustomed to the dark. Stetson's concentration narrowed. Dressed in faded, blue denim overalls, the man's hair was graying around his temples. His shoes needed to be replaced. She could see his large right toe sticking through the leather. As he stood there staring at her with his hands over his head, he looked like a big, benevolent bear. His eyes were as large as silver dollars.

"Who are you?"

"It's me, Missy Stetson. Homer Gee." A broad smile crossed the black man's countenance. He started to relax.

"Keep those hands up, Homer!"

Homer Gee? She knew the name, not the face. Why did she know that name?

"Okay, Homer. Slowly let your hands down. Keep them where I can see them," she dictated.

Homer lowered his hands, ensuring the woman could see them.

"Have you seen Mister Ellsworth, ma'am?"

It came to her. Homer Gee. Of course. She remembered the story, a favorite of Jack Wood's. Jack told it the first night she had met Ellsworth. Jack, recognizing that Kincaid held her interest, bragged incessantly about his friend and his many exploits in the West. Because Jack had been part of this particular adventure, up against the Ku Klux Klan in the backwoods of Kansas, he told the story quite often.

"Homer, how do you know me?" She asked, ignoring the question concerning Kincaid.

"You's Missy Stetson. Mister Ellsworth's genteel lady friend from back East. Blonde and beautiful. Why, everyone know you, Missy. Everyone back home, that is. We all hear 'bout you."

"Why are you here looking for Mister…Er…Uh…Ellsworth, Homer?" His smile was infectious, and Stetson allowed herself to smile back at the big man.

"Why, I hear Mister Jack got hisself in some kinda trouble. Heard it all the way back in Kansas. I knowed, if Mister Jack was in trouble, Mister Ellsworth would help him. I'm here to help Mister Ellsworth, that is, if he needs my help and all."

Stetson eyes began to tear. Not one friend of theirs in this godforsaken town would help them. Yet, all the way from Kansas, this giant, adorable man was willing to help Ellsworth and Jack.

"Homer, Ellsworth and I—and I know Jack as well—appreciate your help. But there's a lot of danger ahead for us. You'd likely get hurt. Ellsworth couldn't forgive himself if you did."

"Ma'am, I can take care of myself, thank you. If there's a fight coming, I'm ready to help."

"Homer, you're not even armed. Please, it would be best if you waited. You can stay at the hotel."

Homer reached into his overalls and pulled out a revolver.

"I'm armed, Missy Stetson." His warm smile beseeched Stetson to allow him to join them in their attempt to find Jack. "Besides, I can't stay in no hotel. They won't allow me in a nice place like that."

"Let me see that thing," Stetson reached for the weapon. Momentarily hesitating, Homer relented and allowed her to take the gun.

Stetson turned the rusty 1858 Remington over in her hand. An old cap-and-ball revolver widely used during the Civil War, the .44 caliber Remington was a reliable, powerful weapon. The solid frame was considered to be superior to the old Colt. The topstrap, pitted and rusty on the gun she held, enhanced its accuracy. She twirled it with her index finger. It was a well-balanced pistol. Turning the cylinder proved difficult. Oxidation was apparent on the octagon barrel and cylinder.

"Homer, this gun isn't safe." She handed it back to him.

"Well, ma'am. No offense, but I done shot it plenty. And it's fine." The pistol disappeared into the large pocket of the overalls.

"Homer, I'll talk to Ellsworth. Tomorrow morning, we'll be leaving early. You meet us here, right where you're standing. We'll all decide how you can best help us. Okay?"

"Yes, ma'am. I'll be here waiting in the morning."

Stetson made her way down the dimly lit boardwalk. She went across the street to the hotel. At the desk, she requested her room key. Separate rooms was a necessity, if for any other reason than her virtue. She smiled.

"Virtuous until I met Kincaid," she thought.

Behind the hotel desk, a young man in his early twenties smiled as he handed her the key. With a quick thanks, she turned and took the stairs to the second story. Glancing at the pocket watch her father had given her; she saw it was past midnight. She knew Kincaid would head out before sunrise. Removing her revolver and pulling off her boots and chaps, she stripped. The coolness of the room touched her naked body. She quickly blew out the light and slipped into bed, mentally calculating the time to meet Kincaid.

* * * *

The batwing saloon doors to Rosita's Cantina burst open.

"Ellsworth?" Stetson scanned the interior of the barroom, not expecting to see anyone this early in the morning. She wasn't disappointed. She turned to exit.

"Morning, Stetson!"

Stetson turned. The faint light made it difficult to see. Again, she surveyed the interior of the tavern. Across the room, sitting on the staircase, was Billy Irons. A smoldering cigarette was between his fingers. His boots were off and placed on the steps beside him. His white-socked feet wiggled as he exercised his toes. A nonchalant smirk sat crookedly on his gray, stubbled face. He looked exhausted. Remembering him ascending the stairs the night before with two vivacious ladies, she wasn't surprised to see him tired.

"Buy you a drink?"

Stetson moved quickly around the many tables toward Billy.

"No, I'm in a hurry. Have you seen Ellsworth this morning?" There wasn't any reason to ask him for help. She understood Bison very clearly from the previous evening. For whatever reason, they were not about to help.

"Can't say I have. Awfully early for most folks to be up." Sitting with his head resting in his hands, Irons had a terrible headache and stomachache.

"If you see him, tell him I'm looking for him."

Irons nodded his acknowledgment, scratched his graying stubble and leaned back. He admired Stetson's silhouette as she hastily headed for the exit.

"She's as handsome as a full house," he thought, smiling.

Then he felt sick again. His half-opened eyes began imagining the saloon spinning around. He groaned.

"Oh, Billy!" The female voice rolled down the staircase like warmed molasses. Irons looked at the ceiling, shook his head, and wondered where he found the energy. With a sigh, he took one last look at Stetson as she exited the saloon, picked up his boots, and headed back up the stairs.

Stetson stood on the boardwalk outside the saloon. She heard a rooster crow.

"Damn him," she thought. "He left without me."

When did he leave? Could she catch him? Sometimes, he exasperated her to no end. She hadn't counted on him leaving without her. He had never done this to her before. She expected an argument, even some shouting. In the end, as always, he would acquiesce to her wishes. She was wasting time. She hurried to the stables to saddle her appaloosa.

Homer Gee stood ahead, waiting patiently as promised.

"Missy Stetson!" he hollered as she approached.

"Homer, have you seen Ellsworth?"

"No, ma'am."

"How long have you been waiting?"

"About two hours."

A two-hour head start, maybe more. She couldn't catch him. That black stallion was too fast. A day-and-a-half ride to Condeza Barajas could be whittled to a half-day on that horse. But he would be vigilant as he got closer to Jack's captors. His cautious nature might be her only salvation. She knew she wouldn't be able to find him. By the time she got close to his proximity, he'd already be shadowing the enemy. Her only hope was for him to find her.

"Homer, do you have a horse?"

"No, ma'am. I ain't." Homer looked pensively at the ground in front of him. He had hitched a ride from Kansas to Texas. He felt the chance of helping his friends evaporate with the question.

"Homer, Ellsworth could still be in town. I've haven't the time to search for him. I need your help."

The customary smile crossed Homer's face.

"Yes, ma'am. You name it."

"Find Ellsworth. Tell him I'm headed for Condeza Barajas and to hurry. Will you do that for me?"

"Yes, ma'am. I'll find him. Is Mister Jack in that place?"

"Yes, I'm afraid he is, Homer."

"If I find Mister Ellsworth, can I come, too?"

"It's up to Ellsworth. I'm sure we'll need all the help we can get. Now hurry, Homer!" She turned and ran to the stable.

Tightening the cinch on Sweetwater, she stroked the horse's neck several times.

"It'll be a hard ride, girl," she whispered to her beloved horse. Grabbing the pommel, she threw her right leg over the saddle. With slight leg pressure, she maneuvered the horse out of the barn. The sun was a speck on the distant horizon.

"Come on, girl. We're burning daylight!"

Putting the horse into a quick gallop, she headed due south.

CHAPTER 24

Dear Elly,

I apologize for not having written sooner, but there hasn't been much to write about. However, I do hope you receive this letter. I have good news. Remember Old Curly? General Custer is having a reunion of sorts. The Army of Tennessee is hosting a grand reunion party in Toledo come October. Grant, Sheridan, Sherman, and some highfalutin gents from Europe will be there. More importantly, old sport, some of the most beautiful women this side of the big muddy will be in attendance. From all over, these young, school-educated girls will be coming to this shindig. They call them debutantes. Don't know if you kept your uniform all these years, but wear it if you did. I will be on my way from Washington, DC, and a return letter will not reach me. I do hope to see you next month.

Your friend,

Jack

Kincaid reread the letter and smiled. It had been a few years since he had heard from his best friend. He was surprised to learn Jack was in Washington. He was the type of man who would easily grow restless in a big city, becoming claustrophobic with the tall, brick buildings and paved roads. Kincaid sat in the saddle while he studied the letter. He had received several letters over the months from folks he had never met. It was easy to find him vis-à-vis written correspondence by simply addressing a letter to the New York firm of Beadle and Adams at 98 William Street, a publisher of several dime novels about his exploits. Some were true, but most were exaggerations.

Kincaid laughed aloud while thinking about joining Jack. It was just like Jack to pull out the old, wool Union cavalry uniform to impress a woman. He remembered Jack as fairly successful with the women. Watching Jack chase a woman was worth a trip to Ohio. Kincaid folded the letter and placed it in his vest pocket. It was time to move on. He was tiring of the work as a ranch foreman on the Kansas frontier. He longed to return to Texas, and a detour to Ohio was in order. He promised himself he'd definitely surprise Jack at the party in Toledo.

* * * *

Kincaid felt out of place in the large ballroom of the Boody House. He had never seen so many high-ranking military officers cloistered in one place, except at Lee's surrender at Appomattox. Kincaid noted many of the men in the room wearing red neckties, symbolizing a bond between those who rode with Custer as a Wolverine in the Seventh Michigan Cavalry.

He tugged at the sleeves of the black waistcoat while scanning the banquet room, searching for Jack. Hungry, he moved in the direction of food, hoping to find someone he knew. He was uncomfortable with walking up to a stranger and starting a conversation.

"Elly! Elly!" Among the horde of people moving toward the buffet tables was Jack, the only person who ever called him Elly. Before he could turn around, he felt a strong slap on his back. Turning, Ellsworth looked into his best friend's broad smile.

"Jack!" The men embraced as if they were two forlorn lovers who had discovered one another. Each gripped the other until it became a contest. Although grown men, when together, the two promptly reverted to their adolescent ways. Their bear hug tightened until both started laughing.

"You look like hell, Ellsworth!"

"Me? Look at you!" Kincaid jabbed at Jack's flat stomach. Both men were at their physical best, and Jack looked gallant in his military uniform.

"Elly, look around. This reunion is one of the best in years."

Kincaid followed his friend's gesture around the room. The ballroom, filled with Civil War veterans, was massive. Many brought their wives or sweethearts. Most of the men, especially those dressed in their military best, came single. Tonight, many men would do their best to innocently flirt and dance with as many beautiful ladies as possible.

"Over in the reception line. Do you see him?"

Jack pointed to the entry where several men had improvised a reception line and were graciously shaking hands with those entering the ballroom to join the party. President Grant, General William T. Sherman, General Phil Sheridan, and

General George A. Custer each took his turn in bestowing a kiss on each lady in the line. The men were having a grand time laughing and hugging an attractive young woman as the women gladly returned the favor. In the far corner, a gentleman sat, sketching the events for the November issue of *Frank Leslie's Illustrated Newspaper*.

"I see him. Old Iron Pants himself," Kincaid said, using the nickname that paid tribute to Custer's stamina in the saddle.

"By the way, where are all the beautiful women, Jack?"

"You must be blind. They're everywhere. Choose one, and I'll introduce you."

The women were beautiful, and their gowns flowed with ribbons and velvet. Their hands were gloved to the elbow in satin. Their exposed shoulders, arms, and necks were as pure as the Montana skies. Disappointed, he didn't see one woman who piqued his interest.

"Ellsworth. Tonight is not the night to be shy. Just choose one."

Jack saw his friend wasn't paying attention to him. Kincaid was riveted. He was staring at several girls toward the rear of the room who were waiting to dance. Kincaid hesitated. He hadn't danced since he was a young officer over nine years ago and could only dance the Texas two-step and Tennessee waltz.

Jack nudged his friend. "Go over there, and ask one of them to dance."

Ellsworth nervously shook his head.

"Want me to ask for you?" Jack asked.

"Don't be annoying."

Ellsworth stared at one particular young debutante. She stood five-foot-five-inches. Slight of build, her blonde hair was piled high on her head, and curls cascaded gently onto her shoulders. Her gown was white, but, unlike the other women, she showed little cleavage. Her appearance was modest, even though her dress looked expensive. She held herself differently than the others. She had self-assurance without appearing self-indulgent, like many of the women. She moved gracefully with an infectious smile. Kincaid settled on stunning to describe her.

"Okay, Elly. You're on your own. I just spotted the true love of my life. It's time to dance." Jack walked away to meet another of the many women he would fancy that evening.

Ellsworth stopped staring at the petite debutante, got into the buffet line, filled his plate with food, and found an empty chair in which to sit and eat.

"Hello."

Ellsworth looked up from his plate and gazed into the emerald eyes belonging to the woman he had been entranced with earlier.

"Hello." Kincaid stood and offered his hand. She shook it with a firm grip.

"My name is Stetson. I saw you sitting by yourself and thought I'd introduce myself, if that's all right?"

Shyly, Kincaid responded, "Yes, ma'am. It's all right."

"Ma'am? Sir, I'm offended. I assumed there wasn't a large difference in our ages, unless I appear older than you."

"No, ma'am…er…uh…no." Kincaid was mesmerized. Her voice was soft, and her smile indicated she was toying with him.

"My name is Stetson. What's yours?" she said softly.

"Kincaid. Ellsworth T. Kincaid." He swallowed hard. Of all the men in the ballroom, she had chosen him to talk to. He couldn't believe his luck.

"Elly!" Kincaid's good fortune changed. His womanizing friend had returned.

"Jack, this is Stetson. Stetson, Jack." Stetson smiled while shaking Jack's hand. Jack winked at Ellsworth.

"An absolute pleasure, Stetson." Jack took her gloved hand, bowed, and kissed it.

"May I get you a drink?" Jack noticed her hands were empty. Kincaid blushed. He felt the fool, which he usually did when he was around Jack and women.

"Why yes, Jack. Thank you."

"I'll get it. Anything particular?" Ellsworth asked.

"Oh, something cool. Some punch would be just fine, thank you."

Having returned with drinks for all three, they stood talking about the party. Kincaid had difficulty making small talk, especially with such a beautiful woman. Jack did most of the talking, which was about himself and his heroics during the war. Stetson feigned interest in Jack's boasting while observing Ellsworth. He was shy and hardly spoke about himself.

"He hardly speaks," she thought. "He seems genuinely interested in Jack retelling his tales."

"Look Elly, Stetson, here he comes." Jack motioned toward the general with the flowing blonde curls.

General George Armstrong Custer sauntered up to the three.

"Evening, gentlemen, ma'am." Custer leaned over and placed a kiss on Stetson's cheek. Ellsworth felt jealous with the gesture. Custer wore the insignia of a lieutenant colonel, but he was often addressed as "General" for his Civil War brevet major general rank.

"General Custer, you are such a flirt for a married man." Stetson poured on the charm while allowing a small amount of facetiousness to show in her voice.

"Lady Stetson, I will declare to everyone this evening that you are the prettiest girl at the ball. Isn't she, gentlemen?" Custer held her hand while ignoring the other two.

"Lady Stetson? You're a lady?" Ellsworth was perplexed.

"Of course she's a lady, lad," Custer laughed, slapping Kincaid on the back.

"It's a long story, Ellsworth." Stetson smiled at Ellsworth's ingenuous question.

"General, these gentlemen have been entertaining me with stories about the war and about you in particular."

Custer glanced again at the two men. "I know you two, don't I?"

"Sir, Lieutenants Wood and Kincaid, at your service, sir!" Jack snapped to attention and saluted the general.

Ellsworth jutted out his hand and added, "How's Tom doing?"

"Of course, my God. Jack and Ellsworth!" Custer turned toward Stetson. "These two saved my brother's sorry butt during the war and, I might add, on more than one occasion." Custer shook hands with Kincaid and Jack.

"How are you two?"

Stetson was immediately impressed, thinking all the boasting about Custer hadn't been true.

"And you, sir, have been an inspiration to me," Custer directed the comment to Kincaid.

"How's that?" Kincaid still thought about Stetson, not Custer.

"All those stories I read about you in the dime novels."

"Stories? What stories, Ellsworth?" Stetson was surprised at this revelation.

"It's a long story, Stetson," Kincaid mimicked her earlier reply to his question regarding she being a lady. She smiled, hoping a repartee was developing between them.

"No, I'm quite serious. Once those dime novelists get hold of you, one cannot tell fact from fiction." Custer's charisma was unparalleled. "I intend to write my own autobiography. It's nearly finished. I'm calling it *My Life on the Plains*."

"Don't let Frank Tousey or John Morrison publish it. That would guarantee pure sensationalism," Stetson added, wanting to join the conversation while also wanting everyone to know she was well-read and knew something about dime novels, even though she had never read anything about the dashing Ellsworth.

"Not to worry, my dear. My beautiful wife, Libbie, has already chosen Sheldon and Company in New York as the publisher. They claim it'll be a best seller," Custer broadly smiled, proud of his announcement.

Changing the subject from him to Kincaid, Custer remarked, "Just hope it's as interesting as that story about you and the Indian attack at Broken Springs. I love that story!"

"Tell me the story, Ellsworth," Stetson pleaded. "Please."

"It was nothing. Like all those cheap dime novels, it's a little fact mixed with a whole bunch of fiction." Kincaid didn't like the attention.

"Nothing? My friend saves twenty lives of the best buffalo hunters who ever lived, and he says it was nothing." As always, Jack was ready to tell the tale.

"How'd he do it, Jack?" Custer loved good stories, especially about Indian fighting.

"It was early in the morning. The sun was just coming up over the horizon," Jack's voice lowered, forcing Stetson and Custer to lean in closer to hear over the band playing in the background.

"It was chilly on the plains in western Texas. You could see your breath and hear the frost crackle with each step. Kincaid had risen earlier than the rest of the men, as usual. He was out scouting for buffalo. As the others slept in the small cabin, a loud, Comanche war cry broke the stillness." Jack paused and looked into Custer's and Stetson's faces to ensure he held their interest. Both nodded to continue.

"Shots rang out. Several of the boys ran from the cabin to see what the noise was and were wounded by the Injuns encircling the cabin. Several others ran to drag them back and were cut down by the murderous redskins. The sky filled with gun smoke that overcast morning as we held off the red devils."

Jack reached around and slapped Ellsworth on the back, "And then our boy here, coming back from hunting buffalo, sees what's happening and charges these Injuns. Must have been a hundred of 'em. He attacks them with complete surprise! They get one look at Kincaid, galloping at them with guns blazing, and they hightail it outta there as fast as they could ride. I know because I was there."

Custer and Stetson applauded at the story's conclusion.

"Bravo, lad," Custer announced.

"How'd you do it, Ellsworth?" Stetson felt herself liking this shy cowboy.

Winking at Jack, Kincaid looked at Custer and then Stetson. He smiled and whispered, "Them Injuns knew I had them surrounded."

Custer and Jack laughed uproariously. Stetson didn't understand. Was the story a joke, or did it happen? Before she could ask, the band began playing *Garry Owen*, the general's favorite.

"Good seeing you boys. Stetson, my pleasure, as always. Tell your dear father and mother hello for me." The general took her gloved hand and kissed it.

"Please give Mrs. Custer my regards, general." Stetson had met her briefly and liked her immediately. George and Libbie Custer were one of the era's great romances.

Turning his attention to Jack and Ellsworth, Custer remarked, "I could use you two with me on the plains. I'm heading to Fort Abraham Lincoln next week. Join the Seventh Cavalry and me. You'll fight more Indians with me than you ever did at Broken Springs."

"Thanks, general. I'll let you know." Jack had another agenda that only he and the United States government knew about.

"I'll pass, too. But you be careful out there, general," Ellsworth warned. "Those Indians fight a lot different now than they did five years ago. They're learning our tactics. They're well-armed, and they don't run off like they used to." Kincaid assumed Custer was as brash and foolhardy as he was during the war. It could only get him in trouble.

"You two think about it. We'll have a grand time with lots of hunting and fishing. Don't worry about me, Kincaid. There's not an Indian who can beat the Seventh." Custer bid farewell to the three and returned to join the other generals watch the band play the final chords to *Garry Owen*.

* * * *

"Pssst! Jack?"

The faint voice woke Jack from a dead sleep, interrupting his dream. He stared at the dark walls surrounding him. He hadn't been sleeping well. De la Caza guaranteed it. He found himself occasionally dozing and hallucinating about old times. They were occurring more frequently. With what little water and rations his captors gave him, he knew he was delirious at times.

"Pssssst!" The sound came through the small, barred window above. He was certain he was hearing voices. It would just be a matter of time before he lost his mind. Perhaps that was what de la Caza wanted. It had been several days since the self-appointed Mexican messiah had come to interrogate him. Jack pulled the moth-eaten wool blanket over his shoulders, drew his knees up into the fetal position, and closed his eyes.

"Jack, you in there?"

Jack lay motionless on the flat mattress. He pushed his long, blonde hair from his eyes and listened intently. Had he lost his mind? Was someone calling his name?

"Pssssst!"

Jack sat upright. He had to be imagining it. Perhaps it was another of de la Caza's tricks, one among many intended to make him paranoid. It was more harassment to break him and make him talk.

"Pssssst!"

It was becoming annoying. Jack stood on the mattress, grabbed the bars of the overhead window, and pulled himself up. He stared out the window. He couldn't believe the face looking back at him.

Jack slid down to the mattress and sat. Putting his elbows on his knees and his head in his hands, he prayed that it was just another dream.

CHAPTER 25

"Mother? Father?" Stetson called as she descended the winding oak staircase of the family mansion. She stopped in the entry hall near the front doors. She had news for them. They wouldn't take the news lightly, and it would surely break their hearts. Yet, she was determined to follow her heart. After all, she was twenty-three, a college graduate, and, unlike her three sisters, unmarried. Of course, the single men in Pittsburgh would have done anything to have her as a wife. However, they wanted her family's wealth and political power. They were nothing like the man she had met in Toledo. They were not as intelligent, courteous, or courageous. They did not have his strength of character and action. Any man in town was not as ruggedly handsome. Best of all, he didn't know her and didn't know of her family's affluence. He was genuinely interested in her and only her. For the first time, she actually trusted that a man's interest was solely centered on her and did not have any hidden agendas. She was delighted!

After the reunion in Toledo, she was to return home the next morning. But he asked her to stay another day. Arriving at the hotel where she and her friend Jenny were staying, he took her to breakfast. They then went to an equestrian center. While dancing the previous evening, he had asked if she could ride. Her answer was an unequivocal yes.

The morning ride along the Maumee River convinced her that she was more than intrigued by this man. He was relaxed and readily spoke about himself and his travels. He was so unlike the reserved, quiet man he had been during the ball. Riding well on the rented gelding, she managed to outdistance him by a hair-breadth on the thoroughfare leading to the river. He found her competitive. She was the best woman rider he had known. Like no woman before, he was quickly succumbing to her intelligence, beauty, sense of humor, and spirit. When he suggested he follow her home to Pittsburgh, she was flabbergasted, but pleased. She graciously accepted him as a suitor.

Within thirty-six hours, he was calling upon her at home. Her sisters had waited all day to meet the man who had stolen their little sister's heart. After a formal dinner, Kincaid joined the women in the kitchen while the men smoked cigars and sipped cognac in the home's exquisite, oak-paneled great room. The men wanted to talk to Kincaid about the West, the continued Indian uprisings, the violence of the outlaw gangs, the greed of the cattle barons, and everything else they had read about in the newspapers. They laughingly pitied Kincaid when the women engulfed him.

With an apron tied around his waist, Kincaid washed the dishes at the kitchen sink while the women talked incessantly, questioning him about the women in the West. They cheerily laughed at his jokes and gasped at his responses regarding Indian outrages that pervaded the local newspapers. His nonchalant responses to the violence surprised them. To Stetson, sitting at the kitchen table watching her sisters agreeing with him, teasing him, and becoming enthralled with the cowboy she had brought home, he was her chivalrous, gallant knight.

Stetson entered the comfortable, unadorned, stonewalled library with the low, Renaissance-style plaster ceiling and stone mantelpiece. It was located in the front of the manor, off the main foyer. The afternoon sun streamed through the three, tall, stained glass windows to her left, lighting the room. A colossal volume of books surrounded the large fireplace, which was opposite the library's entry. Her father's passion, besides his businesses, was reading. His interest ran from the Napoleonic wars, the mummification of the kings and queens of Egypt, and winning at poker. His bourgeois education had always bothered him, even though he was one of only a handful of successful and wealthy businessmen in town. The room smelled of him, the sweet cologne he wore and the occasional cigar he smoked when her mother wasn't looking. Her eyes began filling with small tears, and she turned to exit the empty room.

Hurrying down the Oriental-carpeted hallway toward the rear of the house, she spied into each room as she made her way toward the kitchen. Pushing open the kitchen door, she heard her mother's voice.

"Mother!" Her mother was standing at the chopping block in the center of the white cabinet-filled room, talking animatedly to the maid, Mary, who sat at the linen-covered table. She was listening intently and admiring Mrs. Holovanisin's potato peeling talents while enjoying their reverse roles.

"Stetson, sit by Mary. I was telling her how your father and I first met," Mrs. Holovanisin waved her arm to an empty chair at the table. Stetson glanced at Mary and smiled. Returning the smile, Mary silently mouthed, "Again."

"Mother, where's Father?"

"He should be back any moment. He's in the stables. You know how he loves those horses of his." She studied her daughter and became a little apprehensive.

"Honey, are you all right? Your eyes are all puffy."

Stetson walked briskly to the rear door, passing Mary as she did and softly touching her on the shoulder. She would miss Mary. Mary, a runaway Negro, had been part of the family since the war. Her father helped her escape via the Underground Railroad. It was rumored that her father had helped many slaves escape. He hid them in the basement, fed and clothed them and their families, and ultimately saved them from death and the horrors of slavery. Mary loved the Holovanisin family and stayed with them under her own volition. She helped raise Stetson since she was a teenager, and they had become fast friends and confidants.

"Father! Come to the house!" Stetson yelled toward the stables. She closed the door and faced Mary and her mother. Her heart was pounding. She was already homesick, and she hadn't left home yet. She had to get this done quickly.

"Mother, when Father comes in, might I see both of you in the parlor?"

"Of course, child. Is everything all right?" Her mother was worried, which had always been her nature. At considerable risk to her own health, she had borne Stetson late in life. There was a twelve-year difference between Stetson and her oldest sister, Margie. Stetson remembered asking her mother when she was about ten years old if she had been a mistake.

She would never forget her mother's response. "Why, of course not, Stetson. You were a cherished gift from heaven." She always felt she was her mother's favorite. Later, when she could discuss these feelings with her three sisters and brother, she found that each felt the same way. Each believed they were the favorite child.

"I'm fine, really. I'll be waiting in the parlor." Stetson smiled nervously at Mary and her mother. She then hastily left the kitchen. Tears formed in the corners of her eyes.

"How's my little girl?" Andrew Holovanisin entered the parlor and gave his daughter a big hug. Not a large man, he seemed larger than his five-foot-eight-inches with his robust voice, regal demeanor, gregarious nature, and broad smile.

"Father, please sit on the sofa." Stetson motioned toward the sofa. Accustomed to indulging his children, he sat as instructed.

"Mother, please come and sit by Father," Stetson said nervously as her mother entered the parlor. Margaret Holovanisin removed her linen tea apron and sat next to her husband, placing a light hand on his thigh and glancing lovingly at him.

Stetson saw their love. She noticed how close they sat as her mother's hand touched her father. She hoped she'd discovered the same love these two extraordinary people had found.

"Well, Stetson, you have our attention. What's on your mind?" Her father could quickly get to the point, one of the few work habits he brought home.

"Remember the young man I met a few weeks ago? Ellsworth is his name, remember?" She fumbled for the right words.

"Yes, I remember that rambunctious cowboy. Heard he left town. Good riddance, I say." Andrew did not think any man was good enough for his daughter, especially one who made his way in the savage lands west of the Mississippi River. Margaret nudged him, offering an impatient look. He nodded for Stetson to continue.

"He's on his way back to Texas or Indian Territory or wherever. I'm not sure exactly where he's going." She could no longer hold back her enthusiasm.

"By now, you must know that I love him. I intend to join him. I have to. My heart tells me it's the right thing to do. I hope you understand," she said hurriedly.

"Did he ask you to go with him?" Her father became cold, as if he was negotiating a business deal. But he knew he was negotiating for much more. He was bargaining for his daughter's future.

"No, Father. He didn't ask me. But I believe he loves me and wants me with him. I love him, and I can't bear the thought of not being with him." She held back the tears she knew her father would recognize as a weakness.

"This is preposterous! I'll not hear of it!" Standing, his presence gave him the appearance of being larger than life. "You'll not do this, not to us or yourself. You're throwing away everything—your education, your station in life, the finer things I never had. I forbid it!"

"Father, please understand," Stetson pleaded.

"Why would a beautiful, young lady with a promising future in my company, or any company for that matter, risk her life to travel to the other side of this dangerous country with a man no one knows? Stetson, look at you. You could have any man you want."

Margaret cleared her throat, allowing Andrew to catch his breath. "Father, I believe I understand what Stetson is telling us. It's simple. Listen to her. She's in love."

"I can't believe what I'm hearing from you, Mother! You want her to leave us and live with savages?"

"I'd give anything if Stetson would stay with us forever. Haven't you noticed?" Margaret gestured toward her daughter. "She's a grown woman, a woman in love."

"Margaret, I will not have this."

"Papa, Mother is right. I'm in love." Stetson knew from experience that calling him Papa, an expression from the old country, would soften him.

Andrew smiled and said softly, "Calling me Papa will not work today, young lady. I'm sorry, but this conversation is over."

Andrew Holovanisin slid past his daughter and grimly left the room.

"Mother, I'm leaving. I must find Ellsworth before it's too late. Please say good-bye to Father for me."

"I love you, honey." Her mother stood and gave Stetson a tight embrace.

"You remind me of me at your age. I was in love with your father, and no one could convince me otherwise. He was poor, and my family thought he would never amount to anything. I didn't care. I was in love. Love can get you through the rough times as well as the good times. Follow your heart, honey. Your father and I will always love you."

"I know, Mother. I love you both so much."

Stetson saw the tears in her mother's eyes and felt her own tears swell up again. Her mother reached over and dabbed Stetson's upper lip with a handkerchief. Both laughed and embraced. Stetson turned to walk away. Their grasp fell apart. Stetson left the room and headed for the staircase. She could hear her mother softly cry as she bounded up the stairs to her room to pack.

* * * *

The chill in the air made her shiver. She shook her head once and then again. Stetson was momentarily bewildered. The quarter moon barely gave off enough light for her to gain her bearings. She had been daydreaming and had fallen asleep in the saddle. She was exhausted. Leaving El Paso at dawn, she had ridden her appaloosa hard the entire day. Kincaid was impossible to follow, as she knew he would be. She was grateful she had paid attention to Father O'Brien when he had reviewed the map with Kincaid. Forced to stop several times and allow

Sweetwater to water and rest, she knew she would never catch Kincaid and his relentless black stallion. Her only hope was that he would detect her.

The terrain had been bleak and barren throughout the day. It was just rolling hills dotted with sagebrush and buffalo grass that was turning green with the recent rain. She was now in a passage assembled of massive boulders that, based on the stars, headed due south. She was not far from the mission occupied by the Mexicans. She had not seen or sensed any sentries. Moving cautiously, Stetson and Sweetwater headed in the direction she assumed Kincaid would have taken to the old mission.

After another half hour had passed, she dismounted, walked to a granite wall of boulders, climbed up a small grade of rocks, and peered between two colossal slabs of stone. In the distance was Condeza Barajas, surrounded by a few decaying buildings.

"If Jack is in there, I will find him," she told herself.

The entire grounds surrounding the mission had been cleared of any possible hiding place, no matter how small. A lizard could not get close to the fortress without being detected. Leaving Sweetwater at the granite passageway, she moved quickly, walking directly toward the mission. It was dark. If she was careful, maybe no one would notice her approaching, at least she hoped.

At the entry to the mission, she stopped. She breathed deeply and tried listening over her own panting. It was pitch-black where she stood. The moon barely crested the towering peaks surrounding the area. To her left, she heard horses. She had to move. Which direction? Not knowing where the men quartered, she hesitated, understanding a wrong move may be her last. The old mission stood dead center of the complex. She recalled Kincaid telling her that, when approaching an unknown enemy, a bold decision was sometimes the best decision. She made her choice. Instead of going left or right, she headed straight toward the mission.

Her hand touched the adobe wall of the church. She hadn't seen a sentry. Perhaps the place had been impenetrable for so long that the men within no longer bothered, knowing any approaching enemy faced certain death. It was probably true, and she was foolish for having treaded into their domain. She wondered if she should turn around and head back toward the passageway.

"I've gone this far," she thought. "I'll stay long enough to find Jack. Then I'll find Ellsworth."

It would make it easier for them to rescue Jack if they knew where he was being held.

She slowly circled the mission's perimeter. The area was deathly quiet. She could see her breath in the crisp, cool air. She turned the first corner, scanned the building's walls, and brushed by several barrels smelling of gunpowder. Reaching another corner of the mission, she tentatively peeked around. With another deep breath, she slithered around the corner, watching her footing as she moved. Glancing over the building, she noticed two high, barred windows overhead. What better place to incarcerate a prisoner than an old mission?

With the windows out of reach, she looked around for something that would elevate her. Remembering the barrels, she retraced her steps, moved to the side of the mission, and located the three barrels. Finding each too heavy, she used all her strength and pushed the lighter of the three over. It landed with a heavy thud. She froze while waiting for Mexican bandits to discover her. Not a sound emanated from the surrounding buildings. Putting her shoulder against the overturned barrel, she slowly rolled it around the corner. She paused under the window. Not having the strength to place the barrel upright, she rolled it against the wall, got down on her hands and knees to locate several rocks, and placed a few small rocks against the barrel to ensure it wouldn't roll away from the wall. She then delicately climbed the barrel. Steadying herself against the mission wall, she reached up and grabbed the bar. It was firmly placed in mortar. She pulled herself up and peered inside.

"Pssst! Jack?" Through the darkness, she thought she saw movement.

"God, what if I've awakened a guard?" she thought.

"Psssst!" She was growing impatient. "Jack, are you in there?" If she raised her voice any louder, others would hear her. She listened and waited.

"Psssst!"

She had nearly lost her grip when Jack was suddenly staring back at her. Then he slid out of sight.

Jack sat on the mattress. Putting his elbows on his knees and his head in his hands, he prayed this was just another of his dreams.

"Jack, are you okay?"

He shook the thought off. Somehow, she had managed to get to this mountainous sanctuary and find him. Standing, he pulled himself to the window to stare back at his rescuer.

"Get the hell outta here! Now!"

"Okay, but you're coming with me!" She had forgotten her promise to herself to locate Jack and then race back to find Kincaid.

As she spoke, Jack disappeared again. He sat back on the threadbare mattress. Knowing de la Caza, he understood how she had managed to get to him.

"Jack? We're getting out of here!" Where had he gone? She pulled herself up as much as her drained muscles would allow.

The coolness of metal touching her neck sent a shiver down her spine. Four distinctive clicks distinguished the cocking of a Colt revolver.

"*Buena tarde, señorita.*" Juan Rodriquez Felipe de la Caza was immensely pleased with himself.

She wondered if the man who addressed her would pull the trigger.

CHAPTER 26

"Andy, are you awake?" Wide-awake, Margaret lay in bed. It was half past midnight. Worrying about Stetson, she couldn't sleep.

After years of living in luxury, she was no longer aware of the satin sheets and ruffled feather bed she slept in. She was not mindful of the ten-foot-high mahogany headboard richly adorned in ornate carvings of flowers and angels or the prominent Victorian artwork decorating the walls and eighteenth-century English country furniture covering the Bijar Persian rug. The master bedroom, located upstairs at the rear of the home, overlooked the rose garden and horse stables. The picturesque foothills of the Allegheny Mountains were in the background. The estate consisted of 620 acres of manicured lawns, including the riding arena and play area built years ago for the children. Inevitably, the children grew up, married, and moved away. All except Stetson, they had a spouse and children of their own. Now she too had matured into a young woman and would be leaving them. Hopefully, it would not be under these circumstances, not with Stetson and her father angry with one another.

"Andy?" She spoke softly with urgency in her voice that belied its subtlety. She reached out and touched the sleeve of his flannel pajamas.

"I'm awake." Andrew reflected on the day's events as he stared at the ceiling.

"We're losing Stetson." She was on the verge of tears, and he could sense it.

"I know."

"She loves you very much."

"And I her."

"I'm so happy for her."

"Happy?" Andrew rolled on his side and stared in the dimness at his wife. "Why are you so happy for her?"

"She's in love, Andy. For the very first time in her life, she is actually head over heels in love."

"Maybe she's just infatuated with a man from another way of life that is different from her own. Have you thought of that?"

"Yes, I've given this considerable thought, Andy. Have you looked in her eyes? Have you seen how they sparkle? Oh, it's definitely love. I'd recognize that look."

"How have you become such an authority on love?"

"I saw it first in Margie's eyes when she fell in love with Hank. I saw it again when Mary Ann met Bob and when Monica met Ron. Three daughters falling in love in this household gives me plenty of experience. Why, it's the same look my family accused me of having when I met you." Margaret turned on her left side to face her beloved husband and smiled.

"Andy, I believe Stetson intends to run away from home tonight."

Andrew rolled over on his back and refocused on the ceiling.

"I have the same feeling. Why couldn't she have met a nice, young successful man in town and settled down? Why this man? Why a cowboy?"

"Why a tall, handsome cowboy hero who has novels written about him? We shouldn't be surprised. We brought her up as a tomboy. She could do anything better than most boys at school. She may be a lady in every way, including title, but she can manage very well in this masculine world."

Even though no one in the family took the title seriously, the youngest child of Andrew Holovanisin had acquired the title of "Lady" when she had turned eighteen years of age. The title of honor came from her father's country of Slovakia when a distant uncle, a recluse no one remembered, died and bequeathed a sizable tract of property to the youngest child of Andrew, his favorite nephew. The uncle's estate, worth a small fortune in the old country, identified the youngest child of Andrew as sole heir. The rightful title of nobility accompanied the estate.

"She's a tomboy all right. She can outthink, outride, outwrestle, and outshoot any man in western Pennsylvania. That's my little girl." Andrew smiled, extremely proud of his youngest daughter. As well as she had taken to school and studying, she had taken to the outdoors along with riding, hunting, fishing, and tracking wild game. Her well-rounded education, where she distinguished herself in the male-dominated fields of academia, was indeed one of the best that could be offered. She excelled in every endeavor she attempted. Although she was often rebellious against the formalities of Victorian society, she was still daddy's little girl. Andrew's smile broadened in the darkened room.

"I said my good-byes earlier. But you haven't. You walked out of the parlor so quickly. Please don't let her go without telling her that you love her," she said, hoping he'd come to his senses.

Andrew sat upright and swung his legs over the edge of the bed. The height of the down mattress allowed his feet to hover above the floor.

"Don't worry, Mother. Everything has been arranged. I should be on my way."

"Where are you going at this time of night?"

"I'll tell you when I return. I won't be long."

Andrew slid a few inches down the mattress for his feet to hit the inch-thick carpet. He pulled his trousers over his pajamas, threw on a robe, and left the room.

The double door entry to the Tudor mansion slowly opened. It was past midnight, and the moon spread its golden beams of light through the open crack as it widened. Monica Williams, third youngest sister and eight years older than her sister Stetson, allowed her demure figure to cast an ominous shadow on the marble entryway. She peered into the great house and looked for signs of movement. She knew her family went to bed at eleven o'clock sharp and hoped she had waited long enough to ensure they would be asleep. If her father caught her sneaking around at this hour, he would be furious.

She entered the foyer and slowly closed the door behind her. There wasn't a sound in the house. As she tiptoed toward the sweeping staircase to her right, she raised her hand to muffle a giggle. She cautiously climbed the stairs, remembering the times when she and Mary Ann sneaked throughout the house in the early morning while playing hide-and-seek. She remembered when the two of them and Margie would make hot chocolate in the middle of the night without waking their parents. They'd sit in the kitchen and talk about silly things, including school, boys, clothes, and everything their father thought was a waste of time. As children, it was a wonderful time in the house. Their brother, Andrew Junior, or as they nicknamed him, Sonny, was born when she was four years old. He would also play and sneak around in the great manor with them. Four years after Sonny's birth, Stetson was born. They were excited about another baby they could play with and care for. As Stetson got old enough to run around the house, the girls grew older and lost interest in playing silly games. Margie, the oldest, married and moved out. Two years later, Mary Ann did the same. When Stetson was thirteen years old, Monica married and moved several miles away on the other side of the city. Monica and Stetson remained close. As often as possible, Monica came to the house to play with Stetson. She watched Stetson grow into a rebellious youth and then into young adulthood. She witnessed her bloom into womanhood. She had always been there for her youngest sister. Tonight would be no exception. Monica could sense Stetson was troubled. Ever since Stetson met the attractive cowboy, a change had taken place in Stetson. Monica knew she was losing her best friend and youngest sister to this man. Knowing Stetson, they would never be forever lost because they would always remain close.

Monica passed her parent's bedroom door and stiffened. What would she do if the door swung open and her father was standing there with his hands on hips while waiting for an excuse? Would she lie? Would she act as if she was walking in her sleep? She stifled another giggle. She could never lie to her father. She had tried several times as a child. She had not been successful once. He always knew when she told a falsehood, as he called it. Passing her parents' bedroom, she heard voices. They were awake! She quickened her pace as she moved down the hallway toward Stetson's bedroom.

Stetson was perplexed. Her heart told her she was doing the right thing, but she loved her family so very much. Was she listening to her heart when she should be listening to her head? Love is so crazy. It truly confuses one's senses.

"No," she thought, "don't try to intellectualize these feelings."

"Your family will always love you. Follow your heart and dreams. Follow the man you love," she repeated to herself.

A light knock on the door interrupted her thoughts. Moving to the door, she opened it wide enough to see her sister Monica glancing nervously down the hallway.

"Monica?"

Monica's head jarred back to the sound of Stetson's voice. "Oh, Stetson, I had to come see you," she barely whispered.

Stetson opened the door to allow entry. "What are you doing here at this time of night?"

Monica entered and saw several large bags by the bed. "You're packing to leave already?"

"Monica, you can stop whispering."

Monica looked at Stetson, and both started giggling.

"They can't hear you from here."

Through her laughter, Monica asked, "Are you sure?"

They couldn't stop their silly laughter.

"As kids, Sonny would go to their room. I'd talk at different levels from here. They can't hear us." They collapsed on the bed. Tears ran down their cheeks. They held their voices down while attempting to stifle their chuckles.

Unexpectedly, Monica became serious. "You're going after him, aren't you?" She knew the answer without asking.

Stetson's eyes moved in the direction of the bags and then back to Monica. "I'm leaving home tonight, sis."

Monica's tears of laughter turned to tears of sadness.

"I knew something was troubling you, Stetson. Must you leave so quickly? It's as if you're running away from home."

"I am running away from home. Father doesn't like Ellsworth and has forbidden me from seeing him again."

"Oh, you know Father. His bark is worse than his bite. He would never want you to leave home."

"I love him, Monica, with all my heart. It actually hurts. I love Ellsworth so much. I want to be with him forever."

"I know. I love Ron the same way, but running away doesn't solve anything. You must face Father and tell him exactly the way you feel."

"But I love him too, sis. I don't want to hurt him. I couldn't stand to see his face when I told him I'm going out West with a man I hardly know and leaving everything he has worked so hard to provide me."

"He loves you and will understand."

"Then he'll understand why I'm leaving in the middle of the night. Enough of this, sis. Help me pack, will you?"

They spent the next several minutes packing the few remaining articles of clothing and memorabilia that Stetson could not part with. They reminisced about the past and discussed their hopes for the future.

"Tell me again silly, about the…Oh, you know, the rose thingamajig."

"The Tradition of the Rose?"

"Oh, I love the sound of that. Did he make it up?"

"Uh-huh, I think so. It may have been some other kind of flower in the West, but he used a rose on me." Stetson giggled. "And it worked."

"How does it go?"

"Well, for every rose a suitor gives a woman, he receives one kiss. The stipulation is that he has only twenty-four hours to collect."

"Oh, I like it." Monica put her hand to her mouth to stifle another giggle.

"The rule is that it is not a game of passion, but one of flirtation. Guess he didn't want me to think he wanted to be passionate."

"Go ahead, then…"

"The kiss must be harmless, like on the cheek. The man may never embarrass the woman, thus the kiss must be secretive to others when taken."

"The little devil." Monica grinned.

"Only the woman can decide if the kiss will be placed other than on the cheek. The woman can refuse the kiss or halt the game at any time."

"How many roses did you get?"

"A dozen."

"Oh, you!!!"

"I'm shameless."

"Always on the cheek?"

"Except the last three. Before you ask, promise never to tell anyone, especially the family."

"I swear," Monica said as she crossed herself.

"The last three were on the mouth."

"Shame on you, Stetson!"

"Didn't you ever kiss Ronny on the mouth before you were married?"

Monica smiled a sheepish smile. "Uh-huh."

"He's a good kisser, Monica."

"He sounds very romantic. How does a cowboy get romantic?"

"He reads a lot. His mother, who he adored, taught him to read and write. He's very well-educated. I was surprised."

"In a way, I envy you, Stetson."

"You do?"

"Yes. Your future sounds so exciting. Going off to faraway places we only read about. Danger! Adventure! It sounds so thrilling. Do you plan on settling down? Having a family? Coming back home?"

"I'm chasing after a man I know little about. Does he want to settle down? Does he want a family? Oh, Monica, I pray he does."

Monica and Ron had wanted to have children in the worst way and had tried without any luck. She knew it was the one thing in Monica's life she couldn't have. Both Margie and Mary Ann had been blessed with babies. Margie had four, strapping, young boys. Mary Ann had two beautiful, petite girls and a son who was the spitting image of his father, Bob. Sonny and his wife, Patricia, had two baby girls the family adored.

"Well, I guess it's time to go."

Stetson saw the sadness in her sister's face.

"I'll stay in touch. I promise."

"I love you. You know that, don't you?" Monica's voice quivered.

"Of course I do, silly. I love you and Ron. Please explain to everyone why I'm leaving. Say good-bye to them, okay?"

"Okay. Can I walk with you for a while?"

"No, Monica. Please, if it's all right with you. This is hard enough for me as it is. It's better if we part here. I'm in a hurry. I know Ellsworth left town two days ago. I don't even know how I'm going to find him. But I will. I must. Bye, sis."

She gave Monica a warm embrace and a kiss on the cheek. She picked up the several bags placed near the door. Without looking back, she exited.

Stetson was nearly panicked. She forced herself to walk carefully and quietly down the hallway, not wanting to waste time with an altercation with her father. She hurried down the staircase, turned right, and headed toward the kitchen. Leaving by the rear door would save her valuable time because it was closer to the stables. She would have to steal one of her father's pride possessions. Which way to ride? Oh, why didn't she leave with him? Why did she wait? She had to say good-bye to her mother. Moreover, it was so important to talk with Monica and explain. Monica would explain everything to the family. Yes, it had been the best decision to stay and say her good-byes.

"Now hurry!" she told herself. "Hurry!"

The brick stable complex was immense, like everything her father built. It housed more than thirty pedigreed horses and twenty mares under one roof. It also had a cow barn, attendant rooms and paddock, a greenhouse, an office, a supply room and tack room, and a cottage for the housing of the stablemaster. Stetson entered from the north side, giving her the opportunity to choose one of her father's less favorite ponies. The thoroughbreds, quarter horses, and special-bred horses, including the Arabians and appaloosas, were on the opposite end of the stables. She could always trade later for another horse that was better suited for the harshness she expected to find in the West.

She set her bags down and walked down the center of the stables, looking in each stall for a horse suitable for the arduous ride ahead. The dampness in the air gave the stables a rich, thick pungency of horseflesh mixed with the smell of hay and grain.

Like her father, Stetson loved horses. She learned to ride at the age of five. She was competing in state and national championships by the time she was fifteen. The trophies and ribbons bestowed upon her over the years filled her room. She would miss these animals. Yet, she knew her father and Percy, the stablemaster, would take good care of them.

Nearing the end of the first row of ten stables, she had not made a decision on the horse of her choosing. There were so many to choose from: the Welsh pony, the Assateague, the Morgan, or the Missouri Fox Trotter. She dare not pick from the more expensive purebreds that her father doted upon. She turned around to walk back past the same stalls, promising to choose carefully. She saw a shadow coming from one of the stalls. She breathed deeply. It was Percy. Who else could it be at this hour?

"Percy, is that you?" Her nervous whisper could barely be heard. It had begun to rain outside, and the falling rain was more audible than the whisper.

She recognized the man's shadow that moved across the ground.

"Good evening, Stetson."

Andrew Holovanisin leaned against the stable wall, putting a burning match to the pipe in his mouth. The smoke rose lazily as her father peered over the burning embers of the pipe.

"Should I say good morning? It's awfully late to be strolling in the stables. Isn't it, young lady?"

Stetson swallowed and took a deep breath. "Hello, Father." She was too startled to say anything else.

"Your mind is set, isn't it?" Her father's voice had an edge to it.

"Yes, father, it is."

"You're strong-willed. Just like your old man." He smiled, and his eyes sparkled.

"Yes, father." She returned the smile.

"Not very glib tonight? Can't even say good-bye to your father?" He continued to peer over the pipe, his dark eyebrows raised as if in a question mark.

"Oh, Daddy," Stetson ran the several yards separating them and threw her arms around her father's neck.

He felt his heart breaking as he held her to him. They embraced for several more seconds. Tears rolled down Stetson's cheeks as she gasped for air, choking down her remorse for being angry with this wonderful man.

He put his hands on her waist and gently pushed her away. She stepped back, noticing the tears in his eyes. She rarely saw him sentimental.

"Looking for a good animal to take with you?" He gestured around the stables with the pipe.

"Yes." She was always so articulate. Now she was at a loss for words.

"I believe you're looking in the wrong area of the stables, sweetie. I could've sworn you knew horseflesh better than this."

Turning toward the southern end of the stables, he began walking in the direction she had felt obligated not to go.

"Father, I can't take one of those horses."

"Why not?" He stopped in his tracks and turned to look at her.

"These animals are so...Well, they're so important to you. I couldn't choose one."

"Very well, Stetson. I'll choose for you."

"Hmm, perhaps a quarter horse." He looked at his daughter and continued walking. "Powerful hind legs...Remarkable speed for short distances...Agile and quick...A combination of spirit and small size."

"Not a quarter horse, huh?" he asked lovingly.

He stopped and faced the southern end of the stables. With a deeper, richer, more pronounced voice, he called, "Percy!"

Percy Hannibal emerged from the rear of the stable. Although in his early sixties, the small-framed, five-foot-seven-inch Percy was a good-looking, muscular Negro with closely cropped, receding gray hair that didn't take away from his youthful appearance. Behind Percy followed an appaloosa, the reins in his hands.

"I choose this one. That is, if it meets with your approval." His smile broadened as he looked at Stetson and looked back again to the horse.

"Father, no! I mean, I couldn't possibly take Sweetwater from you. She's your favorite! Please, let me pick another."

"Nonsense, child. Look at her. Beautiful, isn't she?" Her father ran his hand over the shoulder as well as down and across her flank. He patted the horse's haunch.

"She's a purebred appaloosa filly. Strong and high-spirited," he referred to the three-and-half-year-old female horse as if it was a member of their family. "Where you're going, you'll need a sturdy, sure-footed animal."

Stetson looked at the muscular appaloosa. Sweetwater was grayish in color with black-and-white leopard spots on her haunch and thighs. Her eyes were white-rimmed. Her hooves had a splash of black-and-white stripes. Stetson couldn't help noticing that the horse was saddled and bridled.

"Father, you planned this all along, haven't you?" She could hardly hold back the tears.

"Consider it a gift."

He opened his arms for another hug, and Stetson gladly obliged. She pulled back and looked at her father.

"Father, I'm not sure which direction to take. Ellsworth left two days ago. When he said good-bye, I didn't think to ask where he was going. I must hurry. Thank you so much. I love you."

She turned to take the reins from Percy's hands.

Andrew nodded at Percy, who withdrew the reins and held them away from Stetson. Confused, she turned to look at her father.

"Ellsworth left for St. Louis. From there, he's on his way to Texas. I believe he told me around Lubbock, the Palo Duro area. Beautiful this time of year, or so your cowboy told me." Andrew reached inside his left breast pocket of his robe and extracted some papers.

"You're booked on the next train to St. Louis. Percy will take Sweetwater to the station and board her for you. The carriage is outside. There is little time to waste."

He handed Stetson her train tickets for the Pittsburgh to St. Louis ride.

"Father, I don't know what to say."

"Make me a promise, will you?" His voice was momentarily serious.

"Of course, Father. Anything."

"Make your old man proud."

"I promise, Daddy. I really promise."

The rain had ceased, leaving droplets of moisture over the walkway, trees, and flowers. The rain made each appear as if stars were sparkling ubiquitously. Stetson and her father walked from the stables. Percy and Sweetwater followed.

Tying the horse to the rear of the carriage and climbing into the cabin, Percy took the reins of the two hackney horses. Stetson climbed in after Percy. She looked at her father.

"I promise I'll write every chance I get."

"Your mother and I love you, Stetson." He held up his hand to wave good-bye.

"Percy, move along quickly now," Andrew commanded while choking back tears.

Stetson blew her father a kiss as Percy shook the reins. The carriage moved away.

* * * *

The grip on her right ankle tightened. Stetson woke with a start. She had been dreaming again of home. The morning sun shone through a window high overhead in what appeared to be a jail cell. She then remembered the previous night, finding Jack and being captured by the Mexican banditos. They had put her in one of two cells within the mission. She rolled her head in the pillow and looked over at the cell next to hers. Through the bars, she saw Jack sitting on his cot. His arms were wrapped around his knees. He was watching her. The pain in her ankle worsened, and she glanced at the foot of her cot. The man who had directed her into the cell at gunpoint sat there. He sat stiffly upright with his shoulders back. He wore a dark blue, military waistcoat. Its shoulders displayed the ornate epaulets of a military officer. The man was Mexican, but his skin was far lighter than the other three Mexicans standing in the cell looking down at her. His grip around her ankle intensified. He apparently was trying to wake her. He had succeeded.

"Who are you?" Stetson demanded as she pushed herself to an upright position. Her voice was strong, and she tried being as threatening as possible, trying to hide the terror deep within her.

"*Buenos días, señorita.* My name is Juan Rodriquez Felipe de la Caza. Welcome to Condeza Barajas."

His dark eyes stared into hers. She attempted to hold his gaze, but she lost the fight and blinked. She momentarily closed her eyes and hoped it was a bad dream. Suddenly, she kicked her leg hard, breaking the man's grip.

"Let go of me!" she demanded.

De la Caza smiled. "What brings such a beautiful young lady to Condeza Barajas?" His hand rested on her ankle.

Again, Stetson and de la Caza's eyes locked. Slowly, his smile turned into a sneer as his eyes bore into his captive's unwavering glare. De la Caza slid closer to the woman. She was unflinching as he slithered his hand from her ankle and over her knee. He gently squeezed her thigh. No man or woman had held his gaze for this long. He found himself immensely attracted to such a woman. He leaned forward, parting his lips slightly to receive a kiss from the beautiful, resolute American. At the same time, he slid his hand up and between her thighs. He had forgotten the sentries and the other prisoner in the next cell. His only thought was taking this woman, knowing his sensual presence had unnerved her, like so many women before.

Putting her strength behind the blow, Stetson jabbed with all her might, striking de la Caza in the jaw with her right elbow. The sound of bone against bone reverberated against the adobe walls of the cell. De la Caza's head jerked to his right, momentarily dazing him and knocking him off the cot. His right knee struck the adobe floor as he stabilized himself against the cot. The sentries stood motionless, not knowing what to do. They had never seen their commander accosted before.

The Mexican leader held his jaw in his left hand. His left elbow held him upright against the cot. Blood oozed from the swollen lip. Dazed, he waited a moment. His downcast eyes looked up from the floor to Stetson.

"Whore!" de la Caza shouted as he pushed forward. His right clenched fist moved at incredible speed. Stetson blocked the punch, as her father had taught her many years ago. De la Caza was on his feet, screaming obscenities at the woman who had humiliated him in front of his men. With a wave of his hand, he motioned for the sentries to move on her. Stetson moved against the abode cell, bracing herself for the attack.

Jack moved quickly, grabbing the first sentry through the bars of the cell. With one hand on the Mexican's forehead and the other around his neck, Jack wrenched in opposite directions. The sound of breaking vertebrae silenced the room. Releasing his grasp, the dead sentry fell to the ground.

Momentarily frozen, the remaining two guards and de la Caza stared, first at the slumped mound of flesh and uniform at their feet and then at Jack. Forgetting the woman, de la Caza shouted orders while the sentries moved from Stetson's cell toward Jack's.

Jack attacked the first Mexican entering the cell, knocking him unconscious. Reinforcements from outside the mission filled the cellblock. As de la Caza bellowed instructions, Jack was overtaken and severely beaten by the Mexicans while Stetson was dragged from her cell.

The sun was fierce in the desert and beat down upon the mission with intensity. Dark clouds from the west threatened cooler weather and overcast skies within the next twenty-four hours. Stetson shielded her eyes from the sun's glare as she was dragged into the courtyard. Several Mexicans stood watching while others ran from various points within the confines of the mission.

De la Caza entered the courtyard. He held himself with pride while straightening his waistcoat and sash. He dabbed the corner of his mouth with a white handkerchief; already covered with a pinkish hue.

The crowd parted as de la Caza took his familiar stance in the center of the mob.

"Now is not a time for speeches," de la Caza reminded himself.

The two sentries would tell of the American woman striking him and sending him to his knees. Before nightfall, they'd all know of her transgression and be laughing silently. Each would be wishing he'd struck him. An example needed to be set—immediately. No one should believe he, de la Caza, could be confronted without reproach. De la Caza gave the command, and gasps from the hardened men could be heard.

"*El Commandante*, it is asking too much," Carlos Flores stepped forward. Only he, and perhaps Miguel Ignacio, could question de la Caza. Their friendship had been tested many times over the years and endured. Every man needs friends, and this truism was not lost on de la Caza. The three had protected each other over the years. Carlos worried de la Caza would push the men to the brink, risking everything they'd planned and trained for over the last year.

De la Caza glanced around at the semicircle of 200 men. They'd learn quickly, if they hadn't already, that punishment for inappropriate actions against him would be swift and final. De la Caza's eyes fell on his friend, Carlos Flores.

"Juan," Flores tried appealing to his friend and mentor. "Punishing a woman is wrong. The men will hate you. Twenty-five lashes would kill a man. She won't survive. This will make you appear weak before your men."

De la Caza turned his back on his friend and stared at the American woman.

"You hear this? You will not survive twenty-five lashes from the whip. You are going to die. My men will learn that anyone, man or woman, who raises a hand against me, shall perish from this earth. Quite biblical, in a sense, don't you think?"

"Tie her," de la Caza commanded. De la Caza took Stetson by her shoulders and turned her around, facing the direction opposite him. With both hands, he gripped her white blouse, ripped it open, and tore it down to her waist. De la Caza reached through the blouse and gently touched the flushed skin. It was soft and cool. He knew, if she survived, twenty-five lashes would leave hideous scars. Men would turn in repulsion.

Stetson's wrists were tied to an overhang formed by two four-by-four upright poles, connected by another four-by-four overhead beam. Her back faced the semicircle of men. Stetson bit her lower lip, preparing herself for the numbing pain she knew would come.

From the mob of men, a large, swarthy, muscular man with high-polished knee boots, similar to those worn by de la Caza, strode. His shirt had been removed, and the dark hair on his chest and back couldn't hide his muscularity. In his right hand, he carried a twenty-foot-long bullwhip. The man snapped the whip several times in the air, seizing the mob's attention. He smiled. His ability to inflict pain was a learned skill, honed over many years. With a simple flick of his wrist, he could control the tip of the whip to gently caress, instilling fear in his victim. Just as easily, he could dig deeply, driving the tip to the bone, and sending his victim into spasms. He controlled the final outcome. With de la Caza, the finale was always death. This woman would be unfortunately sacrificed.

The man struck the whip into the air several more times to test the strength of the whip. He then faced his victim and the soft, white mound of flesh that was offered as his target. He'd make the crowd wince and de la Caza proud. He would take his time on the woman and bring her to a slow but certain death. His slender, mustachioed countenance contorted in a gnarl. There would be no clemency or mercy for this woman, only savage brutality.

CHAPTER 27

Stetson yanked at the rawhide cord binding her wrists to the overhead banister. She could feel the warmth of the morning sun on her bare shoulders. The courtyard was motionless, nary a word uttered by the men staring at what they assumed to be a masquerade of death. Certainly de la Caza would not kill this woman, an *Americano*, although de la Caza had professed his animosity of Americans many times. But she was beautiful and could make any man among them a pleasing wife. De la Caza had been blessed with a legion of women in his life—rich and poor as well as beautiful and famous. The men presumed he would take this woman for his own. She would fall under his charm as they all did. When he tired of her, they would all scuffle and spar for her attention.

"On with it!" de la Caza dictated as he stepped back to join his men.

The executioner knew the men expected de la Caza to call off the charade. Having been with de la Caza for many years, he knew de la Caza reigned by fear. The woman's death needed to instill undeniable fear into them. The men loathed de la Caza, cowered in fear of him, but his methods produced results for the breed of men he led.

Snapping his wrist, the executioner placed the bullwhip in the dust lengthwise, allowing the tip to gently caress Stetson's leather chaps. The perimeter of men shifted closer, anticipating the slow, agonizing death the woman would endure. No one had the bravado to decry the punishment, to challenge de la Caza. In so doing, they would guarantee themselves the wrath of de la Caza and the executioner.

"Son of a bitch!"

The crowd turned toward the voice. Jack, dragged from his cell to witness his friend's execution, was positioned on his knees. His hands were cinched behind him with leather rigging lashed around his ankles, wrists, and neck, which prevented him from rising without choking. A bandito filled his hand with Jack's hair, holding him up to watch the execution. With a cue from de la Caza, the Mexican pulled on Jack's hair, forcing the leather cord around Jack's neck to tighten and silence him. The men turned their attention back to the executioner.

Knowing de la Caza relished a skillful execution, the executioner deliberately dragged the bullwhip slowly through the dust. The crowd closely observed its serpentine movement. Flicking his wrist, the bullwhip jumped into the air, circling above him. One snap and then another. Another again followed. The tip of the whip broke the still, hot air of the morning. Lunging forward, the whip's tip delicately fingered the woman's golden hair, without misplacing one strand. The executioner confirmed his cunning with the whip to the crowd.

Stetson heard the sound of the whip, but she did not feel anything. She trembled. Her knees weakened, and she bit her lower lip. She'd never known such apprehension. Knowing she was going to die didn't terrify her as much as understanding considerable pain would be involved with her death. Aware she'd never see Kincaid again brought the first tears to her eyes. She steadied herself for what was to come. She prayed she'd be spared any suffering.

The men's eyes were riveted on the executioner's every move. With the back of her blouse torn to her waist, the executioner decided to remove bits of skin from the woman's back, near the base of her spine. The men needed to see the type of heinous wound a whip can create, watch the blood slowly trickle, and see the skin welt. Her exposed flesh was perfect for the reaction he knew he could exact from the audience. If de la Caza coveted fear from his men this morning, then the executioner would guarantee absolute horror for them to witness. He pitied the young woman. She would suffer pain few—men or women—have ever endured. He wanted to delay her death long enough to ensure the men understood de la Caza's message. He lifted his right arm over his shoulder and snapped the whip into the air, keeping it circling overhead as the men looked back and forth between the whip and the woman's tender, white back.

"Deliver the souls of the departed faithful, Lord, from every bond of sin; and by the help of thy grace may they deserve to escape thy just retribution and enjoy the blessedness of ever-lasting light." The man with the Sharp's rifle and long-range Creedmoor sight had discovered that reciting different verses from the Bible provided the indispensable rhythm for loading, sighting, and squeezing the trigger while simultaneously keeping his mind clear for the work at hand. He called it God's work, and he felt it befitting to recite from the Bible when exacting God's vengeance to the fullest extent.

The .44-90 slug trekked across 1,100 yards of terrain, striking the executioner in the left temple. The reverberation of the blast resonated off the cliff walls surrounding the old fortress. The men in the courtyard momentarily froze, not knowing what was happening. The explosion of the executioner's head and his body slumping to the ground answered any questions they may have had. The men began running in every direction, cursing as they dove for cover.

The man on the hillside decided this cadence was insufficient. He had rarely seen men move so quickly. He smiled, enjoying the challenge.

He chose another familiar passage. "I am the resurrection and the life." His right hand moved the lever of the Sharp's rifle downward, opening the breech.

"Whoever believes in me," he uttered aloud as he picked up the next metallic cartridge. "Even if he dies…" His fingers inserted the cartridge into the chamber. "Will live."

Recycling the lever upward, he closed the breech. "And everyone who lives and believes in me…" He cocked the hammer, sighted the next target, and set the rear trigger, "Will never die."

He slowly squeezed the front hair-trigger. The second man went down with a bullet to the chest.

"Quicker," he thought. His mind raced to the next citation. "Eternal rest give unto him, Lord." He placed the lever down and picked up the next cartridge.

"And let perpetual light shine upon him." He inserted the cartridge, placed the lever up, and cocked the hammer.

"May he rest in peace." He sighted the target and set the rear trigger.

"Amen." He pulled the front trigger. The third man went down.

The old fortress was in mass confusion. The men ran from cover to cover. When a man exposed himself, a bullet ripped him open. De la Caza caught a glimmer from the mountain peaks to the west, a flash from an object high in the rocky crevices caused by the mid-morning sun. A puff of black powder moved with the breeze.

"No man could shoot accurately at such a distance," de la Caza thought. He knew the legends of the old buffalo hunters, but no one knew of this old mission. His sentries would have apprehended anyone coming into the area. Yet, someone was up there.

The man muttered the recitations aloud to himself. Occasionally, he lapsed into Latin. "*Misereatur vestri omnipotens Deus, et, dismissis peccatis vestris, perducat vos ad vitam aeternam* (May the almighty God be merciful to you, forgive your sins and bring you to everlasting life)." The fourth man went down.

The Mexican holding Jack was the fourth man killed. Jack lay on his right side. His ankles were cinched so tight that they were touching his buttocks. He watched the banditos being slaughtered. Only one or two men he knew could shoot so quickly and precisely from such a distance. Billy Dixon, a buffalo hunter from his past, was one such man, but Jack had lost contact with him years ago. Only one man had the nerves of steel and dogged determination to find him south of the border. With Stetson held captive, the obvious man was Ellsworth T. Kincaid.

"C'mon Elly, kill the sons of bitches!" Jack shouted.

The Mexicans responded to de la Caza's instructions, firing their rifles in the direction de la Caza indicated, toward the puffs of black smoke. However, no weapon in their possession could reach the long distance.

De la Caza stealthily made his way to Jack. He moved cautiously, waiting until another man had been hit so he could move the few seconds it took the man upon the hillside to reload. De la Caza counted four, maybe five, seconds between shots. The man never missed.

"Who is that?" de la Caza lay next to Jack, ensuring Jack was between him and the hillside where the shots were coming. Jack rolled over and found himself lying face-to-face with de la Caza.

"A friend, *mi amigo*, a friend," Jack shouted over the roar of gunfire.

De la Caza gripped Jack's throat and pulled him closer until they were nose to nose. "Who is that?"

De la Caza relaxed his grip so Jack could speak. "Kincaid. Ellsworth T. Kincaid."

"Do I know this man?" de la Caza glanced to the hillside. "Kincaid? Who is this Ellsworth Kincaid?"

"That's Ellsworth T. Kincaid," Jack laughed, putting the emphasis on the middle initial.

De la Caza looked around. The ground was covered with dead men. He counted seven…no, eight men blown apart. The rest had taken cover. Not one man was firing back as he had instructed. The shooting was futile at such a distance. He looked back at Jack and wondered what he had said. T? The gringo had lost his mind. What was he talking about?

"T?" de la Caza repeated.

Jack smiled. "Yeah, T! Big trouble."

De la Caza saw another man move and die.

"Untie the woman!" He directed.

Several men moved in Stetson's direction. One man was cut down before he had moved three paces. The other two men moved toward her, allowing Stetson to serve as a shield for them and ensuring she was between the hillside killer and them. With a knife, one of the men cut the bonds holding her wrists. She slipped her hands from the overhead rafter and pulled her blouse up, covering herself. The two men moved quickly away. The firing from the hillside ceased.

No one moved for several minutes. Slowly, some of the men moved from behind their shelter. No further shots were fired into the courtyard. De la Caza stood and walked to the center of the courtyard, dusting off his military jacket and red sash.

The man on the hillside waited. His Sharps' breech and barrel were extremely hot to the touch. He knew the weapon's propensity to jam under these conditions. He watched and waited, giving the firearm a needed cooldown.

"*Amigos*! Bring the woman here," de la Caza commanded.

No one moved. Several of the men slowly walked out into the open, partially crouched in fear of another bullet coming from the canyon walls.

"Now!" de la Caza angrily shouted.

Stetson was brought to de la Caza in the center of the courtyard. The men now surrounded them.

"I could kill you, *señorita*. My men provide us cover. Look around you."

Stetson saw the men had circled around her and their leader, shielding them from the unknown aggressor on the hillside. She knew she remained at their mercy. She said nothing. She only gazed back at de la Caza.

"Bring me her horse!" de la Caza had a plan he knew would work.

The appaloosa, found earlier by sentries covering the passageway to the old fortress, was brought to de la Caza.

"Carlos, your knife." de la Caza held out his hand as he issued the order.

Carlos Flores pulled his six-inch blade from its sheath, flipped it in the air, and carefully caught it by the razor-sharp blade. He handed the knife, handle first, to de la Caza.

"Your hand, Carlos." de la Caza glanced in the eyes of his friend, seeking any threads of fear. Carlos Flores readily put out his right hand with his palm up.

"Grip the blade." The men ground their teeth together.

"My friend, grip it with your left hand. Not too tightly. I do not want to cripple you."

Carlos delicately grasped the blade with his left hand. As he did so, de la Caza slowly pulled the knife through Carlos' fingers, ensuring not to sever any fingers. De la Caza watched the emotionless expression on his friend's face.

"Give me your hand, Carlos."

De la Caza snatched Carlos by the left wrist and took his bleeding hand.

"Place your hand here." de la Caza smeared Carlos' blood on the appaloosa's saddle.

"And here." He again smeared blood. This time, it was on the horse's right rear quarters.

"Clear the front gate," de la Caza dictated.

The sentries moved to one side. The men surrounding de la Caza, Stetson, and the appaloosa looked puzzled. De la Caza smiled to the crowd.

"It is very simple. This is the bait." de la Caza motioned to the horse, "And there waits the catch," de la Caza said as he motioned to the hillside where the shots had come.

With this last remark, de la Caza slapped the horse's hindquarters. The horse fled toward the mountainous passageway.

"Now we wait." de la Caza smiled again to his men.

"They can be so stupid," he thought to himself.

Stetson was moved to the makeshift jail within the old church. A large Mexican kicked Jack twice in the stomach. The same Mexican then picked up Jack by his restraints and dragged him to the jail.

De la Caza looked again to the hillside.

"Now we wait," he uttered softly.

Assuming the Mexicans might try to outflank him, the man on the hillside moved on.

CHAPTER 28

It was an hour before dawn. It was an hour before the firing and shelling would resume. It was an hour before the bloodshed would commence again.

Lying on his back, Jack stared at his threadbare canvas ceiling, unable to sleep.

"Psst, Elly, you awake?" he whispered.

"Yeah."

"It's gonna be a bitch come morning."

Kincaid rolled onto his side to face his friend on the other side of the tent, pushing a wad of dark hair from his forehead.

"War's almost over, Jack. Grant's gonna finish it and soon. It'll be hell until it's over."

"Guess we'll be in the thick of it." Jack sighed.

"Watching over that damn, fool lieutenant we will be. One dumbass stupid assignment, if you ask me. Yeah, you can place good money on it. We'll be lucky to get through the day."

"Write your ma?"

"Every week, like I promised her."

"Something happens to me, you'll write my ma, won't ya?"

"Christ, Jack. I was joshing. Ain't nothing gonna happen to us. Get some sleep. The sun will be up soon." Kincaid rolled over on his other side, away from Jack. His face almost touched the small tent's canvas covering. He wished he could fall asleep. He wished he was as sure of their safety as he insinuated.

"Fire!" Captain Stephen Ridley barked the command to the battle-weary men manning the five twelve-inch howitzers stationed to his left. Standing on the front line, the roar of the cannons was deafening. Smoke and the acrid smell of gunpowder hung in the humid air. A small breeze rippled the artillery's blue-and-gold triangular flag that evenly separated the ten cannon ranks, five cannons on either side. Far behind Ridley and the thrashed Union soldiers, wagons rolled, carrying the wounded and dead from the field of battle. Reinforcements quickly marched to the front to fill the vacant positions. Hundreds of corpses still lay within the men's ranks.

"Fire!" Captain Ridley ordered the men manning the cannons to his right. His authoritative presence on the front lines was reassuring for his men and boys fighting to gain another inch of sacred dirt on the bloody Virginia battlefield. On his command, the fuses on the half-ton cannons were ignited. The ground jarred as cannon balls sailed into the morning sky toward the dense, thick line of men clad in gray, only hundreds of yards away.

Captain Ridley stood proud. His every command was shouted above the cacophony of war. The double row of gold buttons on his custom-made military blue frock coat shone brilliantly as the morning sun rose lazily over the green hills. This was his first battle engagement in a war many people thought would last only weeks. Instead, it had dragged on for four years. He thought of his father, Brigadier General Scott C. Ridley, on special assignment as adjutant and strategic war adviser to President Lincoln in Washington, DC. The general would be proud of his son. A brief week-and-a-half had passed since his appointment to the field and his hurried marriage to his childhood sweetheart, Sarah Jane. Now he commanded more than 300 Union soldiers in a tactical maneuver that could possibly shorten this dreadful fight between brothers and ideology. Yet, he hoped the war would not end too quickly. He had dreams and aspirations to fulfill. Promotion to major was his first priority. Then, with the additional military pay, he and Sarah Jane would have children, a dream of hers. They would have a large family and settle in Washington, DC. He would hopefully work side by side with his father, whom he loved and admired. His father had always been his guiding spirit, his source of inspiration, and the yardstick by which he had always measured himself.

"Sergeant Nichols! Over there!" Ridley yelled, pointing to an outcropping of Confederates on the far right who were massing for a frontal assault. "Put your number three and four cannons in that direction!"

"Aye, captain." Sergeant Nichols used the naval jargon drummed into him over the last ten years of his military service. He had requested a transfer to the Army to "see the enemy eye to eye while fighting 'em." Nichols gave the command. The two cannons were rolled into position. The elevation was sighted, and fuses were ignited. Two thunderous bursts from the howitzers shook the sweaty, powder-smeared men. The ground around the Confederates erupted in a fiery inferno, sending earth, armaments, and body fragments skyward. Roaring in excitement, the Yanks threw their hats into the air. A volley from Confederate long rifles rained into them, disrupting their merriment.

"Give 'em hell, boys!" Captain Ridley rallied his men.

Holding his saber high in the air, Ridley dropped it swiftly. The call of cannon shot rang true. Ridley was certain he and his troops would prevail over the lesser-equipped, ill-prepared Confederates. A sense of triumph swelled within him as he envisioned his father's smile and firm handshake for a job well done when two .58 caliber slugs buried themselves into his freshly starched blue jacket. Captain Ridley stiffened, glancing down at his blood-soaked coat. Ridley fell to his knees, feeling dizzy. The sound of gunfire and rebel yelling became dimmer…softer.

With his bloodstained hands covering his mortal wounds, Ridley muttered, "Father, I'm sorry." His body slumped to the ground as another young officer shouldered the command.

"Yeeee Haaaa! Come on, boys! Follow me!" Ebullient and young, Second Lieutenant Tom Custer swiftly rode through the ranks of soldiers as they jumped from the path of horse and rider. The Michigan Brigade understood the general's brother was a reckless daredevil. Not rising in rank as quickly as his brother, Tom Custer competed for medals and the bragging rights that accompanied the decorations pinned to his chest.

Custer cut in and out among them. He rode up the small, grassy embankment where the cannons were located. He grabbed the detachment's flag and then charged the distant birch tree line identifying the enemy's location. He yelled loud obscenities toward the Rebels.

"Shit, Elly. Here we go again." Shaking his head, Jack looked wide-eyed at Kincaid. Jack and Kincaid had been selected to watch over the lieutenant ever since the general hired them to scout for the division. This was the second time the general's younger brother had behaved idiotically in as many weeks.

Without another word, Jack grabbed the reins of his tethered horse, held tightly on the pommel's horn, and threw his right leg over the saddle as his horse neared a full gallop. Kincaid ran toward his horse and slid himself smoothly into the battered McClellan saddle.

The enemy stared in disbelief. Their guns were momentarily silent as both lads put spur to horseflesh, riding in Custer's wake. At a full gallop, Jack and Kincaid quickly caught Custer. Jack angled to the lieutenant's left; Kincaid flared to the right. Riding low in the saddle, Jack came alongside Custer. They were within one hundred yards of the Confederate's muskets.

"Get the hell out of here, lieutenant!" Jack yelled over the pounding of cannon fire while waving his revolver in the air. The Confederates opened fire as the three horsemen drew closer. Musket balls zipped in the air as Custer leaned forward in the saddle. His torso was within an inch of his horse's mane. His blonde, unkempt mustache was stretched into a thin grin. Custer ignored Jack's pleading and rode straight at the enemy's thickest line of defense. The Michigan Brigade's flag flowed in the breeze.

Kincaid rode ahead of Custer. His revolver was aimed toward the mass of men. Jack whipped his horse ahead of the lieutenant, attempting to catch Kincaid. Jack angled for the same point in the enemy's rank as Kincaid.

The two had to generate chaos among the Southern boys in order to create a path of least resistance for the lieutenant. Within ten yards of the gray line, Kincaid and Jack opened fire. Both killed a man with their initial volley.

The enemy's return fire was poorly aimed as men hurriedly lunged to escape Jack and Kincaid as the two breached the makeshift fortification. Kincaid swung his horse around to find Custer. An infantryman grabbed Kincaid's leg, nearly pulling his boot off. Kincaid shot the man through the forehead.

Within seconds, Custer was among them. Several Confederates charged Custer with bayonets affixed to their rifles. Custer impaled two men running toward him, using the detachment's flagpole as a lance. Jack shot a man who jumped on the rear of Custer's horse. Custer rushed the Confederate's flag bearer. He bent forward from his saddle with an outstretched hand to bag another enemy's flag, one more trophy for his brother. As Custer's hand wrapped around the detachment's flagpole, the flag bearer fired his pistol at point-blank range.

A shearing, red-hot ball of flame struck Custer in the face. The seventy-nine-grain round ball passed through the soft tissue and exited his cheek without striking bone. Custer reared his mount, looking for an exit. Kincaid's shot felled the flag bearer before he could fire another shot at Custer.

"Retreat!" the Confederate corporal bellowed at his soldiers.

Jack yelled, "Now, lieutenant. Go!"

Custer laughed. His head was bent backward. His blood-soaked mouth was wide open. Coagulated blood covered his cheek and jaw.

With his last two remaining .36 caliber balls, Kincaid killed the corporal who issued the retreat. As the Confederates pulled away from the three horsemen, Jack reined his horse around, withdrawing with Custer and Kincaid. His horse trampled a Confederate soldier who had fallen underfoot. Another soldier fired a .58

caliber musket ball within inches of a fellow solider. The reverberation of the shot rang in the neighboring soldier's ears, triggering blood to spurt from both ears. The musket ball tore through the right sleeve of Kincaid, now positioned behind Custer to protect him.

"Fire!" Twenty Confederate riflemen had formed, reloaded, and waited for their comrades to safely remove themselves from their line of fire. On the command, a volley was discharged at the three escaping cavalrymen. Black powder from the fusillade rose overhead.

Musket balls perforated the air. One found its target. The gray-colored roan froze as the ball ripped through flesh, sinew, and bone. Rearing its front hooves in the air, she fell as gravity gripped and pulled the dead carcass to earth.

"Jack!" Kincaid, straddling his fallen horse, yelled.

* * * *

"Jack!" Kincaid jolted from his slumber with the recurring nightmare. Sweating profusely and momentarily bewildered, Kincaid glanced around at his surroundings. He quickly recalled his whereabouts in the mountains south of the border, the mountains encircling Condeza Barajas.

Stiff and tired, Kincaid stretched his aching muscles. During his years as a Texas Ranger, he had grown accustomed to sleeping anywhere at any time. When tracking his prey, he preferred working at night and resting during the hottest part of the day. This mission was no different. During the last two evenings, he had reconnoitered the entire area as well as memorized the whereabouts of the old mission, the canyon valley leading to its entrance, and the position of every sentry.

Kincaid rested in the shade of a large boulder, mentally charting his destination for that night when the first shot rang out, the sound echoing through the canyons. Lunging to his feet and grabbing his rifle, he quickly moved to a shadowy fissure, chambered a round, and waited. He counted two, three, and four shots. Each was approximately five seconds apart. The firearm was a single-shot, large-caliber rifle. He first thought that someone had foolishly entered de la Caza's domain to hunt game and would probably die at the hands of the Mexicans. Suddenly, a series of shots from small-caliber firearms rang out. Were the Mexicans killing the hunter? A fusillade of gunfire erupted again and then went silent. The single-shot weapon fired several times and ceased. The hunter was either dead or someone had been caught off guard near the fortress and executed.

Knowing the hillside would be swarming with Mexicans for several hours, Kincaid choose to remain hidden.

He'd lost valuable hours. Disappointed, he sat in the shade of a boulder and sharpened his knife to a fine edge, thinking about Jack and how they had become fast friends, riding for the pony express and joining the Union Army as scouts.

After the war, they had hunted buffalo in the Texas panhandle. He joined the Texas Rangers to defend homesteaders against the Comanche and Mexicans while Jack went home to visit his mother. He lost track of Jack after the Toledo, Ohio, reunion. Rumors circulated that Jack still resided in Washington, DC. Knowing Jack, he was either appointed a general or elected a senator.

"It was probably why de la Caza captured him, for some outrageous ransom to be paid by the United States government," Kincaid thought.

He and Jack had known each other for more than sixteen years. They'd seen the best and worst of times together. Jack had saved his sorry butt a time or two. Now Jack would owe him big this time. Kincaid slowly moved the knife's blade in a circular motion on the wet stone, occasionally touching the sharp edge with his thumb to assure its sharpness.

Kincaid woke after midnight and moved to ensure his black stallion was tethered in its hiding place. The loss of such a horse in this environment meant certain death. Detection of the horse meant his detection as well. Kincaid shifted with the shadows down the mountainside to a dead-end corridor on the valley floor. The horse was where he had left him. Its black coat glistened in the moonlight. Kincaid ran his hand over the horse's mane and stroked its withers. They'd seen a lot of action over the last several years. With a good horse, a good friend, and a good woman waiting for him in El Paso, Kincaid knew he was a very lucky fellow.

Suddenly, the hairs on the back of his neck stood on end. Hearing something, he remained motionless. He was well-hidden. Anyone passing within feet of him would not notice him or his horse. He waited.

A horse came within feet of their hideout. Kincaid drew his knife. If detected, he would have to move silently and quickly. He waited for the horse to pass. Kincaid stopped breathing and listened intently. The horse stopped at the entrance to their hideaway and whinnied. He moved closer, prepared to fight. The horse whinnied again. The horse moved closer, and Kincaid saw its outline. It was riderless.

"The rider must be moving to flank my position," he thought.

The sweat rolled down the center of his back. Relying on instinct, he decided to make a stand and fight. He stepped into the clearing.

Kincaid checked his breathing. It was normal. Even though he knew his adrenaline was pumping, he was calm. He held his knife steady. He moved nearer the horse. It was an appaloosa, similar to Stetson's. Then he froze. Feeling the saddle, he identified the square skirt and double rigging with a four-inch pommel as Stetson's custom-tooled rig. It wasn't one used by any Mexican he ever knew. He took the reins and led the horse out of the shadows. The quarter moon gave enough light to examine the horse and verify it was Sweetwater. Something on the saddle skirt caught his eye. He moved closer. His face nearly touched the leather. It was dark, dried, and flaky. He scratched some off and rolled it between his fingers. Moistening it with his saliva, he smelled and tasted it. Blood. He ran his hand over the saddle, bridle, and then the horse itself. He felt more of it on the rear quarters. What was Stetson doing here?

"De la Caza," he thought. "The butcher had her."

The moment he thought it, Kincaid knew it.

Something stirred deep within him. He had never loved anyone so intensely and so profoundly as he did Stetson. Feeling powerless, he struggled with the urge to scream. De la Caza had her. Perhaps the gunshots he heard were fired at her. She could be dead. The thought induced a reflex to vomit. He felt sick and feverish. She had followed him. He felt the fool. Attempting to avoid an argument about her not coming with him, he had allowed her to become the victim. He should have known she would follow him. Knowing her temperament, she would have definitely come, if only to help him. A fierce, ominous beast of hatred stirred within him, a beast he resolved to unleash.

Cautiously, Kincaid tethered Sweetwater with Cimarron. He looked over his shoulder every few seconds, not believing the appaloosa came without followers.

He intended to move out immediately. There was much to do. The guards he observed were lazy, making his task easier. Kincaid laid out his weapons, checked them thoroughly, and then checked them again.

He hid his provisions. He wouldn't need them tonight. For some reason, he thought of his mother. He wasn't a religious man. Except as a boy, he rarely attended church, and only when his mother forced him. He hadn't thought of God much, even though he understood death, its meaning to the Indian tribes, and their belief in the afterlife. He didn't clearly comprehend what came over him, but he felt the need to pray. On one knee with his head bowed, Kincaid said a prayer. He remembered, as a child, his mother said he could speak to the Lord at any time and the Lord would listen.

He missed his ma. Going home to St. Joseph after the war was over, he found an old colored woman tending to the house and family restaurant. His ma was lying in bed in the back bedroom, thoroughly soaked by her own perspiration. He placed his hand on her forehead and detected a high fever. She opened her eyes, immediately recognized him, and smiled. Her eyes brightened. She reached out for him, and he took her thin, bony, fragile hand. She just stared at him and smiled. Her grip was strong, and she didn't want to let go of him. He leaned forward and ran his hand over her hair. He bent down and whispered he loved her. She continued to smile. He saw a tear run down her shallow cheek. She whispered a question he couldn't hear. He moved closer and put his ear near her mouth. She asked if she had been a good mother. He smiled and held her hand tighter. He nodded and said she had been the best ma ever. He said he loved her with all his heart. She closed her eyes and died. He remembered hearing her last breath exiting her lungs. He cried like he had never cried before. He had lost so many friends during the war and seen so much death, but her passing unnerved him. He worshiped her. She had been a kind, loving, God-fearing person. He stayed with her in her room through the next day until the old Negro woman came in and said his mother needed burying. He couldn't afford much, but he gave her a good funeral. She would have been proud of the number of folks that attended.

Kneeling high in the mountains south of Texas, Kincaid prayed for the safe extrication of Stetson and thanked the Almighty for bringing them together. He then asked for the eternal salvation of his mother's soul. He thought of his best friend and asked God to help him bring Jack to safety along with Stetson. Then, for some reason, he asked God to forgive him, for the things he may have done wrong in his past and for the things he would probably do in the future, if he survived the next several days. Finally, he asked the Lord to forgive him for those he was about to kill.

CHAPTER 29

Kincaid stepped into the clearing from the rocky crevices. The lone Mexican sentry erroneously made a move for his firearm. Even though his death was imminent, a scream to his comrades would have been a wiser choice. It may have saved their lives, warned them of danger, and given them the opportunity to warn the garrison at the mission. A trained warrior, knowing the value of teamwork, would have made the correct split-second decision of alerting the squad while calmly realizing that death was his ultimate fate. For Kincaid, this first man was simply a matter of an execution.

The second and third man, each alone, became conscious of his presence as his knife abruptly slit their throats. Kincaid rarely shuddered. He loathed killing a man with a knife. He preferred a revolver, facing the man one-on-one. Men seldom faced off and fought one another nowadays. Most preferred catching a man off guard, shooting a man in the back, or using a shotgun at close range. Killing with a knife was vicious and personal. The act involved touching the person, feeling his perspiration, smelling his stench, discerning his fear, and experiencing the body trembling in the agony of death. Admittedly, the knife was profoundly effective when performed accurately. The neck and jugular area was the choice target. Piercing the layer of tissues surrounding the throat prevented a man from screaming. He would gulp for air and swallow his own life's blood. Within seconds, he became lifeless. Shoving the head frontward, until the chin nearly touches the chest, stifles the sound of air escaping from the lungs. It was an old Indian trick that worked well.

The next man, cognizant of his surroundings, saw Kincaid coming. Emerging from the shadows, Kincaid beheld the man's panic in his eyes. In the man's incapacity to move hastily, Kincaid advanced swiftly from the boulders, darted across the encampment, and thrust the six-and-a-half-inch blade in the Mexican's jugular, twisting the blade to assure maximum injury before death so no sound could be emitted. The man, more paralyzed from horror than pain, stumbled and pitched forward.

The next two sentries, also alone, endeavored to fight back. But Kincaid's intensity and fury was greater than theirs, and they also perished quickly.

The last two men were unexpectedly together. Both men were asleep. Kincaid had never killed a man in his sleep. He vowed he never would, even though the Indians had taught him differently. He bludgeoned the first man over the head. The second man, lying ten feet away, woke from the sound and began sitting up, just in time to receive a right clenched fist to the jaw, knocking him unconscious. Kincaid began tethering the second man's hands when the first man he had clubbed roused and rushed him. Shifting to one side and sweeping his right leg out, he tripped the oncoming Mexican. Quickly, Kincaid found himself in a life-or-death struggle. The Mexican pulled his knife. Its blade sliced through the air close to Kincaid's abdomen. But Kincaid's knife found its mark quicker, forcing the razor-sharp blade to its hilt. He twisted and pushed while dodging the Mexican's knife that haphazardly stabbed the night.

Bent over the dead man, the other man rushed Kincaid. He was as large as a buffalo. His lips were puffy and bleeding from Kincaid's earlier punch. Kincaid rolled onto his back and kicked upward. His foot struck the big Mexican in his plump stomach, forcing him up and over his position. Kincaid's knife was nestled in the thoracic cavity of the dead man, out of his reach. Kincaid searched in vain for the dead man's knife. The big Mexican was on his feet, rushing him again. He had withdrawn an ominous eight-inch bowie knife from his belt. Kincaid rolled again, out of the path of the oncoming man. Kincaid got to his knees as the other man closed the gap between them, seized the man's wrist, and tried wrestling the knife from him. The Mexican kicked again and again, smacking Kincaid in the ribs and driving the wind from him. With all his strength, Kincaid twisted the knife, bending the man's wrist backward and pulling the large man to the ground next to him. The Mexican held tight onto the knife's handle. With both hands clasped around the Mexican's huge hands, Kincaid purposefully drove the knife through the Mexican's sternum and into his heart. The Mexican stared at Kincaid for several seconds. Kincaid could smell the man's putrid breath. The Mexican's eyes glassed over, and his strength finally dissipated.

Two hours had passed since he had left his mountainous lair. In those hours, he had killed all eight sentries. He killed each swiftly, mostly with minor effort.

He killed as the Indians had tutored him a decade ago, propelling himself with sensibilities filled with rage, hatred, and vengeance. Fortunately, each sentinel was stationed as he had initially found him during his scouting. If the Mexicans had shifted their lookout positions as a matter of course or staked out a perimeter they attended to, his job of finding and killing them would have been much more laborious. The guards were obviously not a trained militia. The natural tendency of man facing the elements is to hunker down, pull a blanket around one's knees and shoulders, and permit one's natural body temperature to keep one warm. A skilled warrior would keep moving, keeping the body warm and the brain alert. Trained soldiers would not have stayed in one place for so long and would have worked as a close-knit crew, in pairs, to prevent any surprises.

Not one of those he killed that evening considered the others. Four of the eight never knew their assailant, never heard him, and never saw him. Kincaid had always postulated fair play in battle, cards, and love. Bushwhacking, back-stabbing, and getting the drop on someone was not a prank he had ever played, considering it had been played on him numerous times. But the blood he had seen on Sweetwater had taken all the gamesmanship and fair play from him. He was on his own, in a country he preferred not to be in. Even as a Texas Ranger, he rarely rode south of the Rio Grande without provocation. Now, both Jack and Stetson's lives, if they were alive, depended upon him and the tactics he employed.

Bruised and sore, his legs aching from the climbing and stooping as he stalked and destroyed his prey, Kincaid quickly descended the mountain.

Standing at the base of the mountains near the entrance to the corridor once known as the Valley of Death, he stared at Condeza Barajas, scrutinizing the safely established fortress across the barren expanse of desert some 700 to 800 yards away. A sliver of moon furnished the only fragment of light, allowing him to see small sagebrushes dotting the terrain. There was no place to hide, and no way to advance on the old basilica unnoticed. He wiped his bloodied knife on the Mexican serape thrown over his left shoulder. He inhaled deeply, filling his lungs with the cool, crisp air of the evening. He slowly exhaled, forcing the air from his lungs until he was starved of oxygen. Then, Kincaid started his resolute walk toward the mission.

CHAPTER 30

Without any other choice, Kincaid hiked the distance from the rocky passageway to the old mission in the clear, realizing an expert marksman could easily shoot him in an instant. He held the reins of Cimarron and Sweetwater in his left hand. A colorful, dirty serape was thrown over his right shoulder, covering the Colt held in his right hand. A faint moon, shrouded in the wintry embrace of whispery cirrus clouds, permitted him to find his footing across the desert floor without stumbling on the numerous scrubs and small rocks that nature had callously flung in the way.

Within forty yards of the mission, he saw a guard leaning against the wrought iron and adobe entrance. Within a few more yards, a rifle in the guard's left hand, its butt resting on his left thigh, could be detected. The Mexican guard casually watched as Kincaid approached.

The Mexican bolted upright from his leaning stance when Kincaid was within fifteen feet. In the dark, it was difficult for the guard to identify the approaching man. The sentry assumed it was one of the men guarding the passageway. Quickly gaining his composure, the guard scrutinized the two horses as the man approached his station. They were not of Mexican stock. The black stallion was a magnificent beast, worth many *pesos*. Its muscularity was easily discerned, even in the low light conditions. As the guard moved to get a better look at the man in the sombrero, the stallion's nostrils flared. The gray, spotted appaloosa was also a beautiful animal. She was smaller than the stallion, but, pound for pound, she was every inch a suitable rival. She looked familiar, but he could not remember from where. Neither horse belonged to anyone in the area because those inhabiting the surrounding area were poor laborers. Such beasts dwelled further south, closer to Mexico City, at the affluent rancheros. The horses instinctively told the guard to be cautious.

"*Que paso, amigo*?" With the question, Kincaid was close to exhausting the extent of his Spanish language skills. He tilted his head up and stared at the Mexican guard from under the large-brimmed sombrero he had snatched off one of the dead sentries. As he waited for a reply, he scanned the mission walls and surrounding area for movement of any kind. He tightened his grip around the Colt, sensing his guise wasn't going to last. The Mexican guard was studying him. Kincaid stepped closer to the guard, and the guard brought his rifle to port arms.

"Halt! *Como sey yama, amigo*?" The guard's index finger closed around the rifle's trigger.

Dropping the reins from his left hand, Kincaid feigned a movement toward the guard's rifle. As the guard moved to block Kincaid's action, Kincaid thrust the Colt up to the guard's temple, cocking it. The guard froze as he felt the pistol's cold barrel softly touching the clammy skin near his left eye.

"Turn around," Kincaid said in Spanish, pleased with himself that he remembered the command in such a tense moment. The guard judiciously followed the command. Bringing the seven-and-a-half-inch barrel forcibly down on the crown of the guard's head, the guard was knocked unconscious. Kincaid caught the man by his armpits, dragged him to the wall, and sat him near where he originally stood, allowing the rifle to nestle in the crook of his arm. Kincaid stepped back. The guard looked as if he had fallen asleep while standing sentinel. Kincaid nodded his approval.

Standing a moment to listen and watch, Kincaid could only hear the horses' breathing and the wind howling through the mountain canyons. He lingered, waiting for his arduous breathing to lessen. Taking the reins, he moved furtively deeper inside the courtyard, throwing the serape over his right shoulder and displaying the Colt. If they came, he'd have little time to react.

The chapel stood before him. Surrounding the church in a 360-degree circumference were other buildings, including living quarters, stables, and storage shacks.

The tingling down his spine warned him of danger. It was a trick or a plot. He had been told that more than 200 Mexican banditos were housed within the confines of the mission walls. Where were they? If Stetson and Jack were here, he had to find them. His best guess was the most obvious, the chapel.

He released the horses' reins, knowing the grounded reins were enough to keep the well-trained horses stationary. The large wooden doors of the chapel were closed. Slowly, yet deliberately, he walked around the building. The moon's low illumination provided sufficient light to see the courtyard and beyond to the surrounding buildings. Shadows shifted and grew deeper as he peered at each building only thirty yards distant. He couldn't distinguish anyone lurking in the shadows.

The building was deeper than he anticipated, and it took several minutes to reach the rear of the chapel. On the back wall were two windows that were high overhead. A thin ray of light illuminated from each. Below one window was a barrel, lying on its side. Kincaid placed a knee on the barrel and pushed his way up. Stretching, he grabbed the windowsill and pulled himself up, peering inside. He smiled. There she was, and Jack as well. Three Mexican guards were sitting around a small table. They were awake, alert, and entertaining themselves with a game of dice.

Kincaid eased himself down to the barrel. Establishing a plan, he jumped to the ground, made his way to the front of the chapel, and walked across the courtyard to the stables. Unbelievably, no one had come forth. No one had discovered his presence, and no one had seen the guard he had knocked out. He almost wished the silence to end in order to know where the enemy was and to engage them. Lady Luck had always been a part of his life. Perhaps tonight was no exception. He accepted it without question. Perhaps Lady Luck was a gift from God. Even though his thoughts were darting back and forth while attempting to formulate a strategy, he smiled. Here he was this evening, first praying for the first time since he was a small boy and now thinking Lady Luck was as much a gift from God as Lady Stetson. He couldn't think of two better ladies he would have asked for from God.

Looking over the wood railing, he saw the stables ran the entire perimeter of the east wall, easily housing the more than 200 horses tethered there. That answered one of his questions. The presence of the horses confirmed the bandit's occupancy. Pushing the thought from his mind, he helped himself to the first mustang, saddled it, and moved back toward the chapel. He allowed the mustang to nuzzle with Stetson's horse as he moved toward the great doors of the chapel. They creaked as he opened them. He hesitated. He needed a few more inches to slide through. He pushed again. Again they creaked. Finally, he was inside the church.

Debris was strewn everywhere. Most was wreckage from the ceiling. The roof had partially caved in. Many of the pews had been ripped out and thrown against the walls. The obligatory church ornamentation was gone, stolen by unscrupulous thieves in years past. Kincaid found himself hurrying, almost running, down the center of the room toward where the crucifix of Jesus would have certainly hung. Doors were on either side of the sacristy. Kincaid chose the one on the right. As he converged on the door, he saw a light coming from below it. Voices could be heard. He had chosen correctly. He knocked.

The voices became silent. The sound of chairs shifting over the hard adobe ground could be heard. More silence. The door was abruptly thrown open, and the three Mexican guards stood with their revolvers in hand. No one was there to greet them, and they looked at each other. With his revolver, one guard motioned to another to move forward and inspect beyond the door. That guard nodded and slowly moved forward. He peered to one side and then the other. No one was there. The other two guards followed, and they also searched about in the darkness. One of the guards shrugged his shoulders, uttered a strained snicker, and turned to reenter the makeshift jail. The other two laughed nervously and turned to follow.

"*Que paso, amigos*?"

The voice came from behind them. Turning in haste, the three guards found themselves facing a man wearing a sombrero. His eyes just showed under the brim, and a serape was thrown over his right shoulder. The light coming from the jail cell behind them lit his face. His dark stubble initially gave him the appearance of being one of their own. Then he smiled, and they recognized he was a gringo. They started for their guns, but the gringo moved quicker. The Colt came from beneath his serape, striking the center guard in the base of the chin as the gun swung upward and broke the guard's jaw. Stopping the upward momentum of the Colt, Kincaid brought it down powerfully, striking the guard to his right on top of the head near the hairline. A clear sound of his cranium cracking shattered the sound of scuffling. The guard to the left leveled his revolver at Kincaid. He smiled broadly.

Surrendering himself, Kincaid put his hands in the air.

The guard motioned for Kincaid to turn over the Colt, which was held high over their heads. The guard was cautious, having witnessed the damage done by the swirling gun. Kincaid allowed the gun to droop in his hand, dangling from the trigger guard on his trigger finger. The guard focused on the gun. As he reached for it, Kincaid kept it high, forcing the guard to move close to him. As the guard reached for the pistol, Kincaid jabbed the guard in the solar plexus. The guard gasped as he took the blow. His attention was now riveted on Kincaid, who was staring him in the eyes.

Kincaid could smell his stale, odious body odor as he forcibly twisted and pushed the knife. A haze formed over the guard's eyes as he exhaled one last time. Then his lifeless body slumped to the ground.

CHAPTER 31

"Warm tonight," Jake mentioned to JJ as he stepped onto the covered porch encircling the house. The Rangers had rented rooms at the old, whitewashed, two-story hostel south of town. The paint was peeling. The roof needed repairs, and the window shutters needed to be rehung. The outcropping of several buildings, including the barn, were in similar condition. It was perfect. No one in their right mind would pay good money for these surroundings. Thus, no one would bother them as they all waited for Bison to make a decision on their next move.

Leaning back in his chair, whittling a piece of oak that had fallen from the large tree in the front yard, JJ didn't respond. Jake pulled up a chair and sat down.

"Hate this waiting around," Jake said. "What's it been now, couple days?"

"Seems a lot longer to me," JJ said without looking up from his whittling.

Tex walked onto the porch to cool down from the heat. "What's got into Bison? Not the same man I rode with years ago."

The Rangers had become morose and irritable. The waiting was rubbing them raw. Bison had decided that staying in El Paso was only welcoming trouble. He told them that there'd be a time when someone in town would recognize one of them or hear them talking. Someone would eventually pick up on the notion they were Rangers. Bison warned there'd be trouble if that happened. Half the population of El Paso was made up of men on the dodge, riding the owl hoot trail and skirting the law. The most honest citizens in town were the Mexicans, and they didn't cotton to trouble. Bison had said there'd be no telling whose side they'd be on if a gunfight erupted. So, Bison rented the sleaziest rooming house outside the city limits. They were not allowed to leave under any circumstances. When they were given permission to leave, they'd go in pairs for self-defense.

"I mean, he's as cautious as a rabbit in a wolf's mouth," Tex continued talking. "There was a time when he'd have ridden down to Mexico all by his lonesome and single-handedly snatched Wood from that de la Caza fella."

"Wood can take care of him. You got my word on that." Irons walked to the porch from the stables, pulled up a chair, stretched his long legs, and lit another cigarette. He tilted his head back and blew a smoke ring overhead.

"What would you do, Billy, if it was you instead of Bison?" Jake asked.

"Wait."

"You'd what?" JJ sat upright from his leaning position.

"No telling what Bison's up against. We found Wood. It's what we were hired to do. Bison was told not to go into Mexico because of their revolt. He's wired the governor for instructions. So we wait."

"He brought us down here to sit on our asses. A hell of a shame is all," Tex added.

"Billy, you know Jack Wood pretty good, don't ya?" Jake asked as he leaned against one of the porch railings.

"Yeah. Rode with him and Ellsworth during the latter part of the war."

"Damn Yankees," JJ interrupted his whittling to facetiously throw a barb at Irons.

"Don't start with me, JJ. At least I joined the side that won."

"You joined the side that brought anarchy to the South."

"JJ, I swear, you keep it going like this, and I'll…"

"Yeah?" JJ smiled, hoping Irons knew he was teasing.

"Ever see a rattlesnake full of venom in the hot August heat?"

"I get your point, Billy. Just joshing with you for Christ's sake," JJ pleaded.

"Yeah, Jake. I rode with the two of 'em when I first signed on as a scout for Custer. That general went through scouts something fierce," Irons said. He had quickly forgiven JJ for his tiresome banter.

"Talking about it brings back a flood of memories." Irons leaned back in his chair, pulled a drag from his cigarette, and continued. "First time I met Jack and Ellsworth was during the war. It was what? Ten, eleven years ago? Jesus, seems like yesterday. I can still smell the gunpowder."

"Here we go again." Tex closed his eyes.

"Jake, don't get him going," JJ begged.

Irons threw his cigarette on the white-faded porch, put his hands behind his head, leaned way back in his rocking chair, and stared at the porch's ceiling.

"It was April 1865. The morning fog had just melted away, and the humidity was tossing a powerful punch." Irons told the story about Tom Custer charging the Confederate lines and Kincaid and Jack rescuing him. The other Rangers listened intently.

Finishing his story, Irons sighed. "Would you believe that fool Tom Custer got the Medal of Honor for that ride. There was nary a mention of Wood or Kincaid. Don't seem right. But, I gotta admit. Those boys loved riding with Custer. Hell, we all loved following that man."

"Riding with Custer meant plenty of casualties, too. The Michigan Brigade suffered the heaviest losses of any Union cavalry unit in the War," remarked Jake, an aficionado of the war.

"Some say Custer was the best damned cavalry general in that war," Tex interjected sarcastically. "If, of course, you overlook J. E. B. Stuart, John Mosby, John Morgan Hunt, and Nathan Bedford Forrest." Tex spat on the ground for emphasis.

"It don't seem right sitting here and waiting." Jake changed the subject of the conversation. "I know Bison has to wait for orders. But Kincaid and Stetson haven't come back yet, and it's been a couple days. They should have been back by now, don't ya think?" Jake commented.

"Maybe de la Caza captured them. Maybe they're dead," JJ replied.

"What do ya think, Tex?" Irons lit another cigarette.

"Tell ya what I think. I don't like it here. I smell evil. It's a terrible smell. You boys ever smell evil?" They all shook their heads, indicating they hadn't.

"I'm tellin' ya, as God is my witness, we're surrounded by evil. In town here, over yonder, across the Rio Grande in Mexico. Evil is meaner than a rattlesnake on a hot skillet. I say we either ride south and get Wood or just plain get outta here."

"I know you boys feel tied down like a bronco to a snorting post," Irons commented. "I know I do. But we need to listen to Bison. It's best we wait, just a little while more."

"If Kincaid don't come back, what then?" Jake asked.

"I know the man. If he don't come back, none of us would've," Irons replied.

"I'm a God-fearing man," Tex interjected. "Not religious, mind you. But I do believe. If we stick around here, I think it's gonna get worse before it gets better. If you boys believe in God, I'd suggest we all bend our brains around praying. If you got the time, and we all have at the moment, I'd suggest praying while you all have a chance.

CHAPTER 32

"Whoa up there!" Bison put his hands on the reins. He stroked the horse's neck as he looked at Jake. "Where you headed, son?"

Jake tried shaking the reins free from the captain's grip. He stared at the captain.

"Don't think you care none." Jake had listened intently to what the other Rangers had said about waiting, praying, and it getting tougher before it got better. It scared him some. They all were itching to help Kincaid get Jack back, but Bison was preventing it.

Bison reached up and grabbed a handful of shirt, pulling Johnson from the saddle.

"What's your problem?" Bison released his grip as Johnson pulled away from him. "Why you sassing me?"

"We're sick and tired of doing nothing."

"For Pete's sake, Jake. It's only been three days."

"Stetson and Ellsworth. It's been two days since they rode out. They might just need our help. They might be in trouble."

"That where you're headed, Jake?"

"Yep."

"Didn't I give everyone orders to stay put?"

"You did, captain. But no one wants to wait anymore."

"Go down there alone. Get yourself killed. Then I'm requested by the president of the United States to go get Wood. What do I tell him? I enlisted a bunch of Rangers who couldn't take orders and got themselves killed? Because of that, now we can't go?"

"The president of the United States?"

"Yep."

"Captain Bison, I didn't know."

"The boys don't know. The governor told me this is a highly secretive mission. I keep going into town to check the wire service to see if the governor or Washington has orders for us. Why ya think I got half a company of Rangers locked up in an old, falling down apartment house?"

"Sorry." Jake flushed.

"Everyone back at our grand hotel?"

"Haven't seen Justus or Crowhorse."

"Crowhorse was with me. He's outside. Justus?"

"Don't know where he is."

"Go grab Crowhorse, get into town, and see if you can find him. Christ, I told all of you not to go into town, especially alone."

"Maybe he's not in town."

"If he's not here, there ain't no other place to be. Hightail it to town, and have a look."

Jake threw his leg over the saddle and walked the horse out of the barn. Jim ran out and gave Crowhorse the same instructions. Jake and Crowhorse galloped toward town.

Justus Strummin had seen the old adobe church the day he came into town. He saw the townspeople and the small children. All looked dirt-poor. Even though it was Sunday, he found the owner of the general store and purchased some books to take to the church that evening. He knew the gifts would thrill the children and their parents. He continued down Seventh Street toward the church. It was dark, and the last congregation would be letting out soon. It was cumbersome carrying the books with the mandolin hanging over his shoulder, but he wanted to play some songs for the children, if it was permissible with the priest, a Father O'Brien, as the owner of the general store had told him. Passing an alleyway, Justus heard someone call out. Stopping, he looked down the shadowy alley.

"Help! Help me!"

Ambling down the dark alleyway, Justus managed not to drop the books. He came to a dead-end, but no one was there.

"Dang kids," he thought to himself.

Turning to leave, he saw two men blocking his exit.

"Hold it, mister," the man in the soiled duster said. He wore a sullied linen duster that hung down to his boot heels. He had a full beard with two white stripes emanating from the corners of his mouth, running parallel down either side of his chin. The duster was pulled back to reveal a revolver. He looked as if he hadn't bathed in months. The man next to him looked the same.

"What's this all about?" Justus asked.

He decided to drop the books and draw his firearm, figuring he could best both men. Suddenly, a hand came from behind him, covering his mouth. Justus dropped the books, trying to turn around. A large knife pierced his right kidney. His eyes widened as he felt the blade. His struggle became sluggish. Attempting to see his attacker, Justus tried turning around, but the blade struck again. Justus clawed at his back. He moaned as the man behind dropped him to the ground.

"Jesus, Jess, you weren't supposed to kill him. Thought we were going to rob him."

"Told you two that's the son of a bitch who hung my partner two years ago down around San Saba," the man with the knife said as he bent over Justus and fished through his pockets.

"Yep, I knew it," he said, holding up a Texas Ranger badge.

"You killed a Texas Ranger? Jess, we're in a heap of trouble."

Jess Turner grabbed Justus by the bandanna around his neck and pulled him up until they were face-to-face. "Told ya I getcha someday."

Justus moaned. Turner released his grip, allowing Justus to fall back on the ground. Jess picked up the mandolin.

"Souvenir," he said to his two conspirators.

"Nate, Boone, let's go. We're done here," Jess ordered. The three men ran down the alley.

Homer Gee heard the scuffling down the alley. He leaned against the side of the gun store and watched. The light was too dim for him to see what had happened. Homer heard footsteps fast approaching, and he saw the three men running directly toward him. He stepped aside to let them pass.

Jake and Crowhorse, walking past the alleyway, bumped into Nate and Jess Turner and their friend, Boone Jackson. All three men looked gruff, dirty, and startled. The Rangers saw the mandolin. The Turner brothers and Jackson stopped. They looked at the two Rangers and each other. They turned and began running down the street in the direction of San Antonio Street.

"Stop them!" Jake shouted and lunged at Nate Turner. Turner brought up a knee and struck Jake in the groin, dropping him. Jess and Nate continued running. Crowhorse pulled his knife from his sheath and was preparing to throw it when Jake yelled for him to stop. Crowhorse turned and looked at Jake, who was holding his groin. Both Rangers saw the big black man holding Boone Jackson in a headlock.

Jake heard a groan from the alleyway. Frowning, he slowly started walking down the dark passageway. Remembering, he turned and asked the black man to hold his quarry until he returned. Homer Gee smiled, nodded in the affirmative, and squeezed Boone Jackson a tad tighter.

"Wonder what's going on?" Jake asked Crowhorse, who walked behind him. His hand was on his knife as he watched the buildings, expecting trouble. He didn't respond to the question.

"Oh my God!" Jake saw the silhouette of a man lying on the ground, surrounded by books. His worst suspicions were realized as he rushed to the prone body. Justus lay staring wide-eyed into oblivion. Crowhorse leaned down and closed the dead man's eyes. On Justus' chest was the Ranger badge that Jess Turner had thrown down.

CHAPTER 33

"Jack!" Kincaid, straddling his fallen horse, yelled. The reins held tight in his hands.

Jack pulled back hard on his horse's reins, drawing her around as another volley of shot from the Confederates searched for intended victims. Whipping the horse with the reins, Jack galloped back for his friend, back toward the enemy.

Hoping to avenge the death of their fallen comrades, the Confederates broke formation and ran wildly toward the downed Union cavalryman. Their bayonets were positioned to kill.

Glancing at the men running in his direction, Kincaid drew his Spencer carbine from its scabbard. In a full gallop, Jack slid to the left of his saddle with his weight on his left stirrup. Catching Kincaid with an outstretched left arm, he swung him toward the rear of his horse. Using his body momentum, Kincaid straddled the horse just to the rear of the saddle.

"Fire! Fire at will!" Sergeant Nichols directed after the second commanding Union officer was killed. "Let's get our boys outta there!"

"Formation two…Fire!" While the first line of Union riflemen reloaded their muskets, the second volley was discharged at the Confederates.

The additional weight of Kincaid slowed Jack's horse as she turned to escape from the gray frenzy upon her. Squeezing the horse around in a tight circle, Jack fired into the rush of screaming Confederates, killing the nearest one. Kincaid struck savagely with the Spencer's wooden stock, striking an approaching Confederate in the face.

The Rebels took the offense as they gathered inner reserves of strength for their final thrust at the Union lines.

Nearing the Union ranks, Custer, Jack, and Kincaid turned and saw the Confederates charging over the green hillsides. Dead men littered the landscape. Many more fell as Union artillery pummeled the invading men. Heavy black-gray smoke hung low in the sky, creating a morning fog. White streaks of daylight filtered through.

Their comrades cheered as the three horsemen jumped the barrier of hay bales, barrels, and overturned wagons. The three exhausted riders moved to the rear of the Union lines. Dismounting, they slumped beside one of the many white, canvas tents. Lieutenant Custer jumped to his feet in excitement as the commanding officer, astride a black stallion, approached them.

Twenty-five-year-old Major General George Armstrong Custer, called the Boy General, had proven himself on the battlefield many times. While his commanding presence, good looks, and bravado gave his subordinates cause for admiration, his arrogance and quick field promotions caused his peers to dislike and distrust him. His style of dress, aided by his wife, Libbie, who sewed many of his resplendent shirts and neck scarves, was flamboyant.

General Custer worked his way through the tent encampment toward the front lines. His horse's stride and her master's posture made an imposing picture. As the general came upon the three horsemen, he stopped and glanced at the two sitting on the ground, wiping the day's dirt and gunpowder from their faces. Tom Custer stood proudly by.

"Autie! We've done it!" Tom spoke to his brother excitedly, calling him by his family nickname.

"That was pure tomfoolery!" A smile crossed the general's face as he made the remark.

"Look what I've brought you!" Tom gathered the tattered Confederate detachment flag along with their own detachment's flag.

"A return of our division's flag, soaked with the enemy's blood. Better yet, another Confederate flag for your collection!" Tom proffered them to his brother.

"You're not to pull that stunt again while under my command!" The general said brusquely.

"Okay, brother." Tom mounted his horse. "At the moment, Autie, I'm no longer under your command! I need just one more guidon for the day!"

As Tom Custer spurred his horse, General Custer reached forward and grabbed the horse's reins. "Corporal, place this man under arrest!"

Two enlisted men, sitting on cots inside a tent, stationed themselves on either side of Tom's horse.

As Lieutenant Custer dismounted, he replied, "Autie, look there." He motioned to the retreating Confederate line. "We have them on the run. I rallied our boys. It was all in fun."

"You're under arrest for the remainder of today's engagement. Now go cool off. Corporal, escort the lieutenant to the rear of the lines."

"Yes, sir!" The two men snapped to attention, saluted, and walked Tom Custer and his horse away.

Jack and Kincaid took in the banter between the two brothers, knowing they often played pranks on one another. They sighed in relief with the arrest.

"You two!" General Custer barked at the two scouts. "Stand when a general is speaking to you!"

Both slowly rose to their feet and glanced upward. The sun shone directly behind Custer's head, giving him the appearance of wearing a halo. Holding their hands up to shield their eyes from the sun's glare, Custer mistakenly thought they were saluting and returned the salute.

"That's better. Now, what in blazes were the two of you doing out there?"

Jack spoke without hesitation. "Watching over that dang fool brother of yours!"

"I'm aware of that. I thank you both for saving his ass again, if I recall correctly. What are your names?"

"Kincaid."

Custer looked at Ellsworth. "Why, you're just a boy!" Then he laughed because he knew it wasn't unusual for boys to fight in the war. "Well, Kincaid, what's the rest of it?"

"Ellsworth, sir. Ellsworth T, sir."

"And you, boy. Your name?" Custer looked quizzically at Jack. Jack had the same blonde hair as both he and his brother Tom. He initially appeared as if he could be related. The blonde fuzz on his face indicated the boy was trying to grow a mustache—without much luck.

"Wood, sir. Jack R."

"As general of the Third Division of the Army of the Potomac, I am granting each of you a field promotion for services beyond the call of duty and for the bravery shown today. Effective immediately, you're commissioned second lieutenants under my command. Orderly, get these two men blouses with the proper rank!"

"Yes, sir, General, but ain't no uniforms out here, sir. Could take weeks…"

"Then take the uniforms from a dead officer!"

"Yes, sir, General!"

"By your leave, gentlemen, I have a battalion to command and a battle to finish." Popping a quick salute, the general spurred his horse and rode toward the front lines.

"Lieutenant Kincaid, by your leave." Clicking the heels of his muddy boots, Jack made a smart salute.

"Hullo, Lieutenant Wood. Fine day for a battle, eh what?"

Returning the salute, Kincaid jokingly used a British accent. Both roared uproariously, slapping each other on the back as they trudged their way through camp toward the battlefield. Two boyhood friends, having lied about their ages to ride for the pony express five years before and having lied again about their ages to scout for the Union army, were now commissioned officers. They couldn't believe their luck.

Walking to the front lines, Kincaid looked over at Jack. "What you did today, I ain't got the words…"

Jack smiled. "Just remember, you owe me big next time."

* * * *

Lying on his back on the worn cot, Jack heard the scuffling and opened his eyes. The door to their jail cell was open. The guards were gone. He glanced into the next cell and watched Stetson staring in disbelief at the open door, biting her lip nervously. Jack knew his friend had arrived. He smiled to himself.

Kincaid stepped over the three bodies and entered the jail cell. The candles placed on the table in the right corner flickered with his entrance, creating dancing shadows on the adobe walls.

"Ellsworth!" Stetson exclaimed with excitement. "Oh God, Ellsworth." She gripped the cell bars and reached out to him.

Kincaid smiled broadly at her. Her clothes, wrinkled and worn, were covered with dirt. Her white blouse hung loose on her shoulders, apparently torn in back. Her hair was pulled straight back from her face. Her cheeks were smudged, and her lower lip was swollen and cracked. She looked as if she hadn't slept in months, yet she was the loveliest vision he had ever witnessed.

He gazed at the hunched over form in the cell next to hers. Sitting on a flimsy mattress, the man leaned against the corner of the cell. His knees were pulled in tight to his chin. He was curiously watching Kincaid. The eyes were swollen and black. Dried blood was visible under his nose and on the right corner of his mouth. The long, blonde hair dangling over the eyebrows and the thick, droopy mustache identified Kincaid's missing friend.

"You look like hell, Jack." A bit of sarcasm and a speck of worry was evident in Kincaid's voice.

"Long time no see, *amigo*. Thought you'd never show. How the hell are ya?" Jack responded clearly.

"We'll have plenty of time to reminisce, Jack. Time to go."

Kincaid moved to Stetson's cell. It was locked! He turned back toward the three bodies and searched each one until he found the keys. Opening her cell, he was rewarded with a big hug and smile.

She held on tightly and brushed her face against his unshaven cheek. He felt good to her. How long had it been since she held him? She didn't want to let go. If only she could just hold onto him, close her eyes, and be somewhere else far, far away…

Kincaid returned the hug. He could feel her tremble. He squeezed hard one last time and then gently pushed her away. He wanted to hold her, but he knew there would be plenty of time for that later. His focus was getting her and his friend out alive. Kincaid moved to Jack's cell. Jack rose slowly from the mattress, supporting himself against the wall.

"Christ, Jack," Kincaid said as he held out a hand to steady his friend.

"It was my fault," Stetson exclaimed. "Jack killed a guard protecting me."

Kincaid glanced at her and back at Jack.

"Only one?"

Jack smiled at his friend as he limped lamely to the cell door. Kincaid gripped him by the arm to support him.

"Where's de la Caza and his men?" Kincaid asked.

"Believe me, pal, they're out there."

Kincaid drew the serape over his head and revealed two sets of gun rigs.

"Christ, gonna fight an army?"

"Only if we have to."

Kincaid unbuckled one brace of Colts and handed them to Jack. He handed the other set to Stetson. Each buckled on the twin set of pistols.

"You armed, Elly?" Jack wondered aloud when he saw his partner without any weapons.

"They're on Cimarron. C'mon, let's go."

"Still riding that black?" Jack shook his head as they headed toward the large, wooden doors.

Quickly scanning the grounds, Kincaid didn't see anyone. He helped Stetson into her saddle and then Jack. Both were weak from hunger, fatigue, and mistreatment. He hoped they had the energy to ride and fight.

From the corner of his eye, Kincaid caught a glimpse of a man's silhouette standing on the boardwalk in front of one of the buildings to his left. The man was casually smoking a *cigarro* as he watched them.

"They're on to us!" Kincaid barely whispered. With the comment, he threw his leg over the saddle and spurred Cimarron into a sudden gallop. The others followed quickly behind.

"Ready!" the smoking man's booming voice roared over the thundering hooves of the three galloping horses. More than a dozen men guarding the entry to the mission cocked their weapons and aimed at the approaching riders.

"Now!" Kincaid yelled. All three drew their firearms and fired at the Mexicans who separated them from the entrance and freedom.

"Fire!" de la Caza ordered. Several Mexicans fired automatically at the command, but most were already dead, dying, or running from the fusillade of bullets coming from the riders. The three riders galloped toward the entry with a pistol in each hand and gunsmoke twirling overhead. Each repeatedly fired at the horde of sombrero-capped men. The length between the church and the entry fleetingly dissolved.

Lights came on in the buildings surrounding the church courtyard. The riders could see shadows scrambling among the several buildings, yet the only firing came from those directly ahead. That firing was sporadic because one of the Americans took down each man that fired.

Suddenly, Stetson reared back on the reins of Sweetwater. She pulled and tugged, trying to restrain the horse now at full speed. She was purposely diverting the horse to her left. The other two horses swept swiftly by as Sweetwater followed the lead given her. She slowed to a canter while drifting to the left of the other two riders.

Kincaid was rapidly guiding the stallion in the same direction as Stetson, away from their escape route, when Jack slapped Cimarron's hindquarters and yelled, "C'mon, Elly! Get outta here!"

Jack waved his gun and motioned for Kincaid to head for the exit while the Mexicans ran in an effort not to be trampled upon. The exit loomed within yards. Instinctively, Kincaid trusted his friend and spurred his stallion toward the wrought iron gates. Jack was close behind.

Heading directly to one of the buildings with the house lights on, Stetson drew Sweetwater to a sliding stop, jumped to the ground, and leaped the three steps to the covered boardwalk. Stopping, she knelt, looked through one of the windows, and saw a small girl staring back at her. Her precious face was pushed against the glass.

Stetson moved closer to the window and placed her hand on the windowpane next to the small, angelic face.

"Katy Marie?" she asked.

The little girl placed her hand on the same pane and attempted a smile. Within seconds, more than twenty Mexicans converged on Stetson.

"C'mon, Elly! Ride!" Jack screamed at his friend.

Kincaid had slowed his horse to a lope while looking over his shoulder. He could scarcely see the frame of Stetson as it disappeared behind the shroud of Mexican men.

"C'mon, man!" Jack continually fought the unyielding Mexican mustang while attempting to get Kincaid and himself out of rifle range.

For two hours, they galloped at full speed in silence until the horses' frothy sweat forced them to slow.

"Jack, what was that all about? Stetson…Why did she…Why did she turn around?"

"Dunno, Elly. I dunno." Jack shook his head. The turn of events confused him. De la Caza could have killed them outright. Plenty of men knew how to shoot in that courtyard. Why didn't he? De la Caza knew they would ride north and warn the citizens of El Paso. Why did Stetson turn to go back?

The two men stopped on a small hill approximately a two-hour ride from El Paso.

"Damnit, Jack, I've got to go back. I've got to get her back."

"No, Elly. Trust me. De la Caza will be heading our way very soon."

"Huh?"

"It's too long of a story, and we haven't time. Trust me, he's coming this way. You understand me?" Jack was forced to talk over his shoulder as the mustang continually turned and fought the reins.

"Elly, I've got to get back to El Paso!"

"Those sons of bitches have her, Jack," Kincaid said without expression, looking south from whence they came.

"Elly, listen to me. Wait here for me. I'll be back. We'll fight those bastards together. Damnit, you wait here for me!"

Kincaid stared at his friend, trying to make some sense out of it all. They should be heading back to de la Caza's lair to rescue Stetson. Why was Jack so impatient about getting to El Paso? Nothing made sense.

"Wait for me, Elly! I'm coming back!"

Kincaid nodded. "You hurry. You hear me, Jack! You damn well hurry!"

Jack pointed at his friend for emphasis. "Wait here. I'll be back before dawn."

Spurring the mustang, Jack headed due north toward El Paso.

"Those sons of bitches have her," Kincaid whispered to himself as he stared back toward Condeza Barajas.

*   *   *   *

"*Buonas noches, señorita.*" de la Caza stared at Stetson. Several banditos now tightly gripped her arms. Stetson tugged at her captors.

"You cannot escape, my pretty gringo. You see…" de la Caza motioned toward the fortress entry. "Even your brave *Americano* has left you."

"Carlos, bring out the little one," de la Caza commanded.

Carlos, holding onto the child's small hand, escorted the little girl, nervously sucking her thumb, onto the covered, wooden boardwalk amidst the men. Burying her head into him, she wrapped her small arms tightly around his leg.

"It's okay, little one," Carlos said softly to her. He knelt down and stroked her blonde hair.

The men surrounding them were silent, watching. Carefully, Carlos removed her arms from around him and pushed her toward de la Caza.

De la Caza squatted and held out his hand for her to come to him. Little Katy Marie looked at the Mexican leader. She began sobbing. Tears rolled down her cheeks. She stood motionless while staring at de la Caza.

"Come here!" he commanded the small, fragile child. Her sobbing became louder.

"You bastard, leave her alone!" Stetson continued squirming against the men holding her.

De la Caza placed his hands on his knees and pushed himself upright. Walking over to Katy Marie, he placed a hand on her head.

"Everything will be fine, child."

He nodded approval to the large group of men that had gathered. For their sake, he loudly repeated, "Everything will be fine."

*   *   *   *

Jack had the mustang at a full gallop. Its legs moved so quickly underneath him that the sagebrush dotting the terrain was a blur as they rushed by.

"Four hours to dawn," he thought to himself. "Not enough time."

If he didn't return by the promised hour, he knew Kincaid would attack the Mexican army without him—alone. Unconsciously, he dug his spurs into the mustang's hide, knowing he couldn't go any faster without killing the horse.

"An army," Jack thought. "de la Caza was leading a trained militia of bandits the Mexican government hired to take Texas away from the United States. They had exact orders that, if captured, the government would disavow any knowledge of them or their objectives. If they succeeded, Juan Rodriquez Felipe de la Caza would be made territorial governor of Texas, appointed personally by the new president of Mexico, Porfirio Diaz!"

Jack moved lower in the saddle. The mustang's mane brushed his face. His thoughts raced as fast as the mustang could gallop.

* * * *

The Mexicans gathered in the courtyard before the provisional headquarters of de la Caza. Torches lit the sky and warmed the cool evening as 200 men filled the quadrant.

De la Caza waited inside. He waited for his men to grow impatient, which they quickly did these last few weeks. They were bored. They were tired from training and tired from being kept imprisoned at the old fortress. They longed for a good meal and good alcohol. They especially longed for a good, warm-bodied woman to lay by their side. De la Caza knew it had been difficult for them, but the waiting was over.

De la Caza stood before the mirror and primped himself. He admired his good looks, the tailored clothing, and the high gloss on his knee-high boots. He tightened the red sash around his waist, just below the bordello jacket that hugged his physique and made his shoulders appear even larger than they were. He held himself proudly erect. He turned from the mirror and scanned the pitiful little room with the many maps thrown about.

Before long, his dream of becoming the governor of the *Tejas* territory would be realized. Then he would set his sights on the presidency of Mexico and oust the petty tyrant, Porfirio Diaz. He would take back the coastal waters of Louisiana and the Florida peninsula for the monetary benefit of Mexico. If ever challenged again by the United States, France, or Spain, his military machine would conquer them.

Turning again, he smiled at himself in the mirror. The time had come. Texas had become his *tierra de oportunidad* (land of opportunity). From his pocket, he pulled the gold watch his father gave him on his ninth birthday, just a year before the *Americanos* killed his father and mother and took his little sister from their *hacienda* for their own purposes. The watch read 2:30 AM. He marched briskly to the door and exited.

De la Caza stood momentarily in the door frame, ensuring his men were aware that he stood before them. He waited until their voices quieted and all eyes were riveted on him.

He flung up his arms and cried, "*Amigos*! *Mi amigos*!"

The men cheered their leader.

"I bring you good news!" de la Caza proclaimed.

"You see this woman, *amigos*?" de la Caza pointed to Stetson, who was tied against the porch railing.

"Because of her, our plans have been altered! Our plans, *mi amigos*, must be modified for the better." de la Caza spoke slowly and clearly, ensuring his men heard every word.

"Because of this *Americano* and her friends, we move on *Tejas* today!"

He shouted out the last two words, knowing his men would rejoice. Their voices were one as they yelled and screamed. They threw their sombreros into the air.

De la Caza stepped forward for emphasis. He lowered his head and looked out at his audience with a scowl on his face.

"*Amigos*, are you ready to fight today?" Again, he emphasized the last two words.

Their response was exactly as he had planned and exactly as he had hoped. He raised his head with a large, broad smile as his men cheered.

"*Si*, *amigos*! You are indeed ready!" He nodded his head as he spoke, verifying to all that the words he spoke were true.

"Today, we march on El Paso! Tomorrow, we burn her!"

The triumphant screams were music to his ears because he knew the murderous cutthroats were ready to obey his every order. Allowing his prisoner to escape, thus giving him a reason to move up the date for the planned attack on the United States, ahead of the plan the Mexican government had carefully laid out, had worked. Everyone here this evening would verify to anyone asking that the attack had to be moved forward. The plan had to be varied because the escaped prisoner would warn the city of El Paso, and the *Americanos* would arm themselves. Many Mexican lives would be saved for moving quickly before the enemy could rise to fight them. He motioned with his hands for his men to be quiet. Once silent, he again spoke loudly and slowly.

"By the end of this week, *amigos*, we shall pierce the heart of Dallas and take back *Tejas* for Mexico!" de la Caza held up his arms as his men cheered. They shot their guns in the air to celebrate. Again, he motioned for silence.

"Save your ammo for the *Americanos*!" de la Caza laughed. His men hollered and laughed with him. He walked over to Stetson and smiled.

"Today you will watch the mass destruction of an American city and the massacre of your people."

Stetson spit in his face. De la Caza smiled as he wiped the saliva from his cheek.

"Then you, *señorita*, will die." de la Caza walked to the steps of the boardwalk. "*Amigos*! Prepare to move within thirty minutes!"

Turning around, he reentered his headquarters as his men cheered, "*Viva La Mexico*! *Viva La Mexico*!"

* * * *

Bison stood on the porch facing the Rangers. He had just told them about Justus' death. Jake and Crowhorse stood with him as the men loitered in the yard.

"Goddamnit!" Tex took off his hat and slapped it against his thigh. He punted a large rock with the heel of his boot, creating a small cloud of dirt as he furiously tramped in a semicircle. The other men were motionless. Staring at him, they were surprised he had used the Lord's name in vain. It was Tex who had talked about praying to the Lord just a few hours ago. The stress of waiting and doing nothing had whittled all of their patience.

"That's it with me, Jim. No more waiting around," Tex announced.

"Me, too," JJ added.

"I'm asking you not leave. We've got work to do here," Bison reasoned.

"We ain't leaving. We're headed into town. If those two men are still there, they'll swing from the nearest pole," Tex proclaimed as he checked his revolvers and put them back in his holsters. JJ pulled his firearm, opened the cylinder gate, and spun the cylinder, ensuring it was fully loaded. He pulled a .45 caliber bullet from the loop of his gun belt and inserted the sixth bullet. He, like most men on the plains, usually loaded only five rounds. For safety, he left the firing pin resting on an empty cylinder. Not only was an accidental discharge embarrassing, it could prove fatal.

"Count me in," Irons inserted.

The men started toward the barn and their horses when Bison called to them. "Those men have probably left town."

"Then we'll hang the one in jail," Tex yelled over his shoulder.

Halfway to the barn, JJ stopped. "Hold up a minute, boys."

The men stopped behind him.

"Hold up for what?" Tex asked.

JJ turned and looked at the others. "Maybe we should wait."

"Get the hell out of my way." Tex slid by JJ and continued walking toward the barn.

"Tex, I'm willing to fight tooth and nail, just like you. But we're here on account of Bison. He's ramrodding this outfit."

"Bison can't make a decision. We've got to make one ourselves," Tex replied.

"Hold on there." Bison stepped from the porch and approached the Rangers. "Folks higher up than me are making these decisions. We ride for them until I say otherwise."

"Make a decision. Fight or wait," Tex demanded.

Bison searched the faces of each Ranger. He shrugged. "I don't want to lose anymore Rangers to this town. We found Wood. Some decisions have to be made about getting him out of Mexico."

"One last time, fight or wait," Tex insisted.

"We gotta wait," Bison stood erect as he addressed the men.

"We're leaving,'" JJ announced.

"If you go against me, you go against the governor of Texas and folks in Washington. If you boys go into town and lynch a man, you'll unravel everything. I can't let it play out like this," Bison said stoically as his hand rested on his pistol grip.

"I'll back your play, captain," Jake stepped from the porch and stood next to Bison, facing the three Rangers.

Crowhorse grunted, walked down the porch's two steps, and joined Bison and Johnson.

Tex, JJ, and Irons looked at each other.

"I'll not fight a Ranger," JJ proclaimed.

"Reckon we wait," Tex said resignedly.

CHAPTER 34

De la Caza exited his quarters exactly at the half hour. His men had prepared well and were waiting. A silence fell over the courtyard as de la Caza walked into the midst of his army. The American woman stood in the center. Her wrists were bound in front of her. He saw her watching him as he approached.

"Arrogant and foolish," he thought, "standing so proud and staring at me."

She defied him. For that, he hated her. Carlos Flores was to her right.

"Carlos, we leave at once." He glanced at the woman and then back at Flores. "She walks."

"Juan, she will slow us down. We will never reach El Paso by sunrise."

"I can ride," she whispered. Her apprehensive voice belied her unflinching countenance.

"There are no horses for you to ride, *señorita*. You must walk," de la Caza spat back.

"I can ride my horse."

"Your horse?" de la Caza questioned.

"The appaloosa."

"Of course, a magnificent animal. Excellent. Carlos, bring us the appaloosa."

Flores shouted an order to one of the other soldiers. Momentarily, the man appeared with Sweetwater.

"She is a most beautiful horse, *señorita*." de la Caza looked at Stetson and back at the horse. He ran his hand over the moist nose of the horse as he drew a five-inch bladed knife from a sheath on his belt.

"My apologies, *señorita*." de la Caza plunged the knife into the horse's chest. The appaloosa bleated loudly, rose up on its hind legs, and pawed the night air.

As the front hooves reached the ground, de la Caza struck again with the knife, severing an artery. Stetson screamed and kicked away from the men standing near her. She moved closer to her beloved horse. The horse fell onto its side. Crying, Stetson threw herself down and put her head close to the head of the fallen horse, softly saying she was sorry.

"Again, *señorita,* you walk." de la Caza turned to Flores. "Have the men mount."

* * * *

De la Caza sat on his magnificent, purebred, white Tennessee Walker, a gift from Regaldo Bustamante, the Mexican secretary of war and a distant cousin on his father's side. The horse was more than sixteen hands high. Its white tail hung within inches of the ground while the ivory mane draped gracefully over the thick, muscular neck. According to many of the ranchero owners, the horse was the swiftest in all of southern Mexico. Silver conchos adorned the saddle and bridle.

De la Caza wore black cavalry boots adorned with silver inlaid spurs and black silver-spotted spur straps. Tight, black, riding trousers with a red stripe running down the outside seam of each pant leg were tucked into the top of his boots. Around his waist were a twin set of engraved, ivory-handled, .45 caliber Schofield revolvers, a gift from a woman who had long since escaped his memory. She knew he had a fascination with firearms, and these top-break revolvers were made for a mounted fighting man. They could be quickly unloaded with all six spent cartridges extracted at once with a simple unlatching of the barrel. Their ingenuity pleased him, and he believed them to be superior to the Colt.

A blue bolero-style military jacket partially covered his silk, crimson shirt. A flowing yellow crêpe de chine bandanna embroidered with black stars hung around his neck. It was knotted with a handmade silver slide in the shape of a sombrero. Lastly, even though he hated hats, especially Mexican sombreros, he wore a black hat with a four-inch flat crown and a five-inch brim cinched snuggly under his chin by a braided horsehair string.

De la Caza turned in his saddle to admire the group of mounted men who had assembled behind him, 200 total. He smiled. The men looked like the ragtag ruffians they were. They were not the punctilious military men he had wanted to lead into combat. Yet, these men were twice the men of any government-trained militia the Mexican army had ever produced. To his left rear, Carlos Flores had half the men under his command. To his right rear, Miguel Ignacio had the other half. Both men were deserving of the command given them, and their pride showed on their faces as each man gave de la Caza the signal that they were ready for the *jornado* into Texas. With a wave of his arm, de la Caza signaled his men to move out. With a slight nudge of his knees, his purebred warhorse pranced from the courtyard of the once famed and now antiquated fortress, the mission that had served him and his men well.

In the rear, one of the banditos on horseback led Stetson, a leather rope tied around her neck, as she walked. With each step, Stetson could feel the yank of the rope on her neck. Katy Marie sat on the rear of the next horse. Her thick, blonde hair bobbed with each horse's step. She was tied at the waist to the saddle to prevent her from falling. Katy Marie held tightly onto the raggedy doll that Stetson had found in the family's Conestoga wagon and had kept in her saddlebag.

Heading north through the passageway, de la Caza estimated the time they would arrive at the southern section of El Paso would be just after dawn, just as the city was waking. He wished the citizens of El Paso could wake to the sounds of a trumpeter playing "*Que Vasta*" and then "*Deguello*." This last melody, played the final, decisive day that General Santa Anna and his army besieged the Alamo, signaled the general's steadfast resolve to give the defenders no quarter. He promised that every man, woman, and child within the old mission would be put to the sword. De la Caza had forgotten that small detail. Nodding approval to himself, he would ensure they had a trumpet upon entering Dallas.

* * * *

Jack galloped into El Paso, still asleep in the early morning hours, and headed for the telegraph office. Upon his initial arrival in town, it was one of the first buildings he had purposely become aware of. Had it only been two weeks since he'd arrived in El Paso with a mandate from the Treasury Department to uncover any counterfeit activity? And what he had discovered: Mexico's covert mission to devalue the dollar along the Texas border and drive local businesses into bankruptcy plus the assembly of thousands of armed Mexicans along the border to attack and destroy key towns, ultimately seizing Dallas and holding her for ransom. Mexico would barter the thousands of Americans taken prisoner for Texas. Yet, he knew de la Caza would take few prisoners. His mission was to humiliate the United States government with the death of hundreds of innocent families, knowing the United States' inability to swiftly counterattack and prevent his wholesale killing. The American president would be compelled to petition the

Mexican president to stop the bloodshed and would be coerced, by a collective national outcry, to turn Texas over to Mexico to save the lives of the American prisoners. Such action would destroy the presidency, preventing President Grant from seeking an unprecedented third term.

De la Caza's destruction of El Paso would signal those waiting along the border to attack key targets. Before America could react, tens of thousands of Mexicans living within Texas would aid their country to oust the Americans from what was once theirs and reclaim Texas. The taking of Texas meant the United States' loss of railroads, cattle, and oil. It would all belong to Mexico and fuel Porfirio Diaz' cause. The Americans would be at a loss to stop him without another war that the United States could not afford.

At the telegraph office, Jack jumped off the mustang and felt the pain shoot in his legs as he landed. Hurriedly, he dashed for the door to the office. It was locked! Jack knocked on the door once and then again. Then he cursed under his breath as he knocked louder a third time.

"Your hoss is plum tuckered out, mister. You just about killed him."

Jack turned at the sound of the voice and saw an enormous black man wearing blue overalls standing next to the mustang. Jack squinted at the man.

"Hey, you," Jack said. "Hey! Look at me!"

The black man dropped the left rear hoof he was studying and looked up. He momentarily froze, studying the man at the door to the telegraph office.

"Homer?"

"Mister Jack?"

"Homer! What are you doing here?"

"Mister Jack! Well I'll be. Mister Ellsworth find you, did he?" Homer stepped onto the boardwalk and walked to Jack. He towered over him.

"Yeah, Elly found me, Homer," Jack said quizzically.

"Hold on, Homer."

Jack turned around and kicked at the door several times. He then jammed his elbow in the door's window. He broke the glass, reached inside, and tugged at the knob.

"Excuse me, Mister Jack," Homer said as he reached around Jack, took hold of the outside doorknob, and twisted it off.

"It be open now, Mister Jack." Homer smiled at his friend.

"C'mon, Homer," Jack entered the dark office.

"Hey, who goes there?"

The messenger, wearing nightclothes, carried a sawed-off shotgun. His hair was ruffled, and his glasses hung on his large, skinny nose.

"I need to send a telegram," Jack responded, slowly putting his hands in the air.

"That anyway to get my attention, knocking down the darn door and breaking the window? I'll expect you to pay for it." The tall, wiry messenger lowered his shotgun.

"Put your hands down. I ain't fixing to shoot you."

The messenger moved over to the desk and sat down.

Jack turned to Homer. "Homer, you know about Elly…er…Mister Ellsworth coming to find me?"

"Yes, sir, I do. I heard you in trouble in Mexico. Missy Stetson told me that she and Mister Ellsworth were riding down to find you. She sure was grieving though. Mister Ellsworth left without her, and she was looking everywhere for him. I offered to go, you being a friend and all. But she wouldn't have any part of me getting hurt. She's a nice lady. Don't you think, Mister Jack? They with you?"

Homer spoke so quickly that his words ran together.

"No, Homer. I'm going back for them."

"They in trouble, Mister Jack?"

"Yeah, Homer, they're in big trouble. Now, what's your name, mister?" Jack turned to face the man behind the counter.

The messenger looked up from his chair with his right hand poised over the telegraph. "Paul, Paul Fix. You ready to send your message?"

"Mister Jack? Mister Jack?"

"Homer, give me a minute. I've got to send this message."

"They being in trouble and all. Can I help?"

Jack turned around, holding his tongue. In a hurry, he didn't appreciate the distraction. Yet, he knew Homer was a faithful, good-hearted friend.

"Yeah, Homer, you can help."

"Thanks, Mister Jack, thanks. I'll go get the Texas Ranger man to help us, too!"

"Whoa, Homer! A Texas Ranger? In El Paso?"

"Yes, sir. Bunch of them in town. Dunno why. Suppose to be a secret, or so they tells me."

"Go and get the Texas Ranger man, Homer!"

"Texas Rangers?" Jack thought. "Thank you, Jesus. And thank you Jonah Walsh."

"God bless you, Jonah Walsh," Jack said aloud.

"That what you want to say in the telegram, mister?"

"No, sorry. Send the telegram to the president of the United States."

"Huh? The…the president?"

"Wait, better yet, send it to Captain Jonah Walsh, Washington, DC. It'll find its way to the president."

"Okay, mister. I'm ready."

Paul Fix visibly shook and had difficulty wiring the message that Jack dictated.

"What's the matter?"

Jack leaned over the counter and saw the messenger's trembling fingers.

"I've never sent anything to Washington or the president before. Guess I'm kinda nervous."

"Stand aside, Paul."

Jack moved behind the counter, sat at the chair the messenger vacated, and began typing the message.

"Lord, I've never seen anyone so fast on that there machine before."

"Uh-huh." Jack was in deep thought. The message needed to be encrypted. Jack concentrated on what he needed to tell Walsh.

"Wood, Jack Wood!" the man announced as he entered the telegraph office.

"Just one second," Jack said over his shoulder as he finished the message.

"Okay, who's asking for me?" Jack stood and turned to face the man who announced his name.

"The name's Bison. Captain Jim Bison, Texas Ranger." Bison smiled and jutted out his hand.

Jack eyed the man who held himself proudly, especially when he said Texas Ranger. He was slight of build and in his early sixties. Gray hair was coming from beneath his silver belly hat with a Montana peak pressed into the crown. His face was sunburned, and his gray mustache was long and turned up at the corners. He wore a brace of revolvers and two gun belts with every loop loaded with ammunition. He looked worn and tired, yet he was ready for a fight. His blue eyes were alert and engaging. He wore the serious look of a man who had seen much in his life.

"Captain, I understand you have other Rangers with you?" Jack asked quickly, wasting no time for pleasantries.

Bison frowned at Homer.

"Yes, sir, I do. Six…er…five men." The Rangers were up in arms over Justus' death. It was all Bison could manage to ensure Boone Jackson was in jail and not swinging from the nearest telegraph pole. "Understand there's trouble brewing south of the border."

Bison was disappointed he hadn't heard from Washington or the Texas governor. If Wood needed help, the Rangers would have to stand down until word came from higher up. He just couldn't believe the man the governor and Jonah Walsh had sent them to find was now standing in front of him.

"My friend Ellsworth Kincaid is down there. Know him?"

"I do. He's a friend. What's he up against?"

"Two hundred murderous banditos."

"Hmm, 200. The odds seem about right." He'd given considerable thought to what Stetson had said. She'd been right. Bison gave an expansive smile.

"Okay, captain, I agree with the odds, knowing Elly. Yet, the Mexs have Stetson in custody and may harm her."

Bison's countenance took on a gray pallor. His smile vanished. "They got Stetson? Damnit! How far south are they?" Upon hearing about Stetson, Bison immediately changed his mind about waiting to hear from the government.

"About a two-hour hard ride."

"You know we have no jurisdiction south of the border, son?"

"I understand. But I gotta head back pronto. I got a promise to keep."

Jack moved past Bison toward the door.

"Hold on a sec. I didn't say we wouldn't help. I only said we had no jurisdiction down there." Bison knew his decision involved the fate of his Rangers, their careers, and the fate of his two friends south of the Rio Grande.

Bison turned to Homer. "Homer, get the boys! Tell 'em to come ready to ride."

"Yes, sir, Captain Jim! Yes, sir!" Homer moved quickly from the office.

Jack walked outside to unsaddle his horse. "I'll need a fresh horse," he commented.

"We'll each need several horses for the ride. I'll requisition a few from the stable."

"How'd you hook up with Homer?" Jack quickly walked the worn mustang that was lagging behind Bison toward the stable.

"Homer helped us out in a situation earlier this evening. That man has just been beside himself about you and Kincaid. Stewing something terrible. He told me how he knew you two boys. I couldn't help but take him into my confidence."

"Why all the Rangers down here in El Paso?"

"Investigating my assumptive tie-in with Jonah Walsh is a good idea," Jack thought.

"You," Bison casually commented. The time for secrecy had ended.

"Me?"

"Just as I thought," Jack said to himself.

"Yeah, tenderfoot, you. People in high places thought you got lost. We were supposed to find you or bury you."

"Why didn't you join Kincaid?"

"Told ya, have no jurisdiction there."

"But you're going now?"

"Things change. Situations change. Life ain't as simple anymore. We wanted to help. My hands were tied, so to speak. I needed an okay from higher up to push south. With Stetson in trouble, that changes the situation."

Jack decided it was time to tell his tale and take someone into his confidence, if anyone would believe his story. They arrived at the stables and started sorting horses for everyone, two to the man.

"Jim, I need to tell you what's going on and what's about to happen."

"Speak your piece, boy."

Jack began his story.

CHAPTER 35

A slight breeze from the northwest chilled the early morn. The air felt damp. Once again, impending rain threatened the area south of El Paso. Autumn rode on the shirttails of a cold front heading toward the southwest prairie. Kincaid pulled up the black corduroy collar of his gray duster to protect his neck from the chilly wind. He rambled around Cimarron again and again. He checked and rechecked the bridle and halter, and ensured the saddle was tightly cinched. He tied and retied the saddlebags securely in place. He firmly fastened the Winchester and its scabbard on the saddle. He hung it at exactly the angle he preferred with the rifle butt facing forward. He cleaned his Colts twice. He inspected each cartridge to guarantee nothing would jam the revolvers. Yet, nothing could prevent his agitation and restlessness about having left Stetson.

Jack promised to return by dawn. If it rained, Jack would be late, and Kincaid had decided not to wait for him. Jack commented that de la Caza would be coming their way. Kincaid trusted Jack, trusted him like no other friend in the world. He was smart and capable. But he had questions concerning Jack. What was Jack doing in El Paso? Why had he been in jail? Why had he affably gone along, at least according to eyewitnesses, with the breakout of a Mexican bandito and ridden south to Condeza Barajas? How did he end up in a jail in an old church? It was all too puzzling. Stranger yet, why had Stetson stayed behind at the last moment, risking her life? Kincaid was mad at himself for taking flight and leaving her behind. But he trusted Jack and knew staying behind was certain death. Being alive now allowed him to formulate a plan. Jack was right to continue their escape. But he had been here for at least two hours and had yet to formulate a strategy to free Stetson from de la Caza. He didn't know if or when the Mexican jackal would come. He didn't know if he'd even take the same direct route to El Paso as he and Jack had taken. He could be standing there forever, and de la Caza and 200 banditos could slip right by him in this limitless prairie.

Kincaid felt tiny droplets of water on the brim of his hat. It had started to rain. Jack would need to hurry if he was to arrive on time. He promised Jack he'd wait until sunrise, and he was obligated to keep his promise. But, at sunrise, he'd head south and transverse the area, looking for 200 men on horseback. For a trained tracker, how hard could that be? He smiled. He'd find her and get her back safely. There was no question in his mind. The waiting was driving him crazy, but he would wait.

* * * *

Miguel Ignacio pulled his serape tighter around him. The sombrero kept his head dry while the serape kept his guns and saddle leather dry. He worried about the woman and small child. He sent one of the men to the back of the pack train with blankets for them.

"On a night like this, walking in this wind and rain," he thought, "is difficult enough for any man, let alone a woman. But she's a tough one."

He would have been very proud to have a woman like her. She had stood up to de la Caza several times, and she had shown amazing fearlessness and determination upon returning to help the little girl. He admired the woman and would discuss her freedom with de la Caza after they captured El Paso. Miguel knew that showing compassion and kindness to others who were weaker and in need set a good example for his men. In time, they would learn what true leaders have always known: ruling with a strong fist along with having a good heart vanquishes enemies and captivates followers.

Stetson began limping. Her feet were blistered from the long march. The gently rolling terrain was dotted with rocks and small scrubs that she couldn't see in the dark, which caused her to occasionally stumble. The leather collar had rubbed her neck raw.

She sometimes heard Katy Marie sobbing. The child was tranquil for the moment. Hopefully, she was sleeping, if anyone could sleep while sitting on back of a horse and tied to a saddle. She wondered where Ellsworth and Jack were, if they were watching them now with a plan to rescue her and the girl. She prayed they were out there, waiting for the right moment. She believed de la Caza would kill her and Katy Marie. After destroying El Paso, there would be no further need for them, if there was even a need now. Then she shuddered. She recalled reading that, during the eleventh and twelfth centuries in Europe, fierce warriors would attack a city with the heads of their captors held high on poles, leading them into battle. The horrified defenders oftentimes surrendered from sheer fright, only to be slaughtered later. De la Caza was a well-read man, and it would not be beyond his barbarism to use such a tactic. She pushed the thought out of her mind. Ellsworth and Jack were out there, and they would rescue them.

A Mexican approached her and offered a blanket. She told him to give it to the little girl. In broken English, he insinuated he had another quilt for the girl. Stetson took the blanket and put it around her shoulders. He offered her water, and she drank from the canteen.

The man bowed slightly and said, "From Miguel Ignacio." He then withdrew. He placed a blanket around the sleeping girl's shoulders and disappeared to the front lines. She knew the man named Ignacio. She had seen him talking to de la Caza. The welcomed blanket warmed her. She hoped she had other friends among these murderers when all hell broke, as surely it must. She figured it would be soon…very soon.

De la Caza witnessed the kind gesture of Ignacio toward the woman. He took in a deep breath. Miguel had been a good friend and loyal confidante for several years. He had proved himself valuable both in battle and counsel. The men willingly did as he instructed, and he set a good example as a fearless warrior. Yet, he had his weaknesses as well. Assisting the woman and girl brought needless notice to them. If the men began having compassion for the woman, it would be dangerous to kill her. The men could become mutinous as a result. It was necessary for his men to think of the woman as the enemy. They could not afford to have emotions on their path to glory. Gratuitous death and destruction was obligatory to warrant victory in Dallas. As word spread of the mass destruction of El Paso, many of the defenders of Dallas would flee. As other Mexican troops moved across the border into Texas and carried out the same havoc, city by city, their arrival in Dallas should be met without incident because it should be abandoned. Texas would literally be given to them without further fighting.

He would need to keep a close eye on Miguel. If necessary, he may need to be exterminated during the fighting at El Paso. If Miguel showed the Americans, any American, any mercy, the decision would be made and carried out.

* * * *

Bison bridled and saddled the last horse when he heard the men approach the barn. Leaving the stables, Bison and Jack went to meet them. Bison stepped up on the boardwalk of the feed store to address his men. Homer Gee, who had retrieved the men, joined Jack. Both men stood behind Bison, watching the Rangers group in front of their leader. Time was running out. Jack knew he would be late and needed to head back. Whether the Rangers decided to go or not was a moot point. He had gave his best friend a pledge he intended to keep.

"Tex, you asked me a question last night," Bison said.

"What was that?"

"Do we wait, or do we fight?" Bison replied.

"Think we all know the answer to that one, Jim," Tex said dejectedly.

Bison held himself tall. "I'm standing here right now to tell you...we fight!" Bison emphasized the last word.

"Heeee haaaa! Christ, it's 'bout time!" Tex exclaimed. He looked at the others with a big grin, as if he had won an argument, not knowing who or what they were going to fight.

"You hear from Washington, captain?" Jake asked.

"No. It don't matter no more. After what I learned this morning, I've made a decision. I hope you boys can live with it," Bison continued. "Men, we've little time. Mexico is on the move to retake Texas, and El Paso is the first target," Bison talked fast, getting to the point the best way he knew how.

"The hell you say, captain," Tex said. The men glanced around at each other at this new revelation.

"Men, this here is Jack Wood," Bison jerked his thumb over his left shoulder to point out the man they had come looking for. The men stared in disbelief.

"He just telegraphed the president of the United States. Men, we need to move out fast. Kincaid is holding the line for us until we arrive..." Bison was cut off.

"Kincaid? What's he holding?" JJ queried. He hadn't forgotten that Kincaid was once a Ranger. He had asked for their help and had been denied. JJ, like the others, believed, "Once a Ranger, always a Ranger." JJ stood with his thumbs hooked in his gun belt, waiting for a reply. The others leaned forward.

"How's 200 thieving, murdering banditos. The ones stealing our Texas longhorns and raiding our ranches. The one's keeping us on duty twenty-four hours a day. The ones, I might add, passing out those counterfeit bills along the border," Bison responded.

As Bison addressed his men, Paul Fix, the telegraph messenger, walked up to Jack and handed him a telegram. "You might want to read this," he commented. The messenger turned and walked away as Jack read the message.

Jack stepped forward. "Men, y'all can chew the fat all day. Kincaid isn't down there to save Texas. He doesn't know anything about what Captain Bison just told you."

"Why's he still down there? He was supposed to get you," Tex asked.

"Heard of Juan Rodriquez Felipe de la Caza?" Jack looked each man in the eye. "Well, he has Stetson."

A deathly silence fell over the men. Not one man looked at the other. Instead, they chose to stare at their boots or the hats held in their hands. Tex finally broke the silence as he started loading cartridges into his Winchester. "Damn right, we're fighting."

"I'm going with Jack," Bison addressed the men again. "I can't order any of you to go. If they catch us, those Mexs will skin us alive. If you go, you go voluntarily. I doubt the old U S of A wants us down there anyway."

"Hell, I'd ride down there just to see that pretty little smile on Stetson's face," Irons volunteered, as he also pulled his rifle from the scabbard and started loading it. The other men followed the lead, pulling rifles and checking ammunition.

JJ stepped on the boardwalk and stood next to Bison. "Looks as if the only thing standing between those Mexs and Texas are us. Don't care anymore if we have jurisdiction. If those Mexs are coming our way, we need to stop 'em." He turned to Jack, "Count me in."

"Ain't scalped a Mex in years. Count me in." A broad smile crossed Crowhorse's face.

The men looked at each other. As if in unison, a smile similar to Crowhorse's crossed each man's face.

"Do we have the talking part done? We could've been down there by now! C'mon, boys, this is what we're paid for!" Tex spoke for the rest of the Rangers.

Homer tapped Jack on the shoulder. "Can I go, Mister Jack?"

"Love to have you along, Homer. Mount up."

The sound of spurs jingling on the boardwalk, boots scraping against stirrups, leather squeaking as saddles were mounted and rifles shoved into scabbards, and horses whinnying as they moved into the streets could be heard in the still, morning air of El Paso. Jack, now mounted, handed Bison the telegram he had received from the messenger.

"Anything important?" Bison asked.

"Nope," Jack replied. Bison stuffed the unread telegram inside his wool vest pocket.

Within a moment, Jack and the Texas Rangers galloped out of town, moving toward Mexico.

* * * *

"*El Commandante*! *El Commandante*!" a Mexican scout was riding hard toward the formation headed by de la Caza. De la Caza held up his arm, signaling the men to halt.

"*El Commandante*!" the scout shouted as he galloped up to the Mexican leader, sliding to a halt in front of him.

"*Si*, *amigo*. What have you?" de la Caza asked matter-of-factly.

"Over the next ridge, there is a rider, an *Americano*."

"How many?"

"Only one man." The scout was breathing hard from the ride.

"Only one man? Show me now!"

The scout spurred the sorrel into a gallop, heading north, with de la Caza and two others following. After a hard five-minute ride, the four men stopped on a small hill. De la Caza unbuttoned his coat because the rain had ceased. He turned and asked one of the men for a spyglass.

De la Caza looked through the brass telescope at the man on the opposite hill, approximately 1,000 yards away.

"It is the woman's gringo." de la Caza shook his head in disbelief. "Tomas, is he alone?" he asked the scout.

"*Si*, he is alone. I have scouted the surrounding area. There are no others."

"He's trying to trick us," de la Caza replied and turned to the other two. "Or he is a very brave, but foolish, man."

"Perhaps the other man has gone to El Paso to warn them of our approach," one of the others suggested.

"*Si*, perhaps you are right. There is no doubt that our Mr. Wood has ridden ahead."

De la Caza took out his gold pocket watch. The sun was just beginning to paint the sky a purple hue, enabling him to read the watch.

"At a full gallop, Mr. Wood has already arrived in El Paso," he smiled.

"*El Commandante*, there is little time. El Paso remains more than two hours away. We are behind schedule," the other rider indicated.

De la Caza used the moment. "*Si*, we are moving too slowly. It is the woman. She has slowed us down past our estimation. Go back, and move the men up to this point. I will determine what to do about the gringo. Go now and bring the men quickly."

Both men moved out at the command. One headed toward Ignacio's group; the other headed toward Carlos' formation. De la Caza turned toward the scout.

"Under a flag of truce, ask what the gringo wants. He will say the woman, Tomas. Tell him she is negotiable. Tell him I will give her to him if he voluntarily turns over Mr. Wood to me. Otherwise, she will die."

"*Si, El Commandante*!" the scout pulled a white bandanna from his saddlebag and tied it to the muzzle of his rifle.

De la Caza nodded to himself as Tomas turned and rode toward Kincaid. He would gladly turn over the woman and the child if necessary, if only to be rid of her. He would not have to kill her and second-guess his men's reaction to her murder.

"After all," he thought, "the gringos will ride back to El Paso and die with all the others."

He knew it was a weak plan to get the woman off his hands, but the gringo on the far hill seemed very simple and was becoming very boring. All he wanted was his woman, the fool, while he, Juan Rodriquez, wanted Texas and the presidency of Mexico.

"Different men have different agendas," he thought to himself.

* * * *

The Rangers quickly crossed the shallow waters of the Rio Grande and entered Mexico. Bison pulled the reins of his horse, holding up his hand for the others to stop.

"Hold up!" he shouted. He looked at each man as he spoke the words. "We're Texas Rangers, and I intend to fight and meet the final roll call, if need be, as a Texas Ranger."

Bison fumbled for something in his vest pocket, found it, and held it up high. It was a Texas Ranger badge. He pinned it on his vest. The others rummaged into various bags and pockets. Each pulled out the badge that they had removed upon entering El Paso.

"Captain Jim?"

Bison looked at Homer. The look on his face brought a smile to Bison.

"Anyone got an extra badge?" he asked.

"Yeah, I got one," Tex leaned back in the saddle, rifled through his saddlebag, and pulled out an older, dented badge. Jake pulled out Justus' badge as well.

"Jake, when this is over, you take that badge back to Justus' family, you hear? You tell 'em he died for Texas." Jake nodded at Bison and returned the badge to his saddlebags.

Tex tossed the old badge to Homer. "It's the best I can do, Homer. Wear it with pride. You see that dent? That badge saved my life once."

"Thanks, boss. Thanks," Homer gladly took the badge and pinned it on.

"Homer," Bison's authoritative voice commanded.

Homer looked up shyly, hoping the captain hadn't had second thoughts.

"I hereby swear you in as a Texas Ranger."

With a rousing Rebel yell, the riders spurred their steeds and headed south to meet de la Caza.

* * * *

Two hundred heavily armed men on horseback amassed on a small hill just under a two hours ride from El Paso. The rain had stopped, and the sun began painting the prairie with a sunburst of colors. The precipitation had quickly turned the sagebrush-and cholla-covered plains green. The lupines, brittlebush, and Mexican gold poppies began flowering. The soil had become damp. A small stream, evenly separating the field of battle, ran between the two gently rolling hills, taking the runoff toward a tributary of the Rio Grande River.

De la Caza and his men filed in formation along the hill facing north, facing Kincaid. They waited for the scout to return with Kincaid's request, a request for the woman that de la Caza would gladly barter.

The scout had spoken only briefly with the gringo as de la Caza had suspected. The scout hurried back to the Mexican formation. The wavering white bandanna was held high.

"What are his demands, Tomas?" de la Caza shouted, wanting all to hear the woman was at stake and he could be benevolent and be willing to barter for her safety.

"*El Commandante*! The gringo wishes to fight you!" the scout shouted as the distance between him and the formation of men closed. "*Mano y mano*!" the scout shouted for all to hear, knowing the ridiculous, laughable request would be met with chuckles and scorn from the men.

"*El Commandante*! The gringo…" de la Caza truncated the scout's attempt to repeat the demand.

"Imbecile!" de la Caza said abruptly to the halting scout. "Shut up!"

The scout looked surprised at de la Caza, knowing the request of the *Americano* was beyond acceptance.

"What about the woman? Does he want the woman?"

"*El Commandante,* he made no mention of the woman."

"And you fool made no reference of her either?"

The scout looked down, eyeing the mane of his horse. "No."

De la Caza turned toward Miguel Ignacio and Carlos Flores. Both stood by their leader and, along with the rest of the men, clearly heard the American's request, the request for vengeance and personal battle.

"Prepare the men. We shall attack and kill the gringo at once. Then we move quickly toward El Paso. Time is wasting," de la Caza ordered.

Miguel stepped closer to de la Caza and whispered so only he, Carlos, and de la Caza could hear him. "You must fight the *Americano,* Felipe."

Carlos agreed. "*Si,* you must answer the challenge."

De la Caza gaped at both with a rage neither had seen before. "You take me for a fool, *amigos*?"

He glared at both men. Carlos looked the other way. Miguel stared back at the man who led them, the man who knew so little in gaining respect and leading others.

"Felipe, the men heard the challenge. You must accept or lose face with the very men ready to die for our cause. You must accept."

"And you, Carlos?" de la Caza turned his gaze at the smaller of the three men.

"Do you agree with your friend here? Must I waste time fighting a man we can simply kill?"

"*Si,* I agree. The men will lose respect for you unless you fight this man and kill him," Carlos said as he continued to look away from de la Caza's glare.

Miguel added, "Fight him, and kill him. These men will then follow you into hell, Felipe."

De la Caza thought about the advice the two men who had befriended him over the years had given him. It would not take long to fight this man. Moreover, he wanted the respect of his men as much as he wanted their fear. To surround himself with those who would gladly give their own lives in his defense could never be bought. He would need such men while governing Texas and ultimately taking the presidency of Mexico by force.

"Very well."

He turned toward the scout.

"Tomas!" He shouted for all to hear. "Tell the gringo I accept his challenge!"

Two hundred men cheered their leader.

CHAPTER 36

Waiting for his advisors, Grant glanced over the pile of reports on his desk concerning the Indian situation. The news was encouraging. Within the last two weeks, General George Crook, assigned to the Department of the Platte since 1875, and his troops, commanded by Captain Anson Mills, successfully engaged American Horse and his tribe of Ogallala and Miniconjou Sioux in Slim Buttes, Dakota Territory. A full account of the incident was forthcoming. As commander of the Department of Arizona from 1871 through 1875, General Crook had experienced many successful campaigns against the Apache. Now he'd be required to execute a victorious finale in the campaign against Chief Red Cloud and Dull Knife in the Bighorn Mountains in Wyoming. Crook's presence in the New Mexico area might need to be reestablished to turn the tide against Blue Dog and his Mimbreno Apaches and the recent threats coming from Mexico near El Paso. Grant made a mental note to look into the matter.

The door to the Lincoln Room opened.

"Good morning, gentlemen," President Grant greeted his Shadow Cabinet cordially as they entered and sat down.

"Very early, if you ask me," John Gilmore, the young undersecretary of war glanced at his pocket watch.

"Captain Walsh asked me to call this meeting as soon as possible," Grant nodded for Walsh to impart his message to the assembled group.

"Morning, gentlemen. I apologize for waking everyone so early, but I've received a telegram from Jack Wood."

Professor Carl Upridge craned his neck and leaned forward, excitedly commenting, "You found him, Walsh! Excellent! Well done!"

Alexander Stewart, secretary of the treasury, glanced at the president. Gifford held his hands together, forming a small temple with his fingers while intently watching Walsh. Gilmore stood up.

"The illustrious treasury agent finally shows himself, huh? About time, for Christ's sake." Gilmore never missed an opportunity to impugn Walsh.

"Sit down, John, and hush," Grant frowned at his undersecretary of war.

Walsh shot a menacing glance toward Gilmore.

"Always on the attack," Walsh thought to himself.

"Jack's back in El Paso. What we feared most is underway, gentlemen. Juan Rodriquez Felipe de la Caza and his army are marching toward El Paso as we speak." Walsh let the words sink in before he continued.

"I knew we should have contacted Sherman on this," Grant imparted.

"Estimated time of arrival, Walsh?" the scholarly Upridge interrupted.

"I'm getting there, professor."

"Huh? Sorry, Jonah. Bad habit of mine. Please continue."

"Approximately around dawn, their time, Wood estimates de la Caza and his men will enter the area just south of El Paso. They are heavily armed. They intend to decimate the city and butcher every American by the end of the day."

"Kill women and children as well? What on earth for?" Upridge, as scholarly a man as any in Washington, didn't understand the nuances of war.

"Professor, I believe Sherman called it the Scorch Earth policy when he burned Atlanta. It is to create total terror and hope others will capitulate," Walsh continued. "Upon notification of El Paso's destruction, Mexicans waiting along Texas' border will invade selected cities and carry out the same plan. What I mean is mass destruction and total butchery."

Walsh paused, knowing he had just confirmed the correspondence between the Mexican Embassy and Mexico City.

"Gilmore, have the armies in Texas and New Mexico been contacted?"

Grant knew the answer before he asked it. Gilmore was comparable to a young whelp. He was always beside him and always reporting the exact details of his actions. He was looking for approbation at each and every moment of the day. He was a most insecure man, but he had a brilliant mind. Grant tired of him, yet he relied on his organizational skills and knowledge. The question was asked for the others to hear.

"Yes, sir. Most of the cavalry was in the field on maneuvers. They've been recalled. Unfortunately, I can't get a sizable force to El Paso until the day after tomorrow."

"Two days too late," Walsh's observation was a reminder that urgency was paramount.

Alexander Stewart spoke for the first time since entering the room.

"Mr. President, I believe everyone recalls my statement that our country cannot afford war with Mexico, or any nation, at this time. We'd surely go into financial ruin. It would take decades for us to recover. There must be another option, another solution than an all-out war with Mexico."

"Can we contact President Porfirio Diaz, Mr. President?" Gifford questioned.

"We've tried to reach him in Mexico City. He's not responding to our telegrams." Grant looked tired and nervous.

"Should de la Caza fail in his attempt I surmise Diaz will readily contact you and disavow any knowledge of a plan to attack El Paso, Mr. President." Walsh had carefully read and understood Wood's lengthy message.

"Sir, if the Mexicans take Dallas and if there is much bloodshed of American lives, we will be forced to negotiate the surrender of Texas to the Mexican government. To repeat myself, our nation is not financially able to declare war. It would be total chaos for the United States, Mr. President." Stewart stood firm in his assessment of the situation.

Grant studied his treasury secretary and replied, "Surrender Texas, Mr. Stewart? Not on my good mother's grave," Grant looked around the room. "Gentlemen, I need options. Give me a reason not to go to Congress and ask for a declaration of war against Mexico immediately. Give me just one option. Do not dare suggest that I consider negotiating with Mexico or that dictator Diaz."

"What are de la Caza's chances of success against El Paso, an old city full of gunmen, prostitutes, and saloon keepers, Walsh?" Gilmore asked.

"Depends. I believe de la Caza is going to run into some interference, gentlemen," Walsh smiled.

"Go on, Jonah. What kind of interference?" Upridge asked, with an appreciative nod from every man in the room.

"Jack Wood is headed back to meet the Mexican army. With him, he has the finest bunch of Texas Rangers ever assembled." Walsh was pleased because he had personally handpicked Captain Jim Bison for this particular mission, and he trusted the old Ranger to pick the very best. Once chosen, he'd personally reviewed each man's dossier carefully. By Walsh's own admission, Bison had indeed chosen the best Texas had to offer.

"Jonah, why'd they head back to Mexico? Wouldn't it be best to set up defenses around El Paso? There must be plenty of gunmen willing to fight off the

Mexicans. Why go into open territory to fight? It goes against tactical strategy." Grant asked. As a former leader of armies, he was curious of the tactic to be used.

Walsh addressed Grant's question. "Jack Wood is going back to help his friend against insurmountable odds, Mr. President. It's as simple as that. There is no tactical procedure being employed, just a code of honor among friends."

"Hell of a friend. Sounds like suicide to me. How many Texas Rangers supporting Wood?" Grant asked.

"Six."

"Six? Six Texas Rangers going up against how many? Didn't you say more than 200?"

"Yes, sir. Simple math, gentlemen, Wood and six Texas Rangers against 200 well-armed butchers. Anyone taking odds?" Walsh queried.

"Bravo to them," said Upridge. "All for the sake of Texas and the United States. I don't have the words to express my feelings."

"Well, professor, not exactly for Texas and the old U.S. of A. But, if they succeed, we'll benefit."

Barely audible, Professor Upridge uttered, "Until the day of his death, no man can be sure of his courage." It was merely a passage he had read or heard, a passage about bravery and courage in the West, a salute to the legacy of every man and woman who helped tame the West, a passage the professor had never forgotten.

Grant looked at Walsh. "Why are they riding to certain death if not to protect their country?"

"Ever hear of a man by the name of Ellsworth T. Kincaid?" Walsh asked.

The room grew silent as each man searched his memory for the name. Heads shook negatively. No one could remember such a name. Finally, President Grant spoke up. "Embarrassingly as it is, I must confess, from time to time, I enjoy reading those dang-blasted dime novels. Full of adventure and bravado. I recall that name in some of those stories. Isn't he some kind of cowboy adventurer, Walsh?"

"Very good, Mr. President. Yes, Kincaid has been written about in those cheap dime novels. But he is indeed a real person, not some fictional character out of the frontier. He's also a good friend of Jack Wood."

"Ah, the independent and self-assured cowboy and his shadowy myth, courageous and carefree, fun-loving and loyal, a walking armory and arsenal. Watchful and suspicious to avoid boot hill, yet fills up graveyards himself."

Grant looked quizzically at his friend, Gifford, who smiled.

"Yes, sir. I admit it. I also occasionally read about the wild and woolly West in those dime novels. I'll have to borrow some of yours and read about Kincaid."

"So, Wood and six Rangers are riding down to help this Kincaid adventurer fight Mexican banditos? I don't get it, Walsh."

"Gilmore, it goes beyond that. De la Caza has Kincaid's girl, or, if you will, his sweetheart, as prisoner. Someone Wood referred to as Stetson. They're not trying to save Texas, gentlemen. Those men are going back to rescue her."

Walsh loved romanticism, and this tale, as true as it was, was full of adventure and romanticism. If the dime novelists ever got wind of such a story, it would be a best-seller. Yet this was a covert assignment, as Wood and the Rangers were fully aware. Kincaid would be thusly informed. No one, beyond those in the Lincoln Room, would ever know…unless de la Caza succeeded and Texas fell.

"Walsh, we've had this discussion before and in this very room. Texas Rangers have no authorization beyond the Rio Grande. Their presence in Mexico is tantamount to a declaration of war with Mexico." John Gilmore stood up and walked over to Walsh. "I'll have you and every one of those Rangers court-martialed, if they survive. You hear me?"

"Sorry, John, but they have the express permission of the president of the United States."

"What?" Gilmore glanced at Grant. Grant shrugged his shoulders.

Walsh reached into his inside jacket pocket and pulled out a telegram.

"Allow me to read this, gentlemen."

Walsh unfolded the telegram and began to read, "Understand urgency of message. Stop. Understand necessity to enter Mexico with Texas Rangers. Stop. Permission granted. Stop. Godspeed. Signed, the President of the United States."

Walsh looked up from the message. He was unable to prevent the small creases around his eyes from deepening as he withheld a broad smile. He winked at Grant.

"Gotcha this time, Gilmore," Walsh thought.

Gilmore took his seat, dumbfounded. He was mumbling under his breath.

Grant looked at Walsh. "Jonah, this Kincaid fellow, you know him?"

"Yes, sir, a bit. Heard about him in the war, know a little history about the man, know some of his friends. That's about it."

"Tell me, does he have the heart of a lion?"

"Excuse me, sir?" The question baffled Walsh.

"Jonah, as commander of the Army during the war, I learned a leader must have the heart of a lion to be victorious on the field of battle. Only then, when facing insurmountable odds, will your troops rally and give you the superiority to crush those overwhelming odds. Tell me, Jonah. Does Kincaid have the heart of a lion?"

Walsh thought about the question, realizing Grant was not only asking him about the man. He was asking about his personal assessment of the success or failure of the mission against de la Caza, about the possible loss of Texas, and what the terrible defeat would mean to Grant's presidency. Walsh understood Grant was concerned how this affair, if made public, would be handled in the history books. Grant, ever optimistic, was looking for more than a simple yes to his question. Indeed, he was asking about the future of the United States.

"I know Kincaid well enough. I know Jack Wood and those Texas Rangers enough to say, 'Yes, sir, the man has the heart of a lion, and I believe they will succeed.'"

"Preposterous. Six, seven men against hundreds?" Gilmore commented.

Grant ignored his undersecretary of war. He then smiled at Walsh, also knowing the meaning behind his answer.

"Gentlemen, we have our option. Thank you, Jonah." Grant clasped his hands as if in prayer and glanced around the room. "May God smile upon us this day."

CHAPTER 37

Confronting de la Caza was Kincaid's only chance of freeing Stetson. If de la Caza refuses or sends fifty or more Mexicans in response to his challenge, all would be lost. As the sun began rising, Kincaid could see the silhouette of the Mexican army covering the hill 1,000 yards away. He pulled his spyglass from his saddlebag and peered through it.

He saw the scout with the flag of truce speaking to several of the banditos. They were hopefully considering his offer. If he won the engagement with de la Caza, what then? Without a leader, would the banditos disband? He doubted it. There would be another to take his place and then another. He could pursue issuing challenges until they were fed up and attacked him en masse.

He thought of Tom Custer during the war and his charge into the Confederates to bag a flag for his brother, George. They all survived that brush with fate. He decided that would be his plan. If successful against de la Caza, he would continue his charge into the very ranks of the Mexicans, momentarily surprising them. They would not expect a full charge from one, solitary man. With guns blazing, he would disrupt them long enough to grab Stetson and hightail it out alive. He knew it was a terrible plan, but it was the best he could come up with.

Peering through his spyglass, he continued to observe the enemy. They were not as orderly as a trained militia. Perhaps that would be to his advantage later. He continued examining the enemy's line, looking for Stetson. Then he saw her. She was alive, although more battered and bruised than he remembered. She was about fifteen feet behind a horse. Its rider held a leather lariat tied to her neck.

Kincaid steadied the spyglass. Someone else, a small girl, was on a horse with another rider. Kincaid speculated for a moment. Was it one of the banditos' daughters? Was it the girl who had caused Stetson to halt her escape? Again, there were questions and no answers. Kincaid focused on the line of men.

There was de la Caza. Kincaid remembered him too well. He looked fit and sat a good horse. He was talking to the scout.

The scout turned and galloped toward Kincaid's position. Soon, the rider stopped in front of Kincaid. In Spanish, he said the challenge had been accepted. He then repeated the message in English, saying de la Caza had chosen pistols, on horseback, at a full gallop. Kincaid nodded his acceptance of the duel's conditions. The rider reared his horse around and headed back.

It was an odd habit to repeat what one had done repeatedly, yet Kincaid pulled each Colt and once again inspected each, ensuring both were loaded with six .45 caliber cartridges. He had now inspected them six times in the past several hours. Years ago, he learned that good habits save lives. He didn't fuss with himself for inspecting the revolvers again. He waited for a signal for the duel to begin.

De la Caza nodded to his friend, Miguel. He then spurred the Tennessee Walker into a trot and filed past his men, waving his hat high in a salute to them. They applauded and cheered him as he rode past. He turned at the end of the line and galloped back to rejoin Miguel and Carlos. Carlos was looking through the spyglass.

"Juan, look at this," Carlos said as he handed the spyglass to de la Caza.

Peering through the glass, de la Caza saw a rider join Kincaid on the hillside.

* * * *

"You're late, Jack," Kincaid jested.

"Yeah, I needed a bath and shave. Suppose you got the situation handled by now."

Jack pulled his horse alongside Kincaid's stallion.

"No worries, you can run along home." Kincaid smiled. He had always enjoyed the affinity the two had shared throughout the years. Through thick and thin along with the highs and lows, they always found a moment to joust with one another.

For several seconds, neither said a word. Then Kincaid turned to his friend and said, "Jack, this isn't your fight anymore."

Jack pulled his horse closer to Kincaid.

"That's a hell of a thing to say."

"Just…"

"Forget it."

They both faced forward toward the enemy. Neither said a word.

Hearing horses approach from the rear, Kincaid turned in his saddle and watched the Texas Rangers file in line behind him.

He remarked to Jack, "Bring some friends along for our picnic?"

"I couldn't keep them away." Jack's voice became serious. "After hearing about Stetson, I couldn't keep 'em away. They're here for you and her."

Kincaid smiled at the men who came to help him. They were men ready to die in the name of friendship.

Bison, sitting on a dapple-gray quarter horse, smiled his familiar smile with his eyes crinkled and his cheeks growing rosy. Like the others, he was well-armed with two revolvers, a rifle, and a shotgun. Two more revolvers were in the pommel saddlebag.

Crowhorse, sitting comfortably on a buckskin filly, nodded at Kincaid. He ran his right thumb along the edge of his twelve-inch bowie knife. Kincaid hoped he'd take many scalps today.

Jake sat on a dun-colored sorrel. His hands trembled. Jake nodded at his friend, hoping Kincaid would forgive him for not coming across the border earlier.

JJ fingered the tips of his mustache and exchanged glances with Kincaid. He gazed across the rolling hillside at the staggering number of Mexicans.

Tex's nervous energy prevented him sitting still in the saddle. He moved from side to side as well as back and forth, apparently talking to his horse. The chestnut quarter horse with two white socks rocked in motion with him. His Colt Walkers hung on his hips like canoes.

Irons relaxed with his right leg thrown over the pommel, sitting sidesaddle on a black-and-white pinto. A cigarette dangled from his lips. He raised his eyebrows at Kincaid.

To Kincaid's astonishment, the last man on horseback was Homer Gee. Homer waved a large hand at Kincaid and gave the broadest smile. His eyes twinkling with glee at the fact that he had arrived to help his friends.

"They're good men, Jack," Kincaid said.

"Every last damn one of 'em, Elly."

"That Homer?" Kincaid asked.

"All the way from Kansas to save our sorry asses. Happy as a little kid pulling a dog's ear when he saw me in El Paso."

"Jack, he's got a family."

"Hell, Elly, they've all got families. Homer can tackle a bobcat bare-handed. He'll be all right."

Kincaid spurred his stallion and galloped in front of the men, nodding at each as he passed them. He stopped in front of Homer.

"Homer, it's good to see you."

"Thanks, boss. I'm here to help you and Missy Stetson."

"I see that, Homer. I appreciate it. But you have a family, a family I care about. Promise me nothing will happen to you. I can't face your family without you."

"Nothing will happen, Mr. Ellsworth. Promise."

"Homer, if something happens to me out there, these boys are going to fight the Mexicans. If something happens to me, I need you to gallop as fast as you can back to El Paso for help. Will you do that for me?"

"Yes, sir. But I don't want nothing happening to you or Missy Stetson." A large tear swelled in Homer's eye.

"Remember, you hightail it to El Paso and tell the sheriff what's going on down here. Hopefully, Jack has warned the town, and they'll be armed and ready."

"I don't think Mr. Jack told anyone in town nothing."

"Watch yourself today, okay?"

"Okay, boss."

Kincaid spurred his horse around, galloped toward the front center of the group of men, and stopped next to Jack.

Kincaid briefed his friend of the duel with de la Caza. Jack nodded his understanding.

"Elly, in case you don't make it…" Jack smiled as Kincaid shot him a disappointing look. "What do you want us to do?"

Kincaid looked over the green expanse of prairie separating the warring factions of good and evil. Kincaid thought about the question before responding. "Get Stetson out of harm's way."

Jack nodded.

Kincaid continued, "Get her back safe to her family in Pittsburgh."

"I promise, Elly. It'll be done."

"One other thing, Jack," Kincaid said as he moved Cimarron into a forward position while waiting for de la Caza to make his move, "kill 'em. Kill as many as you can."

Jack broke out into a broad smile.

* * * *

"Tomas, get the child. Now!" de la Caza ordered the scout.

Galloping down the line, Tomas stopped and reached for the girl. The rider in front of her released the knot restraining her to the saddle. Tomas sat her in front of him and galloped back to de la Caza.

"Stand her over there," de la Caza pointed to an area in front of the line of men.

Katy Marie was gently placed on the ground. She stood there bewildered, sucking her thumb. She was unable to cry anymore.

"Felipe, what do you wish us to do in the event…er…in case you are killed?"

Miguel was the practical one. Carlos would have been too afraid to cast any doubt concerning their leader's success.

De la Caza smiled. "Kill the woman and the girl. Kill these foolish gringos, and attack El Paso. The city must be destroyed today. Do you understand? It is important the plan is carried out at all costs."

"*Si*. But the young one and the woman, must they die?"

"Miguel, if I die, the men will follow you. Do not teach them compassion today. Not today, my friend."

Carlos, supporting Miguel and not wanting to bring harm to the women, added, "But the woman, she is so beautiful. The men would be very sad to see her die without the chance to…" Carlos shrugged and smiled, trying to find a way to save the woman.

De la Caza glanced at both men. "Very well, take her to El Paso if you wish. Allow the men to do with her as they please. Just destroy El Paso."

He had tired of worrying about the woman, no longer cared about her fate. The mission was their priority. He pitied the fools for worrying needlessly about such an insignificant matter.

"Pedro!" de la Caza called to one of the other men in line. The man spurred his horse and approached.

"*Que*?"

De la Caza whispered something to him that neither Miguel nor Carlos could hear. Pedro nodded his understanding and returned to his position.

Turning to both men, de la Caza said, "When the first shots are fired, attack at once. Understood?"

"*Si*," both men answered in unison.

CHAPTER 38

"Ellsworth!" the yell, resonant and clear, drifted from behind the Mexican ranks and over the small basin separating the combatants and clawed at the very souls of the Texas Rangers. The black stallion breathed heavily. His nostrils flared upon recognition of Stetson's voice. He pawed at the ground, unearthing large clumps of sodden soil. His muscular neck bobbed, and the large, raven head moved up and down. The long, silky, ebony mane swayed. Kincaid kept a steady hand on the reins, pulling them in tighter as the large, impatient beast moved restlessly.

The rising sun's crimson streaks strained their way through the drab, gray, portentous clouds of fall. The early morning dimness began to lift. The ground fog dissipated, and the last, final colors of autumn burst forth, giving the rolling terrain a pious tranquility. Moist buffalo grass glistened, and mesquite chaparral gently swayed with the moderate breeze from the northwest. The provisional armies of two nations faced one another. Both were self-assured of their triumph. Both were contemplating the number of lives that would be sacrificed for their cause.

"Jack, we got trouble!" remarked Bison.

Jack glanced at Kincaid sitting authoritatively on Cimarron, restraining the animal with the reins held in his left hand while scrutinizing the enemy lines. Jack then turned and looked over his right shoulder at Bison. The captain of the Texas Rangers motioned with his head toward his right, down the line of Rangers.

Jack's eyes followed the gesture, down toward the arroyo that dipped off to the Rangers' right, fifty yards distant. Astride a pinto sat an Apache warrior, watching the line of banditos. The Apache wore ankle-high moccasins; a long, light-colored buckskin loincloth that displayed dark, muscular thighs; a red neckerchief tied around his forehead; and a Union cavalry officer's jacket. He held a Henry rifle, identified by the brass receiver. Its ornamented stock rested on his left thigh.

"Elly, we got company," Jack said.

"He's a friend," Kincaid responded.

Jack wondered how his friend knew of the Apache's presence. He knew Kincaid hadn't taken his eyes off the enemy. In more than one gunfight in which Kincaid had been outnumbered, it had been rumored, sarcastically, that Kincaid had eyes in the back of his head. Jack smiled to himself, realizing he had read and enjoyed too many of those cheap dime novels about his illustrious friend and the fabled black stallion. He was afraid he was starting to believe them. It was too bad no one would ever be able to write the story of how one man was willing to attack a full complement of Mexican banditos for the love of a woman.

"It would make for one hell of a novel," Jack thought.

"Elly, he's getting in position!" Jack pointed out as Kincaid watched the drama unfold across the rolling prairie.

* * * *

"Miguel, Carlos," de la Caza called over his shoulder, "you have the command, *amigos*. At the first volley, attack in force."

Each man nodded to acknowledge the order.

De la Caza had waited long enough. Time was fading, and El Paso had to be destroyed by nightfall. Within twenty-four hours, word would spread of their triumph. Others situated along the border would strike and plunder their way north to Dallas. Nothing stood in their way of returning *Tejas* to Mexico. Indeed, not even his death. He didn't know the man who had bravely challenged him to a duel. He was unaware of the gringo's abilities as a horseman or *pistolero*. Yet he had never met his equivalent in combat. He had fought many a duel, ordinarily over a woman, with men reputed to be his equal or better. All suffered the consequences. Now 200 banditos faced a half-dozen Texas Rangers. It was suicidal for the Rangers to challenge them to open combat. Regardless of the gringo's success or failure in this inescapable duel, El Paso would be destroyed, and *Tejas* would be surrendered to Mexico within the week.

De la Caza repositioned his gun belt, secured the placement of both pistols, took a deep breath, and spurred his Tennessee Walker.

"Here he comes!" Bison exclaimed unnecessarily.

Kincaid waited and watched, measuring the gait of the muscular horse and the subtle movements of its rider. Jack glanced at his friend nervously, wondering when he'd make his move to meet his opponent.

Within an instant, Kincaid was gone. The black stallion was in a full gallop.

The Texas Rangers and Jack stared in amazement at the speed of the powerful black beast. Its hind quarters clearly lifted the two in the air, as if the horse had wings to spread.

Bison moved next to Jack.

"At my signal, captain," Jack said.

"On my command, men!" Bison shouted to his men.

The men automatically stiffened at Bison's voice. They had fought their own battles over the years. Now each prayed their trained instincts, skill, and pervasive luck would carry them through what lay ahead.

"Jake, stay close by me." JJ and Jake had developed a kinship over the past week, and JJ wanted to preserve Bison's policy of two men together, covering each other's backside. Jake shook his head. His hands trembled.

Kincaid moved swiftly across the expanse of prairie as he measured the distance from the small stream separating the opposing forces. The stream had been exactly equidistant from the banditos and Rangers. But the black stallion was moving much quicker than de la Caza's horse. Kincaid figured they'd have to jump the stream that would be within pistol range of a good marksman. If they stumbled or faltered, an accurate, quick shot would allow de la Caza to declare a swift, decisive victory in the duel.

The terrain raced by. The hooves of the black stallion were a blur to those watching from a distance. Riding in a straight line was impossible for either rider because bushes, cactuses, and rocks stood in their way. The stream flashed before them, and Kincaid tightened his calves against Cimarron. The stallion soared into the air without hesitation, gracefully flying over the creek.

Wrapping the reins around the saddle's pommel, de la Caza drew both pistols. He had never seen a rider and horse as nimble as his opponent. De la Caza marveled at their speed and agility. He withheld his fire. Waiting, he wanted to get closer to his adversary, wishing to see the grimace of the man he was about to kill and witness his bewilderment as he was shot down.

They quickly came together, and de la Caza saw his antagonist's stern expression. As if a fog had lifted from his eyes, de la Caza recognized his challenger as the man who had rescued the little Apache girl, the daughter of Blue Dog, several years ago from the Mexican encampment hidden deep in the Sierra Madre

Mountains. De la Caza dug his spurs needlessly into horseflesh as his animosity overpowered him. His emotions were blurred in passion and fury.

Kincaid held a Colt in each hand. The reins were now hanging loose over the saddle's pommel. Both men moved their steeds admirably toward the other with small nuances of leg pressure and spur. The span between the two riders vanished, yet both men withheld their fire.

The combatants watched each other's subtleties of gunplay. Their thumbs flexed to pull back the hammers of each revolver. The index finger of each hand tightened around the trigger. The hand contracted around the pistol grip. Their eyes narrowed, their jaws tensed, and their arms stretched out in order to aim their firearms. Then, without further hesitation, both men fired simultaneously.

Each man stared at the other. Both expected the other to tumble from his saddle. As they glided past one another, each craned his neck to observe the other.

"Now!" Jack yelled after the exchange of gunshots, spurring his horse into action.

"Charge!" Bison's command was distinct and audible to the Rangers behind him. Bison had issued the command many times during the Civil War. There were times when he led desperate men against insurmountable odds. Most of his Rangers had experienced a cavalry charge against opposing forces, and he was grateful for their experience, knowing the thrill and horror of a charge was indescribable.

Stetson watched and waited, praying Ellsworth hadn't been hit.

The line of Mexican banditos waited as well, having forgotten de la Caza's instructions to engage the Americans upon the discharge of weapons.

Stetson saw Pedro, the man de la Caza had spoken with last, moving forward. He pulled a machete from its sheath and tugged at the reins of his horse. He raced down the line of horses and men. Stetson's eyes followed the intended direction of the galloping horse and saw little Katy Marie standing alone.

"No!"

Her shout was a guttural, unnatural bellow. She moved instantly, without thinking or knowing how she'd save the child. She ran toward the rider holding her bondage as he watched the duel with the others. As she leaped and vaulted the horse's hindquarters, she put a stunt she had practiced so many times during her riding lessons in school so many years ago into play.

She landed behind the surprised Mexican. She threw the lariat around his neck and pulled. The Mexican was strong and cursed as he jerked, almost pulling her off the horse. She pulled a bowie knife from the Mexican's waistband and shoved it deep between his ribs. She then pulled and shoved again. She cut the lariat from around her throat, pushed the inert rider from the saddle, and thrashed her heels against the sides of the horse while pulling herself into the saddle. Slapping the horse on either side of the neck with the reins, she was instantly in a gallop, bounding toward the girl. She knew there wasn't time to save her. She saw Pedro advancing on Katy Marie, the machete held high overhead.

Pedro had ridden with de la Caza for twelve years. In that time, they had formed a demonic association. De la Caza depended on Pedro for the more grisly and offensive tasks, which Pedro faithfully carried out. The simple command to kill the child was an easy bidding. Beheading an enemy was a task he'd carried out many times over the years for de la Caza. He knew the others were well-versed with his skill and did not approve of him, but they feared him, and their fear pleased de la Caza.

Pedro was almost within striking distance of the girl. She stood steadfast while watching him advance.

"This will be a clean kill," he thought to himself, "a perfect decapitation as long as the child does not move." He extended the machete high over his head...

The .44-90 slug hit Pedro hard, slapping him back out of the saddle. His chest cavity mushroomed, and he was dead before his lifeless body hit the ground.

The man peered over the rifle's tang-mounted, Creedmoor sight as the Mexican fell from his saddle. He gave the sign of the cross, quickly saying a prayer. He chambered another cartridge in the Sharps. It would be a busy day.

"Bless the Lord," the man said aloud.

The Mexicans could not wait any longer. Miguel issued a sepulchral command to attack. They began their forward advance against the galloping Texas Rangers.

While Carlos and his charge of men swept around the Rangers' right for a flanking maneuver, Miguel moved directly at them, attempting to catch the *Americanos* in a viselike grip.

Galloping toward the banditos, the Rangers' peripheral vision discerned movement on their right. Seconds later, Blue Dog and more than 200 Apache warriors wailed a war cry as they sprinted past the Texas Rangers.

Homer saw them first and shouted an unnecessary warning because the target of the Apache was banditos, not Americans. The swift Indian ponies quickly overtook the Rangers. The warriors' rifles, bows, and arrows worked relentlessly. A cloud of dust enveloped the Rangers as the Apaches rode past them toward the Mexicans.

"Look at 'em!" Jake yelled at JJ. "Yee-haw!"

"C'mon, Petey!" Tex shouted at his horse. Digging his spurs into horseflesh, he advanced rapidly toward the Mexicans. His cap-and-ball .44 caliber Walker Colts were blazing away. The Indians continued their own barrage, creating hesitancy among the oncoming banditos.

Tex rode hard. A determined expression was on his weathered face. He resolved to penetrate the enemy's line before the Apache. For him, it was a contest, a matter of pride of who breached the line first.

CHAPTER 39

The Rangers and Apaches hurled toward the Mexicans. Alone in the center of the battlefield, astride the standing Tennessee Walker, was de la Caza. He was confused, wondering where the Indians had come from. Why were the Texas Rangers moving so slowly?

"Damn the humidity," he thought.

Feeling light-headed, he pulled at his jacket to remove it. Attempting to unbutton it, he felt a cool dampness. His head slowly rolled down, and he saw blood. Sluggishly, he turned to look at his men. He pulled at the waistcoat until it was around his shoulders. Looking down again, he put a finger each in the two bullet holes surrounding his right breast. Gently applying pressure, his fingers went deeper. He laughed. Where was the gringo?

"Probably dead," he thought.

Pulling his fingers from the wounds, the blood oozed. His body jerked, and he grabbed onto the pommel to prevent himself from falling. He wanted off his horse, but his legs wouldn't move. He saw the Apaches coming directly at him. He tried to spur his horse, but he couldn't. His eyes were heavy and half-closed. He leaned to the side, looking for a way to dismount. The ground was out of focus, as if it was shifting beneath him. Leaning further until his torso was parallel with the ground, he heard an Apache war cry. Looking up, he saw Blue Dog.

Stetson dismounted and shielded Katy Marie. The swirling cloud of dust obstructed her view, but she could hear gunfire and the Apache's shrill cry. She thought she could feel the ground shake. For now, she and the child were the least of the banditos' worries.

Kincaid headed directly toward the center of the Mexican line. He knew Stetson was somewhere off to his left. He wondered about de la Caza. Had he hit him? If he had been a betting man, he would have bet his life savings, which wasn't much, that both bullets hit their target, almost dead center of the upper torso. He hunkered down behind the neck of the swiftly moving stallion. He heard the single shot of a Sharps rifle. A piercing war cry from the Apaches followed. He knew he and the Rangers had received help. Once again, he thanked the good God Almighty.

The Apaches rode straight into the line of banditos, fighting furiously. In hand-to-hand combat, no man was the Apache equal. Behind the Apache, the Texas Rangers punched a hole into the maddening expanse of confusion. Jake and JJ circled around the Mexicans' left to ensure the Apache weren't outflanked. They ran straight into Carlos Flores' command.

Crowhorse swept in from the right flank, firing his Winchester at point-blank range. Sliding from his horse with his bowie knife in hand, Crowhorse chose to fight hand-to-hand.

Tex had beaten the Apache to the front line by seconds. Silently approving his horsemanship to himself, he continued firing at the Mexicans now swarming around him and dragging him from his horse.

Riding the perimeter, Bison looked for Stetson and watched for any outflanking maneuver, clashing into a coterie of Mexicans. Irons breached the fighting and fought side by side with the Apache, who were unmercifully butchering the fierce, fighting Mexicans.

Jack hunted for Kincaid, trying to find him through the confusion. Homer, who hadn't fired a shot, rode far behind. Confused, not knowing which way to ride, his only wish was to help Jack and Kincaid find Stetson.

A horrific war cry momentarily ceased the fighting. Blue Dog hurried toward the center of battle, carrying de la Caza's head. Around his shoulders, Blue Dog wore the Mexican leader's blue military waistcoat. The front was covered with de la Caza's blood. The sight of Blue Dog holding de la Caza's head high, dangling by his hair, put a chill in the bravado of the Mexican banditos.

To the surprise of the Texas Rangers, many of the Mexicans turned and ran. Those who chose to fight met the wrath and hatred of Blue Dog and his warriors.

Katy Marie buried her head in Stetson's leather chaps. Her small arms were wrapped around Stetson's thighs.

"Stetson! Stetson!" Kincaid searched in vain for her.

He saw her through the swirling dust. The black stallion, covered with mud and sweat, slid to an abrupt halt as Kincaid jumped and ran toward her.

"Stetson!" he grabbed her by both arms and looked her over from head to toe. "You okay?"

She nodded in the affirmative and then softly asked, "You okay?"

Kincaid smiled and moved closer to her. As Katy Marie continued clinging to her, Stetson stepped closer to the man she thought she'd never see again. He put his arms around her and brought her to his chest, embracing her. He put his face in her hair and kissed her. He pulled back to look at her again. Her face was smudged, and she had blood on her hands and blouse. To him, she was unconditionally the most angelic, ravishing woman he had ever seen.

"Thank God you're all right," he said between breaths.

She stared at him, overwhelmed with the conflict surrounding them, not knowing what to say and not knowing how to protect Katy Marie any longer. She only knew her man was standing before her. Only now was she willing to allow her tension and fatigue to lessen. She was willing to have someone else be tormented with worry for a while.

"I love you," he said flatly.

She cocked her head to one side and smiled. The three words she had been waiting to hear for so long tugged at her heart. She reached up and ran her index finger down the cleft of his chin. She looked into his blue eyes and saw his determination. To her, the fighting had stopped. The horrors of war were behind them.

"I love you, too." She leaned against him and kissed him hard on the mouth.

"Elly! Look out!"

With Jack's warning, Kincaid turned to shield both the child and Stetson. He knew the life he was willing to give was for them. Bearing down on them was more than a dozen banditos at a full charge. He instinctively drew his Colt and started firing. Stetson reached around and pulled Kincaid's other holstered Colt. She also started firing. Their shots were precise, and seven Mexicans fell from their horses.

Their revolvers out of ammo, they stood with Kincaid shielding Stetson and she guarding Katy Marie. Kincaid drew his Winchester from the scabbard, rifled a round, and sighted the closet target.

"Our Father who art in Heaven…" The man laid on his stomach on a small, rolling hill a quarter-mile away. His rifle barrel rested on the exact competitive tripod he had used to win the competition against the Irish in Dublin the previous year. He squeezed off another round, hitting one of the charging Mexicans.

"Hallowed be thy name…" Another Mexican was blown out of his saddle.

"Thy Kingdom Come…" And another went down.

"Thy will be done." Yet another died as he operated the action of the Sharps with incredible speed.

Kincaid steadily worked the lever of his rifle, hitting those the unknown assailant did not kill.

Sweat poured from his brow. Each bandito the man on the rolling hillside targeted lay in the dirt, immobile. Praising the Lord, he chambered another cartridge while looking for his next target.

Kincaid looked around him, wondering who was firing the fatal shots. The charging Mexicans lay sprawled around them.

Kincaid placed the child on the stallion and started to assist Stetson onto the horse she had taken from the Mexican. An Apache war cry pierced the dust-filled air. Looking up, Kincaid saw two Mexican banditos riding out of the dust cloud, charging them. Each had a shotgun at his shoulder, and the closer bandito was already taking deadly aim over the front sights of the side-by-side twelve-gauge. With virtually no time to react and no ammo, Kincaid plucked Stetson out of the saddle.

Blue Dog slid his pinto between the bandito and Kincaid and faced the man squarely. The Mexican fired the shotgun, aimed directly at the Apache leader.

Blue Dog, blown off his horse, quickly rose and shrieked at the Mexican. With disbelief, the Indian leader was unscathed from the blast. The bandito took a fatal bullet from Blue Dog's rifle.

Those warriors witnessing the event were instilled with fearlessness they had never known. The sacred breastplate Blue Dog wore had prevented the Mexican from injuring their leader, as Blue Dog had seen in his vision. With renewed fervor, the Apache attacked the retreating Mexicans viciously.

The second charging Mexican swept by the grounded Apache chief, bearing down on Kincaid and Stetson. Leaning forward in his saddle for a clear shot, his head abruptly exploded, and he toppled forward. From behind him, Miguel Ignacio looked over his rifle sights, bowed from his saddle at Stetson, and touched the brim of his hat, paying tribute one last time to the fearless woman. Spurring his horse south, he attempted to outrun the Apache.

"Elly!" Jack cried out.

"Over here!"

Through the shroud of dust, Jack found his friends and dismounted.

"Everyone safe?"

Both Kincaid and Stetson smiled, nodding in the affirmative. Kincaid saw that Jack's shirt was bloodstained.

"You hurt?"

"I'll be fine. We need to get back to El Paso. And pronto! Our Apache friends will deal with the Mexicans." Jack never thought he'd be calling any Apache friend.

"The Rangers? Anyone down?" Kincaid asked.

"Dunno. I'll round 'em up." Jack mounted and rode toward the swirling dust. Kincaid loaded his Colts and handed Stetson his rifle.

Jack returned within fifteen minutes. "It's not good," he said quietly. His vacant eyes stared at Kincaid.

Jack gave Kincaid the tally. More than seventy-five Mexicans and twenty-three Apache were dead. Several Rangers had superficial injuries, but he couldn't find them all.

One of the men walking toward them, leading his horse with the reins in his hands, was Billy Irons. He had a deep scratch over his right eye.

"See the others?" Jack asked.

Irons looked around and shrugged.

"Homer? Anyone see Homer out there?" Kincaid queried.

With the questions unanswered, Kincaid and Jack threw themselves into their saddles and headed toward the body-littered battlefield, now vacant from the fighting chaos. The Apaches were following the Mexicans deeper into Mexico.

Toward the southern perimeter of the battlefield, Kincaid saw the outline of Homer on the ground. He and Jack rode toward their friend from Kansas.

Homer sat on the ground, surrounded by many dead banditos, sobbing to himself.

"Homer!" Kincaid slid from the saddle and stood looking down at his friend. "Homer, you okay? You hit?" Homer was covered with blood.

Homer looked up at Kincaid and Jack and nodded.

"They killed my horse. They shot him, Mister Ellsworth," Homer held up his hands to show the blood on them.

"They rushed me. I had to kill 'em Mister Ellsworth, or they would've hurt me." Homer sobbed, visibly shaken. "Why'd they kill my horse?"

"Homer, you did fine." Kincaid knelt beside his friend. Homer had killed ten Mexicans hand-to-hand because they killed his borrowed horse. Kincaid breathed a sigh of relief that his friend was alive.

"Homer, we gotta go," Kincaid put his hand under Homer's arm, but he couldn't budge him. Slowly Homer stood, looking around at those he'd killed, shaking his head and muttering he was sorry.

The three of them started walking back toward the other Rangers.

"You're not bringing those back to Texas with you?" Tex addressed Crowhorse, who had just ridden in and was covered with blood from the many scalps hanging on him.

"I'm taking 'em back Tex. Don't go giving me any grief about it," Crowhorse began cutting away little bits of flesh from one of the scalps.

"Good God Almighty!" Tex turned and marched off in a huff, shaking his head in disapproval.

"Tex! Ellsworth!" Jake yelled from the far edge of the battlefield.

Both men, followed by Jack, Homer, and Crowhorse, ran to Jake. What they saw made the men retch. It was JJ. Kincaid knelt beside the body and looked at a man who was more than willing to fight and die for him and Stetson.

"He saved my life, Ellsworth," Jake volunteered. "I almost got it, but JJ got between us and took the bullet for me. I don't understand why he'd do that." Kincaid thought the bullet Jake was referring to had been a twelve-gauge shotgun blast. JJ's head was nearly completely blown away.

"He did what he thought right, what he thought any Ranger would've done. He saved the life of a friend, a fellow Ranger," Crowhorse commented.

"We'll have to bury him."

"Elly, we got to get back to El Paso. I've got to notify some folks about all of this."

"After we bury JJ," Kincaid said decisively.

"Where's Bison?" Tex asked. Everyone shrugged.

"Spread out. Find him," Kincaid ordered.

The men searched the battlefield, turning over Mexicans and Apache alike to find their leader.

"Over here!" Crowhorse yelled out.

Bison lay on the ground outside the field's perimeter, barely conscious. His right arm hung by a few tendons.

"Jim! Jim!" Tex softly nudged the captain. Blood was everywhere. Bison's face was pale. His skin was pallid and doughy. Bison coughed twice and opened his eyes.

"Hey," he faintly mumbled. Attempting to smile, he coughed up a spew of blood.

Irons examined the right arm. The entire shoulder cavity had been blown away. A few muscles held the arm to the exposed bone. "Seen this kind of injury during the war. Arms gotta come off, or gangrene will set in."

Bison pulled his upper torso off the ground, "You ain't taking my arm."

"Billy, you sure?" Kincaid asked.

"I'm no doctor, but I've seen this kind of injury kill good men. Up to me, I'd take it off."

"Jim, if we don't take the arm, you'll die on us," Kincaid responded.

"Don't care. Just don't take my arm." He coughed more blood.

"Someone get Stetson over here." Kincaid said as he examined the wound.

The men grouped around Bison, talking to him to try keeping him awake. They promised to not take his arm off, anything to appease him.

Stetson and Katy Marie walked up. Katy Marie began crying when she saw the blood covering Bison.

"Can we save his arm?" Kincaid asked.

"Anyone got a sewing kit?" she asked.

Rangers always carried a sewing kit in their saddlebags. In no time, she had the necessary items. She threaded a needle. "We should heat up this needle to sterilize it."

"No time. Do the best you can," Jack told her.

"Hold him," Stetson said as she attempted to suture the nearly severed arm.

Within ten minutes, Bison had passed out from the pain. She sewed the arm the best she could.

"Let him sleep," Kincaid suggested. "Get some shovels."

They buried JJ near where he fell. The men gathered around the mound and bowed their heads.

"He was a good man, Lord, loved by family and friends. He was a damn fine Ranger. We'll grieve his passing. Amen," Kincaid finished the brief service. He didn't know how to express his sorrow. They'd all ridden across the Rio Grande into Mexico to rescue Stetson. One man died, another lost his arm, and others were wounded. He didn't have the words.

"Let's ride!" Tex commanded. He readily assumed Bison's responsibilities, and the others were grateful. As Bison had said earlier, he had leadership written all over him.

CHAPTER 40

The Rangers constructed a travois and anchored Bison to it. They inspected and bandaged their own injuries, mounted, and rode north. They reached the outskirts of El Paso four hours later. Kincaid looked puzzled.

"Looks normal, Jack. You did warn the fine folks of El Paso about de la Caza's pending attack?"

"Wasn't time, Elly. If you'll recall, I was in sort of a hurry."

"Christ, Jack, these folks would have been massacred."

Jack ignored his friend. "I gotta head for the telegraph office. Need to head out right away. Folks in Washington, DC, will be asking questions, and I suspect we'll be needed to explain things."

"Washington?"

"Tell ya later. But we gotta get to the train depot pronto."

Washington? Kincaid had more questions for Jack. He shrugged it off. Jack would tell him everything.

Jack headed in the direction he knew well, mentally reciting the message needed sent to Walsh.

The Rangers took Bison to the nearest doctor. It was almost noon, and the streets of El Paso were bustling. On Fourth Street, they found Doctor Sloane. He said their wounds were superficial and he'd look at them later. He needed to examine Bison immediately.

Their destination was Rosita's Cantina. This time, they wore their badges, hoping someone was looking for trouble.

"Ellsworth?" Stetson asked, holding Katy Marie's hand outside Doctor Sloane's office. "What about Katy Marie? She's going with us, isn't she?"

Kincaid shrugged. "Reckon so. It'll be a hard ride to the depot. We'll most likely be traveling all day and night. It'll be rough on her."

"Wait, I know!" she exclaimed.

With Katy Marie, Stetson headed for the church. Kincaid grabbed his saddlebags, threw them over his shoulder, and followed.

"Father O'Brien, please," Stetson asked one of the parishioners.

Taken to the anteroom behind the sacristy, they waited several minutes before being ushered in.

Father O'Brien sat in a leather chair facing the unlit fireplace. His hair was uncombed and tousled. He appeared out of breath. He stood to greet his visitors. Kincaid noticed smudge marks on the black coat. His white collar was crooked and partially buttoned. Father O'Brien appeared rumpled and unkempt, as if he had dressed in a hurry.

"Hello again." Father O'Brien stood and motioned for his guests to take a seat at the wooden table in the center of the small room. He ran a hand through his hair to flatten it.

"Father, I need your help." Stetson told him her dilemma and solution. Kincaid took notice of the room, as any trained Ranger, or ex-Ranger, would do automatically.

"Of course, I understand. Yes, of course, I will." O'Brien patted Stetson's hand.

Father O'Brien stood. Stetson and Kincaid followed. He reached out and shook Kincaid's hand. Father O'Brien's shake was good and firm. The hands were well-callused, unlike most padres. Dirt was beneath the fingernails.

"They've seen their share of work," Kincaid thought.

Kincaid threw his saddlebags on the table. "I reckon that'll help with Stetson's request."

Stetson looked at him and smiled, knowing the $3,000 they had found in the Conestoga wagon was in the saddlebags. They knew, if they could trust anyone, it was the good padre of El Paso.

Father O'Brien, anxious to end the visit, thanked Kincaid without looking into the bags. Ushered out of the room, Kincaid stopped and looked at the exquisite, finely engraved rifle with the unusual scope hanging over the fireplace.

"Yours?" he asked Father O'Brien.

"An old heirloom. It belonged to a friend of mine who was killed at Gettysburg. His family gave it to me. It's old and good for nothing. I rarely take it down."

Kincaid nodded and accepted the explanation without question. Another quick glance told Kincaid the rifle was a Target model 1874 Sharps, chambered for the .44-90 cartridge.

"This kind of rifle had never seen any usage during the war, having been manufactured almost a decade later," Kincaid thought to himself.

The rifle needed a good cleaning. It appeared to have been used recently. Kincaid took a closer look at the rifle and noticed the tang-mounted Creedmoor sight and the powder smears on the end of the barrel. The sights were also relatively new, thus Father O'Brien wasn't telling the truth. Kincaid read the inscription hanging beneath the rifle. On a brass plate was engraved: "If thou dost what is evil, fear, for not without reason do I carry the sword. For I am God's minister, an avenger to execute wrath on him who does evil." Romans, Chapter 13.

Kincaid couldn't help himself. "Those sights…for long distance, aren't they? They worth a damn…uh…Sorry, Father…they any good?"

"This old rifle is good for shooting rabbits and nothing else. Good day to you, my friends." Father O'Brien smiled and escorted them to the door.

"Thank you, padre. Thank you for everything," Kincaid offered as he left the church, hoping Father O'Brien understood the full measure of his gratitude.

"You are most welcomed," replied Father "Wild Bill" O'Brien, the fighting Irishman, the once famous Texas Ranger, the good padre of El Paso, and savior of souls on the Western frontier.

The Texas Rangers ambled over to Rosita's Cantina. Swaggering into the saloon, they were not surprised to see the cantina practically full. By noon on any day, Rosita's Cantina was flourishing.

"Drinks on me, boys." The gruff, old Texan smiled as he offered to buy a round.

The Rangers, unaccustomed to drinking while on duty, looked at Tex, considering his offer. Hesitantly, they leaned against the bar and waited while the bartender poured each a sour mash whiskey. Irons was the first to toss it down his throat and immediately spat it out. The others smelled the liquid in their glasses and placed them back on the bar. Tex sampled his, gagged, and motioned for the bartender, who was cleaning a pile of glasses with a dirty towel.

"Got any Jack Daniel's Tennessee Whiskey?" he asked. The bartender nodded in the affirmative.

"Nothing less than ninety percent," Tex politely told the bartender. The bartender graciously consented to the more expensive liquor and poured freely. The men held their glasses high. Tex made a toast.

"To life," Tex said, holding his glass high. He'd been in many fights in his long life, but he planned this to be his last. In the past few days, he realized he was getting too old.

"To a woman gently moaning," Irons gladly volunteered. The others laughed at the remark.

Tex looked at Crowhorse and Jake. Neither had spoken. "Boys, make a toast."

Crowhorse was wondering how much money his scalps were worth. Not in the habit of making salutary toasts, he thought for a moment and then raised his glass, "To a sharp knife…and…hmmm…thin skin." The Rangers rolled their eyes, but they raised their glasses.

The men clang their glasses together and tossed the drinks down their throats. Each loudly slammed their glass on the bar top, signaling another round was in order.

"Jake? You're next." Irons wanted to make sure they all proposed a toast.

"Look at me, would ya?" Jake said. He held his hands out in front of him with his palms facing downward and his fingers spread apart.

The others turned from the bar and stared at Jake.

"I ain't shaking! Look, boys, I ain't shaking anymore."

"To Jake," Crowhorse proclaimed.

"Just the same, I'd like to drink one for JJ, a good Ranger and a good friend," Jake said sadly. The men solemnly raised their glasses.

"To JJ."

The Rangers tossed back another, slamming their glasses on the bar top again. Irons excused himself, ran up the flight of stairs, and disappeared behind one of the doors.

"What'll we drink to next?" Jake felt inebriated after just a few shots of whiskey.

"To that," Tex said, pointing to the staircase. They turned and watched Irons lead a bevy of lascivious women down the staircase.

"This one's on me, boys!" Irons proclaimed as he walked behind the girls.

The women gathered around the bar, flirting with the Rangers. Each chose a partner. Suddenly, one of the girls screamed and fainted.

"What the?" Irons caught the girl before she hit the floor.

"This is awful. Sorry, boys, maybe next time." The oldest-looking of the women, the obvious madam of the saloon's soiled doves, walked off. With a wave of her hand, she motioned for the girls to follow her back to their rooms.

"What'd we do, darling?" Irons called out.

One of the girls turned, pointed at one of the Rangers, and pinched her nose.

"If that don't beat all," Irons said.

"What?" Jake asked.

"Crowhorse, those scalps of yours. Do ya need to wear 'em on your vest?" Irons asked.

Crowhorse looked down at the scalps. He smiled sheepishly at the Rangers.

"To Crowhorse," Tex laughingly announced. The Rangers tossed back one after another.

"Just a minute," Jake set his glass on the bar and looked across the room.

"Sons of bitches." Jake began walking across the room.

"What is it, Jake?" Tex asked.

"Those men killed Justus. Wait here," Jake empathetically asserted.

"Howdy, boys," Jake said to the two Turner brothers. "How's tricks?" Jake made the remark to Nate Turner, the man he recognized with the full beard and the two distinctive, white stripes running from the corners of his mouth and down either side of his chin.

"Mister," Nate Turner replied, sipping from his shot glass.

"That's a fine-looking mandolin there." Jake pointed to the instrument leaning against the wall. "Either of you boys play?"

"Nah, belongs to a friend. Watching it 'til he gets here."

"That friend happen to be a Texas Ranger? Name of Justus Strummin?"

Both brothers glanced at each other and then at Jake. Jess Turner recognized the young Ranger he had bumped into while running from the alleyway. "Don't know him."

"This is going nowhere," Jake thought to himself.

"That mandolin belongs to a Texas Ranger. Got himself killed here, day before yesterday."

"Sorry to hear that," cracked Jess. He lightly touched the grips of his revolver under the table.

"I saw you running from the alley the night he was killed."

"Accusing me of something?" Jess asked. Turner slowly began easing his gun from its holster.

Tex walked up behind Jake. "You two wiseacres are under arrest."

"For what?" Nate asked.

"Murdering a Texas Ranger." Tex had his Walker pointed at Jess' head before either brother could move a muscle. "You can go peaceful like or not. It makes no never mind to me. I'd soon kill ya." Tex cocked his revolver.

The Turner brothers stood and put their hands into the air. "Where we going?" Nate asked.

"Town jail, to join your friend. What was his name, Jake?"

"Boone Jackson."

"Let's go." The men headed toward the saloon doors, and Tex looked over at Jake. "You're either too amiable or had too much to drink, Jake. I'm going have to teach you how to talk a man into drawing his gun so you can kill 'em quick." Jake nodded in agreement as both Rangers herded the two murderous brothers to jail.

CHAPTER 41

Jack sent his telegram to Washington, DC, and patiently waited for a reply, which came quickly. Reading it, Jack thanked the messenger and headed toward the saloon. Crossing the street, he spied Kincaid and Stetson heading in the same direction and called to them.

"As I suspected, some distinguished gentlemen in Washington want to see us!"

They assembled the other Rangers and informed them of the need to head out right away. Tex, Irons, Crowhorse, and Jake headed for the livery stable to acquire fresh horses for the group.

Stetson went into the saloon to find Homer. She saw him sitting alone at a card table at the far end of the bar.

"Homer?" she asked as she pulled up a chair.

Homer looked at her and smiled. It was a sad smile, not one she had seen on his face.

"Missy Stetson. I feel real bad about killing those men."

"Homer, you had no choice. They would've hurt you, me, and Ellsworth."

"Reckon so. Reckon I'm missing my family. I need to be getting along home."

"Okay, Homer, we'll get you home as fast as we can."

* * * *

Doctor Sloane frowned and shook his head. Bison's right arm was mangled beyond repair. He told them, if it had not been for the expertly woven stitching by the young lady, the captain would have lost his arm. Unfortunately, the arm would be of little use to him, but he wouldn't lose it. Moreover, it would take several weeks for him to recuperate.

"I can ride, damnit!" Bison protested when they told him they'd have to leave him behind. He insisted until he tried standing and collapsed.

Everyone said good-bye to him. Stetson and Ellsworth stood by his bed after the others left. She sat on the bed and held his hand. "I don't know how to apologize for my behavior with you and the men."

"No need, little lady. It all worked out."

Ellsworth sat on a stool near the head of the bed. "Captain, if it weren't for you and the others...Well, I can't thank you enough."

"Hell, from the looks of it, I'd say we saved Texas, and the authorities will probably lynch us for it." Bison smiled, contemplating what the governor of Texas would say to him for riding beyond the Rio Grande without permission.

Stetson and Kincaid stood. "I'm forever in your debt, Jim. If there's anything I can do, say the word," Kincaid said as he shook his left hand.

"Well, there is something you can do for me," Bison said. He was as explicit as possible.

When he was alone, Bison glanced at the unread telegram Jack had given him before they had ridden across the Mexican border. He read it again.

"Well, I'll be damned," Bison said to an empty room.

The message from President Grant clearly gave the Texas Rangers permission to cross the border and engage the enemy. Bison placed his head on the feather pillow, closed his eyes, and took a well-deserved nap.

* * * *

No railroad ran to El Paso. The nearest train depot was north of Santa Fe. Doctor Sloane bandaged the wounds the other Rangers sustained as best he could and told them to change the dressings daily. That afternoon, they rode due north toward Santa Fe, reversing the path the slain Anderson family took two weeks earlier.

* * * *

The train stopped in Newton, Kansas, for Homer to disembark. The Rangers shook Homer's hand and wished him well. Homer handed the old, dented badge back to Tex.

"Keep it. You rightfully earned it. Keep it safe, just in case the Rangers call on you again. Never know when they'll need help. Someday, you tell your son about your adventures with the Texas Rangers and saving Texas from Mexico. Should anyone ever doubt you...Well, that badge is proof."

Homer smiled and returned the badge to his overalls pocket.

Stetson, Jack, and Ellsworth walked Homer from their train car down the boardwalk to the depot station. Stetson gave the large man a hug as a tear cascaded down her cheek. Both Jack and Kincaid, in turn, shook Homer's massive hand. They all stared at each other. Their eyes filled up as they said their good-byes. The train's high-pitched whistle was their cue. Stetson and Jack turned to hurry back toward their train car. Ellsworth once again put out his hand.

"Thanks, for everything."

Homer smiled. "The missus and me and the kids...Well, we love you, Mister Ellsworth. We'll never forget you." Homer firmly grasped Kincaid's hand.

The whistle blew again for the last time, and the metal wheels began turning, tugging at the train, slowly moving it away from the depot. Kincaid ran toward his car, jumped, and landed on the passenger landing. He turned and waved at Homer. Inside the car, Stetson, Jack, and the Rangers all waved good-bye.

They traveled from Kansas City to St. Louis and on toward Washington. They rested, sleeping for what seemed an eternity. Each of the travelers slowly grew silent, peaceful with themselves while contemplating the events that had happened.

Over the next several days, Jack told them the entire story of Juan Rodriquez Felipe de la Caza, how a dictator named Porfirio Diaz overthrew the incumbent Mexican government, and the tyrant's plan to capture Texas and hold her ransom. The counterfeiting of the American dollar along the Texas border was an effort to create an insolvent state where the Mexican peso would prevail. They were fascinated with the story and their personal involvement. Jack repeatedly told them of the secrecy of the events and had them swear they'd never tell anyone.

* * * *

Upon their arrival in the big city, they were whisked away by carriage to the Windsor Hotel, just minutes from the White House on Pennsylvania Avenue. Kincaid went with Jack to meet Jonah Walsh, who told stories of his own experience in the West, fighting Indians, and his exploits during the Civil War with the

Union Army. Kincaid liked Walsh and knew, if he was a friend of Jack's, they would also become friends.

Walsh arranged for a change of clothing for the travelers and set up an introduction between Stetson and Julia Dent Grant, the president's wife. The two women became fast friends, and Mrs. Grant made sure Stetson received special attention to her wardrobe while in Washington. The president's personal physician, Doctor Ronald Crowel, inspected, cleaned, and properly bandaged the Rangers' wounds, which were healing nicely thanks to the doctor in El Paso.

On two occasions Jonah Walsh held meetings with them, ensuring they understood the secrecy of the recent events surrounding El Paso. On the second meeting, Walsh introduced them to John Gilmore, the undersecretary of the War Department. Gilmore downplayed the entire incident. He referred to the Mexicans' clandestine mission of undermining the dollar, strategizing the takeover of Texas, marching on El Paso, and engaging in the subsequent conflict as, in his own words, a "trifling matter" that had already been "swept under the carpet." Kincaid and the others noticed the obvious animosity between Gilmore and Walsh. They also disliked Gilmore and his trivializing of the matter and their participation.

Everyone made small talk in the splendidly decorated East Room of the White House as they waited for dinner to be called. Kincaid glanced at Stetson and watched as she spoke to President Grant and the men who had been invited to this special dinner party at the White House. She was as lovely as when he had first met her in Ohio, at a party celebrating a reunion of those who had fought in the war. Although absent from the dinner, Mrs. Grant had not spared any expense in having the finest seamstresses in the city outfit Stetson. The Texas Rangers intermingled with those gentlemen not being entertained by Stetson. Jack was talking furtively to Jonah Walsh in the far corner of the room.

The table had been set for a private dinner for President Grant, his entourage, and those who had traveled from El Paso. The mood was festive. Wine flowed freely. The dinner bell sounded for all to take their seats. Jack, Walsh, Stetson, and Kincaid sat nearest the president at the head of the table. Gilmore, Secretary of the Treasury Alexander Stewart, Charles Gifford, and Professor Carl Upridge sat among the Texas Rangers at the long, rectangular table sitting perpendicular to the head table.

Grant stood, and the others followed. He held his wineglass high. "Lady…" Grant smiled at Stetson standing to his right, "and gentlemen. The United States government owes each of you its unwavering gratitude. Washington and I, and my fellow advisors here tonight, salute you. God bless you all."

Crowhorse leaned over to Jake and whispered, "God bless those Apaches." Jake smiled and nodded.

"God bless the United States of America," Gilmore proclaimed.

"God bless Texas!" Tex announced proudly.

"Yes, of course! And God bless Texas," President Grant smiled at the tall Texan and the others as they raised their glasses to their lips.

Epilogue

Sitting on the couch with a silk robe wrapped around her, Catherine Webb's tears ran down her cheeks. Early that morning, Captain Jonah Walsh arrived at her apartment, catching her in bed. He rarely, if ever, visited her unannounced. Their relationship, being private, was unknown to their inner circle of friends and federal agents. They'd been extremely secretive, not wanting their relationship to negatively impact their careers or put either one of them at risk if a foreign enemy should use such knowledge to their advantage.

With President Grant bowing out of the presidential race, Walsh, tired of the big city and its politics, requested a transfer out West, preferably to Texas or Colorado. His timing couldn't have been better. Bison's shoulder injury was forcing him to retire from the Texas Rangers. Kincaid had made a special request of President Grant, who contacted the Texas governor. Bison would be commissioned a United States marshal in Texas, fulfilling Bison's request to Kincaid to wear a badge and not sit at a desk shuffling paperwork for the rest of his life. Walsh would assume command of Company C of the Texas Rangers, an assignment the governor gladly gave as a personal favor to the president.

With two days to report to Waco, Texas, he had rushed to Catherine. He wanted to say the right things to her, having practiced asking for her hand and prepared to get on one knee. He intended to tell her how much he loved her, how he couldn't live without her, and how he wanted to marry her.

In his enthusiasm, he reversed the order of his rehearsed speech. He boasted about his new assignment and how thrilled he was with the prospect of going out West. She started crying. He clumsily proposed to her. She continued crying. Now, he stood in her small apartment waiting for a reply.

Catherine looked at the man who meant more to her than life itself. The fear of heading out West and facing the unknown was insignificant to living without him.

She stood and faced the man she wanted to live her entire life with. Though her tears were happy tears that he would someday appreciate, she nodded in the affirmative, accepting his marriage proposal.

* * * *

The knock on the door was surprising for an early Sunday morning. Andrew and Margaret Holovanisin didn't expect visitors. For the first time in a long time, they had an opportunity to spend time together. The weather had turned brisk with dark clouds threatening another rainstorm. The two had decided to stay home, light a fire in the study, and spend time reading, a favorite pastime for both.

Andrew had just purchased a new, leather-bound book containing prints of ancient Egypt. He was absorbed studying the handcolored, three-tinted lithographs depicting the desert of Gizeh, the Sphinx, the Island of Philae, and other monuments dotting the Egyptian landscape. Margaret was reading the daily *Pittsburgh Gazette* when the knock at the door disturbed them. Andrew stood and walked the few paces from the oak study to the front door. He opened it and was momentarily frightened. His gasp startled Margaret, who came and stood by her husband.

A military officer stood at the door holding an envelope. They were reminded of a recurring nightmare since the Civil War when a young military officer had come to their door. He also carried an envelope. The news concerned their son, Sonny. Sonny had joined the Seventy-Eighth Pennsylvania Volunteer Infantry. Under the leadership of Colonel William Sirwell, he had shown heroism at the battle of Stones River. The January 7, 1863, issue of the *Pittsburgh Gazette* had given a brief, glowing account of the battle, bestowing upon the regiment the distinguished name, "The Gallant Seventy-Eighth." The letter informed them that Sonny was missing in action and presumed killed. It wasn't for another three months that his whereabouts were known. Severely wounded, he and several others had crawled to a local farmhouse. Three of the men died, but Sonny and his friend Gabe recovered and rejoined the regiment to fight again at Pickett's Mill. He was decorated many times during the war. However, those three months of worry were the most stressful months they had ever endured.

"Yes?" Andrew asked apprehensively.

"Mr. Andrew Holovanisin?" the young officer inquired.

"Yes?" Andrew hesitantly answered.

The officer handed the envelope to him and stood waiting. Margaret put her hand on her husband's shoulder to steady herself as he carefully opened the envelope.

"It's Stetson, isn't it?" she asked, holding back her tears.

Andrew read the letter. Then he laughed. He faced the officer.

"Yes, of course. We'll be ready tomorrow morning. Thank you, lieutenant. Thank you very much."

"What does it say, Andy?"

"It's a letter from President Grant. He and Mrs. Grant are requesting our company for dinner and a tour of Washington."

"Read it aloud, Andy."

"Yes, of course, my dear. It is with great pleasure that I ask you to join my lovely wife and me on November 5 for dinner at the White House. Time permitting, we would graciously enjoy taking you on a tour of our fair city the following day. I have recently had the privilege of meeting your daughter Stetson and her fiancé Ellsworth. Without doubt, they are two of the most remarkable individuals I have ever met. This country owes them a great deal of gratitude for their work on behalf of our government. I am sure she makes you both very proud. Please let me know of your acceptance. I look forward to spending time with you and sharing my very favorable impressions about your daughter. Cordially, Ulysses S. Grant, President of the United States."

"He knows Stetson. But how? Why?"

"Well, Mother, we'll find out upon our arrival."

Margaret smiled at her husband. "She makes you proud, doesn't she?"

Andrew returned her smile. "Yes she does. That girl of mine makes me very proud."

* * * *

"Hurry, Ron, I don't want to be late." Monica Williams was nervous as usual. She tidied her bonnet, gathered her shawl, and rushed out the door. Her husband was outside with the carriage.

"You don't think this weather will make us late, do you?" The rain had been falling all day, making the roads leading into town hazardous.

"No, Mon, we'll be just fine. Don't worry."

"The rain won't make the train late, will it?"

"Mon, calm down. The train will be on time, and so will we."

From the outskirts of Pittsburgh to the train depot, the ride took approximately an hour. The rain, although muddying the streets, didn't slow the Williams' progress.

"Right on time, hon," Ron announced as they pulled into the train depot. Grabbing an umbrella, he and Monica headed toward the rail station and waited for the train.

The train's whistle announced its arrival. Monica stood eagerly waiting, fixing her dress. She then turned and straightened Ron's tie.

"Oh, Mon, stop it," he told her. "Calm down, please."

"Do you think they made the train? You don't think they missed it, do you?"

Ron ignored his wife as she continued worrying. The train slowly came to a stop.

People began disembarking. Families greeted relatives. There was laughter in the air and jubilant screaming as people welcomed guests and friends. Monica and Ron waited.

As the last few people left the train, Monica turned to Ron. "They missed the train, Ron. What are we going to do?"

Ron smiled at her. "No, they didn't. Here they come now."

Monica turned back toward the train. Her face burst into a glowing smile. On the passenger platform, a nun stood, holding hands with a small, blonde child cradling a soiled, raggedy doll in her arms. Monica ran to the train, stopped, smiled, and asked, "Katy Marie?"

"Look how beautiful she is, Ron. Look at her."

The child timidly returned Monica's smile. The nun, wearing a white habit, disembarked with Katy Marie.

"Hello. I'm Sister Marcella Gonzales. Yes, this is Katy Marie."

The nun squatted next to the toddler and brushed back a few strands of blonde hair. "Say hello to Monica and Ron, Katy."

The child stood staring at Monica and Ron, not yet understanding that she had finally come home.

"Hi, Katy Marie," Monica said. "You look just like my little sister when she was your age. She's as beautiful as you are. Her name is Stetson."

Katy Marie smiled broadly at the mention of the name. She hesitated and then ran excitedly to Monica to hug her around the neck.

* * * *

Kincaid mulled over the idea. After Jonah Walsh and Jack had spoken to President Grant, a formal offer was made. Kincaid could join Jack as an agent for the Treasury Department. With Walsh assigned to the Texas Rangers, there was a remote possibility Jack would assume Walsh's position as the deputy director. Jack and Kincaid would once again be working side-by-side.

He initially disliked the idea, having always been on his own. He could choose if he would serve as a deputy marshal when called upon or herd cattle to Abilene. His was a wandering soul, and he liked the freedom. But he had more than just himself to consider. He had Stetson. Plus, there were distinct advantages to the job offer. Residing in Washington, they'd be close to her home in Pittsburgh. If he took the job, he knew he would need to do the proper thing and ask Stetson to marry him. He loved her, and he knew she loved him as well. He had dealt with life-and-death situations his entire life. Those decisions seemed comparably effortless to this leap of faith. His only worry was rejection. What if she had thought of a reason not to marry him? After her near-death experience with de la Caza, he wouldn't be surprised to learn she had decided to go home and marry one of the more city-refined gentlemen who had pursued her earlier.

They were to have dinner that night with Jack. After dinner, while walking her back to her temporary apartment Walsh had arranged for each of them, he'd consider popping the question, but only if it felt right. He knew it was a terrible plan, but it was the best he could come up with.

* * * *

Haskell Everett needed to make a decision that his own livelihood depended on. The New York City publishing firm of Beadle and Adams had commissioned him to write a dime novel about an incident in the Wild West that would capture the imagination of their readers. If successful, he'd be commissioned to write a novel, again about the Wild West, which seemed to fascinate the Eastern audience. He had dreams of becoming a novelist, and this dime novel could be his introduction to that dream. He also knew his chief competitors, Colonel Prentice Ingraham and Edward Sylvester Ellis, had also been commissioned for the same subject matter. He knew his publishers wanted frontier violence, blood and guts, and harrowing adventure. All of which, his competitors were excellent and prolific in writing.

He studied his notes in his New York apartment. He enjoyed reading by the fireplace during the winter months with a cup of hot coffee spiked with a little whiskey instead of on the frontier, from where he had just returned.

He had traveled for three months during the worst winter in the history of Texas, from one dirt-floor barroom to another. He had traveled from border town to border town, asking questions, probing for information, and occasionally risking his life when he asked the wrong person or just asked too many questions. He first heard about the incident in Washington, DC, in a bar one evening. All a good writer needs is a few details, and the rest is up to diligent research and a little imagination.

The story sounded interesting, yet unbelievable. During the autumn of 1876, while the Mexican government was under revolt, they hatched a plan to recapture Texas. Several hundred banditos had amassed south of El Paso with plans to destroy the town and head to Dallas. They planned to burn everything in their path and demand, under threat of bloodshed of American hostages, that Texas be relinquished to Mexico. Apache battles, Texas Rangers, and, most appealing, the love of a man and a woman along with their involvement in the incident underlined the tale. Because this one man was willing to fight an army of butchers to rescue her, the Mexican's plans were thwarted. The story contained overtones of true love and the triumph of good over evil, exactly what he needed for his tale.

The other story involved Buffalo Bill Cody. During the summer of 1876, General Philip Sheridan asked Cody to join Colonel Merritt and the Fifth Cavalry on War Bonnet Creek. Yellow Hand and forty Cheyenne warriors engaged Cody and the soldiers. Cody was thrown from his horse, recovered his rifle, and shot and killed the Indian chief. Cody then pulled his bowie knife, scalped the dead Indian, and proclaimed, "First scalp for Custer!" Although Yellow Hand was the only fatality, Everett's imagination could do the rest.

Both stories were true. Both had the fundamental elements, as outlined by the publisher for Western lore. Most everyone knew about the Battle at War Bonnet Creek and would believe the story as it richly unfolded within a dime novel. No one knew of the incident south of El Paso or the machinations of Washington, DC. Some knew of Ellsworth T. Kincaid via several dime novels. But he was not as famous as Bill Cody. However, if Everett's story was written properly, Kincaid would become more famous than Cody or Wild Bill Hickok.

The decision Everett faced was one of dollars. Which story would the public buy? Which story rang true? Could the public follow the Kincaid story, from the dark corners of Washington to the Mexican revolt to a brooding Mexican insurgent to counterfeiting along the Texas border? Would they prefer a story concerning revenge for the famous, immensely popular Custer at the hand of another living legend, Buffalo Bill Cody?

Everett weighed his decision throughout the evening and into the early morning. Finally, he took the heavy volume of notes regarding the El Paso incident, an estimated 300 pages, leaned over, and threw them into the fireplace.

"No one," he thought, "would believe such a story."

978-0-595-37374-1
0-595-37374-7

Printed in the United States
47427LVS00005B/73-99

9 780595 373741